W9-BSL-274

The Irish Duke

The Irish Duke

VIRGINIA HENLEY

A SIGNET ECLIPSE BOOK

Signet Eclipse
Published by New American Library,
a division of Penguin Group (USA) Inc.,
375 Hudson Street, New York, New York 10014, USA
Penguin Group (Canada), 90 Eglinton Avenue East, Suite 700, Toronto,
Ontario M4P 2Y3, Canada (a division of Pearson Penguin Canada Inc.)
Penguin Books Ltd., 80 Strand, London WC2R 0RL, England
Penguin Ireland, 25 St. Stephen's Green, Dublin 2,
Ireland (a division of Penguin Books Ltd.)
Penguin Group (Australia), 250 Camberwell Road, Camberwell,
Victoria 3124, Australia (a division of Pearson Australia Group Pty. Ltd.)
Penguin Books India Pvt. Ltd., 11 Community Centre,
Panchsheel Park, New Delhi - 110 017, India
Penguin Group (NZ), 67 Apollo Drive, Rosedale, North Shore 0632,
New Zealand (a division of Pearson New Zealand Ltd.)
Penguin Books (South Africa) (Pty.) Ltd., 24 Sturdee Avenue,
Rosebank, Johannesburg 2196, South Africa

Penguin Books Ltd., Registered Offices:
80 Strand, London WC2R 0RL, England

Copyright © Virginia Henley, 2010
All rights reserved

SIGNET ECLIPSE and logo are trademarks of Penguin Group (USA) Inc.
ISBN 978-1-61664-046-0
Printed in the United States of America

Without limiting the rights under copyright reserved above, no part of this publication may be reproduced, stored in or introduced into a retrieval system, or transmitted, in any form, or by any means (electronic, mechanical, photocopying, recording, or otherwise), without the prior written permission of both the copyright owner and the above publisher of this book.

PUBLISHER'S NOTE

This is a work of fiction. Names, characters, places, and incidents either are the product of the author's imagination or are used fictitiously, and any resemblance to actual persons, living or dead, business establishments, events, or locales is entirely coincidental.

The publisher does not have any control over and does not assume any responsibility for author or third-party Web sites or their content.

The scanning, uploading, and distribution of this book via the Internet or via any other means without the permission of the publisher is illegal and punishable by law. Please purchase only authorized electronic editions, and do not participate in or encourage electronic piracy of copyrighted materials. Your support of the author's rights is appreciated.

Dedicated to my devoted reader Artist Debi Allen,

and to all my other loyal readers.

I owe it all to you.

ACKNOWLEDGMENTS

I am indebted to the following historical and biographical sources, which provided a wealth of information on Georgian England's society, monarchs, government, and noble families, including the Russells and the Hamiltons.

- A. Graves *Catalogue of the Works of the late Sir Edwin Landseer, 1876*
- Lord Frederick Spencer Hamilton *The Days Before Yesterday*
- Lord Holland *Memoirs of the Whig Party, 1854*
- Princess Dorothea Lieven *Correspondence with Lord Grey*
- John Pearson *Stags and Serpents*
- J. H. Plumb *The First Four Georges*
- J. Preest *Lord John Russell*
- Alice Robbins *A Book of Duchesses*
- Rachel Trethewey *Mistress of the Arts*
- Spencer Walpole *The Life of Lord John Russell*
- The Abercorn Estate Papers, County Tyrone Record 7277 from the *Directory of Sources for Women's History in Ireland*
- "The London World" *New York Times*, August 5, 1894
- *The Tyrone Constitution* newspaper *Ireland Old News* Web site, November 1844
- *Britannica* online encyclopedia
- Wikipedia

The Irish Duke

Prologue

"Wouldn't you *love* to know?" Dowager Duchess Louisa winked at her two great-granddaughters who were whispering about her.

The pair blushed hotly when they realized Lu had overheard them wondering how many lovers she'd had in her eighty-odd years.

The *trés grande dame* was presiding over a levee of her one hundred and one descendants.

"After all, I belonged to the decadent Georgian era. You cannot expect me to even pay lip service to the rigid respectability of the repressed Victorians."

"Is it true, Your Grace, that you declined the office of Mistress of the Robes to her Majesty the Queen?" Maud asked in awe.

Lu threw back her head and laughed. "Not once, but twice. One of my greatest passions is beautiful raiment in brilliant colors, such as red. Just the thought of Queen Victoria's dull and dowdy garments gives me the shudders."

"Her daughter-in-law Princess Alexandra has lovely taste in clothes," Maud said.

"Indeed she has. It will be a most welcome change to have a queen who is fashionable. I cannot wait."

The girls looked incredulous that the old girl expected to outlive Queen Victoria.

The corners of Lu's lips lifted in a wry smile. "I'm not ready to stick my spoon in the wall for another decade. I fully intend to welcome in the next era with gusto." She waved her crimson ostrich-feather fan languidly. "A little decadence never hurt anyone."

The room fell silent as Louisa's youngest daughter Evelyn, Marchioness of Lansdowne, read congratulatory letters from Her Majesty Queen Victoria and His Royal Highness, Edward, Prince of Wales.

The future Duke of Leeds, who was married to her favorite granddaughter, handed her a glass of champagne and kissed her cheek. He raised his own glass. "I drink a toast to the best-looking woman in London."

"I'll give you a toast an Irishman taught me:

> *Here's to you and here's to me,*
> *And if someday we disagree,*
> *Sod you . . . here's to me!"*

Louisa sat in the place of honor so that the speeches could begin. Her great-granddaughter Maud and her cousin returned, eager to learn all they could about their fascinating great-grandmother.

"What is it now, Miss Inquisitive?"

"I heard that you first met James Hamilton when you were a little girl. Is that true, Your Grace?"

Louisa's mind took wing and soared back over the decades to Carlton House. "It was July 1819. . . . I remember it all as if it were yesterday."

"Lady Louisa, will you marry me?"

Louisa Jane Russell, daughter of the Duke and Duchess of Bedford, stared at the boy who had planted himself before her, and saw the determination written on his face. "Who the devil are you?" she demanded.

Nine-year-old James Hamilton, needing to impress the beautiful seven-year-old, raised his chin with pride. "I am the Marquis of Abercorn." He pronounced it *Avercorn*.

"Do you have a speech impediment?"

James drew himself up to his full height. "Certainly not!"

"Then why did you say *Avercorn* when your name is *Abercorn*?"

James hid a smile. He resisted the impulse to correct the dark little beauty and inform her that the letter "b" in his title was pronounced "v." "You may call me whatever you like, if you will consent to be my future wife."

"Isn't Abercorn an Irish title?"

"Yes, it is. My name is James Hamilton. I came into my grandfather's title last year." His heart was doing a jig just looking at her. "You haven't answered my question, Lady Louisa. Will you marry me?"

She raised her lashes and stared at him. "Marry an Irishman with a speech impediment? You must be mad!"

Louisa joined her older sister, Georgy. She eyed the glass of wine in her hand and licked her lips. "Where's Mother?"

"She's in the scarlet drawing room with Jack and Charles. Our insufferable brothers have cornered Prinny and are asking all sorts of ridiculous questions about the decorations on his portly chest. Who was that handsome devil you were talking to?"

"His name is James Hamilton. His good looks are very deceiving. He's actually quite stupid." She dismissed him from her thoughts.

"I'm ravenous. I was too nervous to eat before I performed my dance but now my belly is rolling." Louisa could see that her sister wasn't even listening to her. She was searching for someone in the crowd of young people invited to Carlton House for the children's party. When Georgy darted into the throng of pedigreed youngsters, she sprang after her. "Wait a minute. Where's the refreshment room?"

To Louisa's consternation, her sister stopped before James Hamilton and began talking to him. She turned her back on them and was heading in the direction of the scarlet drawing room when she encountered the Prince of Wales.

"My dear, your Spanish dance was delightful." He touched the red fringe on her shawl with a pudgy finger. "You have your mother's exquisite beauty. What may I do to show you my appreciation?"

"Could you get me some ham sandwiches, Your Highness, and a glass of sugared wine? I'm very hungry."

Prinny hid a smile and bowed gallantly. "Your wish is my command, Lady Louisa. I am always delighted to please a lady."

Louisa decided to follow him and with every step she happily clicked the castanets she'd used in her Spanish shawl dance. She instinctively knew if there was food to be had, the corpulent prince regent would home in on it like a pig unearthing truffles.

Prinny took delight in Lady Louisa's dainty appetite. "All the Russell children are most impressive. Your brothers are such fine young men."

Her brows drew together. *My brothers are young savages.* She swallowed the last morsel. "Thank you for the sandwiches, Your Highness. It was a lovely party. I shall take my wine with me so I may savor it." She sketched a curtsy and departed.

Louisa scanned the ranks of doting parents for her mother but didn't see her. Her eyes, however, met those of a striking-looking woman wearing a white turban decorated with a large ruby. She recognized her as Princess Lieven, wife of the Russian ambassador.

Louisa smiled, and when the Russian noblewoman beckoned, she sat down beside her. "Are you enjoying the party, Princess Lieven?"

"I was overcome with *ennui* until I saw you dance, Lady Louisa." She stroked the silk shawl. "Red is a bold color. Do you like it?"

"I love it . . . it makes me feel alive."

"Red has a power all its own. You should wear it often. It is a striking color for a lady with dark hair and green eyes like yours."

Louisa was enthralled. "Do you have Gypsy blood, Princess Lieven?"

"My blood is quite blue, I assure you. But I do have *psychic* power—the ability to see into the future. It is a gift or a curse, depending on the circumstances."

"How fascinating!" Louisa sipped her sugared wine. "Can you see *my* future?"

Dorothea Lieven ran the tip of her tongue over her rouged lips. "Would you truly want to know your future, child?"

"Oh, yes, please," she said avidly.

"Set your wine down and give me your hand."

Louisa did as she was bidden and gazed enthralled as the wraith-like princess stared down at her open palm.

"You have a long life ahead of you, Louisa Russell. You will live to be almost a hundred years old. You will be a great favorite at Court and will live to see five different monarchs sit on the throne of England."

Old King George is about to die and the prince regent will be king soon. Louisa pictured a plump Prinny sitting on the throne, wearing a glittering crown.

"I see many children surrounding you."

"Yes, there are so many of us that Father calls Woburn Abbey the *rabbit warren*. Mother isn't going to have any more babies, is she?" Louisa asked anxiously. At Christmas her mother had given birth to a lifeless baby boy.

"Georgina, Duchess of Bedford, is a friend of mine. I think it entirely probable she will have more. But I was speaking of your own children surrounding you."

Louisa was horrified. "You must be mistaken. I intend to be a dancer and an actress on the stage. I don't want a horde of children. Perhaps I will consider having just one little girl but no boys, certainly."

Princess Lieven brushed Louisa's dark curls from her serious forehead. "Nonsense. You will have more than a dozen children, all beautiful." She saw the look of dismay on the child's face and hastened to assure her. "There will be more girls than boys."

Louisa jumped up in alarm. Her mother's agonizing screams as she gave birth the last three years in a row echoed in her memory. "I must find Mother. Please excuse me, Princess Lieven."

It didn't take her long to recognize the Duchess of Bedford's hat across the chamber. Her mother always wore the most spectacular creations. Louisa hurried to her side and found her surrounded by young people. Her brothers Charles and Jack, as well as her cousin Arthur Lennox, were conversing with their school friends from Westminster, including James Hamilton. Her sister Georgy was batting her eyelashes at Abercorn in a ridiculous manner.

Her Aunt Charlotte, the Dowager Duchess of Richmond, had brought her three youngest daughters, Madelina, Lottie, and Sophia, since Fife House was close by.

"There you are, Pussycat." Georgina smiled at her daughter. "Your dance was a great success, darling."

Her female cousins looked impressed, but her brothers snickered and she pointedly ignored them.

"Are you hungry?" her mother asked with concern.

James Hamilton stepped forward and fished in his pocket. "I have something you might like, Lady Louisa."

"No, thank you." Her refusal was coolly polite. "His Royal Highness, the Prince of Wales, brought me some sandwiches." Suddenly her eyes sparkled with delight. Sitting in the middle of Abercorn's palm was a sugared mouse. "Oh, how sweet. I absolutely cannot resist it." She took the offered treasure to her mouth and licked it.

As the two duchesses and their families made their way toward the Carlton House door, James gazed after Louisa Russell. Her dance had mesmerized him. Her lithe, graceful movements combined with her dark beauty captured his imagination and made his heart sing. He had lost his heart watching her dance. That she was garbed in red seemed prophetic. The Abercorn ancestral color was crimson.

"I knew I'd have you eating out of my hand. It's a trick I learned when I was taming my Arabian mare." Abercorn smiled.

Montagu House, London
August 1894

At the levee in Montagu House, Dowager Duchess Louisa looked at her great-granddaughter Maud. "Does that satisfy your curiosity?"

Maud nodded. "Thank you for telling us the story, Your Grace."

The duchess sat back as the speeches began, extolling her virtues, but Louisa's memories of Abercorn held her fast. *The next time I saw James, I was suffering from a broken heart, as only a sixteen-year-old girl can.*

Chapter One

"May I see the painting?" Louisa stroked her pony's neck with a loving hand. Her heart beat wildly as she gazed at the handsome young man who was working on her portrait.

"No, you may not, Mistress Impatience. The afternoon light is perfect. Ten more minutes is all I ask."

"Then it will be finished, Lanny?"

"No, it won't be finished." He flashed her an indulgent smile. "Perhaps tomorrow, or the next day. Do you find posing tiresome, Louisa?"

"Oh no!" She felt her cheeks blush and said shyly, "I like spending the afternoon in your company." *I wish you would go on painting me forever.*

Louisa's father, the Duke of Bedford, had been Edwin Landseer's patron for more than four years and had commissioned the talented young artist to paint portraits of his wife Georgina and his younger children.

Louisa had considered the artist a familiar friend of the family. But as she posed for him, holding the reins of her pony, her feelings for the handsome young man underwent an amazing transformation.

"Can you make me as beautiful as my mother?" she asked eagerly. Throughout her life Lady Louisa had been told she was the image of her exquisite mother, but she didn't quite believe it.

"You are the prettiest young lady I have ever painted. With the same beautiful dark green eyes, you are truly your mother's daughter."

Louisa lowered her lashes shyly at the lovely compliment. It was the first real praise she had ever received from a member of the opposite sex, and it made her heart flutter.

Thinking an insect had landed on her face, she brushed her fingers across her cheek. Then she felt something hit her chin and heard a muffled giggle. She swooped down immediately and scooped up her youngest brother, Alex, from beneath the mulberry bushes. She kissed his chubby cheek. "You horrid louts shouldn't be teaching him such naughty tricks."

Cosmo and Henry, eleven and twelve respectively, sniggered loudly and moved a safe distance away, but still within taunting distance. "Catch us if you can, Cracknut!"

"Just ignore them," Edwin advised.

"They think it hilarious to call me by the name of my pet dormouse. The boys have run wild for years since Father has been ill; Mother has spent all her time with him." John Russell, Duke of Bedford, had suffered a stroke in 1822, paralyzing his right side, distorting his mouth, and crippling his arm.

"Because of your mother's devoted nursing, your father is much improved and has regained his vigor." Edwin Landseer wiped his brushes. "That's enough for today. Your older brothers will soon be home from Oxford for the summer. They'll box Henry and Cosmo across the ear if they catch them teasing you."

"No, they won't! They are a brotherhood of demons from hell. Instead of three, there will be six to taunt me, to say nothing of their loutish friends who'll come to stay. The *rabbit warren* will become a *madhouse*! The only one who ever champions me is my half-brother, Johnny, but he seldom visits because of his Parliamentary duties."

"Then I shall be your champion."

Louisa sighed. "Thank you, kind sir." As she watched him carry his paints and canvas toward the house, she pictured him on a white charger, wearing her colors at a jousting tournament.

She set her young brother on his feet. "You may come with me while I put Coltsfoot in the paddock."

"Don't want to. I'm playing soldiers with Cosmo and Henry."

"All right, Alexander the Ingrate, off you go." Louisa led her pony along the manicured path that led to the stables. Her mind was filled with Lanny's handsome image. The teasing look in his blue eyes made him irresistibly attractive. All of her family, except the baby, had dark hair and eyes, and Edwin's fair coloring was striking. *He thinks I am the prettiest young lady he has ever painted!*

As she opened the paddock gate, she saw that her sister Georgy and her groom had returned from their ride. She suddenly felt a pang of remorse at reveling in her own pretty face. Her sister had inherited none of their mother's great beauty and could only be described as plain. Although Louisa never reflected on it, that was the reason she loved Georgy so deeply and felt fiercely protective toward her.

The young groom raised his arms to help Lady Georgianna dismount. As she came down from the saddle, she allowed her body to slide against his and then dropped to her knees in the grass. When she saw her sister, she quickly jumped up and moved away from him. "Lu, are you spying on me?"

"Of course not." Louisa removed her pony's bridle. "Lanny wanted me to pose with Coltsfoot and I'm just returning her to the paddock." She watched Dick lead her sister's mare and his own mount into the stables.

"He's devilishly attractive, don't you think?"

"Yes, I do. I can't wait to see my portrait."

"I don't mean Lanny, for God's sake. I mean *Dick!*"

"Ah." Louisa hesitated. "You shouldn't let him touch you like that."

"Shouldn't I? You're such a prude, Lu. You have no sense of fun. You're a late bloomer—you haven't even begun to notice the opposite sex yet."

Louisa blushed, remembering how her heart had fluttered a half hour ago.

"You're seventeen and I bet you've never even been kissed."

Lu pictured Lanny touching his lips to hers and her cheeks grew hot.

"A wager!" Georgy challenged. "A guinea says you won't experience a kiss before you turn eighteen in July."

"Of course I will, if I put my mind to it."

"Use your breasts, not your brain," her sister advised knowingly.

Louisa changed her dress and hurried downstairs to the Venetian drawing room to have a word with her mother before the evening meal. Dinner at Woburn was at six o'clock and seldom were there fewer than twenty people seated in the formal dining room, which displayed the duke's collection of Van Dyke paintings.

She found her mother conversing with her best friend, Lady Holland, whose Ampthill estate was also in Bedfordshire. "Hello, Aunt Beth." Louisa glanced anxiously at her mother, who had been looking wan and tired lately. Baby Rachel was only two, and when she cried in the night her mother sat rocking her for hours until she went back to sleep. Louisa's concern eased when she saw that she looked both happy and well.

"Hello, Lu. What have you been up to?" Beth patted the blue velvet settee, inviting her to join them.

"Lanny is painting my portrait with Coltsfoot, but he won't show it to me until it's finished."

"Posing with animals can be most trying. I once had my portrait painted holding a fidgety spaniel on my knee. Never again!"

"What happened? Did it pee on you?" Georgina teased. "Edwin

has an affinity for painting animals. His talent is unmatched. When we were in the Highlands in the autumn, he did the most spectacular painting of a stag. Though I've sketched all my life, my artistic ability pales beside his. I wish he could transfer his genius to me."

"Speaking of the Highlands," Louisa said tentatively, "is it true that when you were my age, Grandmama took you on a recruiting mission, where you offered a kiss and a guinea to any male who would join the Gordon Highlanders regiment?"

"It is the gospel truth. It was so successful that we recruited a thousand men!"

Louisa gasped. "You kissed a *thousand men*?"

"Not quite a thousand," Georgina said with a wink. "My sister and mother kissed a couple of hundred, but I got the lion's share."

"I've never been kissed once!"

Louisa's words hung in the air, as Georgina and Beth exchanged a significant glance.

"Your mother loves to tease and exaggerate, Lu. You mustn't take her seriously."

"Darling, a kiss is an insignificant trifle. You'll have kisses aplenty, once you are presented and make your debut. The young gentlemen will be fighting over you."

If kisses have so little importance and Georgy kisses Dick, I'll have to find someone before my birthday. I can't lose a wager with my sister. Trouble is, there's only one person I want to kiss.

"There's the gong for dinner. Your father hates tardiness." Georgina waited until her daughter hurried off and then remarked to Beth, "Lu is so unworldly. That's what comes of living at Woburn instead of London. At her age my four sisters and I were positively bold and sophisticated by comparison."

"Well, you were all brought up by the indomitable Jane Gordon. How could you be other than wise in the ways of the wicked world?" Beth teased.

"Very true. The women of my family were both audacious and shrewd."

By the time they arrived in the dining room, Louisa's brothers, Henry and Cosmo, were already at the table. Alexander's nanny brought in her charge, sat him down, and departed. The Duke of Bedford, with the aid of a walking stick, arrived with his friend Lord Holland and Edwin Landseer. Her father's young physician, Harry Halford, who had resided with them since the duke had suffered his stroke, followed them.

When Henry gallantly held Georgina's chair, then did the same for Louisa, she smiled and said, "Thank you, Uncle Holly." When Edwin performed the same service for Lady Holland, Louisa felt positively envious.

John Russell's dark brows drew together. "Where's Georgy? A lack of promptness is ill mannered."

Her father was displaying what her mother referred to as *Russell firmness.* Louisa cleared her throat. "Georgy was reading," she improvised quickly. "She must have gotten so absorbed, she didn't hear the dinner gong."

"What was she reading?" he asked with skepticism.

"One of your lovely books on botany." Lu managed not to choke on the lie. *The only interest Georgy takes in flora and fauna is rolling in the grass.*

The soup was being served by the time Georgy slid into her chair. Louisa saw that she hadn't changed from her riding dress and there were telltale green stains on her skirt. "Please excuse me," Georgy begged sweetly.

Her father's stern voice rang out. "Georgianna . . ."

To deflect the reprimand, Louisa took her courage in both hands. "May I dance for you after dinner? Georgy will play for me."

"That would be lovely," Beth enthused.

Instead of the usual rude protests from her brothers, Louisa saw

Henry and Cosmo exchange a sly smile and wondered what the young demons were up to.

"Lanny, when you have finished the portrait of Lu with her pony, I would like you to paint her in one of her ballet gowns. What do you think?"

"An excellent suggestion, Your Grace. It would be my pleasure."

Louisa lowered her eyes to the beautiful birds and butterflies that decorated her Meissen soup plate and thought it sacrilege when the footman filled it with consommé. *Lanny wants to paint me . . . It will give him pleasure.* Her heart began to sing. She closed her eyes and her imagination took flight: *They were standing by the fountain in the center of the maze. He dipped his head and gently touched his lips to hers. She raised her lashes and gazed into his adoring, deep blue eyes.* Then Georgy joggled her elbow and her fantasy dissolved. Lu cast a guilty look across the table and to her great delight, Lanny smiled at her. *Perhaps he read my mind!* Her breath caught in her throat.

Before the soup plates were removed and the spring lamb was served, the adults were arguing the merits of breast-feeding. Dr. Halford sided with the Duchess of Bedford, and her racy rejoinders soon had the company laughing. "There's nothing more entertaining than *titillating* conversation at dinner."

Louisa glanced at her father and was relieved to see he'd forgotten Georgy's tardiness. The conversation turned to politics, as it invariably did at Woburn. Tonight Louisa's newly awakened yearnings outweighed her interest in politics, so through the rest of the meal she sat daydreaming about the handsome young artist. *Tonight I will dance especially for Lanny.* When she was twelve, it came as a devastating realization that a duke's daughter could not perform on the public stage. But Woburn had its own private theater, which had helped to blunt her disappointment. When she was onstage dancing or acting a role in a play, she took on a persona of confidence and self-assurance. Her costume became a disguise that masked her shyness and insecurity.

After dinner, the ladies usually withdrew to the blue drawing room while the men drank, but tonight everyone repaired to Woburn's theater to watch Louisa perform.

Alexander trotted beside his sister. "I like watching you dance, Lulu."

"Thank you." She thought him sweet, if only because he was too young to be a hellion.

Georgy took her seat at the harpsichord while Louisa went backstage. In the costume room she lifted the lid of the trunk that held her ballet dresses and slippers. With dismay, she discovered that the ribbons had been cut from all her satin dancing slippers. "Damn and blast the young devils!"

She rummaged to the bottom of the trunk and pulled out a pair of toe shoes they'd overlooked. Though she hadn't intended to perform a toe dance, she quickly changed her plans. She removed her gown and petticoat and donned a white bell-shaped ballet dress. Then she sat down on the trunk, pulled on the shoes, and crisscrossed their satin ribbons around her ankles so they were firmly secured.

Louisa walked to the center of the stage, raised her chin, and posed dramatically. She held still, completely poised, with the composure of a professional performer. Her sister knew only a few dance selections, and Lu had learned to match her steps to whatever notes Georgy played.

When the music began, she rose to her toes and danced *demi pointe*, with dainty little steps that carried her across the stage. She was graceful as a gazelle, swaying with the music as if it were part of her being. She raised her arms, leaped into the air, and landed perfectly on her toes without missing a beat. She was as light as a butterfly as she spiraled across the stage, dancing her heart out for only one person.

The music ended on a crescendo and Louisa swept into a low curtsy, her head almost touching her ankles. When she rose to acknowledge the applause, she gave Lanny a radiant smile. Then she extended her hand toward Georgy and watched her take a bow.

Louisa did not feel the pain until she left the stage. She hobbled over to the trunk and removed her shoes and stockings. All of her toes were raw and bleeding. She winced as she dabbed them with her petticoat and then smiled. *It was worth it!*

Before she went to bed, she made an entry in her private journal. She put down only the important things in her life, like her feelings for Lanny. The diary's clasp had a small lock and key for safekeeping. When she was finished, she carefully put the book away in the secret drawer of her writing desk and hid the key. *No one must ever find it and read it. These are the secrets of my heart.*

Chapter Two

*W*illiam, *I'm afraid I dislike your wife intensely.* Louisa kept a polite smile on her face.

"No one would guess you and Georgy were sisters; there is no family resemblance." Elizabeth Russell was her half-brother William's wife. The couple had spent the last few years abroad and had just returned to England. "She's rather plump and plain."

"I think Georgy is beautiful, and she doesn't say unkind things about people."

"She's twenty . . . on the marriage market over a year, and still no prospects?"

"Nineteen." *For another fortnight.* "Georgy hasn't made her debut yet. Grandfather Gordon died and our mourning postponed her coming out. We are making our debut together in the autumn."

"Your mother is very shrewd to pair you up. She knows that all eyes will be on you and no one will notice your sister's shortcomings."

Louisa was fuming and fought the urge to shove Elizabeth on her narrow arse. She hoped her visit would be a short one. "I hear you have bought a townhouse in London."

"Yes, we chose a house in Cavendish Square. It's not ready, of course. We will be staying at Woburn until it is completely redecorated and furnished. Your mother has offered to help with the refurbishing, but our tastes are vastly dissimilar . . ."

"Yes, Mother has exquisite taste in all things. It is a pity your standards don't run parallel with hers."

They were in the breakfast room, located between the Van Dyke dining room and the Venetian drawing room. "We have Mother to thank for this cozy room. She chose the wallpaper to complement the old English masters and filled the bookcases with Shakespeare and the lyrical British poets. She decided every detail from the Sevres china to the Irish Waterford crystal. The atmosphere is so inviting . . . I love to linger over breakfast, then browse through a book."

"I prefer French or Greek classics." Elizabeth looked down her haughty nose as if she smelled something bad.

The atmosphere was inviting until you arrived, Bessy. I shall linger no more. "Please excuse me. I don't want to be late for my sitting."

"That Landseer fellow is painting your portrait?" Bessy's eyebrows arched in disapproval. "I'm amazed he can tear himself away from his . . . *muse.*"

She means Mother. She cannot hide her envy. "Lanny is painting me in my ballet dress. Perhaps he could do a portrait of your son?"

Bessy stiffened. "I think not. Hastings will be painted by Lawrence, not some wildlife amateur."

Lu jumped up, unable to mask the blazing anger in her eyes. *How dare you disparage Lanny's work? It is pure genius!*

Louisa ran down to the theater dressing room. With outrage bubbling inside, she donned the bell-shaped ballet gown in which she'd danced for Lanny. She'd stitched back the satin ribbons her brothers had cut off her ballet slippers, and she chose a pair of blush pink to wear for her portrait. She brushed her hair and fashioned the dark curls at the nape of her neck. She glanced in the mirror. *I hope he thinks I'm pretty.*

Landseer arrived and set up his easel in the light from one of the tall windows. He suggested different poses and Lu followed his directions to the letter. He did a few quick sketches before deciding which one would be most effective.

As Lu posed, her anger melted away. There was no room in her heart for any emotion but joy when she was with Lanny. *He makes me feel so special. I'm sure he is growing fond of me.* As she posed quietly, she fell into a daydream that took her far away from the manicured gardens of Woburn. *They were riding through a rugged glen in Scotland. Finding themselves isolated in the wilderness, they drew rein. He lifted her from the saddle and they ran toward a bubbling burn. Lanny bent and picked purple heather for her. Her heart beat wildly as he clasped her in his arms and touched his lips to hers.*

"Stop!"

Louisa jumped guiltily. Her lovely vision dissolved and was replaced by Henry and Cosmo chasing after ten-year-old Hastings. A pug and a spaniel followed on their heels, barking furiously.

"What's the trouble here, lads?" Edwin put down his paintbrush.

"We were throwing sticks for Scamp, and then Hastings grabbed one and hit my dog with it," Cosmo shouted.

"Your dog bit me!" Hastings cried. "I'll get Father to shoot it."

Lu took three threatening steps toward him. "We don't shoot dogs at Woburn. Sniveling, spiteful nephews, on the other hand, are fair game."

"I'm sure you can find something entertaining that doesn't include sticks," Landseer suggested.

"Swords!" Henry declared. "Will you play pirates with us, Lanny?" he asked hopefully. "We made a raft, but we need your muscles to help us carry it to the lake."

"Go on, you've twisted my arm," Landseer agreed affably.

Louisa's heart sank. "I can pose again this afternoon."

He gave her a warm smile. "The morning light is better. We'll continue tomorrow."

. . .

"What do you think of William's wife?" Louisa asked her sister as they met on the stairs.

"She's an insufferable bitch who cannot abide us."

"But *why* does she hate us?"

"She's jealous of course. William has always confided in Mother, and Bessy thinks she must compete with her for her husband's love. She loathes the fact that Mother is a queen bee with an endless retinue of courtiers who adore her."

"Mother does have a lot of devoted admirers, but why is Bessy jealous of *us*?"

"We are Father's second family. Since he worships the ground Mother walks on, it only stands to reason he loves us best." John Russell had three sons, Francis, William, and Johnny, before he married Georgina Gordon.

"That's not true. Father loves all his children equally."

"Don't let Bessy upset you, Lu. Life's too short."

"You're going riding. If you wait until I change my dress, I'll come with you."

"Yes, I'm going riding, but the last thing I need is a chaperone. Find your own diversion."

"A chaperone is the *first* thing you need. Behave yourself, Georgy."

"You sound exactly like Wriothesley, delivering a sermon. Having a vicar for a brother is bad enough; I don't need a nun for a sister."

Louisa watched Georgy skip down the stairs and decided to see if the cook had made some lemonade. She cut through the conservatory and passed by the corridor leading to the chamber that Lanny used as a studio. Suddenly she had a yen to take a peek at her portrait in the ballet dress. She knew he wouldn't show it to her until it was completely finished. *I'll just go in and take a quick look while he's down at the lake.*

Louisa opened the door and slipped in quietly. The smell of oil paint and turpentine filled her nostrils. She liked the pungent, piney fragrance because she connected it with Lanny. She gazed about the studio, looking for the painting. There were various sketches on easels, but they were not of her. His worktables held brushes, palette knives, tubes of pigment, and etching tools. Dozens of canvases stood against the walls, with his paintings of animals separate from his portraits of the Russells.

She glanced at a large canvas and found half a dozen smaller ones stacked behind it. The portraits were all of her mother, which didn't surprise her. The beauteous Duchess of Bedford was Edwin's favorite model. Suddenly Louisa drew in a quick breath. She stared in disbelief at a sketch of her mother, lying in repose with one breast bared. The intimate pose shocked her. The naked breast was round and ripe; the look on her mother's face was inviting. *How could Mother have exposed herself like this to Lanny?*

A sense of guilt rushed over her. She had no right to be in the artist's studio, pawing through his paintings. Louisa left the room quickly and closed the door behind her. *Mother breast-fed baby Rachel. I often came upon her in the nursery at feeding time. It's perfectly natural. Perhaps Father wanted her sketched like that.* Louisa blushed hotly and chided herself for being shocked.

She made her way to her mother's sitting room, thinking to share afternoon tea with her. As she approached she could hear William and her mother talking. She hung back to see if she could hear his wife. If Elizabeth were there, she wouldn't join them.

"I show Bessy every kindness, but she treats me as an adversary. I try to overlook her cold, haughty manner because an open quarrel would upset your father."

"I wish you could be friends," William said wistfully.

"She disapproves of everything I say and do, and cannot hide it. It has gotten back to me that in her letters she accuses me of extravagance, but she doesn't refuse my offer to pay for decorating and refurbishing the townhouse in Cavendish Square."

"That is most generous of you, Georgina. You only imagine that she disapproves."

"No, her animosity is real. She even accused me of exaggerating your father's illness. But never mind, I rejoice that he is so much improved. I'm glad you have come to visit him and truly happy you have decided to live in England."

Louisa turned around and went back the way she had come. *Bessy doesn't realize Father is improved because of Mother's devoted nursing.* Suddenly the female who dominated her thoughts emerged from her father's library.

"I enjoy spending time with His Grace. He's so friendly and gallant," Bessy declared.

"He is much improved and we owe it all to Mother. She sat by his bed, often twenty-four hours at a time until he began to recover. She was extremely worried."

"It is perfectly understandable why she was worried. Have you seen Hastings?"

"He is down at the lake with my brothers. I'll take you if you like, Bessy." Louisa fell in step beside her sister-in-law and they entered the garden.

"Your mother was terrified the duke would die, for then she and her children would have no place to go."

Louisa stiffened. "What do you mean?"

"John's oldest son Francis will get the title when your father dies. Woburn, the money, and all the other houses and property will no longer be Georgina's to do with as she fancies. Your mother will do anything to keep him breathing."

"That is a wicked and spiteful thing to say. My parents are devoted to each other."

"Well, she certainly has him besotted. He indulges her every whim. It pays her to keep him alive."

Louisa stopped walking. "I'm sure you'll find Hastings. He's the one squealing like a girl." She turned on her heel and went back to her mother's sitting room.

"Ah, there you are, William. Bessy has gone down to the lake to find Hastings. She would like you to join her," she improvised. Louisa took William's plate and empty wineglass, and pointedly set them on the teacart.

William smiled. "I'd best attend her. I don't want to put her in a pique."

When he left, Louisa confronted her mother. "Bessy says you're frightened to death of Father dying, because Francis will get everything and we'll have no place to go."

"The wretched girl cannot help causing trouble. I have nursed your father so he will regain his health and I am gratified that he has come on so well. It wasn't for any ulterior motive that I did it, though she speaks truth that Francis is heir to your father's dukedom, and of course Woburn Abbey."

"I shouldn't have told you what she said, Mother. I don't want to upset you."

"She's said far worse things than that, Lu. She's possessive of William and jealous that he still confides in his stepmother. She won't be here long. Their London house will soon be ready."

Mother doesn't seem particularly worried about Francis inheriting everything. She seems to take it for granted that Father will take care of us.

"It's Rachel's playtime. Will you come up to the nursery with me?"

"I think I'll go and keep Father company in the library." Louisa headed down the long hallway to Woburn's library. She knocked politely before she entered.

"Hello, Puss. Have you come to choose a book to read?"

"Not really. I have some questions I'd like you to answer for me . . . but only if you're feeling well enough, Father."

"I'm feisty as a fighting cock. Come and sit down." John Russell had a firm manner and spoke directly and to the point.

Louisa did not beat about the bush. "When Francis inherits Woburn, where will Mother and the rest of us live?"

John searched his daughter's face. "A couple of years ago, when I bought Campden Hill in Kensington, I put the deed in your mother's name. She chose it because it is next door to Holland House. I had it modernized and enlarged to accommodate all of you." He smiled ruefully. "Your mother has often complained that Woburn is like a large mausoleum."

Louisa let out a relieved breath.

"She will be free to use the Devon house and estate also. Francis is quite aware that your mother and I built Endsleigh together, and I'm sure he will be generous enough to make no claim upon it. Has someone been alarming you about what will happen should I suddenly die?"

"No, no," she denied quickly. "I have no fear that is going to happen. You have made a remarkable recovery, Father."

"In any case, *your* future won't depend upon your brother Francis. Your husband will be responsible for you, my dear. To ensure that we make an excellent match for you, I have set aside a dowry of five thousand pounds. Suitors will soon be vying for a chance to court you. But you may rest assured. We will only consider an alliance with a powerful, noble family."

"But I have no wish to marry! Being a wife and mother of an unruly horde of children does not appeal to me." Though Louisa loved her father, she thought it the height of male selfishness for him to give her mother ten children, on top of the three sons from his first marriage.

His eyes flickered with amusement. "The alternative of being left on the shelf and having to depend upon the charity of your brothers would be far less appealing, I assure you. Far better to have a grand estate of your own to run as you see fit."

Mr. Burke, her father's steward, arrived to help the duke navigate the stairs, so he could dress for dinner. Louisa left the library and slipped through a French door out onto a veranda. She wandered down to the grotto with the seashell walls. She sat beside the reflecting pool to ponder the sobering things she'd learned from her father.

To Louisa, marriage was inextricably connected with having children. She had questioned her mother about childbirth, but she always told her not to worry; it was natural for a woman. None of her fears had been lessened. Sometimes the unspeakable happened, and babies were born dead. It had happened to her mother, and Louisa dreaded the possibility that it could happen to her. She shuddered at the memory of her recurring nightmare. Since she was a small child she had dreamed of seeing her mother covered in blood. When she became older, it was sometimes herself who was drenched in blood. Finally, last year, she had summoned the courage to ask her mother if she had ever suffered a miscarriage.

"Yes. We were picking flowers in the garden, when it happened quite suddenly. I sent you running for help. But you couldn't possibly remember it—you were only about three at the time."

"What were the flowers?"

"They were lupins, darling."

Louisa was distracted from her dark thoughts when she spotted Georgy returning from her ride. She joined her sister, and together they walked up to the house.

"Did you know that the only home we'll ever have will be our husband's?"

"Yes, Lu, and I'm about to turn twenty. I have far less time than you."

"If we refuse to marry, we will have nothing," Lu said indignantly.

"Well, I shan't refuse to marry. I shall relentlessly pursue every male who crosses my path and enjoy every moment. Husband hunting should be a lot more fun than bagging game."

"I don't want a lord and master who will use me as a brood mare. I would far rather be a dancer on the stage than a wife and mother."

"But even a dancer can't manage without a man to pay her bills. Girls on the stage have lovers to pay for their rooms, and clothes, and carriages."

"Lovers? Men who expect to sleep with you?"

"Men who expect sexual favors. Don't be so naive, Lu. It's far easier to marry a doting husband. Men are putty in your hands when you use the right bait."

Lu glanced down at her sister's grass stains. "You'd best change before dinner, Georgy. If Father ever finds out you act provocatively with your groom, there will be hell to pay."

"I know *you* won't tell him, so how the devil will he find out? Besides, everything I do, I learned from Mother. Men cannot resist her. She feeds on courtly love. I'm just using Dick for practice."

"Courtly love is innocent. Uncle Holly dedicates poems to her beauty. It's platonic."

"Don't be naive. There's no such thing," Georgy insisted.

Louisa changed the subject. "What would you like for your birthday?"

Her sister winked suggestively. "What I'd like and what I'll get are two different things. I'd like some suitors, but until they come along I'll make do with Dick."

A few days later, Edwin finished the portrait of Louisa in her ballet gown and allowed her to see it.

"Oh, Lanny, you have made me look beautiful. It flatters me."

Her pulse was fluttering wildly and she could hear her heartbeat thudding in her ears.

"I but captured your natural beauty, my dear. The bloom of youth on your cheek, the lovely curve of your throat, hint at the budding womanhood beneath your innocence."

She caught her breath. *I think I love you.* She swayed toward him.

"Don't lose your balance." He caught her shoulders in strong hands and steadied her. Then he took the canvas from the easel. "Let's go and show your mother."

Her flesh tingled where his hands had rested. *He touched me. I think he was about to kiss me, if he hadn't thought I was going to fall in my ballet slippers.*

They found Georgina kneeling on the rug in her sitting room, watching baby Rachel ride her rocking horse.

"Lanny finished my portrait. We've come to show you."

"Oh, it's lovely. You've perfectly captured her delicacy."

"Louisa's resemblance to you is unmistakable, Your Grace."

"You flatter me, Lanny."

"You and the baby make such a beautiful picture. Now that she's learning to walk, I'd love to paint you together, helping Rachel take her first steps," he suggested.

"What a lovely idea." Louisa picked up her baby sister and kissed her cheek. "She has the prettiest red curls in the world."

Edwin held out his hand and helped Georgina to her feet. Then she lifted Rachel from Louisa's arms, and when the baby began to chortle, they all laughed with delight.

Elizabeth walked into the sitting room and stopped dead in her tracks when she saw them. "Excuse me. I didn't mean to intrude on such an intimate family gathering."

"Bessy, of course you're not intruding," Georgina said smoothly. "Mr. Landseer has just finished a portrait of Louisa."

"I'm amazed Woburn needs its own resident artist." Her tone was disapproving.

"We are fortunate to have him. Painting the Russells is becoming a full-time occupation," Georgina said lightly. "Edwin has his own residence and studio in London."

"Really?" she drawled, with barely concealed skepticism. "William was out shooting. I just wondered if he'd returned. I'm sure you'll excuse me?"

Baby Rachel was about to burst into tears.

"Bessy has that effect on me too, darling." Georgina tickled her daughter's tummy, eliciting another chortle, and they all gave a relieved laugh.

Louisa picked up her portrait. "I think I'd like to keep this in my bedchamber for a few days before it is added to the picture gallery." She blushed prettily. "Thank you so much, Lanny."

"It always gives me great pleasure to paint you, my dear."

Louisa was walking on a cloud as she carried her portrait upstairs to her bedchamber. She removed a sketch her mother had done, replaced it with Lanny's painting, and stood back to admire it. "He has made me look beautiful. This must be the way he sees me." Her heart sang at the thought. *Lanny is different from other men. He's never arrogant and selfish. He's talented, and funny, and so very handsome. After I make my debut, I hope he will court me. I don't want to marry Lanny, but it might be fun to have him court me.* Louisa went off in a reverie, where a pair of sparkling blue eyes gazed at her with longing, and a pair of lips claimed hers with a possessive kiss.

"It's such a beautiful day; I think I'll go for a ride. Perhaps I'll ask Lanny to come with me." Louisa changed into a green riding dress that showed off the curve of her young breasts. She pulled on her boots and then she brushed her dark curls and pinned on a saucy feathered hat. She winked at her reflection. "A-hunting we will go!"

On her way to the main staircase, Louisa crossed the hall that led into the east wing where William and his wife were staying. The sound of Bessy's shrill voice carried to her and she stopped to listen.

"She's so brazen about it! There she was displaying their love child to him, like some trophy. The woman is scandalous. She brings disgrace to the entire family."

"Keep your voice down, Bessy. The servants will hear you."

"Servants aren't blind, William. One look at those blatant red curls proves the child isn't a Russell. I don't know how your father can turn a blind eye and allow the libertine to live here under the same roof."

Louisa gasped. *How can William's wife say such wicked things about Mother? She's insinuating that Rachel is Edwin Landseer's child!* Louisa wanted to march down the hall and slap Bessy's face for uttering such evil lies. She clapped her hands over her ears so she wouldn't hear any more vile accusations and fled from the house.

Her heart was slamming against her chest as she saddled Coltsfoot and mounted her. She took off at full gallop, scattering the fan-tailed doves as they strutted about the stable courtyard.

She headed to the wooded parkland where a stream cut through the trees. She saw Georgy's horse tethered to a tree and quickly dismounted. Her sister was wading in the water with her skirts tucked up above her bare legs. Dick lay in the grass, watching her.

Louisa jerked her head at Dick, in a gesture that told him to leave. When he mounted his horse and rode off, she looked at her sister. "I have something *terrible* to tell you."

"What's wrong? You look like you've seen a ghost."

Louisa wrung her hands. "I don't know where to start."

"Start at the beginning." Georgy waded from the water and sat on the bank.

"Lanny finished my portrait and we went to show Mother. We found her in the sitting room playing with Rachel. We were all laughing and having a good time when Bessy walked in on us. The happy mood changed instantly, as it always does when she comes on the scene.

"I put up my portrait in my bedchamber and decided to go for a ride. When I passed the east wing, I could hear Bessy saying the most dreadful things to William."

"I think he's afraid to stand up to her. She needs a clout round the ear!"

"By God, I almost rushed in and gave her one. She said that mother was brazenly displaying their *love child* to Lanny. She said that Rachel's red curls prove she isn't a Russell. The evil bitch insinuated that mother and Edwin are having an affair and that Rachel is their child!"

"Oh dear." Georgy sighed heavily. "Lu, come and sit down."

Louisa threw herself down on the grass.

"I must admit," Georgy said tentatively, "that I've thought the same thing."

"What on earth are you talking about?" Lu demanded.

"Father is past sixty and that stroke debilitated him badly. Frankly, I don't think he was up to fathering another child."

Cold fingers crept around Louisa's heart. "What are you saying? That Edwin Landseer is Rachel's father?"

"Well, it's plain to see that Lanny is enchanted with Mother. He's painted more than a score of portraits of her. And he was in the Highlands with us the autumn that Mother quickened with child."

"You think Lanny is in *love* with her?" Louisa cried in disbelief.

"All you have to do is see them together. He's besotted, like all her other admirers."

"But Lanny is only in his twenties. Mother is forty-seven."

"You're so unworldly, Lu. Age has nothing to do with it. Most married women have affairs, especially when they are saddled with aging husbands."

Suddenly Louisa remembered the intimate sketch Edwin had

made of her mother with her breast bared. She felt the cold fingers in her chest begin to squeeze. She knew they wouldn't stop until they had crushed her heart. She let out a sob and got to her feet. Tears blinded her eyes as she rode back to the house.

She dashed up to her room and took the portrait from her wall. She carried it down to the long portrait gallery and left it standing against the wall. She knew that she would associate Edwin Landseer with the smell of oil paint for the rest of her life and the stench of it would make her want to spew.

Chapter Three

"The gang from Oxford will be arriving today. I hope they bring some of their friends with them. We are in dire need of suitors. I shall take pains to dress for dinner," Georgy declared as she rummaged through her wardrobe.

"I might forgo dinner." Louisa shuddered. "The only thing worse than dining with Edward, Charles, and Jack is putting up with their loutish friends." Men were on Louisa's black list at the moment, especially young ones. She had been devastated over the incident with Landseer and totally avoided him. Her feelings toward her mother had suffered a blow as well. In truth, she felt alienated from everyone.

"Oxford men are thought to be the cream of the crop. Most of our prime ministers were educated there and you cannot deny you have a keen interest in politics."

"No doubt some of them possess fine intellects, but tell the truth and shame the devil, Georgy. You have no interest in their politics or their intellects."

Georgy laughed. "No, it's a bit lower than that."

That afternoon, six young nobles sat in John Russell's famed Woburn library, drinking claret. The duke's three sons had each brought home a friend from Oxford for the holidays. His son Edward's best friend was Teddy Fox, whose father was Lord Holland. Both young men had now completed their studies at Oxford.

"Do you plan on making the Grand Tour, Teddy?" the duke inquired.

"No, sir. It is politics for me."

"Do you intend to run for office?"

"That would be an ideal place to start. But eventually I hope to join the diplomatic corps."

"The seat for Horsham in West Sussex is open. I'll speak with your father. With our combined support, you should have no trouble." Though the Duke of Bedford no longer played an active role in politics, he still had a great deal of political clout and used his influence behind the scenes.

"Thank you, sir." Teddy saluted with his glass and drained it.

"Good. I'll campaign with you," Edward Russell promised, "but once you are elected, I intend to pursue a naval career."

"I prefer the army," Charles said, "but I still have another year at Oxford."

John glanced from Charles to his son Edward. "I wish you two were set on political rather than military careers. However, I'll see what I can do. I'll invite the Duke of Clarence to Woburn. Though William is no longer head of the Admiralty, he can still pull a few strings. I'll write him an invitation tonight."

George Grey was pleased. "That's jolly good of you, Your Grace. I too plan to pursue a career in the navy."

The duke's son Jack spoke up. "I haven't decided on a career yet. I have no particular zeal in any direction. The same cannot be said for our friend James, however. Abercorn has a consuming passion."

John Russell focused his attention on James Hamilton. "What is that, Abercorn?"

"Ireland, Your Grace. I've anticipated the honor of meeting you for some years. Irish Catholic emancipation has always been a cause dear to your heart as well as mine, and at long last your son Lord John, as a leading Whig, got it passed."

"Yes, and the king finally signed it into law. You are a man after my own heart, Abercorn. I'm very proud of Johnny's accomplishment, though we should give Wellington's Tory government some credit," he conceded.

"Oh, I do, Your Grace. Wellington was shrewd enough to trust Lord John to get the bill passed."

"Johnny will be visiting us shortly," the duke declared.

"I cannot wait to shake his hand. I hope he arrives before I leave for Ireland. I go as often as I can. It is an honor to be invited to Woburn. I believe I can learn a great deal from you." *Actually, I have two consuming passions: Ireland and your daughter Lady Louisa. I have every intention of making her my wife.*

"Feel free to join me here in the library any afternoon," John invited. "We shall soon be thick as thieves."

"Thank you, sir." His dark countenance lit with pleasure. "I am most gratified."

John Russell looked up as his steward entered the library. "Ah, here is Mr. Burke come to show our guests to their rooms. I'll see you gentlemen at dinner." He signaled to Charles, who remained behind, as the others left with Burke.

"James Hamilton's stepfather is the Earl of Aberdeen—a lofty, dour Scot who has rich estates in Scotland. Yet James's heart lies in Ireland."

"He and Aberdeen don't get along. He doesn't remember his real father. He inherited the Abercorn title from his grandfather, as well as his grand estate of Barons Court in County Tyrone."

"I knew both his father and grandfather. His grandsire and I were both Members of Parliament for Cornwall. He was one of the few aristocrats who held Irish, English, and Scottish titles. The Hamiltons were a great dynastic family. I am glad James takes such pride and interest in his Irish heritage." John took a sip of his claret. "I wanted to ask you about Jack. How is his condition?"

"He's still suffering occasional fits, I'm afraid."

John's brow furrowed with concern. "Jack hasn't passed his exams. He'll never make a scholar. I'm afraid he's wasting his time at Oxford."

"Unlike Edward and me, he has no interest in the military, and unlike you and Johnny, no passion for politics."

"He's a good lad. We'll think of something for him to do."

From the second-floor gallery, the Russell sisters' interest was focused on the young men who had just left the library with their brothers. Or more to the point, they were transfixed by one of them.

"My God, look at his shoulders. His coat does nothing to hide his powerful muscles." Georgy licked her lips.

"He's extremely tall and dark." Louisa shuddered. The male moved with the grace of a panther. He held his dark head high; pride showed in every line of his body. *Without exception he is the handsomest male I've ever seen. He looks like a young god, come down from Olympus to walk among men.* She knew immediately that his male beauty made him dangerous.

"My prayers are answered," Georgy declared. "An eligible man who is so good-looking he makes me weak at the knees just gazing at him."

Louisa wrinkled her nose in distaste. "It is my belief that the handsomest men are also the most arrogant and selfish. They love themselves above all others."

"Oh, Lu, who the devil cares?"

"I see Teddy Fox is here. Why on earth doesn't he go home to his own estate?"

"The same reason his father, Lord Holland, is always here. It's the fatal allure of the Russell women, no doubt. I wonder who Jack brought to Woburn?"

"Lord Rancid Pinchmyarse, if the last one he brought home is anything to go by."

"He was rather randy, but I considered that an attribute rather than a liability."

"Our brothers are a year older now. Let us hope they are more mature and have learned to exercise decorum."

"Our brothers, yes . . . that tall, dark, handsome brute, no. He's got dalliance written all over him."

"Georgy, you are incorrigible."

"Lu, you are incorruptible."

"Mr. Burke will accommodate them with bedchambers in the west wing, close to our brothers' rooms," Georgy surmised.

"Yes, in his wisdom he will keep all the troublemakers together."

"Let's wait for him. Burke will know who they are."

"Surely you recognize George Grey, my lady? He's been here before with his parents. And speaking of Earl and Countess Grey, they are coming for a visit."

Georgy laughed. "I would have recognized him if I'd looked at him, but I had eyes only for the dark, attractive devil."

"Ah, that would be James Hamilton, Marquis of Abercorn." Burke kept a straight face. "If you will excuse me, ladies."

Georgy stared at Louisa openmouthed. "Good God! We met him when we were children at Carlton House. He was good-looking then, but now he is an Adonis." She ran after the steward. "Mr. Burke, be sure to seat me next to him at dinner."

Louisa found Abercorn a little too confident. His black curls and dark eyes alight with laughter would be a snare for Georgy. *I don't want her to have her heart broken, as Lanny broke mine.*

Louisa entered the Van Dyke dining room with trepidation. She did not wish to be seated anywhere near Edwin Landseer. She also was determined to avoid William and his wife, Bessy. She felt alarm however, when she realized that Mr. Burke had seated her on James Hamilton's left, and her sister on his right.

James, towering above her, held her chair while she took her seat and then he did the same for Georgy. When all three were seated, his smile moved from one to the other. "Ladies, at long last, we meet again."

Louisa raised her lashes and stared at him blankly. "We have met before?"

"When we were children . . . at Carlton House. I'm James Hamilton."

"I do not recollect the occasion."

"You performed a Spanish shawl dance."

"Yes, so I did. How strange that I don't remember you."

He held her glance with his dark, compelling eyes. *You remember me, Lady Lu. You remember me well enough to lie about it.* She had a vulnerability he couldn't resist. She fought so fiercely to keep it hidden that he was tempted to wrap his arms around her and keep her safe. Always.

"I remember you, James," Georgy said. "I am delighted that Charles invited you."

The duchess introduced her sons' Oxford friends to the others at the table. "This is Teddy Fox, Lord and Lady Holland's son, and this young man is George Grey. Both sets of parents will be joining us in the next few days. Last but not least is James Hamilton, Marquis of Abercorn. At Oxford he is a champion oarsman." Her smile of welcome was radiant.

"Wasn't your sister Susan's husband a champion oarsman?" Bessy asked sweetly.

Georgina threw her a quelling glance. "We will not discuss the Duke of Manchester at my dinner table." Her smile returned. "There is plenty to keep you occupied at Woburn. More than a thousand acres have been set aside for riding and hunting. There is the lake for swimming or boating. We have a menagerie, an aviary, and tennis courts. There is a maze, a grotto, and a folly. Inside the abbey we have one of the most extensive libraries in England, as well as sculpture and picture galleries. There is a ballroom, card rooms, and a theater, which I hope you will make use of."

Georgy added, "We have a conservatory that leads to a greenhouse." She glanced at Abercorn. "We have some rare camellias I'd be happy to show you, among other things."

"Next Saturday, we will have a celebration. Since Georgy's birthday is at the end of June and Louisa's is the first week of July, and mine shortly after, we will have a grand party to celebrate all three."

"This will be Georgy's *twentieth* birthday, I believe?" Bessy's smile was smug.

Lu was furious. "And this year, I believe you turned *thirty-six*, Bessy." Louisa threw her a pitying smile.

Bessy choked on her wine.

The duchess hid a smile. "I forbid anyone to mention my age. A lady's age should be a mystery. It adds to her allure."

"The most beautiful women are ageless," Edwin Landseer declared.

"Who the devil asked you?" Lu muttered under her breath.

James immediately sensed the tension, but the meal progressed without incident until the strawberries were served. He knew Lady Louisa had a sweet tooth, so he picked up the small sugar bowl and handed it to her.

She covered her strawberries with the white crystals, helped herself to the clotted cream, and carried a spoonful to her mouth. The taste was intense and overpowering. By sheer willpower she stopped herself from gagging, lifted her napkin to cover her lips, and glanced about to see which wretched brother had replaced the sugar with salt.

Across from her, Charles was a picture of innocence, so she suspected him immediately. She wondered if his friend Abercorn had been in on the prank. It was entirely possible. She swallowed without batting an eye and, smiling at her dinner partner, returned to the subject of the earlier conversation. "I think age is relative. It is *maturity* that reveals a man's character. There is nothing in a male quite so unattractive as immaturity."

Her brother Charles immediately agreed. "However, there is nothing in a female quite as attractive as a sense of humor."

Louisa reached for a plum and managed to accidentally tip Charles's glass. Red wine splashed across his white neck cloth. "You are right, Charles. We all needed a good laugh."

All five of his brothers suddenly found him amusing.

Abercorn didn't know exactly what was going on, but he knew it was a game of tit for tat and he secretly longed to be a part of this large, fun-loving family.

After dinner everyone moved into the long gallery. Its walls were lined with comfortable sofas as well as gaming tables for cards. There was also plenty of room to play charades and games such as blind-man's buff.

Charles picked up a pillow and took off after young Henry. When he caught his brother, he began to pummel him. "That was a rat-faced thing to do to your sister. An apology is in order."

Henry held up his arms to protect his head. "I'm sorry, Lu. I won't put salt in the sugar again."

Louisa stood transfixed. "Charles, you are actually sticking up for me. Will you forgive me for drenching you with wine?"

"In the past I've played too many loutish tricks on you. It's childish to pit the boys against the girls. From now on we should all be friends and look out for one another. That's what families are for."

A pillow hit him square in the head and Charles charged after his brother Jack. It wasn't long before the rest of the siblings and their friends joined in the melee. Games tables were overturned to act as barriers against flying cushions, cards, and candles.

James, thoroughly enjoying himself, pulled Louisa behind a card table to shield her from the onslaught. "Lady Louisa, will you—"

"You mocking swine. No, I will not marry you!" She balled up her fists and thumped him in the chest. "I gave you my answer at Carlton House and I certainly haven't changed my mind since."

His dark eyes filled with amusement. "I was merely proposing that you keep your head down, not proposing marriage." His mouth curved into a grin. "You said you didn't remember me."

"I lied. And what's more, you know I lied, you arrogant devil." She blushed. When he threw back his head and laughed, her sense of humor deserted her. She felt humiliated and furious at both him and herself.

Georgy, armed with a sofa pillow, flung herself at Abercorn and began to hit him across the shoulders. Instead of snatching it away and overpowering her, as she was hoping he would, James rolled to the carpet in submission. She went down on her knees before him and whispered, "Damn, I'm the one who wants to roll on the rug."

Louisa jumped to her feet and held up her arms. "A truce! A little more decorum, ladies and gentlemen, if you please. Why don't we settle this with a race tomorrow?"

James got to his feet and towered above her. "I know Woburn has its own racecourse. Will your father allow us to use it?"

"Yes, if we ride our own mounts. We cannot use the Russell racehorses."

They set the event for eleven the following morning and then went about restoring the gallery so they could play cards. Lu felt disturbed by Abercorn's presence and distanced herself from him. She played fiercely against her brothers, determined to win money from them, which she could use to wager in the horse race.

Georgy, on the other hand, was playing for higher stakes. She gambled recklessly with her brother's friends, Teddy Fox, George Grey, and James Hamilton. She flirted outrageously and hinted that she might be persuaded to play for certain *favors*.

Georgy followed her sister into her bedchamber. "It is no wonder James Hamilton has an athletic build if he is a champion oarsman. Muscles maketh the man!"

Louisa did not dare to even think of the Irish charmer, let alone discuss his muscles. She quickly changed the subject. "It was wicked of Bessy to bring up Mother's sister Susan. She knows the divorce caused a terrible scandal."

"From all I've heard the Duke of Manchester was an Adonis like Abercorn. He kept a string of mistresses. Women simply threw themselves at him. Poor Susan had one affair and the vindictive devil divorced her and took away her children."

"Men can be so selfish and cruel . . . especially those who are good-looking. And, unlike women, they never have to pay for their sins." With difficulty, she banished the image of Abercorn from her mind. "The wicked shall flourish as the green bay tree. The Crown appointed Manchester governor of Jamaica."

"I warrant he planted a fine crop of bastards in the islands." Georgy yawned and opened the adjoining door to her own bedchamber. "Goodnight, Lu. I wish you sweet dreams filled with lusty bachelors."

As Louisa lay abed she pondered the wager she'd made with her sister about the kiss. Her birthday wasn't that far away and she had few options open to her. *I shall have to approach one of my brothers' friends and explain about my bet with Georgy. Surely one of them will take pity on me. I've known Teddy the longest—I'm sure he will oblige me.* She thought of Abercorn and stiffened. Under no circumstances could she ever ask the handsome, arrogant Irishman for anything. *His mocking dark eyes strip me of my confidence and turn me into a seven-year-old.*

When Louisa fell asleep, she dreamed that she was in the Highlands on a recruiting mission with her mother and sister. They offered a guinea and a kiss to any male who would join the Gordon regiment. The line of braw Scots stretched out for a mile, but as she offered each one a kiss, he refused and passed her on to the next man in line. To add to her humiliation, they were clamoring to fuse their mouths with Georgy and the alluring Duchess of Bedford.

After a restless night, Louisa arose early and soon forgot her mortifying dream. Before breakfast she intended to go to the stables and take a look at the mounts of her brothers' friends prior to the race. She donned a riding dress, pulled on her boots, and made her way outside.

As she passed by the west wing she glanced up at the bedchamber windows and saw a couple of young men gazing down at her. She lowered her eyes immediately, afraid that one of them might be Abercorn. She felt shy about what they might be saying about her and hurried on by. It was fortunate she could not hear their words.

"Lady Lu and Georgy are a study in contrasts," James Hamilton observed.

Teddy laughed. "One is winsome, and one is willing. One is fair, and one is game."

George Grey chimed in, "One's for wedding, and one's for bedding. Which would you choose?"

Abercorn wished he'd kept his mouth shut. He returned to his own chamber, put on a jacket, and went down for breakfast.

Teddy continued the word game. "One is innocent, and one exceedingly guilty."

George Grey said wisely, "Plain girls try harder."

Teddy laughed. "A dilemma. One pretty, one plain—well actually one's pretty plain!"

In the stables, Louisa assessed her brothers' mounts and then carefully looked over the three horses that belonged to their friends. One animal stood out from the rest and she ran her hand down its sleek neck. It was smaller than the two geldings and it was a mare. The shape of its head was elegant. "It's an Arabian," she murmured with awe.

Louisa sought out Woburn's head groom. "After breakfast, we are all going to race our mounts. Will you take charge of the bets for us, Toby?"

"That I will, my lady. There'll be no cheating allowed today."

"You'll have to watch the devils carefully," she warned with a grin. On her way back to the house for breakfast, she counted her betting money and weighed her odds.

Her brothers and their friends were there already when she arrived in the breakfast room. She took a seat beside her sister, took one look at Georgy's plate, and whispered, "You won't win if you eat all that."

"Men don't like girls who outdo them. By losing, I shall be far ahead in the game. Surely you are not going to place bets on yourself?"

Lu raised her chin. "I may not outdo them, but I intend to give it a damn good try!" She passed over the gammon ham, eggs, and sausage, and chose brown bread and honey. She drank a glass of milk and picked up an apple. When she glanced over at her brothers and their friends, their plates were piled high, as if they were having an eating contest. Louisa didn't think she could win against her brother Edward, until she saw him washing down his breakfast with champagne. That made her change her mind.

When everyone had finished breakfast, they all walked to the stables together. The males engaged in much laughing, pushing, and bragging, and Lu kept a wise silence. When Abercorn saddled the Arabian, she was not surprised.

Teddy Fox and George Grey saddled their geldings and led them from the stables.

Cosmo and Henry dashed in and began to saddle their ponies.

Their older brother Edward challenged them. "Who the devil said you two could be in the race?"

They immediately turned to Louisa for her support.

"They have mounts . . . they have money . . . and their name is Russell. They qualify in every way. What are you afraid of, Edward?" she challenged.

He shrugged his shoulders. "I don't mind taking their money."

Louisa winked at Cosmo and Henry. "You'll have to beat them first, Edward. Toby is looking after the bets. You have to put in an extra guinea to pick the overall winner."

When all the horses were saddled, they led them into the courtyard so they could place their bets. They assessed each other's mounts and Georgy, using size as her gauge, placed only two wagers. She bet that Teddy would be the overall winner, and that George Grey would beat James Hamilton.

Cosmo and Henry each bet that they could beat their sisters, and agreed with Georgy that Teddy would be the overall winner, riding his big gelding.

The three older Russell brothers each bet against every other challenger in the race, and, oozing confidence, each one bet that he would be the overall winner.

George Grey, seeing their self-assurance, wagered that he would beat the girls and the younger Russells, and bet that Edward Russell would be the overall winner.

Teddy wagered against every challenger and bet on himself as overall winner.

Louisa secretly watched Abercorn. Perhaps gallantry kept him from betting against the ladies or the two youngest Russell boys, but he wagered that he would beat all his friends from Oxford and that he would be the overall winner.

"Your turn, Lu. Hurry up," her brother Edward urged, impatient for the race.

To everyone's surprise she wagered that she would beat all except Abercorn, who would be the overall winner. "I've changed my mind, Toby. I'm not betting against Edward. He won't even finish the race!"

Edward hooted in derision as the eleven riders mounted and trotted their horses out to the racetrack. Georgy placed herself between Teddy Fox and George Grey, dividing her inviting smiles equally between them.

They lined up at the starting gate and when Toby dropped the flag, the dust flew from the galloping hooves. For the first quarter they were all neck and neck. Then Georgy fell behind, and at the halfway point the two huge geldings began to pull ahead. To overtake them, Edward urged his horse to the outside, swerved, lost his balance, and tumbled to the track. The rest of the Russell brothers tried to avoid him and lost valuable time. At the three-quarter mark, Abercorn's mare made her move and pulled into the lead. Louisa knew she couldn't catch him, but she kept her head low and sailed past Teddy and George, whose big horses were winded.

As Toby calculated the winnings and prepared to pay the bets, the Russell brothers flung insults at Edward and blamed him for their losses. "Lady Louisa takes the lion's share of the winnings," Toby said with a grin.

"How the devil did you come in second?" Jack demanded.

"Because my horse carried the least weight."

"What on earth made you think Abercorn would be the overall winner?"

She glanced at James Hamilton as he accepted his winnings and when their eyes met, she quickly looked away. "I bet on his horse. Arabians are bred for speed and grace. It had absolutely nothing to do with him." *That's not true. He has a will of iron. Determination is bred into his bones. Despite his beautiful smile and charming manners, if he sets his mind on a goal, I'm willing to bet he will move heaven and hell to achieve it.* Louisa shuddered.

. . .

Georgy followed Louisa into her bedchamber. "Help me out of this damn riding dress. It's much too tight."

Lu unbuttoned the back of the dress, then proceeded to remove her own.

"The very worst thing you can ever do is win a bet against a man. It humiliates him. But if you lose, it makes him feel superior. Don't you know anything, Lu?"

"I know that I refuse to play games in order to attract a man."

Georgy sat on the bed. "Catching a husband isn't a game, Lu. It is a deadly serious business. Hasn't it sunk in that without a husband you'll have no status and no home?"

Lu shivered as she recalled her disturbing dream about being homeless. "Mother often complains about her own mother's obsessive matchmaking. She insists that titles are unimportant and encourages all of us to marry for love."

"Lu, for God's sake, don't be so obtuse. She says these things but she doesn't mean them. Look at the facts! You know the history of the Gordon sisters. They all married titled, wealthy, powerful men. Mother was the youngest and her ambition knew no bounds. She managed to get herself engaged to the Duke of Bedford, the premier duke of the realm. But when Francis Russell suddenly died, she lost no time whatsoever in making sure she would still be the Duchess of Bedford. By marrying his brother, she got the status, the wealth, Woburn Abbey, and most important of all, she got the title."

Louisa was horrified at her sister's words. "She married Father for love!"

"How *utterly* convenient that she loved him."

Chapter Four

"You're looking most elegant this morning." Lu was surprised to see her sister had donned one of her best gowns.

"The Hollands and the Greys will be here soon. I'm determined to make a favorable impression upon the parents of both Teddy and George."

After breakfast, Lord and Lady Holland arrived and an hour later, Earl and Countess Grey showed up. The Duchess of Bedford gathered her guests in the blue drawing room, so the doting parents could be reunited with their sons.

Louisa observed with a jaundiced eye how Earl Grey and Lord Holland fawned upon her mother, each outdoing the other's blatant compliments and outrageous flattery. *They act as if they are courting her,* she thought with disgust. When her brothers Edward and Charles joined the company, Lu saw her chance to escape and slipped out unseen.

She wandered down to the kennels where her brother Jack was visiting his hunting dogs. The moment they saw him, the hounds' baying became deafening. "They have clearly missed you."

"And I've missed them." As he opened the kennel gate, half a dozen hounds and Gordon setters bounded through it and encircled Jack, prancing and leaping ecstatically. "They want to play fetch. Help me find some sticks, Lu."

She joined in the fun, delighted to see her brother enjoying himself. Though he was twenty-one, she realized happily that he was still a boy at heart. She watched as he threw himself wholeheartedly into the game, chasing the dogs and letting them chase him.

Jack's face turned red with exertion and he began to perspire. "They've caught a scent! There they go, off through the woods. We won't see them again until they run it to ground."

"That's good." She threw him a worried glance. "It will give you a chance to catch your breath."

Jack turned around in a slow circle, as if he were disoriented. Then he fell to the ground.

Lu rushed to his side and knelt down. She knew immediately that he was having one of his fits. "Jack! Jack!" With her heart in her mouth, she moved a sharp stone from beneath his head. She heard someone coming through the trees. When she saw that it was James Hamilton, she jumped up instantly, her heart pounding. "It's my brother . . . please leave us . . . he won't want you to see him like this."

Abercorn took hold of her elbow. Her eyes were pleading for him to leave. "It's all right, Louisa. I've seen him have a fit before at school."

Hamilton grabbed a stick and put it between Jack's teeth so he wouldn't swallow his tongue.

Louisa watched helplessly as her brother's heels drummed on the ground, then heaved a sigh of relief as his feet stilled and he lay quietly. Hamilton lifted Jack to a sitting position and her brother opened his eyes. He took the stick from his mouth and said sheepishly, "Sorry about that."

"How do you feel?" Abercorn asked.

"Foolish."

James helped him to his feet. "No need to be self-conscious with me, Jack."

Lu took her brother's arm. She was mortified that Jack's failing had been exposed to Abercorn, but she politely offered her gratitude. "Thank you for helping him."

"Have you ever taken betony for your condition, Jack?"

"No, I usually have a stiff drink afterward."

"Is betony supposed to help?" Louisa asked. "How do you know that?"

"One of our gamekeepers in Ireland suffers from the same complaint, but regular doses of the herb keep it under control."

She knew Jack would feel embarrassed if she fussed over him. "The Greys and the Hollands are here. I should go and visit with them. Good luck in getting the hounds back in the kennel." Louisa intended to look up the properties of betony in her father's collection of botany books rather than visit with their guests.

She made her way to the library and climbed the spiral ladder to the upper level where the prized books were shelved. She perused many of the tomes and became absorbed in the colorful illustrations of the magical herbs and plants. She came across an antique copy of *Culpeper's Complete Herbal*. Louisa marveled at the wealth of information that Culpeper had compiled more than two hundred years before. She sat down on the floor and searched the pages for betony. She examined the illustration with its purple flowers and read through the long, detailed description. She smiled at the quaint language:

Place—It groweth frequently in woods, and delighteth in shady places.

Time—It flowereth in May, after which the seed is quickly ripe, yet in its prime in July.

Louisa ran her finger down the page that listed wood betony's government and virtues. *Here it is: Either the herb or root or flowers taken in ale helpeth the falling sickness or convulsions. It is also good to take away bruises from the fall. The root is bitter, but the leaves and flowers are sweet and spicy and pleasing to the taste.*

Louisa was about to rise and take the book with her, when she heard voices. She recognized that it was her father, and he had James Hamilton with him. She sat still as a mouse and listened to what was said.

"We have some things in common, James. I, too, lost my father before I was three and my grandfather a few short years later. I empathize with you."

"Yes, it is a sad coincidence. I don't remember my father, but I loved my grandfather deeply. He took me to live with him at Stanmore Priory when my mother remarried because he didn't approve of her marriage to Aberdeen."

"Your grandfather's daughter Catherine was Aberdeen's first wife."

"Yes, it's complicated. My father and Aberdeen's first wife were brother and sister. So in effect, my mother married her brother-in-law. It was a marriage of convenience. Both my mother and Aberdeen were left with three small children. Unfortunately my grandfather was right. The marriage has brought my mother little happiness."

"When your grandfather died and you were forced to live with your stepfather, it must have been difficult."

"I was devastated," Abercorn said quietly. "When I turn twenty-one in January, Aberdeen will no longer be my guardian. I count my blessings that I inherited my grandfather's estate in Ireland and his title. It will allow me to be my own man and not depend upon Aberdeen for anything."

"Our deep love of Ireland is another thing we have in common, James."

"Your Grace, I have taken you as my role model. You served as the lord lieutenant of Ireland and it has inspired me to follow in your footsteps. I too have ambitions to become the viceroy one day."

"Bravo! That is a worthy endeavor."

"I am looking forward to taking my seat in the House of Lords when I reach my majority in January."

"Wonderful. I shall make a point of joining you there upon occasion."

Louisa was amazed at the friendship that had developed so quickly between the pair. Their admiration for each other was palpable. *Abercorn wishes that John Russell could be his father and it's obvious that their high regard for each other is mutual. No doubt Father would like James Hamilton for a son.*

She heard Mr. Burke's voice.

"Excuse me for interrupting you, but Her Grace has sent me to summon you to the blue drawing room where she is entertaining the Hollands and the Greys."

"Ah, my duties as host are remiss. Lead on, Mr. Burke."

"Would you mind if I took a closer look at your books, Your Grace?"

"Be my guest, James. It gives me pleasure to share them with another book lover."

Damnation. I'll have to sit here all afternoon. Louisa felt her leg cramp and moved her position, as quietly as she could, to ease it. A minute later, her heart sank as she watched James Hamilton's dark head appear as he climbed the ladder to the upper level.

He stopped halfway and turned his head to look at her. "My instincts were correct."

"I got a leg cramp." She spoke defensively, as if that excused her eavesdropping.

"If you wish to listen secretly to what is said in private, you should wear a less distinctive fragrance. Your jasmine stole to me some time ago." He finished climbing to the upper level and walked toward her.

Her pulse raced. "It wasn't intentional. I came to look up betony." Sitting on the floor she appeared defenseless and completely without guile.

He held out his hand to help her to her feet. She stared at his outstretched palm, wanting to place her hand in his yet hesitant to succumb to his magnetism. He had such a commanding, masculine presence that if she touched him, she feared he might gain some mystical power over her. Instead of her hand, she gave him the book.

"Culpeper's Complete Herbal. This is a rare treasure," he said with reverence. "Does he list the properties of betony?"

She rose to her feet gracefully, without his assistance. "Yes. Let me show you." Without touching his hands, she turned the pages until she found the colorful illustration. Then she deliberately stepped away from him, putting a safe distance between them. Abercorn was too tall, too broad, too dark, too compelling, and far, far too handsome.

Louisa erected an invisible shield to protect herself from the attractive devil.

"Betony is in bloom at the moment. Would you like to go to the woods and see if we can find some?"

Lu swallowed hard. If she refused, he'd think she found him so dangerously tempting that she was afraid to be alone with him. "That would be most kind," she replied coolly. "I'll get a basket and an herb knife from the stillroom."

As the pair made their way through Woburn's formal gardens and across the parkland toward the woods, Louisa steered the conversation along impersonal topics. "What is the name of your estate in Ireland?"

"Barons Court in County Tyrone. The tower house was built in medieval times, but my grandfather built the modern additions to the castle."

She was surprised to learn he owned a castle. "How fascinating. Tell me, is Ireland more like England or Scotland?"

"It is like neither. It is unique. While much of England is ordered and cultivated, and Scotland is wild and rugged, Ireland is an enchanting place. My property is laced with interconnecting lakes and rivers brimming with salmon, trout, and pike. It is lush and green—a veritable nature lover's paradise, carpeted with wildflowers that attract myriad butterflies and birds."

"It sounds like a fairy-tale land. No wonder it has spawned so much folklore."

"Ah, you have heard of our pixies, elves, goblins, and leprechauns. Do you believe in supernatural beings, my lady?"

"Perhaps. Shakespeare writes about them in *A Midsummer Night's Dream*."

"And in his poems: *Where the bees suck, there suck I; In a cowslip's bell I lie.*"

Louisa's mouth curved in delight. *"There I couch when owls do cry. On the bat's back I do fly."* Her smile faded. *He lured me to quote the lines of the poem. I fell into his trap so easily. I must not follow where Abercorn leads.* She moved away and looked around for betony plants.

"I think we'll find them deeper in the woods," he suggested. "It delighteth in shady places," he quoted, leading the way to where the trees grew together more densely.

Louisa hesitated until he beckoned, then followed slowly.

"Seek and ye shall find." Abercorn grinned, slipped a knife from his pocket, and squatted down to cut the betony plants.

Louisa hesitated no longer. She put the basket on the ground, took the herb knife, and crouched beside the purple patch. "They are in bloom, just as Culpeper said they would be. We'll gather the leaves, stalks, and flowers but not the bitter roots."

In a short time her basket was filled to the brim. "I'll take the betony to the stillroom and make the decoction before dinner. I'll use Culpeper's recipe."

"Jack is fortunate to have such a caring sister."

"My brothers are louts, and we seldom get along," she informed him.

"But that's on the surface, and you do it for fun and amusement. Underneath, there is a deep bond of affection and loyalty that is immediately apparent to an outsider."

"I fear you are deluding yourself," she told him as they emerged from the woods.

Georgy, accompanied by Teddy and George, spotted them and rode toward the pair. "We've been sent to find you and bring Abercorn to meet the Hollands and the Greys." She looked from one to the other with speculative eyes. "What on earth have you been doing in the woods?" she demanded.

Louisa, determined to conceal her errand of mercy on Jack's behalf, tossed her head. "I've been minding my own business, which is more than you seem capable of doing."

Georgy's face lit with a sudden idea. "You've been *kissing!* Lu, I underestimated how cunning you could be."

Teddy hooted. "Well, James, you didn't let the grass grow under your feet!"

"You devil, Georgy!" Louisa was outraged. "We were doing no such thing. Hamilton was helping me gather some betony."

Teddy laughed. "More like gathering rosebuds while ye may."

James winked. "I'll never tell."

Louisa blushed, but since it was four against one, she decided to have the last word. She raised her chin and looked her sister directly in the eye. "You owe me a guinea."

"Not likely!" Georgy declared. "I'll have to see the kiss with my own eyes."

Hamilton hid his amusement. Though they had not kissed, Louisa was willing to let her sister think otherwise. He surmised correctly that it was in order to collect a wager.

By the time the young people returned to the house, the Duchess of Bedford's sister Charlotte had arrived with her son Arthur and her daughter Sophia, the only two of her fourteen offspring who were still unwed. Since Arthur Lennox attended Oxford with his cousins and their friends, no introductions were necessary.

James Hamilton introduced himself to the Duchess of Richmond. He took her fingers to his lips. "I am delighted to make your acquaintance, Your Grace."

"Such charming manners. Abercorn, this is my daughter, Lady Sophia."

Sophia threw him a teasing smile. "I remember you very well, my lord. I saw you at Carlton House when we were children, but you had eyes only for Louisa."

He smiled back at her. "Then you must allow me to make amends for such discourtesy, my lady."

"Aunt Georgina, may we have a birthday ball as part of the celebrations this year?"

"Well, I hadn't planned one, but there is no reason why we cannot have an impromptu birthday ball tomorrow night, if the other ladies are amenable."

"I think that's a splendid idea," Lady Holland declared. "Your versatile Woburn musicians can play anything from English country dances to Scottish reels."

Georgy nudged her sister and murmured, "Why didn't we think of that? Balls are the perfect setting for dalliance."

Louisa frowned. *Plainly Sophia fancies herself in the arms of Abercorn.* She wondered why she found the idea so distasteful.

John Russell spoke up. "I had a note from the Duke of Clarence this morning, accepting my invitation to Woburn. He and his wife will be arriving tomorrow. William is a bit long in the tooth for Highland dancing, don't you think?"

"He can sit on the sidelines and watch. I don't imagine you'll be doing any Highland flings yourself, John," Georgina declared. "Princess Adelaide is twenty years his junior and I warrant she loves to dance as much as any other female."

"I could organize a hunt for the following day," Jack suggested. "The royal princes are avid huntsmen, and Woburn offers the best shooting in England."

"That's a splendid idea, Jack." When John saw the look of distaste evidenced by his wife and daughters, he added, "We will exclude the ladies. It will give them a chance to visit and indulge in a little gossip."

The ladies instantly fell into a discussion of what they would wear to the ball, giving the men a chance to escape to the gun room, where they chose their weapons for the hunt and indulged their taste for fine Scotch whiskey.

Louisa went to the stillroom to make the decoction for her brother Jack. She boiled the betony flowers and leaves with wine and honey, and allowed the syrup to cool. An hour later she poured it into a clear bottle and stoppered it with a cork. She took it up to Jack's bedchamber, set it on his nightstand, and wrote him a note following Culpepper's instructions to take a spoonful every morning.

Just before the dinner gong rang, Lord John Russell arrived. He took his stepmother into his arms and greeted her warmly. "I didn't dare be late," he whispered into her ear.

"Johnny, it's so lovely to see you. Your father has been expecting you. We have lots of company and more coming tomorrow, but none more welcome than you, my dear."

Lady Holland kissed his cheek. Johnny Russell was like a second son to her. He had often stayed with Beth and Henry when his parents had visited Europe.

Louisa, who had spotted his arrival, came running. "Johnny," she cried breathlessly, "I knew you wouldn't forget Georgy's birthday. We're celebrating our birthdays together and having an impromptu ball tomorrow night."

"Good, a party is just what I need after those long hours in Parliament." The dinner gong sounded and Johnny linked arms with Georgina and Beth and escorted the two ladies to the Van Dyke dining room. Before they arrived, a covey of males emerged from the gun room.

"Johnny! I told Abercorn you'd be visiting us shortly. I know I sent you congratulations on getting the Irish Catholic emancipation bill passed, but now I have the pleasure of praising your accomplishment in person." The duke embraced his son warmly, and then everyone fell into step behind the pair as they entered the dining room.

Informality reigned as Lord John was greeted by his brothers and their guests.

"This is James Hamilton, Marquis of Abercorn, and a true champion of Ireland. Why don't you sit between us, Johnny, and fill us in on all the details?"

Louisa knew it was a foregone conclusion that before the meal was over, Johnny and Abercorn would become fast friends. *All they have in common is a love of Ireland. They don't know anything else about each other.* Every male in the room, save Abercorn, was a staunch Whig. She cleared her throat and spoke to Johnny. "Are you aware that James Hamilton is a *Tory*?"

The two men looked at each other and then threw back their heads in laughter.

"Lu, surely you know I have built my reputation on bipartisanship?" Johnny asked.

The Duchess of Bedford declared, "My mother, Jane Gordon, was the leading Tory hostess, but she had no objections to my marrying into one of the leading Whig families. Fortunately, there is nothing illegal about cohabiting."

Everyone at table thought the racy rejoinder was hilarious. Everyone except Louisa, of course.

The duke spoke up. "The Duke of Wellington has often visited Woburn since he became prime minister. At the moment, I fully support his Tory government."

"Now that the emancipation bill has been signed, I'm once again campaigning in the Commons for parliamentary reform," Johnny announced. "So far, however, my efforts to introduce a bill to reduce election bribery have been unsuccessful."

"It's unconscionable that small boroughs owned by wealthy landowners have the right to elect more Members of Parliament than large industrial towns like Birmingham and Manchester," Abercorn commiserated.

"At the risk of being thought radicals, we have all supported a change to the voting system for years," Lord Holland declared.

"Without reform, we run the risk of a revolution in Britain, like the one in Europe," Earl Grey warned.

Bessy gasped. "Oh please, let us not speak of revolution. It's the reason we had to leave Europe."

Johnny smiled at his brother's wife. "You'll be quite safe in Mayfair, Bessy. Your townhouse is in the same general area as Russell Square. You'll be neighbors of our brother Francis and his wife."

"Yes, I correspond with Anna Maria." Bessy looked puzzled. "Don't you also reside at the Russell Square house, since you and Francis both sit in the House of Commons every day?"

"My committee work necessitates longer hours than Francis. I lease rooms close to Whitehall, but I visit Russell Square whenever I can."

"Then I shall expect to see you in Cavendish Square," she said archly.

Louisa sent Johnny a surreptitious look of horror that clearly told him to make no promises. He understood the look and hid his amusement.

Abercorn saw the look that passed between them. *Lord John and Lady Lu communicate without words. I envy him.*

"Louisa, are you going to entertain us with one of your spectacular Spanish dances tonight?" Johnny asked his favorite sister.

Her mother jumped in immediately. It was a perfect opportunity for her daughter to display her talent and become the center of attention. "I'm sure we can prevail upon her."

Louisa's eyes lit up. "I'll dance, if Johnny will do a soliloquy from Shakespeare."

His brothers hissed good-naturedly. Lord John could quote numerous passages from Shakespeare with great dramatic flourish. "Since you are so enthusiastic, I'll skip the soliloquy and do Henry V's rousing address to his troops."

"Yay!" Henry shouted, and Cosmo and young Alex banged their knives on the table.

James Hamilton grinned. "You are obviously a disruptive influence." *And you are loved by the entire family. Someday, if I'm lucky enough, I'll be part of it.*

After dinner, the Russell family and all their guests trooped down to the theater. Louisa consulted with Georgy and asked her to play her Spanish piece. Johnny offered to go onstage first, to give Louisa time to change into her costume.

The curtains parted to show Johnny standing in the spotlight. A hush fell over the assembly as they anticipated the dramatic speech.

Lord John Russell threw back his head and his clear voice poured forth as if he were making a speech in the Commons.

> *"Once more unto the breach, dear friends, once more,*
> *Or close the wall up with our English dead!*
> *In peace there's nothing so becomes a man*
> *As modest stillness and humility,*
> *But when the blast of war blows in our ears,*
> *Then imitate the action of the tiger:*
> *Stiffen the sinews, summon up the blood,*
> *Disguise fair nature with hard-favored rage,*

Then lend the eye a terrible aspect,
Let pry through the portage of the head
Like the brass cannon, let the brow o'erwhelm it
As fearfully as doth a galled rock
O'erhang and jutty his confounded base,
Swilled with the wild and wasteful ocean.
Now set the teeth and stretch the nostril wide,
Hold hard the breath and bend up every spirit
To his full height. On, on, you noblest English,
Whose blood is fet from fathers of war-proof,
Fathers that, like so many Alexanders,
Have in these parts from morn till even fought
And sheathed their swords for lack of argument.
Dishonor not your mothers. Now attest
That those whom you called fathers did beget you.
Be copy now to men of grosser blood,
And teach them how to war. And you, good yeoman,
Whose limbs were made in England, show us here
The mettle of your pasture. Let us swear
That you are worth your breeding, which I doubt not,
For there is none of you so mean and base
That hath not noble luster in your eyes.
I see you stand like greyhounds in the slips,
Straining upon the start. The game's afoot.
Follow your spirit, and upon this charge
Cry, 'God for Harry, England, and Saint George!'"

A moment of awed silence was followed by deafening applause and shouts of "God for Harry, England, and Saint George!"

Johnny took a bow and the curtains closed. He left the stage and seated himself beside Abercorn amid rousing congratulations from the entire assembly.

Georgy took her place at the harpsichord and waited until the noise died down. She held her fingers above the keys and then brought them down in one loud chord.

The curtains swung open to reveal Lady Louisa affecting a dramatic pose. Her dark hair was pulled back smoothly, and a large crimson rose was pinned above one ear. She wore a flowing skirt and red silk shawl, and carried a black lace fan that concealed her face below her eyes.

Everyone drew in a swift breath of appreciation as the staccato music began and she raised her hands above her head, clicking the castanets in perfect rhythm to the pounding notes. Her red skirts billowed out, revealing black silk stockings and stiletto-heeled shoes. She danced a perfect *paso doble*, stamping her heels in quick tempo as the music pulsed and reverberated around the audience. The haughty, dramatic look on her face befitted a proud Spaniard. Her performance was theatrical, vivid, and striking. At the end, when she twirled her shawl, the illusion of the bull was tangible.

The applause was deafening as Louisa took her bows and cries of "Brava!" went up in the theater.

"She has a marvelous talent," Johnny declared.

"Yes, she's incomparable," Abercorn agreed. "Someday I intend to make her my wife."

Chapter Five

*T*he affable Duke of Clarence sat quaffing claret in Woburn's library in the company of his host and a crowd of male guests.

John Russell signaled his son Jack, who spoke up on cue. "We have arranged a hunt tomorrow in your honor, Your Highness. The pheasants are particularly plentiful this year. There will be no need to beat the bushes—the dogs will flush them out. You won't get better shooting in all of England."

"Splendid! I was hoping for a game shoot and brought along my guns, just in case."

"Jack has agreed to help me manage the estate. For our many friends who come to Woburn for the game, my son has agreed to organize all the hunts from now on."

"You are indeed lucky to have such fine sons, Bedford. You are blessed."

Abercorn kept a straight face, though inwardly he was amused. The king's brother had sons aplenty, albeit illegitimate. He had fathered five sons with the Irish actress Dorothea Jordan, who all bore the surname FitzClarence.

Once the Duke of Clarence had been fortified with wine and mollified with the promise of a good hunt, John Russell brought up the subject of his son's ambitions for a naval career. "Now that Edward has completed his studies at Oxford, all he talks about is joining the military. I told him he could seek no better advice than yours, William. No man breathing is more informed about the navy than the former Admiral of the Fleet."

Abercorn was amazed at how adroitly Bedford handled the Royal Duke. With a combination of charm, flattery, and familiarity, he induced Clarence to use his influence and put in a word for Edward at the Admiralty, which would ensure a plumb naval commission. *Edward is extremely fortunate to have John Russell for a father. My stepfather, Aberdeen, is so dour and abrasive that he offends everyone he deals with.*

Bedford refilled Clarence's glass. "Drink up, William. It will fortify you against the impromptu ball the ladies have planned for this evening."

In the Venetian drawing room, the ladies were regaling Princess Adelaide about the birthday ball they were holding that evening.

"Oh, I simply love to dance," Adelaide admitted, "but I'm not sure I brought a suitable ball gown." She put her hand up to her hair, rather self-consciously.

"Nonsense, Your Highness. We are completely informal here in the country. We don't wear Parisian fashions at Woburn, I assure you. And if you like, I'll have my maid do your hair in the latest style," Georgina suggested.

"Princess Adelaide, you have such lovely thick, shining hair," Louisa declared. "If it were fashioned into large curls and pinned up high with glittering ornaments, it would be extremely flattering."

"I shall take your advice, my dear. I find it decidedly pleasant to be surrounded by young people. It makes me feel alive," she confided.

Lady Sophia hurried into Louisa's bedchamber. "I hear the pipers and the violins. I don't want to be late for the dancing. Will you help me fasten my gown, please?"

Georgy threw her sister a look of disgust. "I told you our dresses were out of style, Lu. Slim empire gowns are decidedly old-fashioned. Waists are back to their natural place, and everyone in London is wearing full skirts and puffed-out sleeves."

"It won't matter tonight, Georgy. The young men from Oxford won't know what the latest styles are," Louisa assured her. "Mother will have new gowns made for us before we make our debut. She's very fashion conscious."

"We have only three bachelors to partner us tonight, Sophia, so please don't push yourself forward and take advantage. You'll have to seek a husband elsewhere."

"Georgy, I'm not husband hunting. As a matter of fact, I'm being courted."

Georgy's mouth fell open. "By whom?" she demanded.

Sophia blushed. "His name is Thomas . . . Lord Thomas Cecil."

"I believe Cecil's brother is the Marquis of Exeter," Louisa declared.

"Damn and blast! I must be the only twenty-year-old in England without prospects!"

"The night is young—you may very well have prospects before the ball is over."

The musicians had finished tuning their instruments by the time the three young ladies arrived in the ballroom. All the married ladies had their husbands in tow. When Georgina arrived with the duke and saw that the bachelors were conspicuous by their absence, she lost no time in going below and rounding them up. She herded them to the third floor and signaled the musicians.

The first dance was a quadrille, and when Teddy Fox asked Georgy to partner him, she was eager to comply. Then Abercorn bowed before Princess Adelaide. She bestowed a radiant smile of thanks upon him and tripped forth as lightly as a girl.

George Grey partnered Lady Sophia, and Johnny clasped Louisa's hand and led her onto the floor. Lu wasn't embarrassed that her brother partnered her. He was one of the few males with whom she felt comfortable. These four couples formed the first square and went through the eight intricate figures that made up the dance. By the time the quadrille was over, the ice had been broken and everyone was laughing.

Georgina announced that a mazey dance would be next. Teddy Fox bowed before Louisa. "Would you guide me through this one? I'm not sure of the steps."

She smiled at him. "Everyone gets mixed up in this one, though it's simple enough. The ladies and gentlemen form two lines facing one another. Then the top couple raises their arms to form an arch and the other couples dance beneath it."

The dance went smoothly enough until George Grey, who was partnering Georgy, forgot it was their turn to form the arch and the entire thing became a muddle of confusion. Good-natured laughter ensued until they all managed to straighten themselves out and finish the dance.

The duchess and her best friend had concocted a plan. Beth whispered to Georgina, "I think *now* would be a good time."

Georgina held up her hands to gain her guests' attention. "We will now have a cotillion, where everyone changes partners when the music stops. But Lady Holland tells me the latest craze in London is a *kissing* dance. So when the dance ends, the gentleman will kiss his partner!"

Whistles went up from all the males in the ballroom.

Louisa drew in a quick breath and she felt her cheeks grow warm. *Mother and Beth have come up with this plan because I told them I've never been kissed. I should leave!* An inner voice told her this was the only way she could win her wager with Georgy. When George Grey asked to partner her, she was on the horns of a dilemma. *Should I run or should I stay?* For a moment Louisa was rooted to the spot and then George took her hand and led her into the dance.

Each time the music stopped, there was a tangible air of anticipation. When it started again, everyone laughed and changed partners. The dance went on and on, as the musicians played a few bars, ceased playing for a beat or two, then resumed the music.

Georgina watched the couples closely. When at last she saw James Hamilton take her daughter Louisa as his partner, she signaled the musicians to end the dance.

When Louisa heard the music stop, she drew in a swift breath. *Oh, please, please, play on!* She waited as three beats stretched into four and she was suddenly gripped by panic. *This cannot be happening to me!* She glanced up and her eyes met Abercorn's triumphant gaze. Her long black lashes swept down immediately and lay fanned against her pale cheeks. She stiffened as she felt Hamilton's powerful arms envelop her. She could hear her heartbeat thudding inside her eardrums as fear spiraled through her belly.

To Louisa, everything seemed to be happening in slow motion. She felt the pressure of his hands on her back as he drew her close. Her lashes flew up in time to see his dark head bend toward her and his lips descend slowly to take possession of her mouth. She gasped for breath and as her lips opened, her eyes closed and Abercorn kissed her.

She held herself rigid, but gradually his compelling closeness overwhelmed her. She stopped thinking and starting feeling. Her stiffness melted and her lips softened beneath his possessive mouth. His male scent stole her senses and his hard, muscled body pressed against hers, luring her to raise her arms and cling to him. She heard the whisper of her gown as it brushed against his marble-hard thighs. Her lips could taste the raw desire of his mouth as he bent her to his will. And then it was over. She felt dismay that the kiss ended and she staggered as he withdrew his powerful arms from her. She gazed up into his dark eyes. *I'll remember your kiss forever.*

Louisa blinked as if awakening from a trance. *Dear God, you must never let the dominant Irish devil know the effect he had on you!* She raised her hand and slapped his face. She knew immediately it was the worst thing she could have done. He grinned down at her knowingly. The slap told him exactly how devastating his kiss had been.

She heard everyone clapping and her cheeks burned with chagrin. When she glanced around at the other couples, however, she realized they were not looking at her and Abercorn. All eyes were on the Duke and Duchess of Bedford, who were locked in a passionate embrace. Her mother's words echoed in her mind: *Darling, a kiss is such an insignificant trifle.* Louisa now realized that was a blatant lie. There was absolutely nothing trifling or insignificant about Abercorn's kiss. Or her parents' for that matter.

The musicians began to play a slow waltz. Hamilton swept her into his arms and led her around the floor in sweeping circles. Louisa did not protest. She was determined to show him that she was indifferent to both his looks and his charm. One thing was certain. She must never allow him to kiss her again.

John Russell gazed down at his beautiful wife. "I love you, little girl."

Georgina touched his face tenderly. "I know you do, my darling."

"Will you waltz with me?"

"I would love it above all things!" She had more good sense than to ask him if he was up to dancing.

"There's method in my madness," he confessed as he led her slowly about the floor. "After this dance, the Scottish reels will begin, and all hell will break loose."

"I remember the first time you put on a kilt and partnered me in a Strathspey."

"I remember it too—the bloody kilt swung up and revealed my bare arse!"

"You have a very manly arse, old man," she whispered provocatively.

"Flattery, begod!" he teased.

"Well, I'll be damned. My sister Charlotte is waltzing with the Duke of Clarence! I'm willing to wager she is the one who asked him and not the other way around."

"That's a safe bet. The Gordon sisters are all bold as brass."

"Poor John. You got the runt of the litter, I'm afraid."

"I got my heart's desire. Not many men can say that."

Georgina stood on tiptoe and kissed him. "At midnight, it will be Georgy's birthday. I think we should give the girls their presents tonight. What do you think?"

"I want what you want. Always have . . . always will," he vowed.

"And that's the reason I love you." She smiled up into his eyes.

For the next two hours the pipers took over and the dancers became raucous as one Scottish reel followed another, interspersed by lively Strathspeys. It was thirsty work and the champagne and whiskey imbibed by the Russells and their guests induced them to cast aside their inhibitions and celebrate life to the full.

At midnight the assembly moved to the supper room. As a large candle-lit cake was wheeled in, everyone sang *Happy Birthday* to Georgy and Louisa.

Georgina presented the birthday girls with identically wrapped presents. All the guests gathered round to watch the sisters open the gifts from their parents.

Louisa carefully removed the ribbon and paper to reveal a velvet jewel case. She caught her breath as she raised the lid and saw the glittering necklace. She had always been in awe of the famous Russell diamonds and was thrilled that her father and mother were bestowing part of the exquisite collection on her. She glanced at Georgy, knowing she was opening a similar gift of diamonds. In all, there were four necklaces, as well as numerous brooches, bracelets, and pairs of earrings.

Louisa threw her father a radiant smile. As her mother fastened the necklace about her throat, she asked, "How can you bear to part with them?"

"Jewels should be worn, not hoarded away in boxes. Display them proudly, darling, but always remember that your own beauty out-shines any diamond."

As her mother fastened Georgy's necklace about her throat, Lou-isa caught a fleeting look of disappointment on her sister's face. It was gone in a trice as all the ladies gathered round to admire the pre-cious gems, with *oohs* and *aahs*.

William's wife Elizabeth turned on her heel and abruptly left the ball-room. Her husband followed her reluctantly, knowing he would feel the brunt of her jealousy.

"Bessy!" he called after her, but knew she would neither turn around nor wait for him, as she rushed in outrage to their suite in the east wing. The moment he closed the door, she turned on him like a wounded tigress.

"How *dare* she?" She beat her clenched fists against his chest. "The diamond collection is part of the Russell inheritance. She has no right to adorn her wretched daughters with jewels that belong to the Russell family. They are priceless heirlooms. I want you to go to your father immediately and tell him that we object. *Strenuously* ob-ject. The audacity of the woman is beyond belief!"

Elizabeth drew in a swift breath as a low knock came on the door.

William opened the door and admitted his brother Johnny.

Lord John spoke quietly. "The *woman*, as you call her, is the Duchess of Bedford."

Bessy turned away in anger and paced about the chamber. Then she returned to face her husband's brother. "To our great sorrow she is the duchess. But that doesn't give her the right to give away the Russell diamonds."

"She has every right. My father gave her the jewels as a wedding present."

"She has him wrapped about her little finger. Without doubt she is the most flagrantly extravagant woman in England. She entertains as if she were royalty."

"I would give the pair of you a little advice. Don't make Georgina your enemy. Father truly loves her. She has it within her power to get him to change his will. If he chooses, he can disown the sons he had with his first wife and leave everything to Georgina's children."

"What Johnny says is true, Bessy. You must stop being vindictive toward her."

"William, you are weak as water. You don't have the courage of your convictions." She threw Johnny a contemptuous glance. "Why do you champion her?"

"When Georgina married Father, she gave him both love and support—things that were lacking in his first marriage to our mother. She also loved me as if I were her own son. I know she can be extravagant and outrageously outspoken, but her generosity of spirit simply outweighs all her flaws."

"I think our absence will be noted, Bessy. It's best that we return."

"I refuse to worship at the shrine of Georgina and her daughters. You may return and kowtow if you choose, William. I bid you good night, gentlemen."

Caught between the devil and the deep, William chose to return with Johnny. "Unfortunately Bessy has a haughty and unbending nature."

"I warrant she may never feel affection for Georgina, but she would be wise to show a little respect," Johnny advised.

By two o'clock, most of the men were legless with drink and declared they had danced enough to last them a lifetime. Some of the ladies retired, but Georgina and the birthday girls joined the more intrepid gentlemen in the long gallery where the gaming tables lured the revelers to try their luck.

The Duchess of Bedford partnered Lord Holland against her sister and the Duke of Clarence. They played whist for an hour until Charlotte threw down her cards in disgust. "Lud, that time I cheated and still lost."

"The cards are against us, m'dear," Clarence declared.

"Never mind, William, perhaps you'll have better luck in the hunt tomorrow." Georgina knew if the royal duke didn't seek his bed soon, he would be unfit for the shoot.

"I shall retire, if you will be good enough to lead me to my chamber, Your Grace."

Charlotte beckoned her daughter Sophie, who had been playing faro with her Russell cousins. "What about your girls, Georgina? Do you think it prudent to let them gamble until dawn with these young vultures?"

"Charlotte, you know *prudent* isn't in my repertoire." She glanced around the gallery. William had fallen asleep on a couch with a drink in his hand. Johnny was having an animated conversation with young Abercorn, and Georgy was giggling happily as she sat playing faro with Teddy, George, her brother Edward, and her sister. "Georgy is extremely impulsive, but no more than I was at her age."

When Louisa saw that her mother was retiring, she rose from the table. She hadn't been able to concentrate on her cards because her thoughts were filled with Abercorn. The effect of the kiss they had shared still lingered. Though she vowed to put it from her mind and focus on the game, she found it impossible to forget. She glanced quickly in Hamilton's direction and saw he was deep in conversation with Johnny. She joined her mother and kissed her cheek. "Thank you for a lovely birthday celebration, and thank you for the precious gift." She touched the diamonds that lay against her throat. "I will cherish them always."

"I find more pleasure in seeing my daughters wearing the diamonds than in wearing them myself." Georgina took firm hold of the Duke of Clarence, and Lord Holland offered his arms to Charlotte and Louisa.

As she walked from the gallery, Louisa vowed that she would not look back.

At the faro table, Edward had lost every game for the last hour and George Grey hadn't done much better, since they were both three sheets to the wind. "It doesn't seem fair that m'sister is having all the bloody luck."

"Of course it's fair. It's my *birthday*. . . . I can't lose!" Georgy declared.

"In that case, I'm done. My pockets are to let."

"I agree," Grey said owlishly. "Not decent to resheive a drubbing at the hands of a female . . . speshly one dripping in diamonds." He stood up and made his unsteady way from the long gallery.

"I didn't want diamonds," Georgy confessed. "I wanted a new horse. A big male hunter like yours, Teddy."

"In that case, I'll put up my horse against your necklace," Teddy offered.

Georgy picked up her glass of champagne and drained it. "It's my birthday, Teddy. I can't lose," she warned.

"Won't let a female beat me," he asserted aggressively.

Edward let out a loud snore as his head dropped to the gaming table.

It caught Johnny's attention. "I seem to be the last Russell standing." He removed the drink from William's hand and lifted his brother's feet onto the couch. "Good night, Abercorn. I'll see you at the hunt tomorrow."

James Hamilton got to his feet and stretched. He had thoroughly enjoyed his conversation with Lord John. He hadn't been paying much attention to the gamblers since Louisa had retired with her mother. He glanced over at the table and frowned when he saw Georgy was still drinking and gambling. He moved toward the table with a feeling of disquiet.

Georgy's eyes glittered with recklessness as she unfastened her necklace with unsteady fingers and laid it on the table. "You are about to lose your favorite mount, Teddy. I'll cut you for it—high card wins." She reached confidently toward the deck of cards, cut it, and turned up a jack. She laughed with abandon. "Jack is my lucky charm!"

Teddy sat still with a stunned look on his face. Then he reached out unsteadily and cut the deck. When he turned up a king, he threw back his head and laughed raucously.

Furious, Georgy picked up the necklace and threw it at him. "Damn you to hellfire, Teddy Fox! Keep your bloody horse!" She jumped up angrily, knocked over her chair, and began to stalk away.

"Don't be a sore loser, Georgy. I'm sure you will think of some way to persuade me to give you back your diamonds."

Abercorn asked quietly, "You put up your horse?"

"Wouldn't you, for a chance to win diamonds?" Teddy asked.

"I'm rather fond of my horse, but I'd hazard a throw of the dice if you'd be willing to bet the necklace." Abercorn pulled a pair of dice from his pocket and rolled a seven. He gathered them up and handed them to Teddy, who dropped them three times before he managed to get a firm grip on them. James knew Teddy was so intoxicated, that it would be a miracle if he remembered anything in the morning.

Teddy cast the dice and rolled a three. It slowly sank in that he had lost. "Damnation," he cursed. "I didn't want to lose my hunter."

"You didn't lose your horse, Teddy. We were playing for the necklace."

A look of relief transformed his face. "Oh, all right then." He fished in his waistcoat pocket and handed over the diamonds.

Chapter Six

When Louisa fell asleep, once again she dreamed that she was in the Highlands on a recruiting mission with her mother and sister. The line of braw Scots stretched out for a mile, but as she offered each one a kiss, he turned into James Hamilton. He kissed her thoroughly, gave her a look of triumph and passed her on to the next man. Again and again the Scot turned into the wicked Irish devil whose possessive kisses turned her knees to water.

Louisa awoke with a start as her sister rushed into her bedchamber and slammed the door. She sat up in bed. "Is that you, Georgy?"

"Yes, it's me—who the devil else would it be?"

Lu, hearing the near panic in her sister's voice, turned up the lamp. "What's the matter?"

"Nothing! Why do you always think there is something the matter?"

"Because there usually is when you awaken me." Lu saw that her sister's face was unusually flushed and knew she'd had far too much to drink. "Are you going to be sick?"

"No . . . Yes!"

Louisa reached under the bed for the chamber pot. "Where's your necklace?"

"I lost it," Georgy said defiantly.

"No wonder you feel sick! Don't worry; I'll help you look for it. You were wearing it when I came up to bed. It must be in the long gallery."

"We won't find it."

"We'll keep looking until we do. Don't tell Mother you lost it. She would be devastated to think you were careless with the Russell diamonds."

Georgy kicked off her shoes and swayed precariously.

"Better lie down before you fall down. Get into my bed and I'll go down now and look for your necklace." She reached for her robe. "If the servants find it in the morning, they'll take it straight to Mother."

Louisa watched her sister fall asleep the moment her head touched the pillow. She put on her slippers, picked up the lamp, and carefully made her way downstairs. Louisa encountered no servants and she was relieved that they had all gone to bed. When she arrived in the gallery, she saw that Edward was asleep, face down on the gaming table. She set the lamp down and turned up two others. The light fell across William, who was asleep on one of the couches. Carefully, trying not to awaken them, she went down on her hands and knees and began searching the carpet around the table.

She heard a step behind her and almost jumped out of her skin.

"Are you searching for something?"

Abercorn had caught her in her nightclothes and she felt guilty as sin. "My sister lost something." She stood up quickly, too embarrassed to remain on her knees before him.

"Would that something be her diamond necklace?"

Her eyes lit with hope. "Did you find it, my lord?"

"Your sister didn't lose it on the floor. She lost it to Teddy Fox in a bet."

Louisa gasped. "You are a liar! My sister would never gamble away her diamonds." She raised her hand to slap his face.

James Hamilton grabbed her wrist and held it in a vise grip. "You will apologize, Lady Lu. Not for the slap but for calling me a liar."

Her mouth went dry and her knees felt as if they were about to collapse. He towered above her, his dark masculinity threatening to overpower her. She gathered her courage and swallowed her fear. "You delude yourself, Abercorn. I would *die* before I'd apologize to an arrogant Irishman!"

James had been ready to return the diamonds. He released her wrist, reached into his vest pocket, and took out the necklace. The diamonds glittered in the lamplight as he weighed them on the palm of his hand. He returned them to his pocket and bowed formally. "Have it your way, my lady."

"Wake up, Georgy!" Louisa sat beside the bed waiting for her sister to rouse as dawn slowly lightened the sky. For the past hour she had mulled over the possibility that Abercorn had been telling the truth about Georgy. Her patience had finally run out.

Georgy groaned in protest. "What do you want?"

"I want to know if you lost your diamond necklace in a wager with Teddy Fox."

Georgy squinted up at her sister. "I don't know what you're talking about."

"I warrant you know exactly what I'm talking about."

With another groan, Georgy pushed herself up to a sitting position. "It isn't the calamity you imagine, Lu. I shall simply persuade Teddy to give it back to me."

"That will be impossible."

Georgy gave her sister a sideways glance. "You don't know my seductive powers of persuasion."

"Seducing him won't work."

"Why not?"

"Because Teddy doesn't have it anymore."

"What the deuce are you talking about?"

"Abercorn has it. He must have won it from Teddy after you lost it. Georgy, I can't believe you wagered your precious diamond necklace. How could you be so reckless?"

"It was my birthday . . . I didn't think I could lose." She threw her sister a speculative glance. "Perhaps my seductive powers of persuasion can work their magic on Abercorn."

"From my experience with the dominant Irish devil, he's impervious to feminine wiles."

"Well, from my experience, no male breathing is impervious."

Louisa's conscience began to prick her. *Abercorn may have given it back if I hadn't called him a liar. Perhaps if I apologize he will . . . No, he wants something from me.* She chided herself for being fanciful. But deep down, in her heart of hearts, she thought she knew exactly what the Irish devil wanted.

"Don't look so forlorn. I'll have it back by lunchtime," Georgy said with confidence.

"You've forgotten the hunt."

"Then I'll wait until the hunters return. I shall mark my prey."

"If you can't get it back, we can take turns wearing my necklace so Mother doesn't find out you lost it."

"I already thought of that."

Teddy Fox wasn't enjoying the hunt. The Russell brothers and George Grey had bagged far more pheasants, and even his own father had outshot him. His self-esteem was sinking by the hour. He fortified himself from a flask of whiskey he'd slipped into his saddlebag and decided he'd had enough. As he approached the stables, he spotted Georgy Russell and drew rein.

She stood on tiptoe and stroked his horse's nose. "I wish he were mine, but it was foolish of me to wager my diamonds last night to try to win him from you."

Vaguely, Teddy remembered staking his horse on a cut of the cards. "It was your birthday. You should have won." He eyed the full breasts that strained against her tight bodice. "Would you like to come for a ride, Georgy?"

She licked her lips in anticipation. "I would love it, Teddy!"

He reached down with both arms and lifted her before him in the saddle. As he began to slowly canter toward the trees, he could feel her plump bottom between his legs, rubbing against his cock and balls. He became aroused instantly and pressed his hard erection into her soft flesh. "Are you enjoying this, Georgy?"

"Oh, yes." She wriggled her bum. "I love a big animal!"

Teddy transferred the reins into his left hand and brought his right hand up to cup her full breasts. He rubbed his thumb across her nipple and felt it harden with arousal. Fire snaked through his groin as Georgy unfastened the buttons on her bodice luring him to explore her naked titties. With his knees, he guided his horse toward the lake and looked for an inviting spot where they could dismount, so he could finish what she had started.

"I'm not much of a hunter," James Hamilton told Lord John Russell. "I prefer live pheasants to dead ones."

"My brother William is an avid huntsman. My two elder brothers ridiculed me unmercifully because I was such a bad shot. They didn't realize I missed on purpose."

James laughed. "My aim is perfect when I'm shooting at old bottles."

"I've enjoyed the exercise. I don't get enough, sitting long hours in Parliament."

"The weather's been perfect—not a cloud in the sky all afternoon. I know the Duke of Clarence has enjoyed himself."

"Here comes Father." Johnny drew rein and waited. "Are you heading back? I'm amazed at your stamina."

"I've had enough. I can't keep up with that lot. They'll be at it until dark, I warrant."

The three men rode back to the abbey and dismounted in the stables. Johnny refrained from assisting his father. He had too much pride to be helped from the saddle.

"It was a warm ride. I'll give Shammar a rubdown. I'll do the same for your horse if you wish, Your Grace," Abercorn offered.

"That would be most kind, James. I need to get off this leg."

The two younger men removed their jackets and set to work tending the animals. After the rubdown, Johnny led his horse into its stall and returned to admire James's Arabian. "Your mare is lovely. Did you breed her in Ireland?"

"Yes. My stable isn't large, but I value quality over quantity."

"My father's racehorses are bred from Gimcrack, a Woburn champion when I was a boy. Their bloodline is excellent."

"That is evident. I was admiring the pair only yesterday and trying not to covet them." He removed the saddle from the duke's horse, wiped the perspiration from his brow, and picked up the currying brush. "This is hot work. When I'm done, I think I'll take a swim in the lake before dinner. Would you care to join me?"

"I'm not as athletic as you, James. I much prefer the library to cold water."

While the men hunted, the ladies enjoyed a leisurely lunch and then took a stroll through the abbey's renowned formal gardens, which had been designed by Humphrey Repton. The duchess was particularly proud of the Chinese garden with its Oriental pagoda and a carved wooden bridge that arched over an ornamental pond where koi swam between the delicate water lilies.

Later in the afternoon the ladies took tea in the Venetian drawing room as they shared the latest gossip about London's *haut ton*. Louisa saw her sister's look of discomfiture when the conversation turned to

Charlotte's daughter, Sophia, and the grand match that would be announced shortly. Lu wasn't surprised to see Georgy slip away at the first opportunity.

"I would have loved to have a daughter," Princess Adelaide lamented. "I do get to spend time with my niece, however. The late Duke of Kent's daughter, Alexandrina Victoria, though very small for her age, is an extremely intelligent young lady."

"Is it true," Lady Holland asked bluntly, "that the Duchess of Kent is having an illicit affair with John Conroy, the Irish officer who is her private secretary?"

"My husband certainly believes the rumor. All I can tell you is that Conroy is an attractive devil, but extremely dominant. Princess Victoria cannot bear the man."

Another handsome, dominant Irishman! Louisa's mind flew back to her encounter with Abercorn. *I should have used sweet talk last night instead of calling him a liar. I think he is attracted to me. If I apologize profusely, perhaps he will be generous and give me the diamonds. I'll watch for his return from the hunt.*

Louisa made her escape from the drawing room. She saw her brother Johnny as he descended the main staircase. "Ah, you're back from the hunt early."

"Yes. Father had had enough, and Abercorn and I aren't avid huntsmen, so we returned with him. Lord only knows when the rest of them will be back."

"Is Abercorn upstairs?" she asked as casually as she could manage.

Johnny hid a smile. "After he gave Father's horse a rubdown, he went off to the lake for a swim. His athletic build provides him with an excess of disgusting energy."

She tossed her head. "More like an excess of arrogance."

· · ·

As James Hamilton made his way down to the lake, he took off his shirt in anticipation of the cool water. It was only a small lake about a mile across. He knew he could easily swim to the far side and back.

He spotted Teddy Fox's horse tethered to a tree and assumed his Oxford friend had also decided to take a dip in the lake. Just as he was about to call out Teddy's name, he stumbled across a male and female coupling in the long grass. He saw immediately that the naked girl was Georgy Russell, and to his horror, James saw that the man on top of her was Teddy Fox. "Almighty God, what are you doing?"

Abashed that they'd been caught, Teddy rolled off her and pulled up his breeches.

"This isn't a servant girl, Fox, it is the daughter of the Duke of Bedford," Hamilton declared in outrage. "Get the hell out of my sight before I give you the thrashing you deserve."

Fox mounted his horse and took off through the trees.

Georgy grabbed her petticoat to cover her nakedness.

James helped her to her feet and picked up her dress. "The lecherous swine coerced you into this with a promise to return your diamonds. But he no longer has them, Georgy. I do."

She neither acknowledged nor denied his assertion. She donned her petticoat and reached for her riding dress. "Will you return my necklace, James?"

"Of course I will." Guilt washed over him for his role in this sordid affair. If he had given the necklace to Louisa last night, none of this would have happened. "I'll bring it to your room after dinner."

Louisa stood rooted to the spot on the path that led to the lake. She couldn't believe her eyes at the scene she saw before her. A shirtless Abercorn stood holding her sister's dress. *Georgy was stark naked with him until she put on her petticoat.* Lu was shocked beyond belief. Her sister had actually lured James Hamilton to the lake and taken off her clothes in a blatant seduction to get her necklace back. Georgy's words echoed in her brain: *Perhaps my seductive powers of persuasion can work their magic on Abercorn. I'll wait until the hunters return. I shall mark my prey.*

"I told her that James Hamilton was impervious to feminine wiles. How utterly naive I was." Louisa turned on her heel and returned to the house. Her heart was pounding and there was an ache inside her breast. She felt betrayed by both of them—her sister and Abercorn. *I hate him!*

Louisa, needing to dispel her chaotic thoughts, went upstairs to the nursery.

"Lulu!" Rachel greeted her with outstretched arms.

Louisa picked her up and hugged her tightly. Her baby sister's innocence tugged at her heartstrings. Her eyes flooded with tears and she rubbed them away with impatient fingers. "Who's the sweetest, prettiest girl in all the world?"

Rachel touched Louisa's wet cheekbone with a tiny finger. They both turned as the door opened and their mother arrived.

"I've arranged that dinner be put back to seven to accommodate the hunters."

"I think I'll eat with Rachel tonight," Louisa announced. "I'll enjoy bathing her and putting her to bed. I don't spend nearly enough time with her."

"Thank you, darling. I'll have a tray sent up for you. It will give me more time to entertain our guests. Just make sure you don't undermine Nanny's rules."

"Wave bye-bye to Mama. Now, what shall we do?"

"Dobbin!"

Louisa carried her over to her rocking horse and set her down on its back. Rachel swayed back and forth, rocking faster and faster, chortling with glee. When the maid arrived with the food, Rachel refused to get off the horse.

"Let's have a tea party," Louisa suggested. "We can invite your dolls and your bunny rabbit."

"And Cracknut!" Rachel climbed off the horse and ran to her dollhouse, which was a replica of a castle. She pulled out a stuffed animal that resembled a dormouse.

"That's her favorite doll," Nanny said.

Louisa stared at the tattered animal that had been patched over and over with new material. "This used to be mine."

"Mine!" Rachel asserted possessively.

"Yes, darling, Cracknut belongs to you. Sit her down at the table and I'll bring your other guests." Louisa sat the dolls and the rabbit in miniature chairs and her little sister did the same with the dormouse. Rachel took her own small chair and Louisa sat down on the floor. The child refused to wear a bib until her big sister agreed to wear one.

Louisa's stomach balked at the thought of food, but to encourage Rachel she pretended to enjoy the soup and a small portion of cheese soufflé. When Rachel took the carrots from her plate and gave them to her rabbit, it brought a smile to Louisa's lips. "Bunny rabbit can only eat imaginary carrots. *You* have to eat the real ones."

Rachel turned up her nose.

"Carrots are magic. Little girls who eat carrots can see in the dark." *I shouldn't tell her lies. She's so sweet and innocent; she'll believe anything I say.* Louisa's thoughts began to stray to the scene she had witnessed earlier. *Innocence is precious. Life's sordid reality will intrude all too soon—especially if Bessy spreads her ugly suspicions about baby Rachel.* She vowed to spend more time with her little sister and do everything she could to shield her from gossip.

After Rachel ate a raspberry tart and drank her milk, Louisa read her a story. Then she bathed her in a tin tub before the fire and put on her nightdress. She picked her up and held the child in her arms, pressed against her heart. She sang a lullaby and rocked Rachel until she drifted off to sleep. As she laid her in her bed and covered her up, she whispered, "Sweet dreams, darling. If I ever have a little girl, I want her to be exactly like you." Again Abercorn intruded into her thoughts, but she quickly banished him.

Louisa returned to her own bedchamber and stood gazing out into the darkness with unseeing eyes. She vowed that she would not think ill of Georgy. *I mustn't let her know what I saw.* But she knew that a few more of her illusions had been shattered. *Perhaps there is no such thing as love . . . mayhap it is a fanciful illusion. From what I've seen, lust is the compelling force that rules men's lives.*

Suddenly she heard a man's deep voice from the adjoining bedchamber. She hadn't heard the words, but she sensed that it was Abercorn in her sister's room. She hurried across to the door and put her ear against it.

"James! Thank you for keeping your promise to return my diamonds."

"Are you all right, Georgy?"

"Swear you will never tell anyone what happened at the lake?"

"You have my word of honor."

Louisa closed her eyes as a wave of anguish swept over her. *Honor? You have no honor, you lecherous Irish swine!*

Chapter Seven

"Father, if I'm going to be elected as the Member for Horsham, I warrant I'd better start campaigning." Teddy Fox wanted to get away from Woburn. Abercorn's presence made him uncomfortable, and if his parents learned of his intimate encounter with Georgy Russell, they would expect him to make an offer for her.

"I think that's a sound idea," Lord Holland agreed. "The Tories may already have someone running for the seat. In the past I've bought ale from William King, who owns a brewery in Horsham. If we get King and his employees stumping for us, it's in the bag. You'll need to be a resident of West Sussex. I'll come along and lease a house for you."

"Thank you, sir. I'll go and start packing. Edward is coming to canvass with me."

James Hamilton sought out the Duke of Bedford in the library. "I want to thank you for your generous hospitality, Your Grace. Much as I would enjoy spending the entire summer at Woburn, I have plans to visit Ireland before I return to Oxford. I promised to take my younger brother Claud to Barons Court. He has a consuming interest in politics. His ambition is to become a Member of Parliament for County Tyrone."

"A *Tory* Member, no doubt," Bedford teased.

"I'm afraid so, Your Grace. It's in the Hamilton tradition."

"James, I extend an open invitation. You are welcome at Woburn anytime."

When Abercorn took his leave of the Duchess of Bedford, Georgy and Louisa were present. Both girls were relieved that he was departing, though for very different reasons.

"James, I hope you enjoyed your first visit to Woburn and devoutly hope that it won't be your last. You have been a perfect guest. Not only did you make lifelong friends with the duke and Lord John, you gave my daughter her first kiss."

Louisa felt her cheeks burn. She wished the floor would open up and swallow her. "Mother, a kiss is such an insignificant trifle." *Compared to the things your perfect guest has been doing with your other daughter.*

"Ah yes, but a lady always remembers her *first* kiss," the duchess insisted. "My husband tells me you're off to Ireland. I have such fond memories of the time I spent there as vice queen." Georgina laughed. "That sounds so deliciously wicked."

Abercorn kissed her hand. "I deeply appreciate your generous hospitality."

"I shall expect to see you in London at my daughters' debutante ball in September, and you must bring your brother Claud. Until then, I shall bid you *au revoir* and Godspeed on your journey."

He bowed politely and withdrew to bid his friend Charles goodbye.

"Why on earth did you invite him to our debutante ball?" Louisa demanded.

"Darling, we will need all the bachelors we can get. Two of them are departing today. That leaves only George Grey to practice your feminine wiles on." She gave her daughter a look of speculation. "You must admit that James is handsome."

Lu darted a glance at Georgy. "Yes. *Sinfully* handsome."

. . .

The following day, the Russell family and their guests were enjoying brunch on one of Woburn Abbey's shaded verandas. The Duke of Clarence had just been served with a brace of partridge he had bagged in the shoot that had been arranged in his honor. He hadn't taken more than a few appreciative mouthfuls when Mr. Burke appeared with a courier in tow. The man was wearing royal livery.

The messenger bowed to the prince and handed him a missive.

Clarence tore it open and read the letter. His face, usually florid, turned ashen.

John Russell knew something untoward had happened. "Is it bad news, William?"

"I'm afraid it is." The Duke of Clarence hesitated. "My brother— the king—has suffered an apoplexy. He is gravely ill. I've been summoned to Windsor without delay."

"Oh, my dear, we must pack and leave immediately." Princess Adelaide wrung her hands in distress.

John instructed Jack to have William and Adelaide's carriage made ready.

"I shall have my maids assist you, my dearest Adelaide." Georgina added, "And I'll have a hamper of partridges packed for your journey."

After Georgina had instructed her servants and her daughters to help the Duchess of Clarence prepare for her journey to Windsor, she took the courier to Woburn's kitchen and plied him with food and drink. She was a man's woman and prided herself on being able to loosen the tongue of any male breathing.

"I am so sorry you were given the dreadful task of delivering bad news to the Duke of Clarence. These difficult duties are always assigned to those who are the most worthy of trust. The king—dear Prinny—has been an intimate friend of mine all my life. Do you believe he will recover from this cruel attack he has suffered?"

The messenger finished his ale and bent toward her confidentially. "Under the circumstances, Your Grace, that would be impossible."

She refilled his tankard and set another roast partridge before him. "Eat up, my friend. This is likely the last meal you will get today."

Georgina went directly to her husband. "I believe George is already dead."

"If you are correct, my dear, we have just entertained the new king and queen of England."

Discreetly, Georgina passed along the momentous news she had gleaned to her children and her guests. By the time the Duke and Duchess of Clarence descended the stairs, the company was gathered in Woburn's main foyer to bow low and bid a respectful adieu to the royal couple who were now in actuality the reigning king and queen of England.

Within the hour the Duke of Bedford, Lord John, and Earl Grey were conferring in the library.

"If what we believe is true and King George is actually dead, it means an automatic election," the duke declared.

Lord John nodded. "Now is our chance to put the Whigs in power."

"We've all supported Wellington and his Tories, but all that must change now. We must strike while the iron is hot." Earl Grey, who had sat in Parliament since he was twenty-two, cleared his throat. "If I run for prime minister, can I count on your support, gentlemen?"

"Absolutely," Bedford agreed.

"Because the Whigs support reform, we stand an excellent chance of winning." Johnny Russell was convinced they must seize the moment.

"Too bad our friend Henry and his son left yesterday. I'll write him a letter and dispatch a messenger immediately," the duke decided.

. . .

The Russell ladies, Lady Holland, and Lady Grey repaired to the blue drawing room. They were all politically savvy, and the Duchess of Bedford, as the leading Whig hostess, realized that King George's death could put their party in power.

"Though we must all regret poor Prinny's demise, fortune has indeed smiled upon us. The close relationship we forged over the last few days with King William and Queen Adelaide is bound to reap us rewards." Georgina poured wine for everyone.

Mary Grey leaned forward. "I tell you this in confidence, ladies. My husband has entertained ambitions to become prime minister for some time. Now, out of the blue, an election will be called."

Lady Holland could not suppress her excitement. "If the Whigs win the election and Teddy wins the seat from Horsham, both my husband and son will be majority Members of Parliament."

"And it cannot hurt that they will be close friends of both the prime minister and King William," Georgina added.

"Johnny's standing will rise considerably," Louisa pointed out happily. "He will stand a very good chance of getting the reform bill passed."

Georgy listened to the ladies' congratulatory chatter with a look of angry disbelief. "What about me?" she demanded. "Prinny's demise will throw the Court into mourning. Once again my season will have to be postponed because someone died!"

"It is dreadfully inconvenient, darling," her mother said with sympathy. "The Court will observe a formal mourning period, but I warrant the *ton* won't forgo balls and entertainments longer than three months. The coronation of the new king and queen won't likely take place until next spring. But only think . . . after that you will be able to attend Queen Adelaide's drawing rooms at St. James's Palace. When it becomes known that you are a personal friend of the queen, suitors will absolutely fawn on you."

Somewhat mollified, Georgy lowered her voice and spoke to her sister. "We'll be going to King George's funeral. I'll get to see Teddy Fox again."

"Teddy? I thought you had set your cap for James Hamilton," Louisa said coolly.

Georgy tossed her head. "My only interest in Hamilton was getting my diamonds back."

Louisa's heart skipped a beat. *Damn you to hellfire, Abercorn!*

Damn you to hellfire, Aberdeen! This estate belongs to me, thanks to my grandfather. James Hamilton rode into the courtyard of Bentley Priory at Stanmore on the outskirts of London. His stepfather had treated the priory as if he owned it, turning it into a gathering place for Tory politicians. *I shouldn't feel resentment. At least it provides my mother with a lovely home.*

"James! I'm so glad to see you." Eighteen-year-old Claud patted Shammar's neck and led his brother into the stable. "Did you enjoy your visit to Woburn?"

"I enjoyed it immensely. I got on extremely well with the Duke of Bedford and his son Lord John." James dismounted and allowed his younger brother to tend his horse. "How's Mother?" When he had last seen her at Christmas she had not yet recovered from giving birth a month earlier. It was the fourth son Aberdeen had fathered on her.

"Frail looking, I'm afraid. But she's enjoyed my visit, mainly because I don't allow our ugly stepsisters to abuse her."

"By God, they'd better not start while I'm here." At the priory there were three factions of sibling rivalry—Aberdeen's two surviving daughters from his first marriage, Harriet's two sons, James and Claud, from *her* first marriage, and four sons from the couple's second marriage. James thought about the Russell family. He envied the deep affection shared by the siblings and their parents.

The two brothers entered the priory together.

"James, what a lovely surprise," his mother cried.

He enfolded her in his arms. *Frail looking is an understatement.* He smiled into her eyes, masking the concern he felt. "How are you feeling, Mother?"

"I'm feeling stronger every day, James. I'm so happy to have you for a few days. After dinner, you must tell me all about your visit to Woburn Abbey."

He could not help comparing her with Georgina Russell. The Duchess of Bedford was vibrant and blooming with health. *She is brimful of wit and laughter, no doubt because she is deeply loved by her husband.* He silently cursed Aberdeen.

At dinner, Aberdeen's daughters contributed little to the conversation. When they did speak, their manner was petulant. James noticed how thin and colorless they appeared. Their appetites were sparse and he suspected the eldest was consumptive.

After dinner, Claud invited his brother to join him in a visit to the public house in Stanmore village. "The evenings here are an exercise in endless endurance. At least at the pub you get a helping of laughter and music with the ale."

"I'll come tomorrow night. I'd like to spend the evening with Mother. Our brothers' term at Harrow is finished for the summer tomorrow, and once they arrive home they'll demand all her attention."

"You mean our *half-brothers*. For all their superior airs at being educated at Harrow, they can't hide their jealousy of you. Perhaps we should lure them to the pub and get them stinking drunk."

"That would give Aberdeen an excuse to thrash the devil out of them."

Claud waggled his dark eyebrows. "Why do you think I suggested it?"

"Go and enjoy yourself." James was thankful his younger brother had a fun-loving Irish temperament.

James waited until his mother had fed baby Arthur and put him to bed, and then he joined her in her private sitting room. She listened raptly as he described Woburn Abbey and the endlessly fascinating Russell family.

"Do the Duke and Duchess of Bedford have a happy marriage?"

James heard the wistful tone in her voice and it pierced his heart. He decided not to paint the Russells' marriage in brilliant colors. "They tolerate each other well enough. He overlooks her extravagance and turns a blind eye to her admirers."

"That's because he loves her. Just as your father loved me." She sighed and then leaned forward and said earnestly, "James, promise me you will never marry without love. Marriage can be difficult even at the best of times, but when you are starved for love and affection, it eats your heart and deadens your soul."

He squeezed her hand. "That's an easy promise to make." *I made my choice a long time ago. Lady Lu pretends complete indifference to me, but the kiss told me all I need to know. Her innocence and vulnerability are irresistible to me.*

"You have found someone?"

"Let us say that I have my eye on a certain lady."

"James, you are so young. You won't do anything impetuous, will you?"

"Of course not. At least not until I come of age," he teased.

She smiled tenderly. "You are my firstborn and therefore very special to me. Because you lost your father at such an early age, you were forced to mature early, far beyond your years. I am grateful that you are like a father to Claud. The woman you marry will be a very lucky lady."

When the three brothers arrived home from Harrow the next day, they brought momentous news. "King George is dead! Our headmaster got the news this morning from Windsor Castle."

"Poor man," Harriet said with sympathy. "That means the Duke of Clarence will be crowned king. James, didn't you tell me he was a guest at Woburn?"

"Yes. For a royal prince, William was very down to earth. I quite liked the man. When I danced with Princess Adelaide a few days ago, I had no notion she would soon be queen of England."

James's half-brothers glared daggers at him. They already envied him his athletic physique and his titles. Now they were chagrined that he was a friend of the new king and queen of England.

James caught Claud's eye. The two brothers, well versed in politics, knew the turmoil Prinny's death would cause in government circles. The pair went outside so they could speak in private.

"Won't the king's death trigger an automatic election?"

"Yes. Wellington's Tories will have to run for reelection," James confirmed.

"Since Aberdeen is foreign secretary, won't that mean he'll lose his office?"

"For the time being, at least. He'll have to run for reelection and his temper will be foul. The Whigs will give the Tories a run for their money, I can tell you."

"I don't want to be here when Aberdeen arrives. I cannot tolerate the overbearing bastard. Can't we leave for Ireland?" Claud pleaded.

"I hate to leave Mother to bear the brunt of his temper. And we should attend the king's funeral. Try to be patient."

That night, James's mother broached the subject of her husband's return to Bentley Priory. "Aberdeen will be furious at losing his office and consumed with worry that the Whigs will win a majority and form the next government."

"Have no fear. I won't allow him to vent his temper on you, Mother."

"Actually, James, I think there would be less tension if you and Claud weren't here. I am well aware that Bentley Priory is yours, but so is Aberdeen. The underlying currents would fill the very air with strife. Not only his daughters, but also his sons would take sides against you in any disagreement."

"I am a match for them, Mother. The odds don't trouble me in the least."

"But it would be less stressful for me, James."

He felt his throat tighten. "Of course. How insensitive of me." James enfolded his mother in his arms. He thought of Prinny's funeral. He knew Louisa would be there and regretted that he would not see her. "Claud and I will leave for Ireland tomorrow."

Chapter Eight

*D*owager Duchess Louisa turned away from the memories of her past so that she could focus on the family members who had gathered to celebrate her long life.

"Thank you, John Claud." Louisa took a sip of champagne from the glass her son had brought her. She was rather proud that he was aide-de-camp to the queen. "Does Victoria enjoy French wine?"

"She much prefers a dram of whiskey." John Claud winked at his mother.

"Ah yes, a habit Victoria picked up when she and Albert came to stay with us for the second time in Scotland. I clearly remember being mortified at your behavior."

"I was only nine years old."

"Certainly old enough to know better. When I presented you to the queen, you immediately stood on your head. To add insult to injury, you were wearing a kilt! I scolded you profusely and when I brought you back to the queen so you could apologize, you promptly did it again."

John Claud grinned. "Mother, you have an amazing memory."

"It is fortunate for you that Victoria's memory is no match for mine, or she would never have made you her aide-de-camp."

"You never know—she may have admired my arse."

"True. Why should she be different from all the other females you've attracted over the years?" She tapped his arm with her fan. "Shush, here's another speech extolling my virtues. I wonder when they'll start on my vices?" She thought fleetingly of Victoria's consort, Prince Albert, and smiled a secret smile.

Louisa Jane, the Duchess of Buccleuch, raised her voice in an attempt to make herself heard above the chatter and clinking of glasses. "The changes our dear mother has seen in her lifetime are absolutely profound."

Poor Louisa Jane was pressured into accepting the appointment of mistress of the robes to Queen Victoria when I turned it down.

"Did you know that Mother is the last person living to have visited Carlton House, the magnificent residence that belonged to the late King George IV?"

Louisa's thoughts took flight, winging back over the years. *King George's death is indelibly marked in my memory. Not because poor old Prinny turned up his dropsical toes, but because I had just discovered my sister and Abercorn by the lake in flagrante delicto. Oh, how I loathed and detested the Irish devil!*

It was almost a year before I saw him again . . .

Belgrave Square, London
May 1831

"I know the exhibition at the Royal Academy of Art marks the official opening of the season, but I'd prefer not to attend," Louisa confided to her sister.

"Because Edwin Landseer is exhibiting his paintings?" Georgy asked.

"Exactly. Since William's wife, Bessy, has gossiped that Landseer is Rachel's father, half of London will be wondering and whispering."

"If we attend the exhibition it will give the lie to such gossip. If we stay away, it will confirm it. Apart from that, every titled bachelor in London will be there. I've waited two long years for my season, Lu, and I refuse to waste one day of it."

"I didn't mean to be thoughtless, Georgy. Of course I'll attend."

"I knew you would change your mind. I'm wearing blue, so please don't choose the same color. I've heard that men prefer blue over any other shade."

When the Duke and Duchess of Bedford and their daughters alighted from their carriage in Piccadilly, they joined the fashionable throng gathered at the Academy of Art.

Wearing a white dress with a red sash and a matching hat decorated with silk poppies, Louisa stood out from the other ladies in the crowd.

The prime minister's son, George Grey, saw her immediately and greeted her warmly. "It would give me great pleasure to escort you through the exhibition, my lady."

Teddy Fox took Louisa's hand and raised it to his lips. "I prefer that I escort you, though if you insist, I suppose George Grey may tag along."

"Neither of you has any manners," she whispered. "You must include my sister."

Georgy appeared as if from nowhere. "Teddy! Congratulations on winning the seat from Horsham." She suddenly pretended an interest in government affairs. "Lu and I are dying to come to the visitors' gallery and watch you on the floor of the Commons."

"You'll find me on the back row benches, not the floor, I'm afraid."

Georgy rubbed his arm and gave him a saucy glance. "It isn't like you to be modest, Teddy. I'm sure you'll soon *thrust* yourself to the forefront." She pulled on his arm. "Let's go this way. You can explain the paintings to me."

Earl Grey kissed the Duchess of Bedford's cheek. "If John didn't come, I'll be happy to act as your escort, Your Grace."

"Having the honor of being escorted by the prime minister of England will make me the envy of every female here today." Georgina tucked her arm into Grey's. "John did accompany us, but because he's Landseer's patron, they'll tour the exhibition together."

Prime Minister Grey introduced his sister Hannah and her husband, Edward Ellice. He was a Scottish Whig MP, whom Grey had appointed Whip in his new government.

"I'm delighted to meet you. I shall add you to the invitation list for my daughters' debutante ball next week."

Lady Grey greeted Georgina. "We shall all come and you must return the favor. We are hosting a Prime Minister's Ball in June."

"Mary, it sounds *trés* elegant. We will be honored to attend."

Mary lowered her voice. "Don't look now, but I believe the Duchess of Kent and her daughter Victoria are about to join us."

Prime Minister Grey made the introductions, and the duchess spoke directly to Georgina. "Lady Bedford, I know your husband is the patron of Edwin Landseer. My daughter is enchanted with his animal portraits, and we are simply dying to meet him."

"Of course. Mr. Landseer will be honored."

Twelve-year-old Princess Victoria stood gazing at Lady Louisa. In addition to her dark beauty, the colors she had chosen to wear drew every eye.

Lu smiled warmly at the plain young princess. "Are you enjoying the exhibition, Your Highness?"

"Oh yes, especially the animal portraits by Edwin Landseer. They are so lifelike. I would love him to paint my little dog. He's called Dash."

"You couldn't have chosen a better artist," Louisa said truthfully.

The Duchess of Kent swept Louisa with an envious glance. "Come along, Victoria. It's rude to stare. Lady Bedford has agreed to introduce the wildlife artist to us."

. . .

"I sincerely hope that today put an end to the speculation about Lanny and me." Georgina Russell removed her bed robe.

Her husband John came up behind her and kissed the nape of her neck. "To hell with society's speculation. We know better, my love."

"We can only hope that *now*, all London knows better." Georgina climbed into bed.

John followed her and took her in his arms. "You never used to let gossip trouble you, little girl."

"It's just that when it comes from a member of the family, people are more apt to believe it."

"I've made it plain to William that we will not receive Bessy again and that she is unwelcome at Woburn."

"Poor John. I am a sore trial to you."

"You are my heart's desire. I adore you." He captured her lips in a passionate kiss. "Take off that nightgown. I want to make love."

Georgina slipped out of the silk night rail and came over him. John groaned as her lush breasts pressed against his chest and her unbound hair brushed against his face. When her hand moved down between their bodies and she stroked his erection, he cried out at the pure pleasure she aroused in him.

John knew he was the luckiest man on earth. When his stroke left him paralyzed down one side, she had nursed him until he regained his strength. *I was left with a limp and a useless arm. That's when Georgina helped me regain my manhood. She didn't hesitate to take the dominant position and make love to me.*

Heat leaped between them as they lost themselves in the sensual mating dance. They didn't hear the knock on their bedchamber door. They were in the throes of an earth-shattering climax and only became aware of Louisa after they had spent.

"Oh! Forgive me . . . I'm so sorry."

Georgina raised her head and asked huskily, "What is it, darling?"

"I . . . it was . . . it was . . . just a silly question about our presentation to the queen." Louisa backed out of the doorway.

Her mother said softly, "I'll answer all your questions in the morning, Lu."

Louisa returned to her own room. She was shocked at walking in on her parents while they were making love. Yet witnessing the sexual encounter made her examine the conclusions she had drawn that her father was incapable of siring another child. A wave of shame washed over her when she recalled the sinful thoughts she'd had about her mother. The evil suspicions she'd harbored about Edwin Landseer's lechery were even worse. *I am ashamed of my wicked thoughts!* Yet at the same time, Louisa felt joy that her parents still honored their marriage vows and remained faithful to each other.

The next morning, when Georgy awakened, Louisa sat down on her bed.

"What are you looking so smug about?"

"Last night I walked in on Mother and Father making love."

"Well, I'll be damned!"

"So, all those malicious things Bessy said about little Rachel are untrue. We should have known better, Georgy. Father isn't the sort of man who would allow his wife to be unfaithful to him."

"What did you see?" Georgy asked avidly.

Lu stared at her sister in disbelief. *You want to hear the intimate details!* "I saw enough," she said quietly.

Georgina inspected her daughters' appearance before they departed for St. James's Palace. Both were dressed in pristine white gowns with demure necklines, leg-o'-mutton sleeves, and white gloves. "I think it best to save your diamonds for your debut ball. We don't want to outshine Queen Adelaide."

"I'm glad Georgy will be presented first. I have nervous butterflies."

"That seems strange, Louisa. You have no trouble performing on-stage."

"That's different, Mother. Tonight I have to be myself."

"I remember my presentation at Court as if it were yesterday. I wasn't sure my father would come from Scotland. When he showed up, it filled me with confidence and my nerves vanished. You're very lucky girls. Your father wouldn't miss this for the world."

"Do you like my hair upswept?" Georgy asked. "Does it make me look taller?"

"Yes. You look absolutely lovely," Louisa assured her.

At St. James's Palace, they alighted from the carriage and joined the large crowd slowly making its way to the main entrance. Inside they joined the throng gathered in the anteroom outside the presence chamber, where the debutantes were to be presented to Queen Adelaide.

"Dorothy!" Georgina Russell greeted her girlhood friend, the eldest daughter of the late Duchess of Devonshire. "I haven't seen you in a dog's age." They had been debutantes together and had been presented to the queen on the same night. "Don't tell me your daughter Blanche is being presented tonight? What a lovely coincidence." Georgina introduced her two girls to Dorothy, Countess of Carlisle, and her daughter, Blanche Howard. She made a mental note to add their names to the invitation list for their ball.

Charlotte, Dowager Duchess of Richmond, with her youngest daughter in tow, pushed through the crowd toward the Russell ladies. Sophia also was being presented tonight. "Is that Dorothy Cavendish?" Charlotte asked her sister. "Lud, she's still tall and gawky, though not nearly as slim, heaven be praised."

"Her daughter Blanche is being presented tonight." Georgina sighed. "Yet one more debutante entering the marriage market."

Charlotte assessed Blanche with one sweeping glance. "The gel is as plain as a pikestaff. Good thing she has the Cavendish and Howard wealth to lure a husband."

"I remember at the Devonshire's debutante ball you said that all mothers thought their geese were swans . . . even ours."

"Lud, that was a lifetime ago, Georgina. I've managed to marry off six of my geese and I hope and pray Sophia will be no exception."

"Number seven is a lucky charm."

Charlotte crossed her fingers. "If Lord Thomas Cecil doesn't escape, Sophia will be wed in her first season."

The presence chamber doors finally opened and the crowd entered the long room and stood against the wall. It was hung with rich tapestries and royal portraits, with a prominent painting of the late King George taking precedence.

The Royal Chamberlain stood ready to announce the noble families and the name of each debutante being presented, in alphabetical order.

Louisa watched Blanche Howard walk down the long chamber until she reached Queen Adelaide, who sat enthroned at the far end. She replied to a brief, formal greeting then moved on quickly.

Georgy began to fidget with her hair by the time Sophia Lennox's name was announced, and Lu hoped her sister could control her impatience. Because their name was Russell, all the other young ladies would be presented before them.

The Duke of Bedford bent his head and whispered to Louisa, "They're saving the best for last."

Lu looked up into her father's eyes and in that moment knew how much he loved her. It filled her with confidence for what lay ahead.

The best part of an hour went by before the chamberlain announced: "Lady Georgianna Russell, first daughter of the Duke and Duchess of Bedford."

Lu held her breath as she watched her sister make her way down the long chamber. She prayed silently that Georgy would not misstep. She gave a sigh of relief when her sister managed to curtsy without wobbling.

Then it was finally her turn. The chamberlain announced: "Lady Louisa Russell, second daughter of the Duke and Duchess of Bedford."

Louisa straightened her shoulders, raised her chin, and took the first step that would lead her down the length of the chamber to the waiting queen. She knew every eye was on her and when she reached Adelaide, she remembered to smile.

"My dearest Louisa, I am delighted that you are being presented tonight. You are the image of your beautiful mother. I hope you will attend my drawing rooms while you are in London."

Lu made a graceful curtsy. "Thank you, Your Royal Highness. It is a great honor to be here tonight." Louisa was startled when Adelaide rose from her throne seat and took her hand. Then she realized it was because she was the last debutante to be presented.

Queen Adelaide led Lady Louisa and her other royal guests to a reception room where buffet tables filled with canapés, fancy desserts, and fine German wines stood against the walls.

King William greeted John Russell warmly and the pair was soon engrossed in conversation.

"It's very gratifying that we are personal friends of the king and queen of England." Georgy picked up a glass of golden Rhenish wine and sipped it. "This tastes like stallion piss," she murmured to Louisa.

Lu grinned. "Well, at least it's imported stallion piss."

Queen Adelaide kept the Duchess of Bedford by her side. "I have persuaded William to throw a royal ball in July."

"That's a marvelous idea, Your Highness. Now that the country is out of mourning, society is avid to be entertained at Court. Why don't you be daring and make the royal ball a masquerade? Londoners will fight over invitations."

The queen's presentation affair was over by midnight. On the carriage ride back to Belgrave Square, Georgina said, "Adelaide told me she plans to throw a royal ball. I planted the seeds for her to make it a masquerade."

"Costume balls encourage licentious behavior," John said with disapproval.

His wife took his hand and squeezed it. "Yes, I remember."

Georgy nudged her sister with her elbow and whispered, "A guinea says I'll be more licentious than you."

"You've had more practice." The minute Lu said it, she felt bad. "I'm sorry. I didn't mean that. A royal masquerade ball should be great fun. I can't wait."

"I've invited Johnny to accompany us to the theater tomorrow night," Georgina informed her daughters. "We have our own box at Covent Garden."

"Father, is it true you own the theater?" Louisa asked.

"I own the land that both the Theatre Royal and Covent Garden are built on, Lu. That's why we enjoy free tickets for any of the performances."

Free tickets! I shall tuck that information away and make use of it some afternoon.

James Hamilton arrived at the theater an hour before the curtain was due to go up and made his way backstage. He spoke to a matronly woman whose arms were filled with costumes. "I'm looking for a young lady by the name of Kitty Connelly. Could you point me in the right direction?"

"Ye must mean Kitty Kelly. Follow me, m'lord."

The stage dresser opened a door and led him into a room where a dozen females were in various stages of undress. James was amused that none of them appeared flustered at the arrival of a male. He spotted her immediately by her mane of lovely red hair. "Hello, Kitty. I'm just returned from Ireland and promised your mother I'd look in on you." Mrs. Connelly had been the housekeeper at Barons Court, Tyrone, as long as he could remember.

"Lord James!" She fastened her dressing gown and threw her arms around him. "That's so kind of you. I know she worries about me being here in wicked London, but I'm getting along famously. I changed my name to Kitty Kelly—it's a stage name."

"I stopped at your lodging to inquire after you and the landlady directed me here. It's a bit run-down, Kitty, and in a rather rough area."

"It's all right. I can look after myself. I'm only in the chorus—I don't earn a fortune."

"After the show, I'll take you somewhere for supper so we can talk."

"Thank you, Lord James." Her eyes sparkled. "Sure an' all, that would be lovely."

"You never used to call me *Lord James* when we were children."

"That's because I was an ignorant lass who knew no better."

I'm afraid I was the one who was in ignorance. "I'll come backstage for you after the performance."

The Duke and Duchess of Bedford, their two daughters, and Lord John took their seats in their private box at Covent Garden Theatre just before the curtain rose. Every seat in the house was filled because the musical play *The Brigand* had received a good review in the *Times.*

Louisa was beside herself with anticipation. She loved the crowd, the theater trappings, and the atmosphere of eager expectation of enjoyment. She leaned forward as the orchestra began to play the overture and focused her attention on the maroon velvet curtain. When it rose, the ladies of the chorus sang and danced an introduction to the first characters that would appear. Lu was enthralled by the ladies' costumes and face paint.

She imagined herself down there on the stage and knew that she was just as talented as most of the girls performing. She tapped her feet to the music and memorized the words being sung. She experienced a pang of regret when the ladies of the chorus left the stage, but she was soon caught up in *The Brigand's* plot.

As the curtain descended for the intermission, Louisa clapped with great enthusiasm. "Isn't it wonderful?" she exclaimed.

"The hero is rather dashing." Georgy licked her lips over him.

The duchess, always eager to mingle with friends and acquaintances who would gather in the foyer to parade about and exchange gossip, stood up. Lord John, ready to accompany her, got to his feet. The Russell daughters chose to stay with their father, and Johnny said he would bring them back drinks.

When the pair returned, they brought back more than glasses of champagne.

"Look who we bumped into," Johnny declared.

Louisa stared into the dark eyes of James Hamilton.

"Do have a seat, James," Georgina invited. "As you can see, there is plenty of room. Our box can accommodate at least a dozen."

James bowed to the duke. "Your Grace." His glance swept over Georgy and Louisa.

"Ladies." He deliberately took a seat directly behind Lady Lu.

To cover her shock at seeing Abercorn, Louisa took a gulp of champagne. It went down the wrong way and forced her to cough. Johnny gave her a couple of sharp taps on the back and by the time she could breathe again, the lights were dimming and the curtain was rising. *I shall refuse to speak to the lecherous swine!*

Louisa banished the image of Abercorn and her sister as she had last seen them at Woburn's lake. She tried to focus on the dancing ladies of the chorus, as they explained in song what was about to happen. But her attention kept straying to the man sitting behind her. His close proximity was a compelling force that seemed to engulf her. Her heart hammered in her breast and her pulse raced erratically. With difficulty she forced her concentration back to the stage, but she pictured Abercorn in the role of the strutting brigand and totally lost the thread of the story. Frustrated and annoyed, she vowed to come and see the musical play again.

When the final curtain descended and the thunderous applause died down, the Duchess of Bedford invited James Hamilton back to Belgrave Square for a late supper.

"Thank you, Your Grace. Unfortunately, I have a previous engagement."

Louisa heaved a sigh of relief. But as she eyed him making his way backstage, her relief evaporated and was replaced by indignation. *I warrant his previous engagement is with a chorus girl!*

"I thoroughly enjoyed the play." James helped Kitty into her cloak. "I had no trouble picking you out in the chorus."

"With flaming hair like mine, how could you?"

A short walk from Covent Garden Theatre led them to a small hotel on Bedford Street with a private dining room. James was amused when his companion stared about in awe of her surroundings. When she saw only men at the tables, she hesitated. "Are you sure, Lord James?"

"I'm quite sure, Kathleen. Please call me James."

"I'll call you James, if you'll call me Kitty."

"That's a deal. What would you like to eat?"

"You order for me. I'll have the same as you."

James ordered lamb cutlets with mint sauce. It came with new potatoes, baby carrots, and a green salad. He also ordered a bottle of claret. Kitty had a healthy appetite, and James enjoyed watching her eat. As he drank his wine, his thoughts went back to the meeting he'd had with his Irish attorney Rowan Maloney when he reached his majority.

Though he had inherited his grandfather's titles when he was seven, the deeds to Barons Court and the other properties in Ireland, England, and Scotland had been held in trust until he turned twenty-one. The income from these properties would now come directly to him rather than his legal guardian, the Earl of Aberdeen.

James had been pleasantly surprised when his attorney handed him a letter from his grandfather to be read when he reached his majority. The patriarch had attached few strings to his bequests, but he had revealed a secret on the second page:

> *I arranged with my attorney a generous annuity for Mrs.*
> *Connelly. Kate was far more than a housekeeper to me in my*
> *later years. I freely admit to you that I am the father of her*
> *child, though Mrs. Connelly prefers that this be kept from*
> *Kathleen. I charge you to make sure that Barons Court will*
> *always be a home to them.*

"Kathleen . . . Kitty, now that you've had a taste of *wicked London,* as you call it, would you like to return to Barons Court?"

"Oh no, m'lord, I mean James. I absolutely love London! Barons Court is a lovely place, especially for a visit, but I couldn't live there . . . not after living in London."

"Well then, I want you to think of it as a safe haven—if you ever need one. You will always be welcome there."

"Thank you, James. That is most kind and generous."

"Your mother would never approve of the lodging house where you are living. I want to take you back there to pick up your things. Then I'll take you to my townhouse until we can find a more suitable place for you." To forestall her refusal, he had thought up a ready lie. "My attorney in Ireland has informed me that my grandfather bequeathed you a small allowance once you turned eighteen, which I must administer. There can be no better use for it than providing you with a decent, safe place to live."

"Your grandfather? The only thing I remember about him was his curly beard."

"You were very young when he died. He left an annuity for his loyal housekeeper and a small allowance for you."

She gave him a skeptical smile. "I'll believe you—thousands wouldn't."

He glanced at her ruefully. "You can see through my subterfuge."

"It's very generous of you, James. I don't know what to say."

Abercorn grinned. "Say: *I will leave everything in your capable hands, James.*"

Kitty gave him a seductive smile. "It will be my special pleasure to leave everything in your capable hands, James."

Chapter Nine

"I'm so glad I was able to persuade your father to acquire this spacious house in Belgrave Square two years ago. The townhouse in St. James's didn't even have a ballroom."

Georgina fastened Louisa's diamond necklace, then did the same for Georgy.

A knock came on the bedchamber door, and Louisa opened it to find her brother Edward dressed in his naval uniform. "Oh, how very smart you look, Lieutenant Russell. Thank you for coming."

"Wouldn't miss my sisters' debutante ball. I see Jack is here, but do you know if Charles is coming?"

"Jack will be returning to Woburn tomorrow. But Charles arrived from Oxford last night. He passed his examinations with flying colors," his mother said proudly.

"That means he'll soon be wearing a uniform. Lord knows why he prefers the army."

"Cavalry, I warrant. He's mad about horses," Lu explained.

"Well, at least we agree he's mad," Georgy quipped. "I expect your friend Teddy Holland will be here tonight, Edward?"

"Yes, it will be like an Oxford reunion. George Grey will be here, and James Hamilton."

"We saw Abercorn at the theater recently. When I sent his invitation, I included one for his brother, Claud." Georgina glanced in the mirror and tucked in an errant curl.

Louisa's heart began to pound. *Oh Mother, I wish you hadn't invited Abercorn.*

"Our guests will be arriving any moment. Your father has already gone downstairs to greet them." She left and came back again. "Before I forget, your subscriptions for Almack's arrived today, so don't forget to be gracious to Sarah Jersey and Emily Cowper."

"I hope Wriothesley is late," Georgy told Edward. "I'd much rather you promenaded us around the ballroom to thank everyone for coming. The Reverend Bloody Russell is sure to put a damper on everyone's fun."

Edward winked. "The rectory at Chenies is quite a distance from London. He could very well be late arriving."

"Shame on the pair of you," Lu declared, trying not to laugh. "Perhaps we can persuade him to leave off his clerical collar."

"I need a drink," Edward declared. "I'll meet you in the ballroom."

"Lu, did you know that Lady Cowper has been Lord Palmerston's mistress for years?" Georgy was fixated on the *ton's* indiscretions.

"Where on earth do you hear all these salacious rumors?"

"I listen in when Mother and Lady Holland are talking. No one is spared. They gossip about everyone." Georgy looked in the mirror. "Your dress is prettier than mine." Louisa's ball gown was blush pink, with tiny rosebuds around its décolleté neckline. The bodice was gathered in tiny pleats. Georgy, as usual, had chosen blue.

"You look lovely," Lu reassured her. "Remember that gentlemen prefer blue."

"Males have no interest in how a female dresses whatsoever . . . only in the way she undresses." Georgy laughed. "Are you ready to parade your charms on the marriage market?"

Louisa shuddered. "I shall never be ready for that, I'm afraid."

"Don't be such a prude, Lu. Let me at 'em!"

. . .

With a sister on each arm, First Lieutenant Edward Russell slowly circled the ballroom. Georgy and Louisa greeted their guests and thanked them for coming. Two hundred invitations had been sent out, and by the looks of the crowd, most had accepted.

When they encountered Lord and Lady Cowper, the sisters curt-sied. "Thank you for our subscription to Almack's, my lady," Lu mur-mured. She took a surreptitious glance at the earl.

"Lady Louisa, it is my distinct pleasure to approve you and your sister for membership."

When they moved on, Georgy said, "One look at Peter Cowper tells you why Emily prefers Palmerston's bed."

In answer, Louisa merely rolled her eyes.

Edward stopped before Wriothesley and his wife Eliza, who had finally arrived.

"Georgy—Louisa, I apologize profusely for being late. The car-riages are backed up to Kensington Road. I had no idea there would be such a crush."

"Don't worry about being late, Reverend. I stepped in and took over your duties."

Louisa stood on tiptoe to kiss her brother's cheek. "Take no no-tice of him, Wrioth. Edward was dying to show off his new uniform. You look lovely, Eliza. Thank you both for coming."

Georgy looked pointedly at her eldest brother's clerical collar. "I'm sure Father would be happy to lend you one of his neck cloths."

"That remark was unworthy of you, Georgy," Wriothesley scolded. Both Louisa and Edward had the decency to flush.

It took the best part of an hour for the sisters to greet everyone in the ballroom. Then came the ritual first dance. The Earl of Bedford partnered his eldest daughter, while Lord John did the honors with Lady Louisa.

"I predict a most successful season, Lu. There's a plethora of bachelors here to partner you."

"I'd much rather dance alone. I don't enjoy following a man's lead."

Johnny smiled at her. "Someday you'll meet your match and all that will change."

He saw Abercorn across the room. "Perhaps sooner than you think."

Lu deftly changed the subject. "Congratulations on your appointment as paymaster of the forces, Johnny."

"Being a personal friend of the prime minister has its rewards."

"You know damn well you got the appointment on your own merits. Politics is your great passion. I warrant that's why you never married."

"Is that a fact? It just so happens I have my eye on a very pretty widow. And since you brought up the subject of marriage, I know it is anathema to you, but your parents have high hopes for you. Don't reject out of hand all the proposals you'll receive."

"Johnny, are you in love?" she asked eagerly.

"Why do you ask?"

"I once thought I was in love with Edwin Landseer," she confessed. "But it turned out to be a silly infatuation."

Johnny frowned. "He didn't make advances toward you, did he?"

"Good heavens, no! Lanny has always behaved like a perfect gentleman." *For which I shall be eternally grateful. It was wicked of me to suspect he was having an affair with Mother.*

The Duke of Bedford and Lord John switched partners, so that Lady Louisa could be partnered by her father in the first dance of the ball. She saw his mouth tighten and knew his leg was paining him.

Her father stopped before James Hamilton. "Abercorn, I relinquish my daughter into your safekeeping."

Louisa was speechless as the dark Irish devil took her hand in his and slipped his other arm around her. "You look extremely beautiful tonight."

She knew she should accept the compliment graciously or at least smile, but she could not bring herself to respond in any way. In a separate part of her mind, she acknowledged that he was an accomplished dancer and in spite of herself she was swept back to the night of the kissing dance. She stiffened with resistance.

"Lady Louisa, you are radiating hostility toward me, yet I can think of no reason why you should be bristling with animosity. Would you care to enlighten me?"

She raised her lashes and glared into his dark eyes. "The afternoon of the Woburn hunt I saw you at the lake with my sister."

James was taken aback. He had no idea anyone, let alone Louisa, had witnessed his encounter with Georgy. "When I returned from the hunt I went for a swim in the lake. I came upon your sister by accident. We were both acutely embarrassed."

"You didn't exact a price for returning her necklace?" she demanded.

"If that's what you think—if that's what you truly think of me, we can never be friends." The first dance ended. James bowed politely and walked away. Teddy Fox was at her elbow, ready to partner her in the next dance. Her thoughts filled with Abercorn, she allowed Teddy to take her hand and lead her onto the dance floor.

With all the men away on the hunt that day, perhaps Georgy went to the lake to swim. She doffs her clothes at the drop of a hat. Is it possible their meeting was accidental and not a sexual encounter?

"You're completely ignoring me," Teddy complained.

"I'm sorry . . . I was concentrating on the dance steps."

"Is anyone courting you, Louisa?"

"Of course not." She finally focused her attention on him. "Why do you ask?"

He grinned at her. "I want to be in the running. A political wife would be a distinct advantage in her husband's career."

"Your compliment overwhelms me, you silver-tongued devil," she teased. "If wedding the daughter of the Duke of Bedford is vital to your career, I suggest you make an offer for Georgy." The music ended and George Grey was waiting to partner her.

"You are the prettiest lady in London, Louisa. I would lay my heart at your feet, except that there are at least two others ready to do the same."

"And who might they be, George?" she asked lightly.

"Teddy Fox and James Hamilton, of course."

Her heart skipped a beat. "I have no intention of marrying until I'm at least thirty."

George squeezed her hand. "Then perhaps I stand a chance."

Between dances, Louisa sought out her sister. "Georgy, did Abercorn ask you for anything in exchange for returning your diamonds?"

"If only," she said, licking her lips suggestively.

"Georgy, I'm serious!"

"If you must know, Abercorn totally disapproves of me. I don't stand a chance with the handsome devil, Lu. I'm not prim and proper enough for his taste."

He found you swimming naked and could not hide his disapproval. O Lord, James was telling the truth. I owe him an apology.

"Louisa, darling, you remember Henry Petty, Marquis of Lansdowne? He partnered me in the opening dance at my own debut ball. Prime Minister Grey has just named Henry president of the council." Her mother gestured toward a young man who resembled the marquis. "This is his son, Tom, Lord Kerry."

"I'm delighted to make your acquaintance, my lord."

"May I partner you in the next dance, Lady Louisa?"

She gave him a gracious smile, though her heart wasn't in it. "I would be honored."

When the dance turned out to be a cotillion where everyone changed partners, she hoped she would get a chance to again dance with Abercorn. After a few different partners, she found herself face-to-face with Hamilton. When the music began, he made no move to take her in his arms. "James," she said breathlessly, "it seems I owe you an apology . . . an abject apology. Will you accept it?"

"When you beg so prettily, how can I possibly resist?" he teased.

"You devil! I wouldn't beg you for anything, as well you know."

"When you are angry, your green eyes glitter like emeralds." *Oh Lady Lu, someday you will beg me to make love to you. The anticipation is delicious.*

The music stopped and another partner swept her into the dance. She noted that the young Earl of Edgecombe had no chin and a deep sigh of regret escaped her lips. The dance ended and Edgecombe delivered her to Lord John, who was conversing with Abercorn and her cousin, Charles Lennox, Duke of Richmond. Johnny and Charlie had been friends since they were boys.

She focused her attention on her cousin. "Hello, Charlie. I haven't seen you for ages. Perhaps I'll visit the House of Lords while I'm in London." The moment she said it, she regretted it. Abercorn was now in the Lords. *The Irish devil will think I'm attracted to him.* She stole a glance at him and saw the amusement in his eyes.

"In that case, I'll do my duty and dance with the debutante," Charlie declared.

"Your gallantry underwhelms me," Louisa teased.

As the couple glided onto the dance floor, Johnny remarked to James, "She is so like her mother. Both Charlie and I adored Georgina when we were boys."

Just then, Johnny's eldest brother joined him. "Hello, Francis.

I didn't expect to see you here. This is James Hamilton, Marquis of Abercorn . . . James, meet my brother, Marquis of Tavistock."

Francis nodded curtly. "Decided to see for myself how much money the woman is lavishing on her daughters' debutante ball. There must be two hundred here."

James was shocked. The *woman* he referred to was his step-mother and it was clear he begrudged the Duchess of Bedford spending the duke's money on her daughters. The loving camaraderie of the Russell siblings did not extend to the heir.

"Surely launching both our sisters at one ball is rather frugal," Johnny suggested.

"Stepsisters," Francis corrected. "*Frugal* isn't in Georgina's vocabulary." His mouth tightened. "The day will come when she has a catastrophic awakening." Having pronounced his dire prediction, Francis stalked off.

Johnny shook his head regretfully. "When Father became the Duke of Bedford, he found out that Woburn was two hundred and fifty thousand pounds in debt, thanks to his late brother's profligate spending habits. He kept it from Georgina and from us, of course, but when Francis reached his majority and learned of the debt through the attorneys, he was outraged. He lives in fear of inheriting liabilities along with the assets."

An alarm bell went off in Abercorn's head. Georgina's *catastrophic awakening* would come about when the Duke of Bedford died. By the sound of the vindictive heir, he intended to swoop in and disinherit the present duchess and her children. An overwhelming desire to protect Louisa from the avaricious swine rose up in James.

He saw his brother Claud laughing with Charles Russell, so he and Johnny went to join them. "Have you danced with the debutantes yet?" James asked Claud.

"I've danced with Georgy, but Louisa is too much in demand. There's a long line of bachelors vying to partner her, I'm afraid."

Charles gave James a rueful glance. He knew how his friend felt about Lu. "Sorry about that, but you can take solace in the fact none of them have taken her fancy."

James winked. "None except me. She just isn't ready to admit it yet."

Claud thumped his brother's shoulder. "Conceited devil."

"When do the Scottish reels begin?" James inquired.

"Not until after midnight. The guests have to be two sheets to the wind before they are ready to shed their inhibitions and attempt the Highland fling."

"That gives us time to sip the bubbly and taste some of that delicious Spey salmon," Claud suggested.

"Good idea," Johnny agreed. "If we go to the supper room early, we won't be trampled by the crowd."

They each picked up a glass of champagne. "Let's drink to Lord John's appointment as paymaster," James suggested.

After the toast Charles asked, "Who else can we drink to?"

Claud, tongue firmly in cheek, said, "Let's drink to Lord Palmerston. I understand Prime Minister Grey has made him secretary of state for foreign affairs."

The Russell brothers laughed. It was not lost on them that the Hamilton brothers' stepfather, the Earl of Aberdeen, had previously held the post.

"I think I will announce a *kissing dance*," Georgina informed her friend Beth.

Lady Holland laughed. "There's no such thing. I made it up the night of Georgy's birthday ball."

Georgina laughed merrily. "It was the highlight of the evening. I shall announce one and see if it sets a new fashion." She instructed the musicians and then held up her hands for silence. She announced the kissing dance to the guests and explained how it worked. Then she asked Lord Holland to partner her.

Louisa drew in a swift breath as memories of Abercorn's kiss came flooding back to her. Not only had it been her first kiss, it had been her last. She glanced around the ballroom but did not see James Hamilton. Young Lord Edgecombe asked her to dance and she accepted only because she knew she would be constantly changing partners.

The floor was crowded because everyone wanted to participate. Anticipation and laughter filled the air each time the music stopped, then started again.

When the kissing dance finally ended, Louisa found herself dancing with Ned Turnour, the young Earl of Winterton. He grinned down at her. "I have captured the belle of the ball." He dipped his head and pressed his lips to hers.

Louisa waited for the magic to begin. After anticipating her second kiss, she felt only disappointment. Apart from that, she felt nothing. Her head did not spin, her pulse did not race, her heart did not pound, her breasts did not tingle, and her knees did not turn to water. She opened her eyes and saw by the look on his handsome face that Winterton had been aroused by the kiss, though she had been completely unmoved.

Abercorn returned to the ballroom just as the music ended, and less than three feet away he saw Louisa gazing up at her dancing partner. His eyes narrowed as he watched Winterton's head dip and take possession of her lips. To James, Louisa's kisses were no trifling matter. Without hesitation he stepped forward, took her hand, and drew her into his arms. He pressed her close and watched her lashes sweep down to brush her cheeks as his mouth captured hers in a sensual kiss, designed to steal her senses.

Lu instantly experienced myriad sensations. His familiar male scent stole to her, filling her head with delicious fancies. Her mouth softened and her nipples ruched as the hard muscles of his chest pressed against her breasts. She stood on tiptoe and her arms reached up around his neck. She clung to him with an innocent desire she could not control. When the kiss ended, a sigh escaped her lips before she opened her eyes. But when she raised her lashes and saw the look of possession in his dark eyes, it threatened her. She wanted to slap him, but instead she laughed to show him the kiss meant nothing to her but a mere trifle.

Young Earl Winterton stepped toward her, with a frown furrowing his brow.

"Did you want something, Winterton?" James demanded.

Ned stepped back. "No . . . No . . . Not a thing, Abercorn."

Louisa watched Winterton retreat into the crowd. "You intimidated the poor devil."

"Can I help it if he slunk off with his tail between his legs?"

"He's not a hunting dog."

"Oh, he was hunting all right and had scented his prey."

"You are the last person I want to ride to my rescue."

His eyes filled with amusement. "I shall be the first . . . and the last."

"You arrogant Irish devil!"

He winked. "You're half right."

Louisa left him and went to find her sister. "Georgy, you look extremely pleased with yourself. Who got to kiss you?"

"It was William Cavendish, Lord Burlington. He's heir to the Duke of Devonshire! Wouldn't it be absolutely fabulous if he offered for me?"

"Don't get your hopes up if you've only just met him, Georgy," Lu cautioned.

"I warrant he's the best catch here tonight—in fact, he's the best catch in England. My kiss completely aroused him," she whispered.

"When he pressed his cock into my belly, I slipped my hand between our bodies and squeezed it."

Louisa was at a loss for words. She wanted to caution her sister about being promiscuous but knew she would call her a prude. "Be careful, Georgy."

"Don't worry. I shall be discreet. I have more sense than to let anyone see the cunning tricks I get up to."

Georgina Russell spoke with the musicians and raised her hands. "Choose your partners for the Duchess of Bedford strathspey, ladies and gentlemen."

"Your beauty overwhelms me. May I partner you in the reel, Lady Louisa?" Adolphus Seymour, heir to the Duke of Somerset, gazed at her with adoration.

Louisa gave him a radiant smile. "It would be my pleasure, Lord Seymour."

He raised her hand to his lips with reverence and led her onto the floor. The Scottish strathspey began with a slow, dignified tempo, but the rhythm picked up and went faster and faster as the reel progressed. The dancers picked up their heels and threw caution to the wind as they abandoned themselves to the music. The tune ended, leaving the dancers breathless but ready for more fun and laughter.

Louisa curtsied to her partner and turned with concern to her brother Jack, who had been dancing close by. She thought his eyes had a glazed look. "Are you all right, Jack?" She took his arm and led him from the floor. "Did you take your medicine?"

"I remembered to bring it from Woburn, but I forgot to take it today."

"I'll come up with you. Can you manage the stairs?" Louisa's heart was in her mouth until they reached the top step. She opened his chamber door, sat him down in a chair, and found the betony syrup. She couldn't find a spoon, so she held the bottle to his lips. "Jack, you'd better rest for a while until you're feeling better."

Louisa closed the door softly and made her way along the hall. When she passed the bedchamber she shared with Georgy, she heard something move inside. Assuming it was her sister, she opened the door. In the dimness she saw the outline of a male and as her eyes adjusted to the shadowy light, she saw her sister crouching before him on her hands and knees. She could not see what Georgy was doing, but it must have been some sort of sex act. Lu closed the door quickly, deeply shocked at her sister's reckless behavior. *She didn't see me—she had her back to the door. Whoever he is didn't see me either. He was too busy moaning with pleasure.* Louisa didn't know what to do. She was loath to cause a scene, but in all conscience she wanted to put a stop to whatever was going on. Finally she rapped sharply on the bedroom door and hurried back to the ballroom.

Louisa kept watch for her sister's return. Georgy entered the ballroom alone, so Lu did not learn her partner's identity. It wasn't long before she discovered it, however.

Georgy, looking like the cat that had swallowed the cream, confided to her sister, "I have engaged the attention of the most sought-after bachelor in London. William Cavendish is hot for me!"

"Please be careful. He may promise anything to get what he wants."

"What he wants is *me*!" Georgy tossed her head and walked away.

The next strathspey was the "Duchess of Richmond." Neil Gow, the famous Scottish fiddler, had composed it especially for Lady Charlotte Gordon when she was a girl. Louisa stood with her brother Charles, as they watched both their mother and her sister Charlotte dance the strathspey with amazing gusto.

"I took Jack upstairs," Louisa confided. "He looked a bit glassy-eyed."

"When the reel ends, I'll go up and check on him."

The "Gey Gordons" was announced and everyone began choosing a partner. William Cavendish bowed before Louisa. "It is high time I partnered the beauty of the family."

She stared at him, aghast, and made the first excuse she could think of. "I am so sorry, Lord Burlington. I promised the next reel to Abercorn." She looked around in a panic. "Ah, there he is with my father. Please excuse me."

She hurried to Hamilton's side. "Would you partner me in the 'Gey Gordons,' James?"

"It would be my pleasure, Louisa." As he led her onto the floor, a teasing light came into his eyes. "You must have an ulterior motive, Lady Lu."

She raised her chin and looked him directly in the eye. "Oh, I do. I want to see how well you acquit yourself in a Scottish reel."

"We were dancing reels and jigs in Ireland long before the Scots laid claim to them."

"Name me one," she challenged.

"'Fig for a Kiss' is a popular one. Then there's my favorite, 'The Ladies' Pantaloons.'"

Louisa tried not to laugh, but she didn't succeed. "You are a vulgar devil."

He grinned. "And then some."

Chapter Ten

"Here's the announcement!" Louisa read aloud from the *Times*: "*The Dowager Duchess of Richmond is pleased to announce the engagement of her youngest daughter, Lady Sophia Lennox, to Colonel Lord Thomas Cecil, son of the late Henry and Sarah Cecil, Marquis and Marchioness of Exeter.*"

"He's only a younger son," Georgy pointed out. "Sophia will never rise above the title of '*Lady*.' She's the daughter of a duke. Surely she could do better."

"That is most uncharitable, Georgy," her mother scolded. "Happiness is far more important than securing a great title."

"You became a duchess. Can't you have both?"

"I married your father for love, not his title," Georgina declared.

"How *utterly* convenient that you loved him, Mother."

"You have a saucy tongue, Georgy. Gentlemen much prefer young ladies to be sweet rather than sarcastic."

"Mother, there are one or two gentlemen of my acquaintance who adore my saucy tongue." Georgy winked at her sister.

Louisa blushed and prayed their mother didn't grasp the double entendre. To distract her, she handed her the newspaper. "There is no mention of a wedding date."

"Charlotte said the date hasn't been decided yet."

"Let's hope Lord Cecil doesn't slip out of the noose."

"Stop being facetious, Georgy, it is most unbecoming in a debutante. Have you decided what you will wear to the Prime Minister's Ball?"

"I want to see what Louisa is wearing before I choose. Let's go up now and decide on our ball gowns."

After the girls went upstairs, a footman announced that the Marquis of Lansdowne was paying a morning call.

"Henry, you're out and about early." Georgina knew that as the newly appointed president of the council, Petty was interested in the reform bill. "Did you wish to see John? He's in the library."

"Well, actually, my formal call this morning concerns both of you. But I did want a word with you first, my dearest Georgina." He took her hand and lifted it to his lips. "My son, Lord Kerry, is very taken with Lady Louisa. Would you object if he paid his addresses to your daughter?"

"Henry, how can you possibly think I would object?"

"When you were a debutante, you rejected me when I proposed to you, Georgina. If there is no chance, I'd prefer that my son didn't make a fool of himself."

"Henry, darling. Surely you didn't think you made a fool of yourself when you proposed to me? I was highly honored. I was very fond of you. My mother was the stumbling block in our relationship. She had set her mind on my marrying a duke and that was that."

Henry chuckled. "The Duchess of Gordon was a woman who must be obeyed."

"My dear friend, there is no need to consult John about this matter, unless you are bringing us a proposal for Louisa's hand."

"No, no, I just wanted to be sure you had no objections to my son paying his addresses to your daughter."

"No objections whatsoever. I have two daughters, you know.

Since it's too early for tea, how about a dram of fine Scotch whiskey to whet your whistle?"

"You always did know the way to a man's heart, my dear."

"I don't know what I was thinking when I was being fitted for my gowns," Georgy complained. "All three are different shades of blue. Everyone will think I'm wearing the same dress! The lavender silk you are planning to wear is a hundred times prettier than mine. Would you consider lending it to me, Lu?"

Louisa could never refuse a plea from her sister. "The color would look lovely on you. Let's ask Mother's sewing woman if she can alter it to fit you."

Two weeks later, the bodice of the lavender silk had been enlarged to accommodate Georgy's fuller figure. Louisa donned her gown of pale green tulle that she had chosen to complement her dark green eyes.

"Do you think Lord Burlington will attend the Prime Minister's Ball?"

"Of course he will," Louisa replied.

"What makes you so sure?" Georgy asked anxiously.

"Because the Duke of Devonshire has been appointed Lord Chamberlain by Prime Minister Grey. Since Lord Burlington is the duke's heir, he is bound to be there."

"I can't keep this political stuff straight. Your head must be crammed full of it, Lu. No wonder you don't attract the opposite sex."

"I don't want to attract the opposite sex. I have no burning desire to marry."

Georgy shook her head in wonder. "You are an unnatural female, Lu. It's every woman's goal to marry, and marry well, I might add."

"A sound basic knowledge of politics could help you reach your goal. This is the first time in twenty-three years the Whigs have been in power. It is a glorious time for Earl Grey and his ministers."

"It is a glorious time for me to finally make my debut." She lowered her voice. "Speaking of Earl Grey, did you know that when he was young, he was the Duchess of Devonshire's lover? He got her with child and her furious husband expelled her to France. She had a baby daughter and Earl Grey took the illegitimate child home to his parents. They named her Eliza Courtney and brought her up as his sister."

Louisa was astonished. "Earl Grey's sister Eliza is really his daughter by the Duchess of Devonshire? Wherever do you hear all this gossip?"

"By keeping my ears open and hiding around corners." She picked up her fan. "Hurry up, Lu. I cannot waste a moment of tonight's ball."

The Prime Minister's Ball was being held in the great hall of ancient Westminster Palace. The Bedfords alighted from their carriage in the palace yard and made their way through the labyrinth of corridors to Westminster Hall.

Prime Minister Grey and his wife, Mary, were stationed at the hall's entrance to greet their guests. Earl Grey kissed Georgina warmly and then spoke to John. "I warrant it's been years since you attended Parliament." Both the House of Commons and the House of Lords were in Westminster Palace.

"Once Johnny presents the reform bill and it is sent to the Upper House, I intend to be there for the debates every day."

"These things move slowly, but I want to be sure the timing will be conducive to getting it passed." Grey reached for Bedford's hand and shook it. "Let me be the first to congratulate you, John."

"Congratulate me for what, pray?"

"You are to receive the Order of the Garter. I proposed your name to the king and he agreed. It's the least I can do for all the help and support you have given me."

"I deeply appreciate receiving the coveted blue ribbon. It's most gratifying. I warrant Georgina will be pleased."

The prime minister's son, George Grey, greeted Louisa and her sister. "You both look lovely. I shall put in my request for the first and second dance before you are swamped with requests. Unfortunately there won't be any Scottish reels tonight."

"You may partner me in the first dance," Georgy declared, taking his arm. "Do you know if Lord Burlington has arrived yet?"

"I haven't seen him. When he arrives, would you like an introduction to him, Georgy?"

"Heavens, no. We are already intimately acquainted."

Teddy Fox spotted Louisa and walked a direct path to her. "I'd like the first dance, if you haven't promised it to anyone."

Georgy spun about when she heard his voice. "Teddy! I promised my first dance to George, but I'm sure he won't mind if we switch partners." She dropped George's arm and took hold of Teddy's.

Louisa was acutely embarrassed that her sister showed her preference for Teddy Fox so blatantly. She took George's hand and squeezed it. "You're such a good dancer . . . I always enjoy it when you partner me." The orchestra began to play a waltz and George led her onto the floor.

"Teddy wanted to dance with *you*. I could see the disappointment on his face."

Louisa tactfully changed the subject. "Now that your father is prime minister, don't you have a desire to go into politics, George?"

"No, it's still the navy for me. When I was a small boy, Father was First Lord of the Admiralty, and I suppose that sparked my desire to become a sailor. As a politician, he didn't wear a uniform, of course, but he exercised command over the Royal Navy. He occasionally took me to the shipyards and took me aboard a few vessels."

"You are fortunate to be able to fulfill your childhood dreams. When I was a young girl I wanted to be a dancer on the stage, but alas, that is quite impossible."

"You dance beautifully, but the public stage is out of the question."

When the dance ended, George fully expected that Teddy would be waiting to whisk Louisa away from him. His glance searched the large hall for his friend, but when the music began for the second dance and Teddy didn't come to claim the prize, he was more than happy to partner Louisa once again.

"Would you like me to show you where I sit in the House of Commons, Georgy?"

"Are you trying to get me alone, Teddy?" she whispered provocatively.

He bit her ear. "Absolutely—I can think of far more amusing things to do than dance."

"Let's slip away before the music stops; then no one will notice. Westminster Palace must be a fascinating place to explore. It has more than a thousand rooms."

They ducked through a small archway in a shadowed corner of the hall.

"I can take you places you've never been before," he promised suggestively.

"New experiences always excite me, Teddy."

Hand in hand they made their way through the labyrinth of corridors until they reached the darkened House of Commons. He opened a door and they slipped inside, and stood against the wall. The vastness of the chamber and the high vaulted ceiling echoed every sound, and they instinctively lowered their voices to whispers.

"Men have often voted for war here, but how many women can say they made love in Parliament?" he murmured.

Her arms snaked up around his neck. "Let's set a precedent!"

He shoved her against the wall, pulled up the lavender silk and the petticoats beneath it, and covered her mons with his palm. "You are always ready for me, Georgy."

Her fingers stroked his hard cock beneath the fabric of his breeches. "What about you, Ready Teddy? I warrant we are a very well-matched pair."

He opened his trousers, freeing his erection, then thrust himself up inside Georgy's sheath, pinning her against the wall. When he felt her hands grasp his buttocks and squeeze, he groaned with pleasure. The sound echoed eerily about the vaulted chamber.

Each time he impaled her, Georgy's bum thumped against the paneled wall. The acoustics in the empty chamber magnified the sound, turning it into a rhythmic drumbeat. She giggled, and the echo made it sound like a disembodied spirit from above was laughing at them. The muscles of her sheath tightened and Teddy immediately spent with a low moan of satisfaction. He withdrew, leaving her still aroused.

While Teddy tucked himself back into his breeches, Georgy advanced into the chamber past the tiers of green benches and stood on the floor in the center. At one end was the Speaker's Chair. She made her way toward it and sat down.

"We should go." Teddy, having achieved what he came for, was reluctant to linger.

Georgy, however, was not finished with the Member. "I'm enjoying myself." With her finger she beckoned him closer. "What would it take to persuade you to stay?"

He stopped beside the Table of the House that was located in the middle of the floor. "Someone might come."

Georgy made a play on words. "And someone might come *again*," she promised.

He felt his cock stir.

She stood up from the Speaker's Chair. "If the mountain won't come to Muhammad . . ." As she walked toward him, she asked, "What's this line down the center of the floor?"

"If a Member from either party takes the floor to speak, he cannot cross the line."

Georgy jumped playfully from one side to the other. "I never toe the line."

"That's what I like about you, Mistress Russell."

She ran her hand along the top of the massive wooden table. "I'm going to lie down, close my eyes, and imagine the benches are filled with the Honorable Members."

Teddy watched her hike up her skirts and slide her bottom across the polished oak. He knew he would never be able to look at the table again without imagining her lying there in open invitation. He opened his trousers and climbed on top of her. He felt himself harden and lengthen, as he brushed against her gleaming white thighs. "How do you like this *Honorable Member?*" He plunged down and took her cry of pleasure into his mouth.

Georgy climaxed a moment after he spent. As he collapsed on her, she bit his ear and whispered, "The Honorable Member for Horsham has presented an *Act of Fornication* before the House. All in favor say *Aye.*"

"May I have the pleasure of this dance, Lady Louisa?"

Lu smiled. "The pleasure is all mine, Lord Kerry. Isn't Kerry an Irish title?"

"Yes, my father became Earl of Kerry when his cousin died without issue."

"I see. I know your father has been appointed president of the council. Forgive my ignorance, but are you also a Member of Parliament, Lord Kerry?"

"Yes, I am the MP for Calne, in Wiltshire. Won't you please call me Tom?"

"Since your father and my mother are such good friends, why not?"

"Did you know that my father once proposed marriage to your mother?"

Louisa's eyes widened. "She turned down the Marquis of Lansdowne?"

"He wasn't a marquis at the time—he was Lord Petty."

Ah, that explains it. "I'm glad they remained friends all these years."

"So am I. If they had wed, I might be your brother."

"Good heavens! I have too many brothers now. I don't need another." *Oh no, he's gazing at me with longing. I said the wrong thing.* "On the other hand, Tom, I think you would make a very nice brother." Louisa saw his longing change to disappointment. She quickly thanked him for the dance and retreated to her brother's side.

"Johnny, thank goodness you've arrived. I think Lord Kerry is smitten with me. He told me that his father once proposed to my mother and I was terrified that he was on the verge of following in his father's footsteps."

"Marriage isn't a fate worse than death, Louisa. The whole idea of a debutante having a season is to receive offers."

"The thought of marriage frightens me and having children terrifies me. A female has so little control over her own life. There is no freedom to do as she pleases. She goes from her father's home to her husband's. A man has complete control over his wife. I realize Mother and Father have always seemed happy, but everyone knows that most women aren't so lucky. And Aunt Susan's husband divorced her and took her children from her."

"A clever woman can wrap her husband around her fingers. Look at your mother. I warrant she gets her own way ninety percent of the time," Johnny declared.

"But that's because he adores her and can deny her nothing."

"Then there's your answer, Louisa. Find a man who adores you." He glanced up to see James Hamilton and his brother Claud. "Speak of the devil," he murmured.

Louisa raised her chin. "Devil is right." She addressed Abercorn. "What are Tories doing at the Prime Minister's Ball?"

Johnny chided, "Don't play ignorant, Lu. You know Earl Grey is prime minister over both parties and both houses."

"Such a pity," she taunted.

"May I have the next dance, Lady Louisa?" Claud asked.

She gave him a radiant smile. "I would be delighted."

"My brother enjoys your teasing. He has an amazing sense of humor."

"You seem to idolize him," she said lightly.

"There's no doubt about it, my lady," Claud said seriously. "James has been like a father to me. I couldn't have endured it without his steadfast care and concern."

"Endured losing your father at such a tender age?"

"Endured having Aberdeen for a stepfather. He was a tyrant with a heavy whip hand. James protected me by taking the blame for all my boyhood transgressions. Many are the beatings he took on my behalf." His eyes gleamed with satisfaction. "The bully doesn't dare raise his hand to us these days. He knows it's more than his life is worth."

Louisa shuddered. She had always sensed a dangerous quality about Abercorn. *He keeps his temper under a tight rein, but if he ever lost control and unleashed his fury, it would be deadly.*

Lord John and Abercorn watched the couple dance. "Louisa feels safe with your brother, James. If she thinks someone is interested in her, she holds him at arm's length."

"She fights fiercely to hide her vulnerability."

"Yes, she is skittish about marriage and terrified of having a child. She's afraid of a husband having control over her. The thought of being a wife was always anathema to her. When she was a little girl, she vowed she would be a dancer on the stage. When she was about twelve, she learned that a duke's daughter could never perform on a public stage. Poor Louisa was devastated. It ruined her life for at least a year."

"I realize I will have a lot of competition for her hand. I take it I will have to add Lord Kerry to the list?"

"Don't worry. She suspects that Kerry is smitten and will try to avoid him."

Abercorn grinned. "Rivalry will only spur me on and harden my resolve."

At the end of the waltz, Claud returned Louisa to Johnny's side. She expected James to ask for the next dance and was looking forward to denying him. When he did not offer to partner her, she was acutely disappointed.

The Earl of Edgecombe bowed before her and begged her to dance. She smiled sweetly and allowed him to lead her onto the floor. She willed herself to stop thinking about his lack of chin. *The poor fellow couldn't choose his ancestors.* She found herself thinking of Abercorn's square jaw and felt annoyed at herself. *He's obviously from a long line of dominant Irishmen!*

When the dance was over, Louisa was approached by the handsome Earl of Winterton and happily followed as he led her onto the floor.

"I am a great admirer of your late uncle, the Duke of Richmond. Lennox was a renowned cricketer." He leaned toward her as if he wanted to impart a confidence. "We have much in common. Lennox played for Sussex, and I play for Sussex. He was a right-hand bat, and I am a right-hand bat."

"How extraordinary," Louisa murmured, as her eyes glazed over. Her Aunt Charlotte's husband had been deceased for over a decade and she had never seen him play. She connected cricket with her brothers, who wielded hard wooden bats as weapons to whack each other, as well as anything else that impeded their rowdy fun and games.

When Georgy returned to the ball, she glanced about the crowded room looking for Lord Burlington. When she found him, she threaded her way through the guests until she was standing beside him. Searching for something interesting to say, she remembered Louisa's words about politics. "Hello, William. I understand your kinsman, the Duke of Devonshire, has been appointed Lord Chamberlain by Prime Minister Grey."

"Yes indeed, Georgy. The ruling Whig families have finally returned to power." He gave her a speculative look. "Would you care to dance? I quite enjoyed *partnering* you at your debutante ball."

She went into his arms with a coy glance. *You'd like me on my knees again, wouldn't you, Willy? I'll hold out the possibility as a lure. You were easy to hook, but the trick will be keeping you on the line until you are caught.* "You showed me some exciting dance steps. You are a wonderful teacher . . . I quite enjoyed my lesson."

"We both seem to enjoy the same things. If we practice, we may achieve perfection."

"Yes, I agree we are a well-matched pair." She licked her lips suggestively.

"Shall we see if we can find a secluded spot where we can . . . communicate?"

"How can I resist such an alluring proposal? But first, let's indulge in a drink."

"'Tis said that champagne lowers the inhibitions."

"And tickles the tongue."

Burlington's cock bucked at mention of her tongue and he led her into the crowded supper room to ply her with champagne.

Georgy accepted the glass he offered and toyed with it in a provocative manner. She ran her finger around the rim, dipped it into the wine, then popped it into her mouth and sucked on it. "Mm, delicious!" She repeated the provocation, then drained the glass.

Burlington reached for her hand.

"I'd like another, before you lead me into temptation," she murmured seductively. She accepted a second glass. "Thank you. This will really whet my appetite." Georgy glanced around the supper room looking for a plausible excuse she could use for not following through on a sexual encounter with Burlington. Tonight she did not want to leave him satisfied; she wanted to leave him craving for her luscious mouth.

"Teddy, please forgive me. I completely forgot I had promised the next waltz to you. I am so sorry you had to come looking for me." She drained her champagne glass and murmured to Burlington, "He's a close friend of the family. I don't dare disappoint him." She glanced down at the bulge in William's trousers. "I'll smoke that cigar later."

Teddy led her from the supper room. "What was all that about?"

Georgy decided to play one against the other. "He's totally captivated. I have reason to believe he's considering a match with the Duke of Bedford's daughter."

"Damn good thing he doesn't suspect what we were up to earlier."

"Oh, I don't know. He might find a wife with experience extremely rewarding."

It wasn't until the last dance in the early hours of the morning that James Hamilton offered to partner Lady Lu. She had fully expected him to seek her out all night. When he did not, she asked herself if she felt relief or disappointment.

His eyes smiled down at her. "I've saved the best for last."

"Flattery, begod." She gave him back his own words. "You must have an ulterior motive."

"Self-preservation. If I'd asked you earlier, you would have turned me down."

"You are an astute devil."

"Is that a criticism or a compliment?"

"I suppose it is both. I admire your shrewdness yet detest the fact that you know me so well. Your powers of observation are much keener than those of other men."

"Here is what I have observed about you, Louisa. Though you have your mother's exquisite beauty, you are not a social butterfly. You don't really enjoy these balls."

"I find having a season offensive. Debutantes are presented on a tray like fancy desserts so that gentlemen can take their pick. To me, it is demeaning."

"You prefer dancing alone on a stage to dancing in a crowded ballroom with a man partnering you and forcing you to follow his steps. You like to be admired from afar."

"And here is what I have observed about you, Abercorn. Your charming surface masks a will of iron. You have a dominant and determined nature, and you enjoy being in control. Yet underneath it all, you yearn to be part of a large, loving family."

"Then you may as well say *yes* now, and have done with it."

She caught her breath. *Are you proposing to me?* She saw the teasing light in his eyes. *No, you are laughing at me, you Irish devil!*

Chapter Eleven

"Madame Madeleine's, on Bond Street." Georgy gave the Russell coachman the address of the fashionable modiste. Since she had ruined the lavender silk by spilling something sticky on it, she was to be fitted for a new ball gown.

"I'm not coming in with you," Louisa informed her sister.

"You sly puss, you have an assignation! Who are you meeting? Not Teddy, I hope."

"Don't be daft, Georgy. If you must know, I'm going to the theater to see the matinee performance of *The Brigand*. When the coachman drops us off, I'll take a hackney to Covent Garden."

"But you've already seen it."

"I could see it every day for a month and still not tire of it. I love everything about the theater."

"But I wanted you to help me pick a style and a color. You have better fashion sense than I have. Besides, Mother would be furious if she knew you were wandering about London on your own."

"I'm trusting you not to tell her. But I'd wager that when Mother was my age, she went wherever she pleased."

"Well, you can return the favor when I have something to hide. But I still think it's selfish of you to abandon me to Madame Madeleine."

The sisters alighted on Bond Street and the coachman went to find a nearby place where he could park the carriage. As soon as he drove on, Louisa crossed to the opposite side and hailed a hackney.

"Kathleen . . . Kitty, you seem to have settled in quite nicely."

"James, how will I ever thank you for providing me with such a fine place to live?"

"I consider it my duty to make sure you are safe while living in London, Kitty." He looked around the apartment he had leased for her in the respectable house on Maiden Lane. He didn't tell her that he had paid the landlady to keep an eye on her. "I'm glad you like it here. Since you have a matinee performance this afternoon, why don't I escort you to the theater? I believe Covent Garden is within walking distance."

"That's one of the things I love about it. Maiden Lane is handy to everything."

James helped her with her cloak then watched her lock the door with her own key. They walked past Rules Restaurant at the end of the street. "I believe this is the oldest eating house in London. I'll take you to dine here one night after your performance."

"That would be lovely. It's very elegant. Lots of famous people dine here."

James smiled. "You may be famous one day. I'll be able to say that I knew Kitty Kelly when she was in the chorus."

Kitty laughed, imagining herself the toast of the town, and perhaps Lord Abercorn's mistress, if she were lucky enough.

As they crossed Covent Garden toward the theater, James was surprised to see Louisa Russell alight from a hackney cab. As he watched her approach the box office, he realized she would be attending the performance. Moreover, she was entirely alone. He escorted Kitty to the stage door entrance and bade her good-bye.

As he walked back to the front of the theater, it didn't take him long to decide to buy a ticket to attend the matinee performance. He entered the theater and gazed up at the Russell family's box. It was empty and he concluded that Louisa must be sitting in the audience. He waited until the lights went down and the curtain began to rise; then he walked down the aisle, scanning the patrons. He saw her sitting close to the stage in the front row and quietly took a seat behind her. She was completely focused on the performers on the stage and totally oblivious of the people around her.

James smiled to himself as he heard her quietly singing the lyrics. He knew that she longed to be up there performing. She was enjoying herself, so he decided to wait until intermission to make his presence known. As the curtain came down and the audience clapped and whistled its appreciation, he bent forward and murmured, "Lady Lu is obviously stagestruck."

Startled, she turned and glared at him. "You simian dolt! I almost jumped out of my skin."

He grinned. "Because I caught you doing something wicked."

"I have never done anything wicked in my life," she hissed.

"Not yet you haven't . . . but wouldn't you just love to?" he teased.

"I'd love to stab you in the eye with my hatpin!"

"Bloodthirsty wench. Wouldn't it be more exciting to go backstage after the performance?"

Louisa caught her breath. "Would that be possible?"

"I might be persuaded to arrange it."

She raised her chin and challenged, "At what price?"

He waggled his eyebrows suggestively. "What price would you be willing to pay?"

"You devil!" She turned her back on him and made her mind up to completely ignore him. *Could he really take me backstage?*

She sat with her back straight, staring at the maroon velvet curtain. She wasn't looking at him, but that didn't mean she was unaware of him. *How dare he follow me into the theater!* His presence behind her was both compelling and disturbing. *What is it about Abercorn that arouses my anger?* She knew the answer. He was far too perceptive. *He can read me like a bloody book!*

After the intermission, the lights went down and the curtain rose. Once again she became so absorbed in the performance that she almost forgot he was there. Almost.

His presence, however, did not detract from her enjoyment. If anything, it was engagingly provocative and added a certain piquancy.

When the musical ended and the final curtain came down, Louisa applauded with great enthusiasm. She became aware of Abercorn clapping behind her and glanced over her shoulder at him.

"I take it you don't wish to go backstage?"

She hesitated for long moments, then blurted, "You know damn well I wish to go."

James masked his amusement. "Then I shall take you. Without any strings attached . . . this time."

Her pulse raced with excitement. They stood together in the aisle until the audience filed out. Then Abercorn led the way backstage. Her heart hammered as she gazed about, drinking in the behind-the-scenes magic. There was a clutter of ropes, scenery, stage props, and costumes. Actors and performers of both sexes mingled about, laughing, cursing, and singing. All seemed a blur of vivid, colorful confusion that filled Louisa's senses with exhilaration. Just to breathe the same air as the performers filled her with excitement. She inhaled the exotic scents of makeup, sweat, and musty garments as if it were the elixir of life. "It's all so thrilling!"

James watched the wonder on her face and it filled him with pleasure. He knew he had made her happy and he realized he wanted to do it every day for the rest of her life. "This way." He walked a direct path to a door marked *dressing room* and knocked.

"Enter," a chorus of female voices sang out.

Abercorn opened the door and ushered Louisa inside where a

bevy of females were in various stages of undress. Mirrors lined one wall and in front of the mirrors was a long shelf that held makeup and wigs. Costumes were strewn about everywhere.

"James! You stayed for the performance." Kitty was clearly delighted.

"Yes. I brought my friend . . . Jane . . . to meet you. The stage fascinates her." He looked at Louisa and again used her middle name. "Jane, I'd like you to meet Kitty Kelly."

Louisa gazed at the pretty girl's lovely red hair. "I'm thrilled to meet you. It must be so exciting to sing and dance before an audience. I've seen *The Brigand* twice and fully intend to come again. I already know all the words to the songs you sing and all the dance steps."

"Sure and I'm glad you enjoyed it, Jane."

She heard the lilt in the girl's voice. *She's Irish. That's how he knows her. Perhaps she's more than a friend.* Louisa's blood slowed in her veins as her sister's words came back to her: *A dancer can't manage without a man to pay her bills. Girls on the stage have lovers to pay for their rooms, and clothes, and carriages.* She felt her heart constrict. *Kitty is his mistress!* She told herself that all young men had mistresses. *It matters naught to me . . . I don't care if Abercorn has a dozen!*

She was covered with chagrin as it dawned on her that he hadn't followed her into the theater after all. He had come to watch Kitty Kelly perform. Louisa turned to address Hamilton. "Thank you for bringing me backstage. It was very kind of you. I mustn't take up any more of your time. Good afternoon, Abercorn. Good-bye, Kitty."

She turned and walked from the dressing room. It was a full minute before she realized that James was following her. "Please stay. I don't wish to interfere with your plans."

"Kitty and I have no plans."

"Kitty . . . what a perfect name for an Irish chorus girl," she said lightly.

It suddenly dawned on him that Louisa was jealous and his heart began to sing. "I do have plans, however, to see you safely back to Belgrave Square."

"That isn't necessary. I'm not a child, Abercorn."

"I don't think of you as a child, Lady Lu. To me you are a desirable woman. One who shouldn't be walking the streets alone."

"I have no intention of walking."

"You'd trust yourself alone in a carriage with me?"

"Don't be absurd." She tried not to laugh but failed. "You are insufferable. Why do you enjoy tormenting me?"

"For the sheer pleasure of watching your face. When you are angry, your green eyes glitter like emeralds. Your nostrils flare, and you draw your lips back from your teeth, as if you are going to bite me. You have a wild beauty that I cannot resist."

"You are a madman!" She pretended outrage, but she was extremely flattered. She watched him hail a hackney and her pulse raced as she wondered if she could trust him in a carriage. When he took the seat opposite her, rather than sitting beside her, she wasn't sure if she felt relief or disappointment.

Silence stretched between them, as James looked out the window. A passing church jogged his memory. "My stepfather, Aberdeen, has a house on South Audley Street. When I was a boy, he made us walk to his church in Drury Lane and back home again. He was a strict Presbyterian and the use of a carriage on Sunday was strictly forbidden."

"South Audley to Drury Lane and back? That's several miles."

"It didn't harm Claud or me, but it was very taxing for my mother, at certain times."

He means when his mother was with child. Louisa felt outrage. "Aberdeen is a monster, and all in the name of religion. Why is it that husbands feel the need to exercise complete control over their wives?"

"Not all husbands, Louisa. I warrant your father doesn't control his wife."

She laughed. "He sometimes tries, but he seldom succeeds."

"You are very fortunate, Louisa, that your parents have a loving relationship. I would wager that is the secret of a happy marriage."

"Marriage doesn't appeal to me," she said quickly in an attempt to erect a barrier between them.

"You'd rather be a dancer on the stage than a wife and mother."

"A thousand times over! But that's impossible," she said wistfully. "Do you still live on South Audley Street when you are in London?"

"Not a chance! I have my own townhouse on Half Moon Street."

The hackney stopped in Belgrave Square and James opened the door, stepped down, and helped Louisa alight. "I take it you will be attending the matinee performance again next Wednesday afternoon, so why don't you allow me to escort you?"

"How can you so easily discern my intensions?"

He smiled into her eyes. "Irish intuition, I suppose."

She hesitated, but the lure he held out was too tempting to resist. "I shall accept your kind offer. You may call for me next Wednesday."

Louisa had been home for an hour before she remembered the sugared mouse he had offered her at the Carlton House party when she was a child. *He offered me something I couldn't resist and today he did it again. You are a shrewd Irish devil, Abercorn!*

At dinner John Russell addressed his daughter. "Louisa, was that James Hamilton who escorted you home this afternoon?"

Louisa blushed. *Damnation, he must have seen us from the library window.* "Yes, Father." She held her breath, hoping he wouldn't ask where she had been.

"Why on earth didn't you invite him in? That was rather ill-mannered of you."

Georgy was furious. "You said you didn't have an assignation!"

"I didn't. Abercorn and I met by accident."

"How very clever of you, darling." Georgina threw her daughter an approving glance. "Have you arranged any more accidental meetings?"

"No!" Louisa had to backtrack immediately. "Actually, Abercorn is escorting me to a matinee performance at the theater next Wednesday."

"How lovely. Having a marquis pay his addresses is a feather in your cap. Did I mention that after your debutante ball, the Marquis of Lansdowne called to ask if his son Lord Kerry could pay his addresses to you?"

Louisa stole a quick glance at her sister and saw her face was like a thundercloud. She could not bear the thought of Georgy's feelings being crushed. She improvised quickly, "Yes, Mother, you did mention that Lord Kerry asked if he could pay his addresses to Georgy and me."

The Duke of Bedford smiled. "Did you girls know that Henry Petty, Marquis of Lansdowne, once proposed to your mother? Now it seems the Pettys are after my daughters." He chuckled. "I suppose hope springs eternal."

Georgy looked somewhat mollified, but the duchess was aware that her remark had hurt her eldest daughter and she deftly changed the subject. "The Royal Masquerade Ball is next week. We really must see about costumes tomorrow."

"I can wear my Spanish dancing costume," Louisa offered.

"But darling, everyone will know it is you," her mother objected. "The whole point of a masquerade is to hide your identity."

"I could wear your Spanish costume, Lu, and everyone would think I was you."

Louisa felt alarm. Georgy got up to all sorts of promiscuous behavior.

"We will go to the *costumiers* tomorrow and see what strikes our fancy," the duchess declared. "When I was your age, I went as Diana, goddess of the hunt."

"Don't encourage our daughters to be licentious, Georgina." John Russell frowned his disapproval. "Provocative costumes invite provocative behavior."

"Yes, darling, I remember it well," Georgina teased.

The following afternoon, the duchess and her two daughters were busy trying on costumes. Bedecked in a large lace ruff and a stomacher, Georgina gazed into the mirror. "I don't believe the Virgin Queen suits me and I know damn well your father would refuse to wear tights. I don't think he'd demur at being King Charles Stuart, however."

"That's an excellent idea, Mother."

"There's method in my madness, Louisa. If he is Charles, I can be Barbara Castlemaine, Duchess of Cleveland. A king's mistress is sure to cause a stir and I can wear one of those fabulous cavalier hats with a sweeping ostrich feather. I shall also need a silk mask and some face patches." She moved toward the dressing room to remove the Elizabethan gown. "What have you chosen, Louisa?"

"It's a dancer's costume," she said evasively, "but not Spanish."

"Is it a famous dancer, darling?"

"If you must know, it's pretty, witty Nell Gwyn."

"Oh, how very droll. King Charles and *both* of his favorite mistresses. The *ton* will be agog. Best not mention it to your father ahead of time." She laughed wickedly. "Better keep it as a surprise." She called out to her other daughter in the next room. "What have you chosen, Georgy?"

"Like Lu, I shall keep it as a surprise."

Louisa and her mother rolled their eyes and went off in a peal of giddy laughter.

"Dressed as King Charles Stuart, you are tempting as sin." The Duchess of Bedford stood on tiptoe and kissed her husband. "I think it's the slim mustache that attracts me."

"I know what attracts me," John said, running his finger across the swell of one half-exposed breast. "Trouble is it will attract every other male bent on seduction."

"Then I make a perfect Barbara Castlemaine. She was never faithful to Charles."

John turned as his daughter descended the stairs in a flowing white robe. "Now there's a costume I fully approve of. You make a lovely novitiate nun, Louisa."

"It is Georgy!" She lifted her white silk mask.

"Good heavens, darling, I never would have expected you to choose a nun's habit," her mother declared. "The wimple covers your lovely hair."

"This is a perfect disguise. I'm going to have great fun tonight."

When Louisa came down, she was wearing her cloak, which completely covered her costume. She had tucked her dark hair beneath a wig of saucy red curls.

Her mother laughed with delight. "Now I know what baby Rachel will look like when she grows up. The carriage is waiting . . . we'll be fashionably late as usual. I wonder what Queen Adelaide will be wearing."

Saint James's Palace was lit up like a Christmas tree for the Royal Masquerade Ball, and even the liveried servants wore masks. The Russell sisters, eager to distance themselves from their parents, melted into the crowd of costumed revelers. Louisa spied Red Riding Hood and knew immediately that it was Lady Holland. A man in a wolf mask hovered behind her. Louisa tapped him on the shoulder. "Hello, Uncle Holly."

He turned to stare at the pretty redhead dressed in a short skirt that showed off her legs and a corset laced provocatively beneath her breasts. When he saw her green eyes through the black mask, he realized it was Louisa. "How on earth did you know it was me?"

"I didn't. It was Beth I recognized. If you hadn't been together, I would never have known you. Will you partner me? I'd love to dance with a wolf."

Henry led her onto the dance floor. "You remind me so much of your mother. Your saucy costume is exactly the sort she would have worn at your age."

"I'm Nell Gwyn. I'll have to keep away from Father. He would never approve."

"Teddy has been looking for you. He came as Robin Hood. My son is quite smitten with you, my dear."

"We've known each other since we were children."

"Exactly. Nothing would please Beth and me more than seeing you and Teddy make a match."

Louisa drew in a quick breath. "Teddy and I are friends . . . I don't feel ready for marriage, Uncle Holly."

"No rush, my dear. But when you are ready to play Maid Marian to his Robin, we'd love to have you as our daughter."

When the dance ended, Louisa thanked him and melted into the crowd as quickly as she could. *Good God, I hope Teddy isn't seriously interested in me. Georgy would be devastated.* She recognized King William, who was aptly wearing an admiral's uniform. She curtsied before him. "Your Majesty, I warrant you have salt water in your veins."

"I'm far more at ease on the deck of a ship than on the dance floor, m'dear." When he learned it was Louisa Russell, he confided, "Just between us, I prefer a ship to the throne, if truth be told."

"I don't see Queen Adelaide."

"She's off dancing. Just look for Queen Cleopatra."

Louisa laughed. "This is such fun. We are all indulging our secret fantasies tonight." She spotted Charles Stuart heading toward the king and moved away quickly.

. . . .

With the tenacity of a terrier, Georgy was on a manhunt for Lord Burlington. She had eluded his amorous advances at the Prime Minister's Ball, playing him like a trout on a line to whet his appetite. Tonight she intended to reel him in. When she recognized the Duke of Devonshire, she focused her attention on the man beside him. He wore a black cape with a red lining and a devil's mask complete with horns. She knew she had viewed her prey. When Devonshire headed toward Sailor Bill, she moved in.

"The only man here who could lead me into temptation. *Devil take me!*"

Burlington thought he recognized her voice. "Georgy, is that you?" He threw back his head and laughed. "What on earth are you doing masquerading as a nun?"

She licked her lips provocatively. "I am every man's fantasy. What male breathing hasn't imagined unfrocking a nun?"

"Christ, it makes me hard just thinking about it."

"Well, think about this. I'm stark naked beneath my robe."

"Lord have mercy! Why don't we find a private place where you can save my soul?"

She took his hand. "Follow me, and I will give you a religious experience."

They left the crowded ballroom, hurried through an antechamber, and made their way down a palace corridor until they found a dark empty room.

Burlington's hands seized the hem of her robe and lifted it high. Then he caressed her naked breasts, belly, and thighs. "Will you get down on your knees and . . . pray for me?"

She unfastened his trousers and took hold of his hard erection. "Mm . . . For what you about to receive, may the Lord make you truly thankful." She sank to her knees and sucked his cock into her mouth.

"Ahh . . . Ahh . . . Ahmen," the devil groaned, as she drained away his sins.

As she tucked his limp cock out of sight, he heaved a deep sigh of satisfaction. "You're the best, Georgy."

"Indeed I am, William. We make a perfect couple. If you were wed to me, you could enjoy this every night of your life."

"Ah, you lead me into temptation, sweetheart."

"I warrant the only reason gentlemen marry is to have sex on a regular basis. The lucky ones find a wife who is insatiable." She took his hand, raised her robe, and pushed his fingers into her hot, wet cleft.

"An insatiable nun!" Burlington's knees went weak at the thought.

It was announced that at midnight, all masks were to be removed and the guests' identities revealed. For the remaining hour the lights in the palace ballroom were lowered. This added to the risqué atmosphere and encouraged the gentlemen to act boldly.

Lady Louisa found her dance partners trying to steal kisses. Since her mother had declared them insignificant trifles, she allowed a few liberties in the spirit of fun. It wasn't hard for her to discern the identity of the young lords who kissed her. She knew Earnest Winterton because he had kissed her at the last ball, and she identified Lord Edgecombe because of his receding chin. It took a little longer to guess that the pirate was actually her friend George Grey. She was surprised that his kiss was rather pleasurable and put it down to the bold buccaneer's disguise.

Two males stood before her wanting to partner her. One was Robin Hood and the other was Caesar, wearing a Roman toga and a laurel wreath. Since Lord Holland had told her Teddy was Robin Hood, she chose to dance with Caesar. The minute he put his powerful arm around her, Louisa knew it was James Hamilton. "I come to bury Caesar, not to praise him!"

"Lady Lu, is that you? Your red wig disguises your identity completely. You are dressed as Nell Gwyn, unless I miss my guess."

"Abercorn, you are the only one who knows who I'm supposed to be!"

"Well, knowing you, it had to be a dancer. A guinea says you can't sing one of Nelly's infamous ditties," he challenged.

"You're on! Find us a private spot and I will prove you wrong, noble Roman."

The pair made their way to a well-lit antechamber. Louisa curtsied low, then executed a saucy dance, kicking up her legs to show her frilly petticoat and warbling, *"It's rolling in the dew that makes the milkmaids fair."*

As James watched her delectable performance, a daring idea occurred to him. "Lady Lu, what if I came up with a way to make your fondest dream come true?"

"You are Caesar, not Merlin."

"I keep my magic wand well hidden," he teased.

"You rude Irish devil!" She laughed in spite of herself. "Tell me more. How do you propose to make my fondest dream come true?"

"I'll divulge the secret when I call for you on Wednesday." He waggled his eyebrows suggestively.

Chapter Twelve

A footman from Campden Hill, the Russells' estate in Kensington on the outskirts of London, handed the Duchess of Bedford a letter.

"Oh dear, Rachel's nursemaid says she is fretful and may be coming down with something." When the Russells came to London for the season, they had brought their two youngest children to stay at Campden Hill. "I shall pack some things and go immediately."

"Would you like me to come with you, Mother?" Louisa offered.

"No, no, darling. You're going to the theater with Abercorn this afternoon. Besides, baby Rachel may have something contagious. I don't want either you or Georgy to come down with anything that would keep you from socializing."

"What about Almack's tonight? I have captured the attention of a certain eligible noble who will likely be there," Georgy declared. "Can't you wait and go tomorrow?"

"No, I can't wait. Your brother Charles will escort you. Who might this noble gentleman be?" her mother asked eagerly.

"He shall remain nameless until I am sure of my conquest. Actually, I have two young men paying their addresses to me."

"What a clever girl you are, Georgy. Don't do anything I wouldn't do, darling."

"You are my role model in everything I do, Mother."

Louisa knew her mother hadn't the faintest notion that Georgy was promiscuous. "Please send us a note to let us know how Rachel is. I hope it's nothing serious."

Lu, wearing an afternoon dress in a delicate shade of peach, picked up her hat decorated with pale green ribbon and descended to the entrance hall, where she paced about waiting for James Hamilton. She heard a carriage and opened the door, but was surprised to see it was her father. "Oh, I thought it was Abercorn."

"When he arrives, don't bolt off, Louisa. You must invite him in. I've just had lunch with Johnny and the prime minister. I have something I'd like to ask Abercorn. I'll be in the library."

Georgy descended the stairs. "If you are wise, you'll let a footman answer the door and keep Abercorn waiting. Anticipation whets the appetite."

"Don't be silly. He's not courting me. He's acting as my escort to the theater because he knows I have a passion for it."

"Don't be naive, Lu. He's after kindling your passion, but not for the theater."

"Then he'll be disappointed, won't he?"

"I doubt that. I'd wager the dark devil is tenacious as a terrier."

The thud of the doorknocker made Louisa jump. She ignored her sister's advice about making him wait and opened the door. "Good afternoon, James."

"Lady Louisa, you look exceptionally lovely today."

"Thank you. I'm sorry, but Father would like to see you in the library."

"Don't be sorry, Lu. I thoroughly enjoy your father's company."

More than mine, likely. "The library is this way."

John Russell stood when he saw Abercorn. "Do come in, James." He glanced at Louisa. "Where's your mother?"

"She left you a note. She's gone to Campden Hill. Rachel's nurse-maid thinks she's coming down with something."

"Oh dear." He glanced at his desk and spotted the note. "Here it is." He picked it up. "I won't keep you, James. I don't want you to be late for the performance. I had lunch with Johnny and Earl Grey. Before Parliament recesses for the summer, I'd like to visit the Lords and wondered if we could go together?"

"I'd be honored, Your Grace."

The duke scanned his wife's letter. "I think I'd better drop in at Campden Hill. Tell you what—when I get back, I'll be in touch and we can arrange a date to visit the Lords together."

"I shall look forward to it. I hope there is nothing seriously wrong at Campden Hill, Your Grace."

Louisa settled back against the leather squabs in Abercorn's carriage. "I don't expect Mother to be back for at least a week. She worries when Rachel is unwell. We all do, actually. Mother lost a baby boy once. The fear of losing a child never leaves you."

Abercorn had a revelation. This was the reason Louisa was skittish about marriage. *She's terrified of having a child!* "The Duchess of Bedford is a devoted mother. She'll nurse little Rachel through all her childhood ailments, have no fear."

"Will you be returning to Ireland in August when Parliament recesses?"

"Actually, I have business in Scotland that needs my attention."

Damnation, we usually go to Scotland for part of August and September. I'd better take care not to divulge that to you, Abercorn.

"Before that comes the boat race between Oxford and Cambridge. Since I'm now a graduate, this will be the last year I'll be allowed to row. It's held at Henley-on-Thames. I'm sure your brother Charles will attend. I'd love you to come and watch, Lu."

"Do you think Oxford will win this year?"

"I *know* Oxford will win. Cambridge doesn't stand a chance."

It must be wonderful to have so much self-confidence. "Cocksure devil!"

"And then some," he said with a grin.

Inside the theater, Louisa led the way to her family's box. When the curtain went up and the chorus danced onto the stage, she sang the words perfectly along with the performers.

James smiled into the darkness, feeling confident that Louisa would not be able to resist the plan he was about to propose.

At the intermission, she applauded with gusto. "I enjoy it more every time." She leaned forward to look at the audience below. She was fascinated by everything about the theater.

When the intermission was over and the chorus danced out again, Lu glanced at him knowingly. "There's your red-headed friend."

"Do you believe you could do her part, if you were down there on the stage?"

"Of course I could." She tossed her head. "I could do it better than Kitty!"

James leaned close. "Cocksure devil."

Her lips twitched, but she refused to look at him. Instead she focused all her attention on the performers. When the musical was over, Louisa stood up and applauded loudly. "Thank you for bringing me. It was exceedingly kind of you."

"I had an ulterior motive."

She went still. *If Kitty was your ulterior motive, you can go to the devil!*

"Lady Lu, I have thought of a way to make your fondest dream

VIRGINIA HENLEY

come true. What if I could arrange for you to sing and dance on Covent Garden's stage for just one night?"

"That's quite impossible. My parents would never allow it."

"They'd never know. No one would know. If you wore a red wig, everyone would assume you were Kitty Kelly."

She drew in a swift breath and her eyes filled with wonder. "You could arrange it?"

"Absolutely. Are you up to the challenge, Lady Lu?"

His proposition was almost too tempting to resist. "At what price?"

James looked deeply into her eyes. "What price would you be willing to pay?"

She thought about it for a full minute. As she hesitated, her longing threatened to overwhelm her caution. But she guessed exactly what price Abercorn was asking. She raised her chin and said primly, "My answer is no."

When the carriage arrived in Belgrave Square, Charles rushed out of the house to speak to his friend James. He flourished a piece of paper. "I got confirmation. I've been accepted into the Household Cavalry as a first lieutenant."

"Congratulations, Charles. Your fondest dream has been realized," James replied.

His choice of words was not lost on Louisa. He was subtly pointing out that dreams could be realized, if you went after them. "I'm very happy for you, Charles." She turned to James. "Thank you for your escort, Abercorn."

Her brother did not follow her into the house. He remained outside talking to his friend. Louisa went upstairs, removed her hat, and washed her hands. When she came back down, her sister was waiting to hear all the details.

"Was I right, or was I wrong? Did Abercorn try to kindle your passion, or was it strictly platonic?"

Louisa blushed. "Don't be silly, Georgy. We're not even friends— we're more like antagonists."

Charles came into the house. "I was on tenterhooks about being accepted into the Household Cavalry. The regiment has height restrictions. At five feet, eleven inches I just made it."

"Being accepted had more to do with who you are than your measurements," Georgy asserted. "Our family is friends with both the king of England and the prime minister. There was never any doubt you'd get into the regiment of your choice."

"That's a damned lie, Georgy. I'm an honors graduate of Oxford and meet all the academic and physical requirements. Watch your tongue, or I won't escort you to Almack's tonight."

Louisa looked surprised at his authoritative tone and Georgy rolled her eyes. "Charles thinks he's in charge because Father has gone to Campden Hill. Mother sent a note that Rachel has chicken pox, and she thinks Alexander has caught it too."

"Oh, poor little monkeys," Louisa sympathized.

"She says they are not very ill. She's having a devil of a time keeping them in bed."

"Since they don't want to bring the infection to their precious daughters, they won't be returning to London for at least a week. In the meantime, I'm the authority figure here, so don't you forget it."

Both sisters gave him a mock salute. "Aye-aye, Lieutenant Bloody Russell."

"Don't expect me to dance attendance on you tonight. I'm only going to gamble."

"And to brag about your commission!" Georgy taunted.

"I invited James to join me."

"Why the devil did you do that?" Louisa demanded.

"Misery loves company—that's why. The place will be filled with matchmaking mothers, desperate to unload their simpering daughters."

"I'm neither simpering nor desperate," Lu declared. "Perhaps I won't go."

"Don't be selfish! The season is so short; I can't afford to pass up any opportunities to socialize with the opposite sex. I plan to wear my new ball gown."

In spite of having threatened not to attend, Louisa was ready and waiting by the time Charles came downstairs wearing the requisite knee breeches. She had been preoccupied with James Hamilton's proposal ever since he made it, but she was determined to put it from her mind. She reasoned that a night at Almack's would surely divert her thoughts.

It was almost ten o'clock when they arrived. Charles did his duty by his sisters and remained in the ballroom for half an hour before he disappeared upstairs.

Louisa kept a sharp watch for Abercorn's arrival while she filled out her dance card and was led onto the floor by various partners. She agreed to dance with Ned Turnour, Earl of Winterton, and was pleasantly surprised when he did not speak of cricket. Next she danced with Lord Seymour. He was a Whig Member of Parliament and spoke of the reform bill that her brother Johnny was sponsoring.

"I'm sure Lord John will welcome your support, Adolphus. He shouldn't have any trouble in the Commons, but when it goes to the Lords, it is not a certainty."

"I'm sure my father will follow my lead, Lady Louisa."

She smiled at him. *The Duke of Somerset is a leader, not a follower.*

By eleven o'clock when Abercorn had not arrived, she knew that Almack's doors would be closed and no more patrons would be admitted. Disappointment clouded her mood and she accepted Lord Kerry's offer to escort her to supper.

It was one o'clock in the morning before she saw her sister. "Are you enjoying yourself, Georgy?"

"Most of the men dancing are second sons, looking for heiresses. I danced twice with Maurice Berkeley, before I realized it was his brother who is the earl. I walked past the gaming rooms and all the interesting gentlemen are playing cards, not dancing."

"I don't suppose Charles will be ready to leave for hours," Louisa guessed.

"I thought I had a lively prospect when the young Duke of Queensberry asked to partner me. But after the dance, Lady Cowper made a point of telling me the lecherous devil took a wife last year."

"Speaking of Lady Cowper, her husband is nowhere to be seen, but Lord Palmerston is dancing attendance on her."

"So I see! The patronesses of Almack's are supposed to be beyond reproach, but Cowper proves that's a load of codswallop," Georgy said, laughing.

"Hush, she will hear you," Lu warned.

Because James Hamilton was absent, the hours dragged for Louisa. In her mind she relived her afternoon at the theater with him over and over. Finally, around four in the morning, Charles came downstairs to take them home. His pockets were to let, and he vowed that was the last time he would ever attend Almack's.

Louisa lay abed but sleep proved to be elusive. Abercorn's offer to arrange for her to dance at Covent Garden loomed more tempting with every passing hour. She had longed to do this all her life. She knew she could fill the role and even surpass Kitty's performance. The only thing stopping her was paying Abercorn's price.

Girls on the stage have lovers . . . men who expect sexual favors.

Lu turned over and thumped her pillow. *It boils down to two things—either you want to perform onstage or you don't.* She knew she wanted it more than anything she'd ever wished for. *It's a chance of a lifetime. Will you grab it with both hands, or will you take the coward's way out and primly refuse?*

Louisa made up her mind in an instant. With the dilemma resolved, she fell promptly asleep and didn't awaken until afternoon.

"I'm going to visit Aunt Charlotte and tell her that Mother has gone to Campden Hill and will likely be there for at least a week because of Rachel's chicken pox. Would you like to come with me, Georgy?"

"And have to sit there and listen to Sophie rabbit on about her wedding plans? Not bloody likely."

Louisa smiled her secret smile. She knew that was exactly the answer her sister would give her. That was the reason she'd chosen Fife House as her fictitious destination.

She left the house, opened her red parasol, and walked down Grosvenor Crescent. She strolled through Green Park, then crossed Piccadilly. Though Half Moon Street was very short, she had no idea which townhouse belonged to Abercorn. She went up the steps and knocked on the door of the first residence.

A servant answered. His eyes swept over her and focused on the red parasol. Since she had no maid with her, he decided she was no lady. "Yes, Miss?"

"Does the Marquis of Abercorn live here?"

"No, Miss." He tried to shut the door.

Louisa pushed it back open. "Do you know which house is Abercorn's?"

"Yes, Miss." Again he tried to shut the door.

"Damn your insolence, sir." She closed her parasol and, holding it as a weapon, threatened him. "Point out his house to me, or you will feel my point!"

The servant pointed his finger at the house across the street then slammed the door.

Louisa crossed over and knocked on the door. When a manservant answered, she was ready for him. With the light of battle in her eyes, she pointed the parasol at him. "Lady Louisa Russell to see the Marquis of Abercorn. Announce me, or else."

He grinned. "Or else ye'll give me the Chinese torture. This way, m'lady."

She followed him into the front hall. "What, pray, is the Chinese torture?"

"Sure an' that's when ye shove yer closed parasol up my arse and pull it down open."

Before Louisa could whoop with laughter a voice from above thundered, "Phineas!" James Hamilton rapidly descended the stairs and dismissed the servant. "I'm sorry, Lu. Please come upstairs."

She didn't try to hide her amusement. "One Irishman apologizing for another, begod! What is the world coming to?" She followed him up to a tastefully furnished sitting room but did not take the seat he offered.

James knew exactly why Louisa had come. He had been waiting for her. He had proffered the sugared mouse, and though it had taken a little time, he was sure she would not be able to resist the bait.

"I've decided to do it!" she said quickly, before she could change her mind.

"Do what, Lady Lu?"

"Take over Kitty's part at Covent Garden Theatre for one night. That is, if you can arrange it for me."

"I can and I will," he promised.

If Kitty will do whatever you ask, she must be your mistress.

"Which night would you prefer? Choose one when you can be away from home all night, without arousing suspicion."

Louisa almost asked *why*? Then she remembered she would be spending the night with him. She told herself it was a small price to pay to achieve her lifelong dream, but she didn't convince herself for one minute. She couldn't decide on a night.

"How about Wednesday? You can watch Kitty at the matinee and then take over for her at the evening performance."

"Yes . . . yes. Wednesday would be best," she quickly agreed.

He glanced at the parasol she was clutching. "Why don't you put that down and have a seat?"

She knew she must look ridiculous and attempted a joke. "You wish to render me defenseless."

"Your weapons are useless against my powers of persuasion, Louisa."

In that case you may as well take me to your bedchamber now, you Irish lecher! She did not voice the sarcastic remark but said sweetly, "Ah, will you stay me with flagons?"

"I won't offer you wine, but I beg you stay for tea."

"Thank you." She took a seat and pretended nonchalance. "I have an ulterior motive."

"Would you care to enlighten me?"

"Of course. I want to see if Phineas is capable of making and serving tea."

In a remarkably short time after James spoke with his manservant, Phineas rolled in a teacart. Over one arm was draped a starched linen towel. There was an assortment of dainty watercress and cucumber sandwiches and some *petits fours*, along with the tea things. He proceeded to set up a small table beside her, with a damask napkin, a porcelain plate, and a small cream and sugar pot. Then he poured tea into a matching cup and saucer and handed it to her. "Will there be anything else, m'lady?"

"No, thank you, Phineas." She could see the china was Spode. It had a claret border with a gold rim and Louisa was impressed, not just by the porcelain but also by the man who served it.

When he withdrew, James smiled. "Never underestimate an Irishman, Lu."

She looked him in the eye over the gold rim of her teacup. "Forewarned is forearmed, Lord Abercorn." She changed the subject to something less personal and spoke of the reform bill that Johnny was working on.

"Lord John has the potential to hold high office," James declared.

"Father hopes he will be appointed to the cabinet. Prime Minister Grey includes him in cabinet meetings when the reform bill is being discussed."

"And rightly so. I predict he will go far."

Louisa had a sandwich and two cakes. She dabbed her lips with her napkin, then rose and picked up her parasol. "Thank you for the tea," she said formally. "And for . . . the arrangement," she added awkwardly.

"Your wish is my command," he said lightly.

Until after my performance. Then your command will be whatever you wish, no doubt. "Good-bye, my lord. I hope to see you on Wednesday."

On Tuesday night, Louisa retired early. She practiced her dances and the words to her songs for hours. When she went to bed, she was far too excited to sleep and went over her performance in her mind's eye again and again. To keep her fear at bay, her thoughts did not stray beyond the curtain coming down.

After lunch on Wednesday, James picked her up and took her to Covent Garden Theatre. Before they went through the stage door, Louisa put on the red wig and tucked in all her dark tendrils.

James escorted her into the dressing room, where Kitty greeted them eagerly.

"You can watch the matinee from the wings, Jane. I've told the other girls in the chorus that you're performing in my place tonight, and the principal actors won't notice. They never look at lowly chorus dancers."

"Thank you, Kitty." Louisa was so excited she could hardly breathe.

James removed Louisa's cloak and asked, "Will you be all right?"

She nodded eagerly, her eyes shining like stars.

"I shall leave you to it then." He whispered in her ear, "Knock 'em dead, Lady Lu."

She looked at Kitty in her scanty costume. "How did you and Lord Abercorn meet?"

"We played together as children in Ireland."

Lu felt weak with relief. *They are childhood friends. She isn't his mistress after all!*

The signal came for the girls to take their places, and they hurried out to the stage. Louisa followed and stood in the wings. She mouthed along with the words to the songs but as she watched she thought the dancing lacked lively spontaneity. The girls of the chorus seemed to be simply going through the motions, as if it had all become routine.

When the principal characters of *The Brigand* came onstage, however, they did their parts with great enthusiasm. Louisa thoroughly enjoyed watching the performance from her advantageous position in the wings. When the musical ended, everyone gathered onstage to take the final bow. She followed the girls of the chorus into their dressing room, where most of them collapsed onto their stools.

Kitty removed her costume and hung it up. "I'm more than ready for a night off."

"Before you go, I want to thank you sincerely, Kitty."

"Don't mention it. I'd do anything for James."

Some of the girls removed their costumes and slipped on silk wrappers to cover their nakedness. A lad, who looked about twelve, came in to collect tuppence from each girl who wanted food to eat between shows.

A half-hour later he came back and handed each chorus girl fish and chips wrapped in newspaper. Louisa was thrilled. She used her fingers and realized she had never eaten anything that tasted quite as delicious in her entire life.

The girls' conversations centered about the men in their lives. All of them were trading sexual favors for various things, from meals to presents. The lucky ones had regular admirers who were paying their rent.

I wonder if James is paying Kitty's rent. The thought was disturbing. She chided herself for her unworthy suspicions and firmly put them out of her mind.

About an hour before the evening performance, Louisa donned her costume and sat before the mirror to apply her stage makeup. She felt butterflies start to flutter in her belly. When she was ready, she gazed at her reflection and knew none would ever recognize her as Lady Louisa Russell—not even members of her own family. The realization filled her with confidence and she smiled her secret smile.

When the cue came that the curtain was about to go up, Lu felt a surge of excited energy. She jumped up, eager for her first performance on a public stage. Though Kitty was not the lead chorus girl, Louisa led the way. She took a deep breath and plunged into the performance.

As her feet carried her across the stage, her nerves vanished like snow in summer.

As she sang *The Brigand's* lyrics, her beautiful clear notes soared above the other voices.

Her gestures were eye-catching, her dancing was perfection itself, and her performance was far more professional than any other girl onstage. She put her heart and soul into her presentation and in essence became the character she was playing.

James Hamilton sat in the audience, mesmerized by Louisa. Her beauty and her talent were breathtaking. It was a great pity that she could not become a professional actress and dancer, for she had all the qualities that would make her a star.

His feelings were proprietary. He had arranged this for one night only. He could never share her with the world. She would belong to him alone. *If I'm lucky enough.*

Chapter Thirteen

Being bathed in applause is the most glorious feeling in the world! Louisa stood onstage as the final curtain descended, filled with triumph. *I did it!* She spread her arms wide and then wrapped them around her body, as a feeling of joy engulfed her senses. Exhilaration spiraled through her belly, making her breasts tingle and her spirits soar. Happiness flowed about her as she floated in a sea of bliss.

She was the last one to leave the stage and when she entered the dressing room, she was oblivious of the resentful glances and dirty looks of the chorus girls.

James opened the door and strode in with an armful of brilliant red roses and carnations. "You did it! And you did it superbly!"

Louisa laughed up at him as she took the flowers. She buried her face in them and inhaled, drinking in their intoxicating fragrance.

Freed of the flowers, he opened his arms and Louisa eagerly went into his embrace.

"Thank you, James. Thank you for making it all possible."

The other girls in the room, changing from their costumes, stared enviously at the handsome noble wearing evening clothes and the girl on whom he was lavishing his attention. The couple was unaware of their audience as the onlookers faded away and left them in a world of their own.

"Let me unhook you," he offered.

She set down her flowers and turned her back toward him. "I hate to take it off." She slipped out of the costume and donned her own petticoat and dress. Then she sat down on the stool and unselfconsciously drew on her hose and garters.

James knelt and helped her put on her shoes. "You can remove your makeup later." He took her cloak from its hook, placed it around her shoulders, and then took her hand.

She picked up her flowers and was surprised to notice that the room was empty. "Where did everyone go?"

James led the way back to the stage and they crossed it to walk behind the curtain. "I know you must be reluctant to leave. Why don't you take another bow?"

Louisa felt euphoric. There was no room for sadness that this would be her last time onstage. She dipped down in a graceful curtsy and bestowed a radiant smile on him when he applauded. She stopped worrying about what was to come. Nothing could erase the joyfulness that filled her heart. This was a fantasy and she didn't want it to end. She had experienced her glorious moment in the sun and was ready and willing to pay the piper.

Eventually they became aware of someone clearing his throat. They looked over at an elderly stagehand, hovering in the wings.

"Beggin' yer pardon, m'lord, I'm waitin' to put out the lights an' lock up."

"I'm sorry, Lady Lu. Your Covent Garden performance has come to an end."

"Don't be sorry, James. I shall take the magic with me."

When they left the darkened theater, they walked past the Covent Garden flower sellers. Phineas had brought Abercorn's carriage at the appointed time. James opened the door and followed Louisa inside. He sat opposite her so he could enjoy her radiant beauty. Her eyes were filled with stars and her lips curved with the exquisite pleasure of her once-in-a-lifetime experience.

"I had a terrible attack of butterflies fluttering in my belly, but once I stepped onto the stage, they disappeared like magic."

"Your performance was so professional you made the other girls look like amateurs."

"I loved every single moment of it and basked shamelessly in the applause."

"You earned it."

"Thank you . . . for the compliment and for making it all possible."

"Making you happy gives me pleasure, Louisa."

The carriage was bowling down Piccadilly far too fast to turn onto Half Moon Street, and Louisa thought he must be taking her home to Belgrave Square. But at the last moment Phineas took the corner on two wheels and reined in the horses in front of Abercorn's townhouse.

She laughed. "Is he drunk?"

"How can one tell? He's Irish." They laughed together.

James jumped from the carriage and helped her to alight. They went up the front steps together and he opened the front door with his key. He removed her cloak and hung it on the hallstand, then gestured toward the staircase. "After you, m'lady."

She gathered up her skirts and ascended the stairs. As he followed her, his closeness took her breath away. She touched her cheek. "I should remove my stage makeup."

"Why don't I draw you a bath? Phineas has gone round the corner to Shepherd's Market to get us some supper." He guided her toward a bathing room and turned the taps on a huge claw-footed bathtub. "You'll be finished by the time he's ready to serve us."

Louisa stared at the closed door. *He gave me no chance to refuse. And why the devil should I refuse? I need to bathe after my energetic performance.* She glanced around the room, noting plenty of towels and a man's green velvet robe. She felt the temperature of the water and turned off the taps. She removed the red wig, undressed quickly, picked up a tablet of sandalwood-scented soap, and stepped into the tub. She washed her face three times to get rid of the greasepaint. As she washed her arms and legs, she sang the male lead's song from *The Brigand*. She was proud that she had learned all the parts.

Louisa pulled the plug, stepped from the water, and picked up a thirsty towel. Instead of dressing, she decided to be bold and pulled on the robe. She glanced in the mirror and saw that her dark hair had formed tiny tendrils about her face from the dampness of the room. Without the red wig, she looked like herself again. She suddenly became aware of her nakedness beneath the robe. She almost lost her nerve and decided to put her clothes on, but something stopped her. *I am an actress about to play the role of a lifetime. This is my one chance to be wild and wicked.* She admired her seductive smile in the mirror. *This is my night. I shall outperform Kitty Kelly in every way!*

She was still exhilarated from performing at Covent Garden, and her euphoric mood had not diminished one iota. She radiated happiness and, amazingly, she did not dread what was to come. Rather, she looked forward to the challenge. Nothing could compare with the pleasure Abercorn had given her and she was perfectly willing to pay the piper. *I enjoyed the kisses I shared with James.* She refused to dwell on thoughts of further intimacy. *A night with the attractive devil will cure me of my naïveté.*

She opened the door and immediately detected a spicy aroma in the air that she identified as curry. Then she saw Abercorn. He had removed his formal jacket and neck cloth, and the whiteness of his shirt contrasted against his tanned face and black hair. She saw his eyes take in the dark green robe, and her heart skipped a beat.

"Are you hungry, Lu?"

She suddenly realized that she was starving. "Yes, indeed I am."

He led the way into a small dining room and she saw that he had put her flowers in water. He held a chair for her and when she sat down, he dropped a kiss on the top of her head then moved around the table to sit opposite her. He removed a silver cover from a brace of roast partridge and another from a dish of curried rice with chestnuts. He poured champagne into two crystal flutes.

"It smells good." Louisa noted that Phineas was nowhere to be seen.

He picked up his glass. "I propose a toast to Lady Lu's smashing performance."

"Thank you." She picked up her glass and sipped the champagne. "What's a fitting toast to an Irishman?"

He grinned. "Here's to you and here's to me, and if someday we disagree . . . sod you, here's to me!"

Louisa threw back her head and laughed. She realized it felt wonderful to laugh. "I love irreverent humor."

"Most Irish humor is irreverent, I warrant." He served them each with a partridge and a heap of curried rice. "Eat before it gets cold." He tore off a leg and bit into it.

Louisa, using her fingers, did the same. "Mm, the skin is so crispy." She devoured the leg and tore off a wing. "My appetite is insatiable tonight. I had fish and chips earlier at the theater."

"Were they wrapped in newspaper?"

"Yes! I never experienced food served in newspaper before. It was delicious."

"I wager there are many delicious things you've never experienced."

Louisa blushed. She took a swig of champagne to give her confidence.

James finished his food long before Louisa did. He leaned back, enjoying the dainty way she ate. When she was done and declared she couldn't manage another bite, he uncovered dessert.

Her eyes sparkled. "I cannot resist blackberries and cream."

After her first mouthful, James came around the table, lifted her, and sat her in his lap. He picked up a spoon. "Let me feed you?" he asked huskily.

She could feel the heat from his thighs through the robe. Her skin began to tingle and she wondered if it was the wine or Abercorn that was affecting her so strangely. She opened her mouth and almost melted at the exquisite taste of the blackberries and cream.

When she licked her lips, he captured her mouth in a long kiss. He pushed the robe from her shoulders and his hands caressed her silken skin. "Ambrosia," he murmured. Then he lifted her glass to her lips and she sipped the champagne.

She thought of the Song of Solomon. *He is staying me with flagons.* "Let him kiss me with the kisses of his mouth," she whispered.

He picked her up, deftly leaving the robe behind, and carried her to the sitting room where a cozy fire had been lit. With one arm still firmly around her, he let her slide down his body, until her soft breasts rested against his powerful chest. When he captured her mouth, she felt his marble-hard erection against her soft belly.

Her arms glided up around his neck and she stood on tiptoe so that her mons rested against his cock. His embrace made her conscious of every pulse of her blood. She was completely intoxicated with the role she was playing. A frisson of desire spiraled through her, until she wanted to scream with excitement. *This is truly a night for new and thrilling sensations!*

James slid to his knees before her and kissed the sensitive silken skin beneath her breasts. He pressed hungry warm lips to her belly and dipped his tongue into her navel. Then he pulled her down to lie on the fur rug, spread her hair out, and gazed down at her with adoring eyes.

The luxurious fur against her naked flesh made her feel seductively beautiful for the first time in her life. She loved his male scent and the feel of his hand as he caressed her breasts and her belly. Then it moved lower to toy with the curls on her high mons. She gasped as his fingertips slipped into her woman's cleft and when he circled her tiny bud, she arched up with a cry of arousal.

James wanted to bring her to climax without tearing her hymen, which called for very gentle and delicate manipulation. He must touch her with the delicacy of a butterfly's wings and control his lust to plunge inside her. As the pads of his fingertips stroked her softly, over and over, he felt her shudder with longing. He knew a need to taste her and his lips took possession of hers. He slid his tongue inside the delicious cave of her hot mouth and thrust in and out, imitating what he ached to do with his cock.

The velvet magic of his tongue aroused her desire, and her woman's center began to throb with the insistent strokes of his fingertips. Her pleasure went higher and higher in ever-widening circles of intensity. She felt as if she were floating in a sea of bliss, then suddenly she erupted and dissolved into a thousand delicious fragments.

His palm gently cupped her cheek and he gazed down into her slumberous green eyes. "Lady Louisa, will you marry me?"

She came out of her trance in an instant, and pulled away from him sharply. "Of course I won't marry you!"

His dark brows drew together in a frown. "You promised to pay the price."

"I *am* willing to pay the price. I will spend the night with you."

He looked at her with regret. "I don't want you for one night, Lu. I want you for a lifetime. With me, it's all or nothing."

Louisa gasped. She was humiliated at his rejection. Suddenly all the beautiful magic of the night was melting away and she hated him for destroying her happiness. "Then it's nothing! Go to the devil, Abercorn."

She was halfway to the door before she realized she was naked. She was mortified that she had discarded her clothes along with her inhibitions. Without looking at him, she raised her chin and marched to the bathing room. She put on her petticoat and gown, fastened it, and then pulled on her stockings and garters. She wanted to fly at him and rake her nails down his cheeks. *That would destroy your last scrap of dignity,* her inner voice warned. *If you want to keep your pride, simply ignore the Irish swine.*

She left the bathing room and retraced her steps. There was no need to ignore Abercorn. He wasn't there. In his place stood Phineas.

"I have instructions to take you home, my lady."

The lump in her throat made it difficult to murmur her thanks. She followed him downstairs to the front door, where she donned her cloak and stuffed the red wig into her pocket. She had been right all along. The handsomest men were by far the most arrogant and selfish. She vowed that she would remember this lesson in humiliation so that she would never be tempted to repeat it.

James Hamilton stood at an upper window, ruefully watching his carriage depart for Belgrave Square. Arranging for Louisa to achieve her heart's desire had made her the happiest female in London tonight. He knew that would be his sole reward. He was sorry he had snatched her joy away but regretted even more her refusal to marry him.

Her euphoric mood made her so desirable, I was sorely tempted to make love to her. She was perfectly willing to let me have my way for one night. He smiled wryly. *There was only one thing that stopped me. I don't want Lu to be promiscuous like her sister. I want her to remain sweet and innocent until she becomes my wife.*

Her dream began happily enough. She was in Woburn's beautiful garden picking flowers. Their heady fragrance filled her senses. She gathered an armful of blue lupins and their peppery scent floated in the air about her. Suddenly, she looked down and saw that her white dress was covered with blood. Her lovely dream had turned into a nightmare. She dropped the lupins in shock. She was obviously having a miscarriage and losing her baby. It was the thing she feared most. She heard screams, and fear for her mother rose up and threatened to overwhelm her. *No! No! Help me . . . please help me.* Then she realized it was not her mother's screams she could hear, it was her own.

Louisa awoke in a panic. She pulled down the covers and examined her nightgown. Relief swept over her when she saw the pristine white garment was not covered in blood. She drew up her knees and wrapped her arms around them. It slowly dawned upon her why she had had the nightmare. Abercorn had asked her to marry him, and she equated marriage with having children. When you bore a child, you risked having a miscarriage or even a dead baby.

Fate saved me tonight. If I had allowed Abercorn to make love to me even one time, he could have planted his seed. She got out of bed and turned up the lamp. She saw that Georgy's bed was empty. Lu took the key to her secret desk drawer from its hiding place and took out her journal. She dipped her pen and wrote: *Tonight I had the terrifying recurring dream where I am covered with blood. It began as usual in the garden picking lupins. It used to be Mother who suffered the miscarriage, but lately I have taken her place. I realize it was Abercorn's proposal of marriage that brought on the nightmare. I have a mortal fear of marriage and all it entails.*

Louisa's feelings of dread left her once she had written in her journal. Her thoughts winged back to Covent Garden Theatre. *Tonight I fulfilled the dream of a lifetime.* The corners of her mouth curved in a secret smile. *I'll write about singing and dancing on the stage tonight. I want to relive the feeling of bliss it gave me. I must never forget the euphoria I experienced when the entire audience applauded my performance.* She dipped in her pen and began to write. By the time she finished, she had recaptured all the joy and magic of her experience on the stage. Her heart overflowed with happiness. Louisa locked her journal away and began to dance.

The Duke and Duchess of Bedford returned to Belgrave Square a week later.

"Rachel was a good little patient, but Alexander behaved like a savage. He scratched the tops off all his chicken pox and refused to take his medicine," Georgina declared. "He disobeyed all the doctor's orders and now insists he will be a physician when he grows up, so he can give the orders."

"You are a marvelous nurse, darling," her husband declared. "You have more patience than any woman in London."

She's had lots of practice, Louisa thought silently. "I'm glad they are recovered."

"Did anything interesting develop while I was away?" Their mother looked expectantly at her daughters.

Georgy looked like the cat that had swallowed the cream, but she refused to divulge a specific name. "I wouldn't be at all surprised if Father doesn't receive a formal call in the near future from a certain noble who has been dangling after me."

Her mother looked pleased and asked archly, "I take it that if he receives an offer for your hand, you would like him to accept it?"

"I do, I do, indeed I do!" Georgy said emphatically.

Her mother looked at Louisa. "What about you, darling? If he receives an offer for you, do you want him to accept it?"

"I don't, I don't, indeed I *do not!*" she said emphatically.

"Lu, darling, I have no idea why you are so averse to the opposite sex. You certainly don't take after me. Men are my favorite people, with the exception of Lady Holland, and now I come to think of it, I even prefer Henry to Beth."

"These invitations came while you were away, Mother." Georgy handed her the cards. "I took the liberty of accepting the one from your friend Dorothy Cavendish, Countess of Carlisle. She's hosting a ball at Devonshire House tomorrow night."

"Oh, how lovely. It is years since I've been to Devonshire House. You will be astonished at its opulence. Her husband, George Howard, is Lord Privy Seal in Grey's government, so of course the Greys will be there." Georgina gave her daughter a speculative look. "Is it by any chance George Grey you are hoping will offer for you?"

Georgy laughed. "Though it would be a feather in any lady's cap to snare the prime minister's son, I'm hoping for a far more noble catch."

I wager that Georgy is talking about William Cavendish, Lord Burlington, who is heir to the powerful Duke of Devonshire, Louisa thought. *She's eager to go to Devonshire House tomorrow night because she hopes someday to own it.*

"Well, there is no harm in aiming high, so long as your affections are involved." Her mother glanced through the rest of the invitations. "I can't believe it's mid-July. Where has the summer gone?"

I'll be glad when the season is over. I'm looking forward to leaving London's marriage market behind and going to Scotland. Lu had more sense than to voice her thoughts aloud.

The Russells arrived fashionably late at Devonshire House the following night. Georgina caught up on old times with her childhood friend Dorothy Howard, and John was soon discussing politics with her husband, the Earl of Carlisle. Both men had recently received the Order of the Garter.

Georgy took it upon herself to explore the magnificent mansion and could not disguise her proprietary air. When she spotted Lord Burlington, she made her way around the ballroom floor until she was standing beside him. She gave him an inviting sideways glance and ran the tip of her tongue around her lips.

William winked at her as his hand surreptitiously caressed her bottom.

He's imagining his cock in my mouth right now. But he knows the only way to get what he wants is to offer for me.

George Grey asked her to dance. She threw William a provocative glance and replied, "I'd love to."

Supper was to be served at midnight, but before everyone left the ballroom, the lights were turned up and the Earl and Countess of Carlisle ascended the dais where the musicians were playing. Dorothy held up her hands for silence. It took a few minutes for the noise to subside.

"The earl and I have an announcement to make. Our beloved daughter, Blanche, has consented to marry William Cavendish, Lord Burlington. Needless to say, our family is delighted with the match."

Blanche Howard and William Cavendish ascended to the dais amid thunderous applause.

Georgy stood stunned, like a bird flown into a stone wall. Her ears began to roar as the blood rushed to her head. She felt her gorge rise. *The bastard! The bloody bastard! I'm going to be sick.*

When Louisa heard the announcement, her heart filled with anguish for her sister. She looked about the ballroom and saw Georgy standing wide-eyed as if she were rooted to the spot. *I must go to her.* She crossed the floor and took her sister's arm. "Are you all right, Georgy?"

Her sister stared at her blankly and Louisa knew she was far from all right. She gently led her from the room and found her a seat. Then she went in search of her mother. "Georgy has taken ill. She needs to go home, I'm afraid."

"Oh dear, I hope I didn't carry the chicken pox infection home to her."

"No, Mother, I don't think it's that. She feels faint and has a dreadful headache. I'll go home with her and put her to bed. You and Father must stay. Georgy will be fine tomorrow." Lu knew that her sister would not be fine. Her dream of marriage and someday becoming the Duchess of Devonshire had just been shattered.

A footman took a message to the Russell coachman, and Lu led her sister from the Devonshire mansion. Georgy sat huddled in silence as the carriage bowled along Piccadilly, slowed as it entered Grosvenor Crescent, and came to a stop in front of their house in Belgrave Square.

When they entered the house, a maid came forward wondering what was amiss that the Russell sisters were returning from a ball at such an early hour. When she saw Georgy's pallid face she gasped. "Oh, my lady, you're ill. Will I send for the doctor?"

Louisa put her arm around her sister. "That won't be necessary, thank you. Just make sure that we are not disturbed."

Once the bedroom door of the room they shared was closed, Georgy began to scream. Lu sat quietly as her sister tore at her clothes and flung things about the chamber. She knew Georgy had to get it all out. After she had screamed for half an hour, her screams turned to sobs. Louisa put her arms around her sister and held her tightly. Then for the next hour she rocked her.

Chapter Fourteen

The following day Louisa urged her sister to come downstairs for lunch. "If you are absent, you'll be subjected to all sorts of scrutiny."

When Georgy entered the dining room, her mother searched her daughter's face with anxious eyes. "You missed breakfast, darling. Are you feeling all right?"

"I'm fully recovered, thank you, Mother." Georgy suppressed a shudder.

"I realize now why the Howards threw a ball at Devonshire House. It was solely to announce the engagement of their daughter Blanche."

"Blanche Howard isn't even pretty," Georgy said with disbelief.

"That's an understatement. But when I analyze it, it's no surprise that they made a match for her with William Cavendish, Devonshire's heir. Since the couple are distant cousins, the marriage will keep their great wealth in one family."

Louisa glanced at Georgy. "Perhaps William had no choice in the matter."

"Oh, it's undoubtedly a marriage of convenience," their mother declared. "Still, I have high hopes we'll have an announcement of our own soon." She gave Georgy a conspiratorial wink. "Do give me a hint who it is, darling."

The blood drained from Georgy's face, and Louisa took her hand and squeezed it under cover of the tablecloth. Georgy couldn't bear her sister's pitying touch. She took a deep breath and forced a smile. "I'm surprised you haven't guessed that Teddy Fox is pressing me to make a commitment."

"Oh, darling. Nothing would make me happier than a match with Teddy."

"He keeps begging me to visit the House of Commons and watch him from the visitors' gallery. Perhaps Lu and I will go tomorrow."

Louisa quickly changed the subject. "Where is Father? He's never late for lunch."

"He and Abercorn are dining out today, before they attend the Lords." She gave Louisa a speculative look. "James is an exceedingly handsome man. He has everything to recommend him . . . title, wealth, and that irresistible Irish charm."

Lu tossed her head. "I have no trouble resisting him."

Her mother smiled archly. "Methinks you protest too much."

That night both Edward and Charles Russell dined at home.

"I've been assigned to the HMS *Britannia*. I've come to say good-bye. She'll be sailing to the Mediterranean shortly." Edward couldn't stop grinning.

His father and mother offered their congratulations because they knew this was what their son wanted.

"I propose a toast." Louisa raised her glass. "To a safe voyage, Edward."

"Not too safe," her brother declared. "I'm looking forward to some action."

Charles, needing to share the limelight, said, "I might be posted to India."

"*India?*" Georgy could not hide her revulsion. "That's halfway around the world, and you'll find the people and the food disgustingly foreign."

"Oh, I love curry." Louisa blushed as she thought of her rendezvous on Half Moon Street. She could actually smell and taste the piquant spice, and feel Abercorn's hands caressing her body.

"Well, it's not definite yet," Charles admitted. "It's just a rumor, really."

"In that case, I take it you will be attending the boat race?" John asked his son.

"Oh, I wouldn't miss it. Teddy Fox, George Grey, and I are going to watch our friend James Hamilton. He's rowing for Oxford, you know."

"Yes, I spent the afternoon with James. He's leaving tonight for Henley-on-Thames to get in a week's rowing practice. He invited us all to go and watch the race."

"Oh, please let's go," Georgy urged.

Her mother realized the presence of Teddy was the reason her daughter was keen. "Perhaps we can make up a party with Henry and Beth." Georgina's eyes suddenly lit up. "Oh, I've just had a brilliant idea. If I can persuade Queen Adelaide to join us, perhaps we can all stay at Windsor Castle."

The next day, Louisa watched her sister avidly gaze down on the members of the House of Commons. "I'm so glad you've recovered from your disappointment over William Cavendish."

"I'll *never* recover from my disappointment, but I don't have time to waste feeling sorry for myself." She pointed her finger. "There's Teddy sitting on the back bench."

Louisa was far more interested in watching her brother, Lord John, as he conferred with Prime Minister Earl Grey. *Perhaps someday Johnny will be prime minister.*

By the time the session ended it was after five o'clock and the sisters descended from the visitors' gallery. As the members were leaving, Louisa greeted Johnny, while Georgy rushed over to join Teddy Fox.

"Looking down on the floor of the house brought back some sinfully delicious memories, Teddy."

"Christ, I can never look at the Table of the House without getting an erection."

"I always knew you were a man of parts, Teddy. We must get together again, sometime soon."

"I'm hard now, just thinking about it."

"I know the cure for that. Do you have your carriage here?"

Teddy glanced over at Louisa. "But you're here with your sister."

"Just because we came together, doesn't say we have to leave together." She gave him a provocative glance. "Coitus in a carriage over bumpy cobblestones sounds rather thrilling. But it's entirely up to you, Teddy."

When Louisa turned around, her sister was nowhere in sight. Nor was Teddy Fox. "Wherever did Georgy go?"

"She left with Edward Fox. Do you have a ride home, Lu?" Johnny asked.

"We came in a hackney."

"Come on then, I'll get you a ride." Lord John took her arm and led her toward a gentleman she knew very well. "Mr. Prime Minister, would it be convenient to drop my sister off in Belgrave Square?"

"Lady Louisa, it would be my pleasure. I take it you were in the visitors' gallery this afternoon. Did you enjoy the session?"

"I did. Everything about politics fascinates me, Lord Grey."

On the drive to Belgrave Square he told her the Greys planned to attend the boat race. Louisa told him her family was also making plans to go and watch the boat race between Oxford and Cambridge, so when they arrived at her house, he came inside.

The duchess greeted him effusively. "John and I would be honored to have the prime minister stay for dinner."

"And if I were not prime minister?" he teased.

"I'd show you the door immediately."

Before the meal was over, Earl Grey agreed to join the Russells for the Oxford boat race. When Georgina told him they might all get an invitation to stay at Windsor for the weekend, he said he'd drop Sailor Bill a note and urge him to attend. "In an unofficial capacity, of course. That way, the royal couple can dispense with all that stultifying formality."

John laughed. "With the two of you coercing them, I warrant a stay at Windsor will be a *fait accompli*."

Georgy didn't arrive home until long after dinner. When her father asked where she had been, she replied, "The session at the Commons didn't finish until late. When I turned around Lu had left without me. Johnny was kind enough to give me a tour of Parliament, and then he put me in a hackney cab."

Louisa, who knew she was lying, didn't have the heart to deny she had left her sister behind. Georgy, crushed by Lord Burlington, was now concentrating all her efforts on Teddy Fox. Lu prayed that he would make an offer for Georgy.

The Duke and Duchess of Bedford, their two eldest daughters, and their son Charles arrived at Windsor on Friday evening. They made their way to the State Apartments, where a royal footman led them to the grand reception room. King William and Queen Adelaide greeted them warmly. The Russells were familiar with Windsor because they had been there in June when the duke had received the Order of the Garter. The Greys arrived accompanied by their son George and were followed shortly by Lord and Lady Holland, and their son Teddy.

The three Oxford graduates gathered in a corner to discuss the boat race.

"What are the odds?" Charles asked.

"Cambridge is favored because of their weight. The heavier crew usually wins."

"Not this time, George. Oxford has Abercorn."

Teddy grimaced. "God doesn't favor Irishmen."

Charles grinned. "No, but the devil does!"

George laughed, but Teddy wasn't amused.

"How about a private bet?" Charles challenged. "A hundred guineas says Oxford takes it."

"Done. I shall look forward to cleaning you out," Teddy boasted. "George?"

"You're a disloyal swine to bet against Oxford. I could never do that."

"Loyalty is for fools, gentlemen."

At that moment dinner was announced, and the royal guests moved into the king's dining room. The Verrio painting on the ceiling depicted a banquet of the gods in their full naked glory. It immediately prompted Teddy Fox to move forward and take a seat between Louisa and Georgy Russell. "You look lovely tonight, Louisa."

She frowned because he hadn't complimented Georgy.

"A thorn between two roses," he said fatuously.

"I can almost feel your prick," Georgy said outrageously.

Teddy leaned over and whispered in her ear, "And shall before the night is over."

After dinner the ladies moved into the adjoining chamber known as the queen's drawing room, while the men accompanied Sailor Bill to the king's closet for cards and brandy. Neither the ladies nor the men made any mention of the fact that Georgy Russell and Teddy Fox were missing from the company.

"Hurry and dress. We need to be at Mortlake so we can see the finish of the race," Charles Russell informed his sisters.

"Is it not possible to be at Putney to watch the start of the race, then take a carriage to Mortlake to watch the finish?" Louisa asked.

"Hell, no! There will be such a crush of spectators along the river, we'd be stampeded by the crowd."

Georgy grumbled, "The race isn't until this afternoon. What's the bloody rush?"

"We have to stake out our spot this morning. If you're not ready in ten minutes, I shall leave without you. It's not just me—we're joining George and Teddy."

"Uncle Holly chartered a boat for the adults," Lu told Charles, "so they can follow the boat race down the Thames."

"Private vessels on the river will be thicker than whores at Vauxhall. There are boat accidents every year. What a lark if the royals get tipped into the water."

"Charles, since you're in the navy, I wouldn't make jokes about sinking boats." Lu suddenly remembered breakfast.

"No time for that. There'll be plenty of hawkers selling food and drink."

The Russells joined Teddy and George, who were pacing impatiently at the Quadrangle. George, the prime minister's son, had bribed a Windsor coach driver to transport them in a royal phaeton.

They all alighted from the carriage at Chiswick Bridge. Georgy took George Grey's arm, and Louisa wondered whom she was trying to fool, when she had disappeared with Teddy for half the night. When Teddy attached himself to her, Louisa thought it rather odd. "Haven't you got the wrong Russell?" she said lightly.

Teddy gallantly kissed her hand. "Lady Louisa, you know how I feel about you."

Lu kept a wise silence.

People were already beginning to gather in the area, and the three males decided they had better find a bookmaker. Teddy offered to place bets for the sisters, and when Louisa wanted to wager on Oxford, he tried to talk her into betting on Cambridge.

A vision of Abercorn came full-blown into her mind. "Not a chance," she said.

"I surrender to your superior judgment, Teddy," Georgy declared.

When the men returned from placing the bets, they bought food from the hawkers. They started with sticky Chelsea buns, then moved on to meat pasties and steaming mugs of black peas, followed by roasted chestnuts. Stag Brewery, which was located at Mortlake and supplied the army, rolled barrels from the brew house and flogged pints of beer to the gathering merrymakers.

Ribbon makers were doing a brisk business selling rosettes in university colors: white for Cambridge and blue for Oxford. Charles, George, and Louisa sported Oxford blue, while Teddy and Georgy proudly displayed white ribbons, not caring that they were dubbed *traitorous turds.*

Mummers, stilt walkers, and acrobats entertained the crowds for thrown pennies. Time passed quickly as everyone had fun in the holiday atmosphere. Teddy paid chivalrous attention to Louisa all day long, and before the race started he took her hand. "You know, Lu, it is my parents' fondest wish to have you as their daughter. If I offered for you, you wouldn't refuse me, would you?"

She stared at him aghast. "Oh, Teddy, please don't offer for me. Georgy would be devastated. You must know she is mad in love with you."

"I know she's in *lust* with me," he murmured.

Just then a roar went up in the distance and everyone knew the race had begun in Putney, more than four miles away. As people jostled her, Louisa surreptitiously moved away from Teddy toward her brother Charles.

The excited voices of the crowd moved closer apace with the rowers. Finally the two boats came into view in the distance. They were just specks at first, but as they grew larger, Louisa could make out that Cambridge was in the lead. "Oxford! Oxford! Oxford!" she chanted.

The skulls drew close enough that the splashing of the oars could be heard above the noise of the crowd, and Louisa could clearly make out James Hamilton. Steadily, the latent strength of the Oxford men pushed their boat past their competitors. Louisa held her breath as the Oxford Blues increased their gain. She watched James's powerful arm and shoulder muscles ripple and bulge and glisten in the sunlight, and thought him the most attractive male she had ever known. As the Oxford team outdistanced their competitors, the Cambridge men lost heart and stopped rowing short of the goal. "James! James! James!" she cried happily.

Charles, deliriously happy, picked up Lu and swung her into the air. "We did it! Come on, let's go and congratulate James."

Suddenly she felt reluctant, but Charles and George were gungho to join their triumphant friend to celebrate his victory, and she went with them. She saw that Teddy's face looked like a thundercloud and realized he was jealous of Abercorn.

There was such a crush of Oxford men gathered about the rowers that Charles and George had to fight their way through. When the males saw a female, they gallantly moved aside and allowed her to reach the riverbank.

James was wiping his glistening perspiration with a towel. He was grinning from ear to ear at his brother, Claud, and still trying to catch his breath.

"You've just won me a hundred guineas from Teddy Fox and another fifty quid from the bookmakers," Charles cried happily.

"When Cambridge was ahead, did you fear you would lose?" George asked.

James smiled into Louisa's eyes. "Not for a minute. When I set a goal, I never doubt myself. If I did, I'd be defeated before I started."

She did not dare think of the last time they had been together. Instead she thought of the horse race at Woburn. Lu had known since then that Abercorn had a will of iron and that determination was bred into his bones. *Once he sets his mind on a goal, he will move heaven and hell to achieve it.* Louisa shuddered.

Suddenly Teddy was beside her. He took hold of her arm in a familiar, proprietary way. "I cashed in your winnings, Lu. Because of the bet I placed for you, you're twenty pounds richer."

"Thank you." She stuffed the money into her pocket. "Where's Georgy?"

"She lost her bet—said it made her feel sick," Teddy explained.

"You shouldn't have left her up on the bridge. I'll go and find her."

"Do you want me to come with you, Lu?" her brother asked.

"No, of course not. All you Oxford men will want to go and celebrate with Abercorn and his teammates. Don't worry about us; we'll be fine."

"I'll stay with you until you find her," James's brother volunteered.

"That's very kind of you, Claud." She glanced at James and found his eyes upon her. In his moment of glory in achieving his goal, she could not deny his irresistible attraction. She gifted him with a smile. "Enjoy your victory."

James could not take his eyes off Lu. Standing beside the river in the sunlight, her cheeks flushed with excitement, she looked like a beautiful water sprite. Their friends and the cheering spectators receded, and it seemed as if there were just the two of them. He fantasized sweeping her up in his arms and carrying her to his boat, then rowing her across one of his private lakes in Ireland.

When they were secluded, he undressed her, slowly removing one garment at a time, until she stood before him in naked splendor. She smiled seductively and beckoned to him. He threw off his clothes and closed the distance between them. She came into his arms eagerly, sweetly, her lovely emerald eyes brimming with love.

"Come on, let's celebrate our Oxford victory." Charles and George Grey linked arms with James, and the lovely vision of Lady Lu disappeared in an instant.

. . .

On the last day of July, Parliament recessed for the summer. When the duke arrived home for dinner, he asked if the family was packed and ready to return to Woburn the following day. "We'll spend a few days in Bedfordshire before we start our journey to Scotland. I accepted Earl Grey's invitation to break our journey at Howick as we do every year."

"The Greys are very hospitable and Northumberland is lovely in August. The packing is almost complete," Georgina said. "We'll be able to leave for Woburn tomorrow, after we pick up the children at Campden Hill."

"James Hamilton was in the Lords this afternoon. Believe it or not, he has business in Scotland, so I invited him to travel with us. He thanked me very much and said he'd join us at Woburn in a couple of days."

Louisa opened her mouth to protest, then closed it again. She had been particularly careful not to mention that they were going to Scotland, and she was dismayed that he had somehow ferreted the information out of her father.

The duchess was elated at the news. Neither of her daughters had received an offer and the season was over. "Without Abercorn, Oxford would have lost the boat race." She gave Louisa a speculative glance. "James is a particular favorite of mine."

After dinner, Georgy took her sister aside. "I want you to do me a favor, Lu."

"Of course I will."

"When we get to Campden Hill tomorrow, I want you to find some way to get Mother to stay overnight."

Georgy's face was so earnest that Louisa felt concern. Since their house in Kensington was next door to Holland House, she surmised that her sister was desperate to have one more try at making Teddy Fox offer for her. "I'll think of something," Louisa promised.

"Thanks, Lu. I knew I could count on you. Will you help me finish packing?"

The following day when their traveling coach arrived at Campden Hill, Rachel and Alexander ran out to meet them. "Mama! Lulu!"

Georgina swept her little girl into her arms and Rachel covered her mother's face with kisses.

Alex unbuttoned his shirt. "Lulu, look at my chicken pox marks," he said proudly. "I'm going to be a doctor when I grow up."

Louisa examined his chest with great interest. He was no longer the chubby-cheeked six-year-old. Now that he'd turned seven, he was growing quickly. "Each scar is a badge of honor that attests to your bravery."

"Oh, jolly good. I didn't realize they were *scars*! Georgy, have a look."

"You are a horrid lout. They are repulsive."

Alexander looked inordinately pleased and trotted into the house after his father.

"Rachel, why don't you show me the garden?" Louisa took her little sister's hand. She led her across the lawns so they could dabble their fingers in the fishpond. Rachel giggled when the carp glided over to nibble their fingertips. "Shall we go next door and see Aunt Holly?"

They were climbing the steps of Holland House when Beth came through the front door. "Hello, Louisa. I saw the carriage turn down the drive and was just coming over."

"How lovely. I'm sure Mother would appreciate an invitation to dinner tonight. That way we won't have to drive all the way to Woburn this afternoon."

"What a good idea. I expect Henry and Teddy will be here in time for dinner."

. . .

In the Hollands' dining room, Teddy sat between the Russell sisters and told them how much he would miss them when they were in Scotland.

Georgy felt enormous relief that he had arrived from London, and that because of the Hollands' dinner invitation they wouldn't be leaving for Woburn until tomorrow. By the time dessert was served, her uncertainty had vanished and was replaced by a feeling of confidence. She had been worried that she wouldn't have a chance to talk to him, but sitting beside him made her anxiety vanish. Her mouth curved in a self-satisfied smile. *They'll all be so surprised when he offers for me.*

When the meal was over and Lady Holland led the way to her sitting room so they could enjoy their wine, Georgy murmured to Teddy, "Go into the garden, and I'll follow you in a minute or two."

He winked at her knowingly.

Georgy spied her chance, and when the conversation turned to politics, she slipped from the room and made her way into the night-scented garden.

As she approached him beneath the willow tree, he said, "Not here—they'll see us from the window."

"Wait, Teddy . . . I have something to tell you."

"Well, hurry up."

"I think . . . I think I'm going to have a baby," she murmured.

He took a step back from her. His face turned to stone. "What the devil does that have to do with me?"

Georgy felt the blood drain from her face. "Teddy, it's your baby."

"Just because you're in trouble, don't try to pin it on me."

"Teddy, you're the baby's father. You'll have to offer for me!"

"Offer for *you?* You must be jesting. If I were to offer for anyone, it would be Louisa."

Georgy recoiled as his cruel words hit her in the face. She dashed toward him and clawed at his cheeks. "Louisa wouldn't have a swine like you!"

He took hold of her wrists in a cruel vise. "Girls like you are for bedding, not wedding. It's the oldest trick in the game. Credit me with some sense. I'm not about to fall into your tawdry marriage trap."

Chapter Fifteen

My monthly courses are only a few days late. I'm likely worrying over nothing. Georgy closed her bedchamber door, thankful that Campden Hill was large enough that she didn't have to share a room with Louisa.

She undressed in front of the mirror and rested her hand on her flat stomach. *I'm not having a baby . . . God wouldn't be that cruel to me.* She stared at her reflection and wiped the tears from her cheeks. *I was so sure that Teddy Fox would marry me. I can't believe what a cold, cruel bastard he is.*

Georgy thought about her sister's aversion to marriage. She'd always accused her of being naive and advised her to marry a doting husband. Now Louisa's response echoed in her mind: *"Perhaps you are the one who is naive. I don't suppose doting husbands grow on trees. From what I've seen, men are arrogant and selfish."*

Arrogant and selfish describe Teddy Fox exactly. She clenched her fists and smashed them against her reflection in the mirror. She gasped as the glass cracked. She stared in horror as her distorted face gazed back at her. *Teddy doesn't want to marry me because I'm ugly. He wants to marry Louisa. I hate her! I hate her!*

An hour later, Louisa closed her bedchamber door. *I wonder if Georgy is still out with Teddy. I hope with all my heart that he asks her to marry* him. *Her dearest wish in life is to be a wife. I suppose going to Scotland is the last thing Georgy wants to do. I warrant she'd much rather stay here so she can be close to Teddy.*

As she undressed and got into bed, Lu's thoughts drifted to James Hamilton. *I wonder if the Irish devil really has business in Scotland. He won't let up in his pursuit. He is tenacious as a terrier!* She reminded herself that he was only traveling with them, and not staying with them at the Doune, their Scottish house in the Cairngorms. *I refuse to let thoughts of Abercorn spoil my holiday in Scotland.*

The moment Louisa began to dream, however, Abercorn appeared. She was dancing alone in the center of a vast stage. The delicate notes of the music lent themselves to graceful steps that carried her swaying and spiraling across the boards. She leaped into the air, light as a dragonfly, and as the music ended in a crescendo, she swept into a low curtsy and bent her head to touch her ankles.

The applause was deafening, though Abercorn was the only one in the audience. He was in the front row, tossing dozens of red roses to her feet and shouting, "Brava!" He jumped up onto the stage and took her in his arms. "Lady Lu, you were superb!"

A feeling of joy engulfed her senses. Exhilaration spiraled through her belly, making her breasts tingle and her spirits soar. Happiness flowed about her as she floated in a sea of bliss. She gazed down into his eyes. "James, I owe it all to you."

He took possession of her mouth in a sensual kiss designed to steal her senses. His familiar male scent stole to her, filling her head with delicious fancies. Her mouth softened and her nipples ruched as the hard muscles of his chest pressed against her breasts. Her arms stole around his neck and she clung to him with an innocent desire she could not control. When the kiss ended a heartfelt sigh escaped her lips. But when she raised her lashes and saw the look of possession in his dark eyes, she felt threatened.

"Marry me, Louisa!"

In a flash, her happiness turned to fear and she woke up trembling.

In the morning Louisa finished her packing. When she saw her sister, Georgy made no mention of Teddy, and Lu knew that he had not proposed.

"I can't wait to leave," Georgy said brightly. "Scotland will make such a welcome change of scene."

Louisa felt awful about her sister's disappointment, but she kept a wise silence.

"I'm so glad you're traveling with us, James. I need another man I can rely on beside my husband. It will seem strange not to have Edward and Charles with us, and Jack has decided to stay at Woburn to look after things in our absence this year."

"It is my pleasure, Your Grace."

"Pleasure?" Louisa didn't try to hide her amusement. "Cosmo, Henry, and Alex will make it their business to ruin your pleasure."

"I know what boys are like—I have a younger brother."

"Claud?" She laughed merrily. "Please don't delude yourself. Claud is a gentleman—my brothers are savages."

Jack came into the breakfast room. "The three carriages are ready, and all your luggage has been loaded onto the baggage wagon."

"Thank you, darling. I don't know what we'd do without you." The duchess kissed Jack's cheek. "We shall see you sometime in September."

The family went out to the courtyard. The drivers were mounted on the traveling coaches and grooms stood at the head of each team, gentling the horses until the passengers were seated. The Duke of Bedford was already in the saddle, and he held the reins of Abercorn's Arabian mount.

James helped Lady Bedford into the carriage, then picked up Rachel and set her inside. Then he helped the nursemaid.

"I'm not sitting with Rachel and her nursemaid," Alex declared. "I'm going in the coach with Cosmo and Henry."

"No you're not, you little pissant." Henry pushed him away.

"You are fighting already," Lu scolded. "If we let the three of you travel together, the coach will be demolished by the time we get to Northampton."

Mr. Burke, Woburn's steward, came out with a large food hamper and handed it to the second female servant who was traveling with the Russells. Georgy immediately climbed in beside her, drawn by the thought of food.

"Alex, I'll give up my seat and let you ride with Georgy," Louisa coaxed.

"I'm not riding with her—she called me repulsive!"

"Georgy is right. You've turned into a horrid lout just like your brothers."

Alex grinned from ear to ear.

His father soon wiped the grin from his face. "Bloody hell! Alex, get in the coach with your brothers. They have my permission to clout you round the ear if you misbehave."

Just as Louisa was about to climb in beside her sister, Georgy declared she had changed her mind. "The smell of the food is making me feel queasy. Lu, put it in the next carriage."

Louisa took the food hamper and handed it to Cosmo. Then she took her seat beside Georgy, the grooms took their places beside the coach drivers, the duke and Abercorn cantered from the court-yard, and the three carriages lurched forward on the first leg of their journey.

After two hours, Bedford drew rein in a lovely shaded spot be-neath some copper beeches, and motioned for the carriages to do likewise. While the grooms watered the horses, the duchess retrieved the food hamper. She opened the lid and stared at her sons in disbelief. "It's empty! What happened to all the food that Mr. Burke provided?"

"We thought it was for us." Cosmo wiped his mouth on his sleeve. "Don't you have your own hamper, Mother?"

Lu came up behind her mother and gave her brothers a withering glance. "I shall add *gluttony* to the litany of your sins."

"Well, at least we can have a drink. There are cases of wine and ale in the baggage cart." The duchess directed one of the grooms to locate the libations. "Lu, would you inform your father there's no food? He's less likely to smite you, darling."

Louisa approached her father. "We are only stopping for a drink. We're not making good time, I'm afraid." She threw Abercorn an apologetic smile.

"Nonsense, James and I want something to eat."

Reluctantly, she explained. "The boys devoured everything in the hamper."

"Goddamn it. Oh well, we'll just have to wait until we arrive at the Northampton manor. It should only take us another hour. I shall sit in the coach with the reprobates. You can ride my horse, Louisa." He handed her the reins.

She glanced at Abercorn, who was doing his best to hide his amusement. "Shall we water the horses?" he asked with a straight face.

Lu felt embarrassed. "I warrant you wish you hadn't agreed to travel with us."

"Not so. What more could I ask, than having you beside me in the saddle?"

He was so dangerously attractive that she wanted to erect a barrier between them. She bit back a terse remark, knowing it would be less provocative if they remained friends. At this slow pace, it would be days before they even reached the Greys' Howick Hall.

It was considerably longer than an hour before the Russell entourage reached their estate near Corby in Northamptonshire. Since it was late afternoon, the Duke and Duchess of Bedford decided they would have dinner and stay overnight.

"James, I'm sorry we've only covered about thirty-five miles today."

"Don't be sorry, Louisa. I enjoyed every one of them."

She tried her best not to blush. "Let's make a pact. If you don't importune me to marry you on this journey, I promise not to get angry and bite your head off."

"To me, you are desirable whether you are angry or not," he teased.

She thumped him in outrage, and he threw up his hands. "All right, I surrender. I shall pretend we are just friends." He winked. "After dinner, will you take me on a moonlight tour of the property?"

"You are an Irish devil!"

"*Mea culpa*, Lady Lu."

After dinner the Duke of Bedford stood up from his chair. "I give you fair warning. We leave at the crack of dawn." Implicit in his words was the threat that those not ready would be left behind.

As Louisa led Abercorn from the dining room, her brothers followed. "I'm giving James a tour and you're not coming. I suggest you have an early night."

At their loud protests, James said simply, "I want to be alone with Lu."

They hooted and made kissing noises.

John Russell stopped them with one word. "Bed!"

Outside, Louisa explained, "The only time I ever come to this estate is when we are on our way to Scotland, so I can't really tell you much about it."

"Then allow me. This landholding provides much of your father's wealth. The rolling hills are perfect for grazing sheep. The farmers who occupy the cottages on your father's land are shepherds who tend large flocks. The only farming they do is sowing and harvesting hay crops for winter fodder. Each family has its own cow, pig, hens, and a treasured, indispensable shepherding dog."

When they came to a stone wall, they both climbed on top and sat down to gaze across the hills and vales that the moonlight showed were dotted with sheep.

"You knew all that without me telling you. Let's see—what else?" James mused.

Louisa's mouth curved into a smile. "The children laugh and have rosy cheeks."

"That's because they are happy and well fed. Your father is a good landlord."

She watched his face change as if a shadow fell across it, and knew he had a troubling thought. "What is it?"

He shook his head.

"Tell me! Friends share their thoughts," she said adamantly.

"Aberdeen owns Haddo House and a vast tract of land in Scotland about thirty miles south of Gordon Castle. My stepfather turned off all the tenants and cleared the land of their humble cottages, so he could run thousands of sheep."

"But who looks after the sheep?"

"No one. They look after themselves. They remain on the craggy mountain slopes year round, foraging for heather and huddling together in winter storms. But even the flocks fare better than the people Aberdeen turned out to starve."

"No wonder you hate him."

"No more talk of Aberdeen. I want you to be happy."

Louisa wanted to make him laugh. "I am happy. I survived my first season without being sold on the marriage market."

When James slipped his arm around her and hugged her close,

she held her breath and waited for him to kiss her. In fact, she had anticipated his kiss from the moment they stepped outside into the moonlight. When he withdrew his arm, she felt the loss acutely.

Masking his amusement, he lifted her from the wall and set her on her feet. "We have to be up early."

Irish devil!

Three days later the weary travelers arrived at Howick Hall. It was fortunate that the stately home was spacious. Apart from their large family, the Greys always entertained guests during Parliament's summer recess.

Earl Grey's sister Hannah and her husband Edward Ellice greeted them. "We're on our way to Scotland. We are interested in buying an estate, not too far from the Doune."

"Oh, I do hope you decide to buy. It would be lovely to have you as neighbors," the Duchess of Bedford declared. "I love to entertain."

"Isn't George here?" Georgy asked as they took their seats for the evening meal.

"No, my dear," Mary Grey replied. "He received his lieutenant's commission from the naval office and is waiting for his assignment."

Georgy was visibly crestfallen.

Countess Grey made the introductions. "You know our eldest son, Henry, and his wife, Maria." Their son was the Member of Parliament for Northumberland. "I'm not sure if you know Henry's friend, Charles Bennet. Lord Ossulston is the Member of Parliament for North Northumberland."

Georgy immediately perked up. "Lord Ossulston, I am delighted to make your acquaintance. I believe your father is the Earl of Tankerville."

"That is correct, my lady." His admiring glance returned to Louisa.

Georgy poked her sister. "Invite him into the garden," she whispered.

After dessert, Louisa smiled at Charles Bennet. "Please excuse us. My sister and I need to stretch our legs after sitting in the coach for so many days."

He jumped up immediately. "Allow me to show you the gardens, Lady Louisa."

James Hamilton stood. "Why don't the four of us have a stroll along the terrace?" He offered his arm to Louisa.

She took it so that her sister would be paired with Ossulston. She glanced up at James. *Abercorn, you know exactly what I am up to and are taking advantage.*

As they strolled along the herbaceous borders of the terrace, James spoke to Charles. "I too am a Tory. It's refreshing that Prime Minister Grey is so nonpartisan."

Charles Bennet laughed. "Earl Grey's son Henry and I have been friends since we were boys. There was never any question that we would follow our father's footsteps into politics, so he became a Whig and I became a Tory."

"Politics fascinate me." Georgy improvised. "Do you ever visit Scotland, Charles?"

"Not as often as I'd like, my lady. Hunting and fishing in Scotland is unsurpassed."

"Charles, allow me to extend an invitation to visit us at the Doune. It's near Kinrara on the River Spey. My parents love to entertain guests. My uncle, the Earl of Gordon, always visits us there in August," Georgy gushed.

Ossulston gave Louisa a speculative glance.

To annoy Abercorn she said, "Oh, we would love to have you, Charles. The salmon fishing in the River Spey is incomparable."

Georgy gifted her sister with a brilliant smile. "Before it gets too dark, I'd love to visit the church and look at the gargoyles that Maria has carved." She stepped from the terrace and pulled Lord Ossulston after her.

Abercorn said smoothly, "Enjoy yourselves. We're going the opposite way. Lady Louisa wants to walk out to the headland to view the North Sea."

Lu was torn. She knew Georgy was doing her best to be alone with Ossulston, but that meant she'd be alone with Abercorn. She weighed her choices; Georgy won out.

Louisa walked slowly beside James. "Howick is such a beautiful coastal property."

They stopped a few feet from the edge of the cliff and looked down at the waves washing ashore. The light from the rising moon made the sea glitter like silver.

"It is at this time of year, but in winter the wind and sea must lash Howick relentlessly. The harsh northern climate is unforgiving in its cruelty. Wisely, the Greys spend most of the year in London."

"Maria is left here year round, while her husband sits in Parliament," Lu declared. "No wonder she sculpts gargoyles, poor lady."

James threw back his head and laughed.

"Men can be as relentless and cruel as the weather, especially to their wives."

"That never seems to deter your sister."

"Georgy will go to any length to please a man." Louisa's hand flew to her mouth. "Oh, that was cruel of me. I only meant that she knows full well the land is boggy down by the church, yet she will brave it to please Charles Bennet."

"Lucky man. If only my lady would brave bogs and gargoyles to please me."

"I am *not* your lady!"

"You know you are, deny it how you will."

Louisa raised her chin in defiance and moved away from him to the edge of the cliff.

James had to clench his fists and muster every ounce of his iron will to keep himself from pulling her to safety. With his heart in his throat, he watched her spread her arms and pirouette, taunting him with her devil's dance.

Louisa flung back her head and laughed.

"I won't take the bait, Lady Lu. You want me to grab you, and shake you, and kiss you, so you can take perverse pleasure in denying and rejecting me."

She stopped still. *Is that what I want? Is that what I'm doing?*

"If you want to be kissed, all you have to do is ask."

She flew at him and kicked him. "You arrogant Irish sod!"

When the pair returned to the hall, John Russell noticed his daughter's flushed cheeks. "James, come and have a drink with us. The prime minister wants you to reassure him that you will support the reform bill once it gets to the Lords."

Two hours later, when the duke emerged from the library, he was approached by Charles Bennet. "At the risk of sounding presumptuous, Your Grace, may I inquire if your daughter, Lady Louisa, is spoken for?"

"I'm sorry to disappoint you, Ossulston, but I have reason to believe my daughter's affections are engaged."

When Georgy retired, Louisa was abed and almost asleep. Georgy turned up the lamp, and her sister knew she wanted to talk.

"I ruined my slippers, but it will be worth it if Ossulston offers for me."

How can you jump from Teddy Fox to Charles Bennet in the blink of an eye? "Are you sure, Georgy? I thought you were in love with Teddy."

"Love? What the devil does love have to do with marriage?"

"Georgy, I know you had deep feelings for Teddy. You had your heart set on becoming his wife. It will take a little time to get over him."

"I don't have time. Time is my enemy!"

"Georgy, you make too much of your age."

She bit her lip, for once not even thinking of her age, until Lu brought it up. "I'll be twenty-two on my next birthday. That's considered an old maid." She finished undressing and got into bed. "I invited Ossulston to the Doune and gave him *every* encouragement. He's heir to the Earl of Tankerville. I'd be quite happy to be his countess, in spite of his countrified Northumbrian accent."

"Then I hope he accepts your invitation."

"When he comes, I want you to stay away from him. You are adept at stealing my thunder." She imitated her sister's voice: *"Oh, we would love to have you, Charles. The salmon fishing in the River Spey is incomparable."*

"I'm sorry, Georgy. I was only trying to help."

"I can manage without help from the *Great Russell Beauty!*"

It was hours before Louisa could sleep. Her heart ached for her sister.

Every morning when Georgy awoke, the first thing she did was examine her nightgown for a smear of blood. Today was her seventh disappointment. *I was certain that riding in the carriage over rutted roads would bring on my menses.* She pushed away her nagging apprehension. *Today I'll do something more strenuous.*

At breakfast she ate porridge, unable to look at the eggs and gammon ham the others were consuming. Even the smell made her nauseous. When the servants cleared the table she threw Charles Bennet a provocative glance. "I feel like doing something daring today. I shall climb down the cliff path and wade into the sea. Anyone care to join me?"

Cosmo, Henry, and Alex immediately chorused, "I will! I will!"

Georgy's face fell. *I should have known better than to announce my plans in front of the young savages.* She glanced hopefully at Charles Bennet, but he didn't take the bait.

"How very adventurous you are," Maria Grey declared. "Henry and Charles have promised to put up my latest gargoyles on the north side of the church."

Georgy felt thwarted. "Careful you don't get stuck in the bog down there."

The Duchess of Bedford heard her daughter's snide remark. "Georgy dear, keep your eye on Alexander on your escapade. You know how uncivilized your brothers can be."

Abercorn smiled at the duchess. "I'll join them, Your Grace. I'll see they come to no harm. How about you, Lady Louisa?"

She glanced at her sister's scowl. "No . . . Perhaps I'll walk down to Howick burn."

"It's all bog land down there," her mother pointed out. "Do climb down the cliff with the others, darling. How often do you get a chance to wade in the North Sea?" She threw James Hamilton a speculative glance. "You don't want to miss all the fun."

At the top of the cliff, Abercorn insisted on taking the lead. He grinned. "I'll break your fall if any of you slip." He knew the Russell boys would be on his heels and decided to give them a run for their money. He flew down the steep cliff and reached the sand a full five minutes before the savage louts, who whooped and screeched with excitement all the way down. He stood at the bottom and waited for the sisters to make their descent.

Georgy came down like a cart horse at full gallop, disregarding all danger. He prayed she wouldn't fall. Behind her, Louisa made the climb down look easy. She had a natural lithe grace that reminded him of his beautiful Arabian.

Behind him, the wild devils threw off their clothes and ran naked into the sea. James knew he had no choice. He was responsible for their safety. While he waited for Georgy and Louisa to reach the sand, he removed his shirt and shoes. The minute the sisters were safe, he tore across the sandy, pebbled beach and plunged into the sea in his breeches.

James joined in the water games and invented a few of his own, allowing the boys to climb up onto his chest so that he could flip them into the sea. He even balanced them on his broad shoulders so they could dive.

Louisa was amazed at the good-natured patience he showed to her young brothers. She took off her shoes and stockings and waded in up to her calves. Georgy took off up the beach on a strenuous run, while Louisa stood bemused watching the water play.

After an hour, her brothers straggled from the water one by one to scramble shivering into their clothes. The North Sea was cold even in August.

James, still in the water, approached Louisa. "Would you like to come in?"

She shook her head. "I can't swim."

"Can't swim?" he asked incredulously. "Why not? You have a lake at Woburn."

"You've seen what the wild savages are like. Whenever I ventured into the lake, they pulled me under and held me there without compunction. Edward, Charles, and Jack were even worse than Cosmo and Henry."

Her vulnerability cried out to him. "Sometime I'll teach you to swim, Lady Lu. I'll make sure there are no monsters lurking beneath the surface."

Louisa glanced at his naked chest. "Aren't you cold?"

"I'm lucky—I don't seem to notice the cold." He put on his shirt and shoes.

"Come on, James!" the Russell boys chorused.

"They're ready to climb back up."

"They will worship you from now on. They are at an impression-able age."

He grinned. "Would that you were, Lady Lu."

"Here comes Georgy. She's full of disgusting energy today."

The boys were halfway up the cliff before the sisters began their ascent. This time James brought up the rear in case any of them slipped. Near the top, Georgy stumbled but caught herself before she fell, and James breathed easier.

"Georgy, you have blood on your skirt," Louisa pointed out.

"Really?" Georgy's hopes soared. Then she felt her knee begin to sting. She lifted her skirt and saw that she had scraped her knee when she stumbled. He heart plummeted as her hopes were dashed.

Chapter Sixteen

"I wish you were coming with us to the Doune, James," Henry Russell said wistfully. "You have become leader of the pack."

Abercorn smiled ruefully. "So do I, Henry. But my business is here in Edinburgh. You can take over as leader."

The Russells had stayed overnight at the Gordon townhouse, which was now owned by Georgina's brother George, Duke of Gordon. The duchess insisted that Abercorn use it while he conducted his business in Edinburgh.

James helped the ladies into their carriage and bade them goodbye. "I'll see you back in London in October." Though he spoke to the family in general, Louisa knew his words were meant especially for her.

Once the Russells arrived at the Doune, there were a multitude of activities to occupy them. They fished in the River Spey, hunted in the ancient Caledonia forest, and rode the mountain paths of the Cairngorms. They exchanged visits with George Gordon and his wife, who were at their farmhouse in nearby Kinrara. And in late August, Edward Ellice and his wife, Hannah, bought the estate next to the Doune. Every week Georgina hosted a dance, where fiddlers and pipers played reels and Strathspeys. Not only were their neighbors invited but also their servants and gillies.

Georgy was sorely disappointed that Charles Bennet had not accepted her invitation to visit. Her disappointment turned to silent hopelessness and then she became morose, realizing that in Scotland she was completely cut off from any eligible man she could entice as a prospective husband. She refused to join Louisa on her rides or any of her siblings in their varied activities. Though her sister was aware of her bouts of nausea, Georgy kept it hidden from her mother. She became withdrawn, wan, and deeply depressed. Louisa was beside herself with worry over her sister.

In Edinburgh, James Hamilton interviewed half a dozen attorneys. Finally he retained Angus Murray, the head of a long-established law firm specializing in inheritance law.

"I have competent lawyers in Ireland who look after my Irish estates, but I have need of a Scots attorney for lands in this country that I inherited from my grandfather, the Marquis of Abercorn."

"It would be a great honor to serve you, Lord Paisley."

James smiled. "I warrant I've chosen the right man." Lord Paisley was the Scottish title he had inherited. "As you may or may not know, my stepfather, the Earl of Aberdeen, became my guardian. Since I celebrated my twenty-first birthday in January, I want his guardianship declared null and void. Legal documents need to be filed in my name for all my Scottish property."

"Absolutely, my lord. I shall look up the records and make sure the deeds are registered in your name."

"I would like an accounting also. I have reason to believe some of the income from my properties has been misappropriated over the years."

"My investigation will be both thorough and discreet, my lord. Do you know the extent of Aberdeen's legal holdings in Scotland?"

"He owns Haddo House and a considerable amount of land in

Aberdeenshire. Any lands in the vicinity of Paisley are mine, bequeathed by my grandfather."

"Does Aberdeen own any land in England, my lord?"

"None that I know of. For many years he has leased a London townhouse on South Audley Street. He occupies Bentley Priory in Stanmore, about ten miles from London. I own it, but because my mother prefers living there to the rigors of Haddo House in the Highlands, I have no objections."

"And do the rents from the Stanmore tenants come to you, or to Aberdeen?"

"I receive no money from Stanmore. If he uses the rents for the upkeep and my mother's comfort, I have no objection."

"Nevertheless, it is imperative that you have a detailed accounting. With your permission I will investigate your holdings in both Scotland and England."

"I hereby grant you that permission, Murray."

"I shall report to you in a week's time at your Edinburgh address, Lord Paisley."

"Georgy hasn't taken breakfast with us for a week. Where does she go on these early morning rides?" her mother asked Louisa.

"She isn't out riding. She's in bed."

"Whatever is the matter with her?" Georgina arose from the table.

"She's tired. She is lethargic and has no energy."

"Louisa, why didn't you tell me? She must be ill."

Lu followed her mother upstairs. *Georgy made me promise not to tell.*

When they entered the bedchamber they were met with the miasma of vomit. Whenever her sister had thrown up, Louisa had discreetly emptied and cleaned the chamber pot.

"My darling, you've been sick!" Her mother was alarmed. She sat down on the bed. "Do you have a fever?" She felt her forehead.

"Sometimes I feel hot, and sometimes I shiver," Georgy improvised, knowing full well her mother would detect no fever.

"We must send for the doctor."

Georgy felt panic. "No, no, I feel better now. I was just about to get up."

"You will do no such thing. You are to stay in bed until the doctor comes. I shall send one of the gillies for Dr. Nicol. Louisa will sit with you."

When her mother left, Georgy demanded, "Why the devil did you tell her I was ill?"

"I didn't. I told her you were tired."

Georgy was almost hysterical. "I don't want the doctor examining me! I'm not ill."

No, you are heartsick. First, William Cavendish spurned you; then Teddy Fox didn't propose, and now Charles Bennet is avoiding you. You feel hopeless and crushed. "I'll empty the chamber pot. The doctor won't be here for hours—he lives thirty miles away."

When Louisa returned she asked, "Do you want to talk, Georgy?"

"No, I don't! What do you know about how I feel?"

"I know you are unhappy."

"Everything is ugly. Food has lost its taste. I hate all my clothes. When I look at the mountains they are brooding and forbidding. I hate my life—I have nothing to live for."

"Things may seem bleak at the moment, but you have everything to live for."

"What does the *beauty* of the family know about it? Leave me alone!"

Louisa moved toward her own bedchamber. "I'll leave the connecting door open. If you want anything, just call out."

Terrified that the doctor would suspect she was with child even though she denied it was possible, Georgy held the covers up to her chin. "I feel much better, thank you."

Dr. Nicol stuck a thermometer in her armpit and then took her pulse.

Georgy shivered with fear.

He looked at the numbers on the glass instrument. "No fever at the moment. She is chilled—she is having a rigor." He looked at the duchess apologetically. "I must examine her body to see if she has a rash, Your Grace."

Georgy pounced on his suggestion. If he diagnosed an illness, she would be safe. "I did have a rash, doctor. But it is all gone now. There were red spots all over my chest and arms yesterday. I showed my sister. But they are faded now," she said desperately.

The doctor looked at Louisa for confirmation and she nodded uncertainly.

He got up from the bed and beckoned the Duchess of Bedford from the room. "Your Grace, I don't wish to alarm you, but there has been a cholera epidemic in the North for the last year." He saw the horror on her face and tried to reassure her. "I don't believe your daughter has cholera, but she could very easily have picked up typhoid fever. The symptoms are vomiting, fever and chills, and a red rash."

"*Typhoid*? But typhoid can be fatal and isn't it highly contagious?"

"Perhaps she should be quarantined to be on the safe side."

Georgina wrung her hands. "I must tell her father. You will stay for the night, doctor. Perhaps you can be more certain of a diagnosis in the morning."

"Yes, thank you, Your Grace. She must be kept in bed and given lots to drink. Get one of the maids to make some barley water, and I'll give her a fever powder."

Georgina hurried down to the library. "John, were you aware that there is a cholera epidemic in the North of England and Scotland?"

"Good God, surely Georgy doesn't have cholera?"

"No, no, Dr. Nicol doesn't think it's cholera, but he thinks it could be typhoid fever, which is almost as bad, from what I've heard. He'll know more in the morning. I shall have the maids pack the children's things, just in case. It would be best if you took them home to Woburn. It's mid-September so they'd only be here another two weeks anyway."

"But I can't leave you here on your own," he protested.

"I don't want any of the others to fall sick. Typhoid can be fatal, John. I'm quite used to nursing sick children, and you are not. Better to be safe than sorry."

Upstairs in her bedroom, Georgy and Louisa heard the maids scurrying about. "Go and see what the doctor told Mother and come straight back."

Louisa hurried downstairs. "What did the doctor say?"

"He suspects typhoid fever. Pack your things, darling. It's very contagious, so your father is taking everyone home."

"No . . . I'm not leaving Georgy." Louisa was covered with guilt because she had not told her mother that Georgy had been vomiting. "I thought she was despondent because Teddy Fox didn't offer for her."

"It's more serious than that, I'm afraid." She picked up Rachel, who had begun to cry. "Louisa, go to the kitchen and have them make some barley water." She brushed Rachel's red curls back from her forehead. "Let's gather up your toys, darling."

"Louisa!" Georgy called. "I need you here when the doctor comes."

It was seven in the morning and Louisa, who was already up and dressed, went into the adjoining room. "You slept all night. How are you feeling?"

"Awful!" Georgy really did feel ill as fear knotted inside her. She was still not convinced that she had conceived because her belly was still flat. But she was terrified that the doctor might somehow jump to conclusions and say that she was with child. "Here comes Mother and the doctor!" She could feel her heartbeat pounding in her eardrums.

Dr. Nicol took her hand and placed his fingers on her wrist. He spoke to the Duchess of Bedford. "Her pulse is very rapid and her face is flushed."

"My ears hurt!"

The doctor nodded. He took an instrument from his bag and looked into both ears. "Deafness is often a symptom of typhoid fever. We can only hope it won't be permanent. I prescribe a drop or two of warm olive oil."

Her mother's hopes sank. "So your diagnosis is confirmed." She rallied her spirits. "We must be thankful that it isn't cholera. Can you remain another day, doctor?"

"I have a good many patients in need of my services, Your Grace. One more day is all I can spare in good conscience."

"Thank you so much, Dr. Nicol."

An hour later, two coaches and the baggage wagon piled high with luggage were ready for the journey south. The Duke of Bedford put his three sons into one carriage, while Rachel and her nurse occupied the second carriage with him. John Russell masked his apprehension and kissed his wife good-bye. He turned to his favorite daughter. "Won't you change your mind and come with us, Louisa?"

"Both Mother and Georgy need me right now. We'll come home as soon as she is recovered. Try not to worry, Father. We won't let anything happen to her."

They waved until the carriages were out of sight. "Louisa, I want you to ride over to Kinrara and tell your Uncle George and Aunt Elizabeth that under no circumstances are they to visit the Doune. Tell them that we suspect Georgy has typhoid. Then you must ride to the Ellice estate and give Edward and Hannah the same message."

"You just missed the Duke of Bedford, my lord. But he left a letter for you." The butler at the Edinburgh townhouse handed James Hamilton an envelope.

"Thank you." James had expected the Russells to remain at the Doune until early October. He tore open the letter and read it.

Dear James,

I was here overnight on the return journey to Woburn. I'm sorry I missed you.

My daughter has fallen ill and the doctor suspects typhoid fever. My wife insisted that I take the rest of the family home as a precaution, and though I was loath to leave, I know it is the sensible thing to do. We are all praying for her recovery.

I hope to see you when you get back to London.

John Russell

James felt his gut knot with apprehension. The duke had not indicated which daughter was ill, but he feared the worst. "Was Lady Louisa with his grace?"

"No, my lord, only his sons and Lady Rachel."

Abercorn had just returned from visiting his lands in Paisley after receiving Angus Murray's report. He had hired a coach and driver for his journey, and fortunately both were still at his disposal. James made the decision immediately to go to the Doune.

"Lu, please don't force any more barley water on me. I cannot keep it down. Some wine would be nice, but failing that, bring me some small ale."

For the umpteenth morning Louisa emptied the nasty contents of Georgy's chamber pot. She was extremely anxious about her sister. Though she did not seem to be fevered and had no rash, she was pale and listless, and she still vomited every morning.

"You should try to eat something. What can I get you?"

"No ham . . . in fact, no meat of any kind. Just the smell makes me nauseous."

"How about a poached egg or a scone with some honey?"

"All right, I'll try." Georgy was deliberately reducing her food intake. The last thing she wanted was to put on extra pounds that would cause comment.

Louisa went down to the kitchen and was surprised to see her mother. She usually rested in the mornings because she sat with Georgy most of the night. "I think we have reason to hope. At least she's no worse. She's going to try some food."

"Georgy slept most of the night, so I take that as a good sign. I believe she's slowly recovering. Her lethargy worries me, though. Perhaps bed rest will take care of that." She glanced out the window. "Damnation! A coach has just driven up. Darling, go outside and see who it is. I'm unfit to receive visitors. I'm still wearing the clothes I had on yesterday."

Louisa went outside and hurried toward the stables where the coach was standing. The last person she was expecting to see climb from the carriage was Abercorn.

"Louisa! Thank God, you are recovered." He closed the distance between them and took her into his arms.

She shuddered at the feel of his powerful arms. She had forgotten how darkly handsome the Irish marquis was. His closeness mesmerized her, and she found it difficult to break the spell of his compelling presence.

Finally she struggled until he set her free. "It's Georgy who is ill. What are you doing here?"

"Your father left me a letter telling me his daughter had contracted typhoid. He didn't say which daughter, but that didn't matter. If your sister has it, you are in danger."

"I couldn't desert Georgy and Mother."

"Of course not. Your mother must be frantic."

"She's coping very well, and Georgy seems slightly improved."

"That's very good news." He began to walk toward the stable. "The horses are tired. We drove all night."

"You can't come in, Abercorn. The Doune is under quarantine."

"Nonsense. If you are willing to risk infection, so am I, my dearest Lu." He gave his driver orders to unhitch the team and take them into the stable.

When the pair entered the house, the Duchess of Bedford looked from one to the other. "James, you shouldn't be here, you know. But I fully understand your concern for Louisa. It was very gallant of you to come rushing up here." Her hand went to her hair. "I'll go up and change. You may stay for lunch, but in all conscience I cannot allow you to stay here overnight. Louisa, after lunch you must take James to Kinrara. My brother George will be happy to accommodate you."

"You are very kind, Your Grace."

"Louisa needs a change from nursing the invalid. She is looking pale and peaked."

James glanced at Louisa and hid his amusement. Her face was a pretty blush pink.

During lunch, she sat quietly and let her mother and Abercorn converse. She knew both her parents thoroughly approved of him and would like nothing better than to welcome him as a son-in-law. She pushed the threatening thoughts away. *Mother would never push me into marriage.*

After lunch she ran upstairs to change into a riding dress.

"Louisa!" Georgy summoned. "Someone arrived in a carriage. Who is it?"

She hopes Lord Ossulston came. "I'm afraid it was James Hamilton." Georgy's face fell.

"Abercorn came to see how you were."

"No, he didn't. He thoroughly disapproves of me. He came to see you, Mistress Prim and Proper. Your virginity draws him like a lodestone!"

"That's not true! I once offered it to him and he refused me," Louisa blurted.

Georgy's mouth fell open.

"Choose a mount." Louisa began to saddle a sure-footed cob for herself.

"I'll ride the roan," he said decisively and then lifted the saddle onto its back. He took a traveling bag from the coach and filled the saddlebags with his clothes and toiletries. She followed him from the stables and hung back for a moment, watching him. When Abercorn rode he was one with his horse, reminding her of a centaur.

Louisa was immensely flattered that he had rushed up to the Doune when he thought she was ailing. This young noble had everything to recommend him: gallantry, looks, personality, wealth, and title. He was perfect. And therein lay the trouble.

I must guard myself against his irresistible charm. He wants to be my husband, but I do not want to be his wife, nor any man's wife. A wife meant being a mother and the thought of that terrified her. She had built an iron carapace around her heart but feared that sooner or later James Hamilton would cleave it asunder and leave her vulnerable and helpless to resist his will.

Side by side they rode along a mountain trail. They came to a clearing in the pines and a magnificent vista opened up before them. James stopped to drink in the beauty of the loch and the heather-covered mountains dotted with sheep that sloped majestically down to the water that reflected the deep blue sky. "Now I understand why you love the Highlands."

Louisa sighed at the sheer beauty. "It holds a special place in my heart."

James smiled into her eyes.

> *"I love your hills, and I love your dales,*
> *And I love your flocks a-bleating;*
> *But oh, on the heather to lie together*
> *With both our hearts a-beating!"*

"If you must compose doggerel, need it be so lustful?"

James laughed. "That is John Keats, my ignorant little lass. But I agree that his romantic poetry is visually sensual."

Louisa blushed, not at Keats's lines but at her own thoughts that the poetry provoked. The scent of the purple heather seemed to dance around them, perfuming the very air they breathed. She felt the wild beat of her heart and tried to deny that Abercorn was the cause of it.

When they arrived at Kinrara, James was out of the saddle in a flash before she could dismount. He held up his arms in invitation. Louisa came down to him in a flurry of petticoats, and he reveled in the embrace, holding her captive against him for an indecorous length of time. He smiled down into her eyes. "The ride has brought the roses back to your cheeks."

It wasn't the ride, you bold Irish devil, and well you know it!

.   .   .

James watched the Duke of Gordon emerge from the stables and noticed the family resemblance immediately.

"How is Georgy?" George Gordon scanned Louisa's face anxiously.

"She is much improved, Uncle George. Mother and I believe the worst is over." She introduced Abercorn to her uncle, the Duke of Gordon.

James shook his hand warmly. "Your Grace, I am delighted to meet you. Your sister, the Duchess of Bedford, allowed me to stay at your Edinburgh townhouse and now sends me to Kinrara to beg your hospitality. I am doubly indebted to you."

Louisa saw that the two men would soon become fast friends. They spoke of Gordon Castle and its proximity to the Earl of Aberdeen's land.

James wondered what Gordon thought of Aberdeen. *I'm sure our low opinion of the man is mutual.* James would not broach the subject in front of George's wife, Elizabeth, or Louisa. He would wait until they were private to discuss the swine and the shameful way he had cleared his land of his tenants.

After an hour's visit with Elizabeth, Louisa said her good-byes.

James stood up. "I can't stay long. I have business in Edinburgh, and then I must return to London."

Louisa said breathlessly, "Well, I shall see you before you leave. You left your coach and horses at the Doune."

"Yes. I'll see you tomorrow or the next day at the latest. I hope Georgy is much improved by then. Ride carefully, Louisa."

"I'll have one of the gillies accompany her." George went with his niece to the stables and when he returned he said, "Louisa tells me you came rushing to the Doune, not knowing which sister had the typhoid."

"I feared for both of them, but knew I would not have a moment's peace until I had seen Louisa with my own eyes."

"How very gallant," Elizabeth declared. "Have you known each other long?"

James smiled. "I proposed to Lady Louisa when she was seven years old. My feelings have never changed. I have every intention of making her my wife."

Chapter Seventeen

"We are fortunate the snow hasn't arrived yet. It often comes as early as November." The Duchess of Bedford tucked in the traveling blanket around Georgy as their coach crossed the border from Scotland into England.

The return trip to Woburn that would reunite them with the rest of the family had been delayed until her mother was absolutely sure that Georgy was free of all infection.

"I'm actually looking forward to seeing the young savages again," Louisa admitted.

Georgy did not join in the conversation. She often pretended she was deaf to the things her mother said.

Louisa, doubtful that the fever had left her sister hearing impaired, and even dubious of the typhoid diagnosis, suddenly felt mischievous. "Perhaps Georgy would benefit from an ear trumpet?"

Roused from her lethargy, Georgy cried, "I'd rather die than use an ear trumpet. It would make me a laughingstock!"

"I'm sorry, Georgy. I was only teasing." Louisa looked at her mother. "Father will be glad to see you, and I'm sure Rachel has missed you terribly."

"Yes, though we wrote faithfully, letters are a poor substitute. Your father didn't mention if Johnny had had any success with the reform bill. But I don't believe the prime minister will present it until he feels sure the Lords will pass it." Her next thought brought a smile. "When we get home, we must start making plans for Christmas."

"Johnny always comes to Woburn for Christmas. He says it rejuvenates him so he can work full bore when Parliament reconvenes in the New Year."

Louisa saw that her sister had fallen asleep and with the monotonous rocking of the coach it wasn't long before both she and her mother gave themselves up to the arms of Morpheus.

It's true. I can't deny it any longer. "Holy Mother of God," Georgy whispered, "what will I do?" She stood before her mirror with clenched fists. She raised them intending to smash them into her reflection, when she suddenly stopped. *Hellfire, I cannot break another mirror. That's why I'm having such rotten bad luck!*

Tears filled her eyes, as she began to frantically count the months since she'd fucked with Teddy Fox. This was the third week of November. As far as she could remember their last fateful coupling had been around the third week of July. "Four months!" She drew in a ragged breath. She placed a shaking hand on her belly and hated the small mound she felt beneath her tight riding habit. "I must get rid of it somehow. I cannot wait any longer."

For the next week she rode every day, galloping like a madwoman in an attempt to shake it loose. But it clung like a leech and every night she cursed heaven and hell. When December dawned and Georgy had received no divine intervention, she made a decision.

She put a warm cloak over her riding dress to cover the burst seams and went into her sister's bedchamber. "Louisa, would you like to go riding with me?"

Lu was surprised. Her sister always rode alone these days and seemed so withdrawn and unhappy. "Yes, I'd love to go with you. Do you think I'll need a cloak?"

"Yes, I think you should wear one. There's frost in the air, and if we are dressed alike, it won't draw attention to me."

In the stables Louisa saddled her own horse and saw that Georgy struggled to do the same, refusing the help of a groom.

Georgy galloped madly through Woburn's park toward the woods and Louisa followed. Once she reached the cover of the trees, Georgy reined in and dismounted. She sat down on a fallen log and gestured for her sister to join her.

"I want to share a secret with you. But first you must promise me you will not breathe a word to anyone."

Lu sat down. *At last she is going to tell me what has been troubling her.* "Of course I won't tell anyone. Your secret is safe with me, Georgy."

"I'm going to have a baby."

Lu stared at her sister's pale face and frightened eyes in disbelief, shocked into momentary speechlessness. Suddenly all the puzzling pieces of her sister's strange behavior fell into place and began to make sense. The enormity of her situation made her heart ache. She took hold of her hand. "Georgy, I'm so sorry."

Her gentle sympathy opened the floodgates. Georgy buried her face against her sister's shoulder and sobbed.

Louisa held her tightly and decided not to ask the unkind question about who had fathered the child. Instead she asked, "How long have you known?"

Georgy drew in a long shuddering breath and allowed Lu to wipe away her tears. "I suspected it before we went to Scotland, but then I pushed the terrifying thought away and refused to believe it. Even after I missed my menses for a couple of months, I kept denying it. I prayed that the jolting carriage or long gallops in the mountains would start my bleeding. I can't deny it any longer. I'm four months gone. Will you help me?"

Your vomiting was morning sickness. You never had typhoid fever.

"No wonder you've been so withdrawn and worried. I'll help you any way I can, Georgy."

"I want you to help me keep it secret. I wore the cloak because I split the seams on my riding dress. Promise me you won't tell Mother."

"I cross my heart, Georgy." *If you are four months along, you won't be able to hide it much longer.* "We can let out the seams on all your dresses and enlarge them."

"Thank you, Lu. You have no idea how relieved I am to share it with you."

Louisa and Georgy got to work immediately letting out her clothes. For the next week Georgy wore a paisley shawl over her gowns as the family made preparations for the Christmas festivities.

"Are you cold, darling?" Georgina asked her daughter.

"Yes. I seem to feel the cold more since I had the typhoid."

"I shall crochet you a shawl. I have some lovely soft wool I brought from Scotland."

That night when the sisters retired, Georgy came into Louisa's bedchamber. "You have to help me, Lu." She took a crochet hook from her pocket. "You have to help me get rid of it."

Louisa recoiled. "I can't do that!"

"You promised to help me," Georgy cried desperately.

"We've both heard the stories of servant girls dying from doing that."

Georgy sank down on the bed. "Whatever am I to do? I cannot face the scandal. I'd rather *die* than have anyone find out."

Louisa sat down beside her and put her arm around her. "Have you told the father?"

"He won't marry me! And if this gets out, it will ruin my chances of *ever* marrying. Swear to me again that you will never reveal my shameful secret!"

"I swear on my honor, Georgy. Go to bed and get some rest. We'll get up early and go for a good gallop. Maybe that will do the trick."

The following day the sisters saddled up and galloped through Woburn's park. As Louisa headed north, Georgy stopped her. "I don't want to ride to Ampthill. I don't want to run into Uncle Holly or Beth. Let's ride south."

It's Teddy she doesn't want to see. Georgy's words rang in her ears: *"He won't marry me!"* Louisa could not believe their friend would be that cruel and dishonorable. "It's Teddy Fox, isn't it? Have you told him?"

Georgy laughed bitterly. "Yes, I told him. Would you like to hear his reply? He said: *'If I offer for anyone, it will be Louisa.'*"

O my God! Lu was covered with guilt that Teddy Fox preferred her to her sister. *He is a selfish bastard like all men.*

Georgy took off, galloping like the wind. She spurned the road and took off across the barren, rutted fields. Louisa did her best to keep up. They rode hard for two hours before Georgy stopped and dismounted. "I have to pee. I can't hold it these days."

She pulled up her petticoats and examined them minutely for any smear of blood. Furious that she could not bend nature to her will, she jumped into the saddle and rode hell-for-leather across the fields, back the way they had come.

Two hours later, they arrived back at Woburn Park. Louisa was relieved that her sister had slowed to a canter, then was horrified to see Georgy let go of her reins and fling herself to the ground. *O my God! She's trying to kill herself!*

Lu reined in, dismounted, and ran to her sister who lay in a crumpled heap. She fell to her knees. "Georgy, Georgy, speak to me!"

"I want to die."

"No, you don't, Georgy. I won't let you die!" She lifted her to a sitting position. "Where does it hurt?"

Georgy closed her eyes in abject misery. "Unfortunately, it doesn't hurt anywhere except my knee and my back."

"Can you walk, or shall I get help?" Lu asked frantically.

"Don't . . . you . . . dare." She glared at her sister with unconcealed hatred.

"Rest for a few minutes while I take the horses to the stable. Then I'll come back and help you up to the house."

When they entered Woburn, their mother was busy putting up Yule decorations while the Russell brothers erected an enormous Christmas tree.

"Everything looks lovely," Lu declared. "As soon as I change my clothes, I'll be back to help you decorate the tree."

The sisters managed to climb the stairs unobserved. Georgy limped into her bedchamber and Lu hung up her sister's cloak. "Lie down and I'll rub your back."

Lu removed her sister's boots and gently massaged her back. "Georgy, you frightened me to death. Promise you won't do anything so reckless again?"

"It didn't work," she said dully.

"I'll bring you up a tray. I'll tell them you are tired from the ride."

"I'm not hungry." Georgy closed her eyes and lay still.

Downstairs, Louisa went through the motions of decorating the Christmas tree with her brothers, but her thoughts were focused on Georgy. The chatter was all about presents and games and who would be Lord of Misrule this year, and none noticed that Lu was preoccupied.

At the evening meal when her father asked about Georgy's absence, Lu had her story ready. "I'm going to take a tray up to her. She's busy wrapping presents, and after dinner I'm going up to do the same."

"I invited my sister Charlotte and her entire clan, but it's possible they will hold Christmas at Fife House," Georgina announced.

"Johnny, however, has sent word that he will be here until New Year. I've invited the prime minister and his wife, and of course the Hollands." She glanced at Louisa. "I sent an invitation to James Hamilton and his brother Claud. I do hope they'll come."

Louisa's anxious thoughts of Georgy crowded out everything else. *Woburn will be filled with guests. How will Georgy face everyone? I love her so much. If only I could find a way to help her.*

Lu set the tray down by Georgy's bed. Her sister had undressed and put on her nightgown. "How are you feeling?"

"My knee is bruised and my back hurts."

"I have some angelica salve that will take away your bruises."

Lu brought the pot of ointment and rubbed it on her sister's knee. Then she raised her nightgown to look at her back. "It's black and blue, but not nearly as bad as I feared. That was a very hard fall." She anointed her sister's back. "Drink your wine; it will help you sleep."

Lu saw that Georgy's hand trembled as she lifted the wineglass to her lips and her heart went out to her. "We'll face this together, Georgy," she pledged.

"Will you stay with me for a while?" Georgy picked at her food.

"Of course I will."

Georgy set down her fork. "I'm so sick and tired of everything."

"Get into bed. You need rest. I'll stay with you until you fall asleep."

Lu sought her own chamber once her sister slept. She put on her nightgown and climbed into bed. Distressing thoughts filled her head. *Georgy hates me. She thinks no one will offer for her, and blames me. It devastates me that she is in such a mess. I'll stand by her, no matter what.* Tired by her ride, she drifted into slumber.

Two hours later, Louisa awoke when Georgy shook her arm. "Lu, I don't feel very well. I don't want to be alone."

Louisa slid out of bed and turned up the lamp. "Are you going to throw up?"

"No, I don't think so." She shivered. "I'm in pain . . . I hurt all over."

"You're cold. Get into my bed. It's nice and warm." Lu took the chamber pot from the cupboard in the night table. "Just in case."

Georgy lay down and pulled up the covers. She moaned softly to ease her misery. All at once, she bolted upright. She pressed a fist against her mouth to smother a scream, as a sharp pain tore through her belly. She felt a tearing sensation, followed by a gush of warm wetness between her thighs. She threw back the covers and saw that she was bleeding.

Louisa's eyes went wide. "O my Lord, you're having a miscarriage!"

"Thank God! Thank God! What shall I do?" she whispered frantically.

Blood was spreading everywhere, drenching Georgy's nightgown and staining the bedsheets.

"Is the pain unbearable?" Lu was terrified for her sister.

"The agonizing pain has stopped." She panted with relief and with fear.

For an hour they sat together while Georgy cramped and bled into towels Louisa had brought. When the cramping eased, Louisa helped her sister from the bed. "Here put this towel between your legs and squeeze them together."

Three towels later, the bleeding subsided. Louisa cut a fresh towel into smaller squares. She removed her sister's soaked nightgown, then brought water and washed her. "I'll get you a fresh gown." Lu pulled the crisp white nightgown over Georgy's body and handed her the squares of towel. "Here, use these as pads."

Georgy was weak with relief but still shaking with fear of discovery. "Promise you'll keep my secret, Lu?"

"I promise no one will ever know. I'll burn these sheets tomorrow and put fresh ones on the bed."

"Swear to me you won't tell anyone." Tears streamed down her face. "I'll kill myself if anyone ever finds out I was with child!"

"Georgy, I swear on my life I will keep this secret. Surely you know you can trust me? No one will ever know." Lu looked down at herself and saw her nightgown and hands were covered with blood, just as in her nightmares. Her nerves were stretched to the breaking point and she let out a sob.

Suddenly the door opened and their mother walked in. "What on earth—"

The three females stood staring at one another.

"Oh, my darling." Georgina closed the distance between them and enfolded Louisa in her arms. "My poor, poor, darling. You're having a miscarriage."

"No . . . Mother . . . I—" Lu saw her sister's face, pale as death and she couldn't betray her. Georgy had tried to kill herself once and she would do it again rather than face the shameful scandal. *I'm stronger than Georgy.*

The duchess stripped the sheets from the bed and put on fresh ones. Then she took a clean nightgown from the drawer and gently eased the blood-stained one from her daughter's body. "You will need to rest." She led Louisa to the bed and glanced at Georgy. "I want you both to listen carefully. No one must ever know about this. Not even your father—*especially* not your father." She bundled up the bloodied nightgowns, sheets, and towels. "I'll tell the servants that I had the miscarriage. I've had them before. We will keep this secret between the three of us. No one else must know."

The duchess saw that Georgy was swaying on her feet. "Go back to your own bed, dearest. I'll look after your sister now."

She bent and placed a tender kiss on Louisa's forehead. "These things happen, darling. We'll get through this together."

. . .

Montagu House, London
August 1894

"The name is the destiny," Dowager Duchess Louisa murmured as she watched her daughter, Georgianna Susan, move toward her through the throng of guests. *I named her after my sister Georgy, never dreaming that my baby girl would turn out to look exactly like her aunt. Never mind, darling. Your plain face didn't stop you from becoming the Fifth Countess of Winterton.*

Louisa smiled a secret smile. *I could have been the Fourth Countess of Winterton. Earl Winterton panted after me and I might have succumbed if he hadn't been such a boring cricket fanatic.* "Georgy, darling. Do you have something of import to impart?"

"Yes, Mother. The press wants permission to take photographs for the newspaper."

"My vanity compels me to grant permission. Pass the word and gather everyone together . . . my sons and daughters first, then my grandchildren, and then my great-grandchildren. Make sure no one is overlooked, Georgy."

As Louisa gazed after her daughter, she felt a tug on her heart-strings. *She is the spitting image of my dear sister, Georgy. The devastating night my sister miscarried is indelibly stamped in my memory as if it just happened.*

That was the night that changed my life and my destiny . . .

Chapter Eighteen

"Henry! Beth! I wish you a Happy Christmas, and many more to come." The Duchess of Bedford greeted her dearest friends warmly. "Don't tell me Teddy isn't coming!"

Beth threw an apologetic look at Georgy and Louisa. "He's gone to Horsham in West Sussex. He said he felt duty bound to visit his constituents while Parliament is in recess."

"How very noble of him," Louisa said sweetly.

"Actually," Lord Holland confided, "we are extremely pleased that Teddy has begun to take his responsibilities seriously."

"Uncle Holly, you always manage to make me laugh." Louisa glanced at her sister and gave her a reassuring smile.

Georgina lamented, "With George Grey and our sons Edward and Charles off serving their country, there will be a shortage of bachelors to celebrate Christmas with us this year. I made a special point of inviting James Hamilton and his brother, but apparently they've gone to Ireland." She glanced at Louisa and saw her blush.

Mother is annoyed that Abercorn won't be coming, but I'm relieved. If he were here, she and Father would aid and abet him in his pursuit of me. "Johnny arrived yesterday and Jack has volunteered to be Lord of Misrule." Lu smiled at her brother. "He'll make sure everyone has a good time."

"Why don't I organize a hunt for this afternoon? We have no snow yet, and I'm sure the ladies would enjoy a good gallop."

"Organize it for just the men, Jack. You forget that Georgy is recuperating from that dreadful bout of fever." The duchess glanced at Louisa with concerned eyes. "Your sisters are helping Johnny write a Christmas play they are going to perform."

Beth took a seat next to Georgy. "How are you feeling after your illness, my dear?"

"Sometimes I get a little tired."

"Yes, you appear much thinner than you did before you went to Scotland," Beth said with sympathy. "You gave us quite a scare, my dear."

An hour later, Earl and Countess Grey arrived, and the conversations were repeated.

That afternoon, Jack included his younger brothers Henry and Cosmo in the hunt. Even Alex was given permission to accompany the men, though for everyone's safety he was allowed no weapon.

The ladies gathered in the Duchess of Bedford's blue drawing room, where they indulged in Christmas confections, champagne, and gossip.

The prime minister's wife, Mary, kept them enthralled with stories of King William's illegitimate offspring. "Though Queen Adelaide accepts them without a qualm, the Duchess of Kent, Princess Victoria's mother, does not. John Conroy has informed the king that his bastards should be banned from Court, to protect the morals of young Victoria. Can you imagine such bare-faced hypocrisy, when all London knows Conroy is the Duchess of Kent's lover?"

"Because she has no children of her own, Adelaide enjoys young Victoria's company," Georgina remarked. "The queen will be devastated if she is deprived of her niece's company."

"William and Adelaide are the king and queen for God's sake,"

Lady Holland declared. "They should rule the Court as they bloody well please!"

"It's because Princess Victoria is heir to the throne that the Duchess of Kent acts so high and mighty. She pretends her farts smell of roses," Mary said vulgarly.

Beth laughed. "When the season begins you should throw a masquerade ball and invite the Duchess of Kent and the king's by-blows. Think of the fun we'd have when the masks were removed at midnight!"

Louisa kept a watchful eye on Georgy. When she began to look fatigued, Lu set down her glass and made their excuses. "We'd better find Johnny and finish writing the play. We're going to give Rachel a walk-on part."

When they left the drawing room, Louisa urged her sister to go up and lie down until it was time for the Christmas Eve dinner.

At the evening meal the conversation naturally gravitated toward politics. It was Lord John's opportunity to discuss the reform bill with the prime minister away from Parliament and get the input of both his father and Lord Holland, who fully supported it.

"Though I've tried often enough to introduce a bill to reduce election bribery, I've never been successful," Johnny said ruefully.

"That's because it would reveal too many skeletons in too many closets," Holland remarked. "Present company excepted, of course."

"I have a feeling the time is ripe to get the reform bill passed in the coming session," Johnny declared.

"There will be no problem getting it through the Commons," Earl Grey assured them. "It's the damned Tories in the Lords who will be the stumbling block."

The Duke of Bedford warned both his son and the prime minister, "You shouldn't send it on to the House of Lords until you are absolutely sure it will get enough votes to get it passed. I will go to

London in January and rally support for it. Henry will help me. It won't be the first time we've used our influence to bring about much needed change."

The Duchess of Bedford smiled at the prime minister. "Your son's friend Charles Bennet is a Tory. I'm sure Lord Ossulston will give you his vote. I should have invited him for Christmas. When we visited you at Howick, he was quite enamored of Georgy. And of course you can count on our dear friend Abercorn's support."

Johnny threw a glance at Louisa. "I'm so sorry James Hamilton decided to go to Ireland for Christmas. I was looking forward to his company."

The Duke of Bedford nodded. "As soon as he returns I'll be in touch with him. I'll invite him to sit with me in the Lords when they debate the reform bill."

Louisa finished her dessert and sighed. *O Lord, not long after Parliament is in session, the season will start and once again Georgy and I will be put on the marriage market.* She closed her eyes and made a wish. *I hope Georgy receives a proposal, and I hope that I escape the marriage trap!*

For Louisa, the Yule festivities seemed to go by in a flash. Jack, as Lord of Misrule, made sure the days were packed with fun and games. Christmas morning was taken up by the exchange of presents and followed by the traditional presentation of gifts to all the people who served Woburn. Jack made sure that the servants enjoyed themselves every bit as much as the Russells and their titled friends. In the evening there was the customary feast, followed by Christmas carols.

On Boxing Day, the Russell siblings performed their annual play for their parents and friends. They used old scenery that Edwin Landseer had once painted, reproducing the Old Bailey. Lord John, with a thick German accent, acted as the judge, while his brothers and sisters were brought before him on various charges of breaking the law.

Louisa, wearing a policeman's hat and a mustache and wielding a truncheon, brought in the culprits, while Georgy played ominous notes on the harpsichord.

Henry and Cosmo had been arrested for being drunk and disorderly, and were still inebriated when they arrived at Court. The judge could see nothing wrong with their behavior. "Zey look pervectly normal to me. Caze dizmizzed!"

The audience cheered the verdict.

Alexander, carrying a doctor's bag and a stethoscope, was charged with practicing medicine without a medical degree. The judge held up his hand. "I have ze cold and ze cough. What do you prescribe, Doktor?"

Alex put the stethoscope on the judge's chest and then, stroking his long beard, declared, "An enema every hour on the hour. A dripping bum is the only antidote for a dripping nose." He opened his bag and pulled out a rubber syringe. "Bend over."

"Guilty as charged!" roared the judge. "I zentence you to a doze of your own medizine."

Louisa confiscated the syringe and hauled Alex behind bars. When the prisoner held his hands over his bottom, the audience was helpless with laughter.

Next, Louisa escorted Jack before the judge. He was wearing a farmer's smock and a floppy bumpkin's hat. Under his arm he carried a mounted stag's head purloined from his father's library. Louisa read the charge: "Hunting game out of season."

The judge pointed to the evidence. "Wrong game! Zis zeason, only game allowed iz spin ze bottle!"

Jack grinned in agreement and produced a bottle of champagne, spun it, and immediately tried to kiss the policeman. Louisa hit him with her truncheon and hauled him behind bars. She tore off his smock to reveal a convict's black and white stripes.

"Just az I zuspected . . . a repeat offender. Zeven years hard labor!" The judge picked up the champagne, offered the policeman his arm, and the pair exited the stage.

The minute they left, little Rachel appeared carrying a cake. She set it on the floor in front of the prison bars and pulled a huge key from the confection. She mimed turning the cardboard key in the cardboard lock, and the prisoners escaped.

When the audience cheered, Rachel walked to center stage and took a bow.

The young people called for the adults to perform, and the Duchess of Bedford went up on the stage to sing. She was soon joined by Lady Holland and Mary Grey, and the trio raised their voices in Handel's *Messiah*. Not to be outdone, the men sang a rousing rendition of "Good King Wenceslas."

Finally, at everyone's urging, Lord John recited his favorite passage from Shakespeare's *Henry V*: "Once more unto the breach, dear friends, once more."

He finished to deafening applause, and his audience demanded more. To everyone's delight he moved on to the next act of the play and recited "This day is call'd the feast of Crispian."

The prime minister declared, "My boy, if you present the reform bill as if you were delivering Shakespeare, we'll have no trouble getting it passed."

In February, the Duke of Bedford received a letter from his son that filled him with elation. He called the family together to share the news.

"Johnny informs me that the reform bill has passed its second reading in the Commons!"

"Father, that's wonderful," Louisa declared. "I shall write him a letter to congratulate him on his accomplishment."

"The bill will be sent to the Upper House next month and I fully intend to be there for the debate."

"Darling, are you sure you're up to sitting through the long hours of debate?" his wife asked. "You could simply attend when it's time to vote."

"I wouldn't miss this debate for all the tea in China. I never felt better in my life."

"Then we shall all go up to London." She looked at her daughters. "Our wardrobes need refurbishing before the season starts."

"I shall write to Abercorn and invite him to attend the debate with me."

When her husband headed to his library, Georgina spoke to her daughters. "I don't like him to go alone. Louisa, are you feeling recovered enough for a trip to London?"

Louisa glanced at her sister. She felt guilty and virtuous at the same time. She hated deceiving her mother, but protecting her sister was both worthy and admirable. "You must stop worrying about me, Mother. I feel quite well, thank you."

"It is my responsibility to worry about you Louisa. In the past my duty toward you may have lapsed, but I have no intention of shirking it in the future."

When their mother left the room, Louisa said, "I hope I gave the right answer. Are you feeling recovered enough for the trip to London?"

"Yes I am, Lu. I can't wait for the season to start. This time it will be different. I'll have a new wardrobe, and I won't be as generous with my sexual favors. Lu, why do you think Teddy Fox treated me badly and refused to marry me, when I gave him everything he wanted?"

"Georgy, most men think themselves superior to women. If you have sex outside marriage, your value is diminished, while theirs is not. You must value yourself more."

"You are right. From now on the price for my sexual favors will be marriage."

That isn't what I meant. But I suppose we all have our price. Mine was performing on the stage at Covent Garden.

The Duchess of Bedford found her husband at his desk. "John, darling, since you are writing to Abercorn, why don't you invite him to Woburn? Then he can return to London with us. I warrant Louisa was most disappointed that he didn't visit us at Christmas."

"Good idea. An invitation may hint that we approve of the match."

Trust me, darling. Most men need more than a hint.

James Hamilton had just returned to his townhouse on Half Moon Street. He and his brother had spent Christmas and January in Ireland. Claud was exploring the possibility of running for Member of Parliament for County Tyrone, and James had spent time with Rowan Mahoney, his Irish attorney, going over the income and investments from Barons Court. He brought him a letter of introduction from Angus Murray, his Scots attorney, so they could coordinate his business affairs in both countries.

Abercorn was interested in buying an estate in the Scottish Highlands. The idea had come to him on his short visit to the Doune and Kinrara, where the magnificent vistas were breathtaking, and he had seen how much Louisa Russell loved the beautiful mountains and lochs of the Cairngorm region.

"Here's a letter for you bearing the Duke of Bedford's crest." Claud Hamilton handed the envelope to his brother and waggled his eyebrows.

James laughed at his brother's gesture and opened the letter. "It's from the duke. Lord John's reform bill has passed its second reading in the Commons, and he thinks it will go to the Upper House next month. He invites me to attend the Lords with him for the debates."

"A political invitation, when you were no doubt hoping for a personal one from Lady Louisa. It's too bad you missed spending Christmas at Woburn to further your pursuit."

James held up his hand. "There's more. He tells me both Lord John and Lady Louisa were disappointed that I was unable to spend Christmas at Woburn. He also says that the duchess was most upset with me but is willing to forgive me if I pay them a visit before they come up to London."

"Well, well. It seems the Duke and Duchess of Bedford think the sun shines out your arse, James."

"I wouldn't go that far. But I can't deny that I get on very well with the Russell family. I have reason to hope they will look favorably on my suit to wed their daughter. I shall reply, accepting their invitation and let them know I'll arrive a week from today."

When the Duke of Bedford received Abercorn's reply, he told his wife that James had accepted their invitation and would be arriving at Woburn on Monday. The duchess was glad that Jack would be away, taking Henry and Cosmo back to school. She kept the news to herself and didn't even inform the steward until the day Hamilton was to arrive.

"Mr. Burke, when James gets here would you bring him into the blue drawing room? I'd like a visit with him before my husband gets a chance to monopolize him."

"Very good, Your Grace."

Georgina took Rachel's hand. "Let's go and find your sisters."

She found them still in the breakfast room. Louisa was reading, while Georgy was on her third helping of French toast. "I'm so glad you have your appetite back, darling. When you are finished I want you both to go through your wardrobes and decide what you will take to London. Each of you make a list of the new clothes you'd like and bring it to the drawing room."

Two hours later, the Russell ladies were having an animated discussion of how many ball gowns were necessary for the London season, when Mr. Burke escorted the Marquis of Abercorn into the blue drawing room.

"James, I am delighted you came." The duchess rose and greeted him warmly. "It's been far too long since you visited Woburn."

"Your Grace." He kissed her hand. "The pleasure is mine." He saw that both Louisa and her sister were surprised to see him.

What on earth are you doing here? Louisa felt her pulse race and her cheeks grow warm. *It's obvious that Mother was expecting you, but she never said a word!*

James spoke to Georgy first. "I am so glad to see that you have recovered your health, my lady."

"Thank you, my lord," she murmured politely.

He smiled at Louisa. "You look radiant, as always, my lady." He could see that she hadn't been told he was coming.

When Rachel recognized him and began to chatter, the duchess picked her up and handed her to Georgy. "Take her up to the nursery, darling. I'd like a private word with James." When Louisa got to her feet, her mother said, "I'd like you to stay, my dear."

Georgy carried Rachel from the drawing room and the duchess closed the door. "Do sit down." Her smile was enigmatic.

He glanced at Louisa and their eyes met and held.

The Irish devil is so darkly handsome that my insides are melting.

The duchess sat down facing the marquis. "I was most upset when you didn't come for the Yule holidays, James. The week before Christmas when you were off enjoying yourself in Ireland, Louisa lost your child in a miscarriage."

The blood drained from Louisa's face, utterly devastated at her mother's words. She saw the look of stunned disbelief in Abercorn's eyes. Then she saw it change to raw, black fury. "Mother! How could you?"

"Very easily, I assure you, darling. I love you deeply. Your well-being is my first priority. I realize you are far too reticent and shy to even broach the subject, but James has every right to know. I am certain he will wish to do his duty."

Abercorn jumped to his feet and towered above them.

The duchess stood. "Her father is in complete ignorance, and that is the way it must remain. The news would kill him. It will be our secret. No one else must know."

I thought Georgy's nightmare was behind us. I thought the tragic secret would never be mentioned again. How utterly naive I was! As her mother left the room, Louisa's heartbeat thundered in her ears at the thought of being alone with Abercorn. Clutching her hands before her, she stood up to face his terrible wrath.

Chapter Nineteen

*T*he silence in the room was deafening.

Be careful what you wish for, lest it come true. James tried to control his anger but failed completely. Inwardly, he knew it was a good thing. His black fury obliterated the earth-shattering pain that had smote his heart and threatened to fell him.

"Who did this thing?" His hard features were set in stone.

Louisa pressed her lips together, closed her eyes, and shook her head in anguish.

"I will kill him."

Her eyes flew open. His dark face told her that he would keep his promise.

The irony was not lost on Abercorn. *Since I was nine years old I've had a consuming desire to make Louisa Russell my wife. Lady Lu has steadfastly refused every proposal. Now she will be forced to marry me . . . if I'll have her.*

Her breasts rose and fell from distress, her lips trembled, and she lowered her lashes to her cheeks.

James asked himself if he wanted to marry her. The answer came back a resounding *yes!* If this was the only way he could get her, then *so be it.*

She had been his exquisite ideal for so long he would not, *could not,* let her go. Her plight gave her an ethereal beauty, yet at the same time lent her an earthy quality. Her vulnerability cried out to him, so he put an iron clamp on his emotions. *I'll be damned if I'll propose to you again, Lady Lu. You are prideful enough to throw it in my teeth.*

Abercorn allowed the silence to stretch between them, waiting for her to look at him.

Finally the long hush compelled her to raise her lashes.

"I shall go and ask your father for your hand in marriage." He bowed formally and left the drawing room.

Louisa ran to the door intending to throw it open and scream, "No! No! No! I will not marry you, Abercorn!" But when her hand touched the doorknob she stopped. If she obeyed her impulse she knew she would have to betray Georgy and she could not bring herself to do that. Her love and loyalty to her sister were inviolate. She could not go back on her sacred promise, no matter the tangled web that their deception would create. *Georgy couldn't face the scandal. She would try to kill herself again. God only knows what that would do to Mother. Father could have another stroke . . .*

Alone in the empty room, Louisa faced a monumental dilemma. Finally her hand dropped to her side. *This is the lesser of two evils.* But as she thought about James Hamilton, she knew she was not fully convinced of it.

"James! I'm delighted to see you, my boy." The Duke of Bedford arose from behind his desk and came forward to shake Abercorn's hand in a warm welcome.

The duchess was telling the truth. He has no inkling of the sordid affair. "Your Grace, I had just returned from Ireland when I received your letter."

The duke bade him sit down. "Good news on the reform bill. I am counting on you to join me in the Lords for the debate. We can all travel up to London together."

"The news is most encouraging. However, I am here on another matter."

John Russell slanted an eyebrow at his formal tone.

"I am here to ask for Lady Louisa's hand in marriage."

"James! Nothing could please me more. I must confess that her mother and I have been hoping for the match. We have every confidence you will do all in your power to make Louisa happy."

Happiness is elusive, like trying to catch lightning in a bottle. "Our attorneys will have to confer before they can draw up the marriage contract." Abercorn placed Angus Murray's business card on the duke's desk. "This is my Edinburgh attorney. We'll also need input on the contract from Rowan Maloney, my Irish attorney who handles the estate affairs of Barons Court."

Bedford laughed. "Financial negotiations can get hectic and are best left to the attorneys. I'll pass these names on to my Woburn lawyer, Horace Woodfine, and ask him to get the ball rolling."

"Excellent . . . and I'll do likewise, Your Grace."

"Well, I warrant we should join the ladies. A congratulatory toast is in order."

The duke summoned his steward. "Round up the ladies, Mr. Burke, and fetch us some champagne."

Louisa, who had been staring out the drawing room window with unseeing eyes, spun around as if awakened from a trance. Her father was smiling broadly, though Abercorn was not. She could not read the expression on her mother's face, but Georgy looked curious as a monkey as Mr. Burke carried in two bottles of champagne.

John Russell handed out the wine that Mr. Burke poured. "This is a joyous day. James has asked for Louisa's hand and I have consented." He raised his glass. "Let's drink a toast to the happy couple."

"Oh, that's marvelous." The duchess raised her glass. "Congratulations, James. Lu, darling, I wish you every happiness."

"Thank you, Mother." *Why are you acting surprised?* Louisa glanced at her sister and saw a look of displeasure on her face. She did not need to look at Abercorn. She could feel his cold anger. *I'm caught in a forked cleft—damned if I do, damned if I don't.*

"Mr. Burke, plenish a room for James and ask Cook to arrange something special for dinner." Georgina radiated warm approval.

Abercorn set down his glass. "I'm sorry, Your Grace. I cannot stay over. I have pressing business in London."

"Well, in that case, I'm sure you'd like to be alone with your future bride. Lu, darling, why don't you take James into the conservatory where you won't be disturbed?"

Louisa walked quietly with downcast eyes. Abercorn nodded with formal politeness and followed her from the room.

Bedford grinned at his wife. "Good heavens, James is rigid as a board. Surely he didn't fear I would turn him down?"

"Abercorn is Irish. I warrant he doesn't have a fearful bone in his body."

"You're right, of course. That's one of the reasons I like him so much."

Georgy spoke up. "This goes against all tradition. The *eldest* daughter is supposed to marry first."

"The Russells don't follow tradition. We set the fashion," her mother declared.

John winked at his wife. "*We* certainly did."

The scent of camellias filled the air. James saw Louisa's nostrils flare as she turned to face him. He masked his anger but it was still there, goading him beneath the surface. "I have your father's blessing, and your mother's condemnation."

"I'm sorry, James."

I'm the one who's sorry. You never responded to my advances because there was someone else. He could not bear the thought that she loved another, nor that the swine had let her down. The knowledge that she had given her heart, and obviously far more, was like a knife twisting in his gut.

"Under the circumstances," she asked softly, "can we not be friends?"

Under the bloody circumstances? "No, I fear not!"

The pleading look in her eyes made him regret his sharp reply. *I'm a self-righteous bastard. She needs me. How can I reject her when she comes to me as a supplicant?* He tried to smile. "At least we can be civilized. Let us have a truce, for the sake of our families."

"A truce . . . yes."

He sought for a token to pledge their truce and reached out to pluck a camellia. His hand hesitated above a creamy white flower but then moved on to pick a crimson bloom because it was the ancestral Abercorn color.

The flare of pain in her green eyes made him aware of the insult he had inadvertently offered her. White was the symbol for a bride and her purity. Red could mean a fallen woman.

She laughed defiantly and plucked the red camellia from his fingers. "You Irish devil! You don't offer a truce—you offer war." She inhaled the crimson bloom's heady fragrance. "Red is my favorite color. War it is!"

James grabbed her shoulders and pulled her into his arms. His lips came down to ravish her mouth and show her who would be the victor in this battle of the sexes.

She pulled her mouth from his. "If you think to bend me to your will by force, you are deluding yourself, Abercorn. It will take a far greater weapon to overcome my defenses."

He felt the hot throb of his erection and pressed it against her to show her how rock hard he was. "I have such a weapon; never doubt it, Lu."

Her eyes flashed fire. "That's *Lady* Lu to you, Irishman!"

"The outraged innocent . . . I must admit you play the role well."

At his words, he glimpsed the hurt in her eyes that she quickly masked. His heart softened and he immediately regretted wounding her. "I promised to be civilized, then did the exact opposite." James cupped her face tenderly and touched his lips to hers. *She needs a protector, not an adversary.*

"Lady Louisa, will you marry me?"

"Your gallantry overwhelms me," she said sweetly.

When she tried to pull away, his hands tightened on her shoulders. "You haven't answered my question."

She glanced up into his dark eyes. *I won't. I can't.* She was covered with guilt. None of this was his fault. He was being trapped every bit as much as she was. She suddenly realized how much the proposal cost his towering pride. "Yes. I will."

On impulse she tucked the crimson camellia between her breasts. It matched the bright spots of color in her cheeks as they emerged from the conservatory.

At dinner they were seated next to each other. Jack had returned from London and offered his sincere congratulations to James. It was plain to everyone that he admired Abercorn and welcomed him as a brother.

As always at Woburn the conversation turned to politics and James felt relief. "Lord John won't have an easy time of it when the reform bill goes to the Upper House. The majority in the Lords are Tories."

"Yes, with Wellington leading the way. The prime minister and I agree that we need more Whig votes. Tomorrow I intend to write to King William and urge him to create fifty new peers."

James was reminded once again how much influence the Duke of Bedford had in politics. "That's a very shrewd suggestion, Your Grace."

"That's generous praise from a Tory," Louisa declared.

You are deliberately emphasizing our differences. James did not take the bait.

John Russell, however, couldn't resist. "Ignore her teasing, James. Mixed marriages can work out. Georgina and I are proof of it, though we sometimes came to blows."

"Lively disagreements add spice to a marriage and keep boredom at bay." Georgina raised her glass and saluted her husband.

"I warrant there will be nothing dull about our marriage," Louisa warned lightly.

James took up the challenge and raised his glass. "I'll drink to that."

Shortly after dinner, Abercorn bade the Russells good-bye.

"I shall see you in London." The duke was about to accompany James to the door until his wife took him by the arm. "I think Louisa can manage without your help, darling."

In the front entrance hall, James put on his caped greatcoat and picked up his hat.

"I'm sorry if that was difficult for you," she murmured.

"It wasn't difficult. Your family and I get along splendidly."

She raised her chin. "I'm the only fly in the ointment."

He placed his fingers beneath her chin and studied her face. "A beautiful dragonfly perhaps." He plucked the camellia from between her breasts and placed the crimson bloom in her hair. "Good night, Lady Lu."

When Louisa went upstairs, Georgy followed her into her bedroom. "You never told me that James was coming to propose to you!"

Louisa stared at her sister. "Surely you know that Mother coerced him into it? She believes I'm the one who had the miscarriage and concluded James was responsible." She was surprised that Georgy couldn't put two and two together. "Because of you, Abercorn and I are both compromised."

"You've always insisted you didn't want to marry. Why did you accept his proposal?"

"He swept me off my feet." Louisa could tell the sarcasm went over Georgy's head.

"You will be the Marchioness of Abercorn, and mayhap a duchess someday." She couldn't hide her envy. "I warrant he's a magnificent lover, too. It isn't fair that you have everything, and I have nothing!"

The hour was late when James arrived at his townhouse on Half Moon Street, but Claud hadn't yet retired. "That was a quick trip. I didn't expect you."

"I proposed to Louisa Russell and she accepted."

"Congratulations! Is the engagement official? Will it be announced in the paper?"

"It won't be announced until the marriage contract has been negotiated."

Claud grimaced. "I forgot a dynastic marriage has to have a legal and binding contract, even when it's a love match. Mother will be happy for you."

The muscle in his jaw clenched. "Yes, I must write her a letter."

When James sat down at his desk, however, the first letter he penned was to Angus Murray. After the salutation he wrote:

I am contemplating marriage with Lady Louisa, the second daughter of the Duke and Duchess of Bedford. John Russell's attorney, Horace Woodfine of Woburn, will be contacting you to negotiate the marriage contract. I am asking Rowan Maloney, my attorney from Omagh, County Tyrone, to come to Edinburgh to take part in the negotiations, and hope you will have no objection. I of course will be there when you draw up the actual contract.

In the meantime, Angus, I would appreciate it if you would do a thorough search of the Duke of Bedford's holdings, income, liabilities, debts, and mortgages. If it is within your power, I'd also like to know what is in his will.

Bedford's heir is Lord Francis Russell, Marquis of Tavistock. I would appreciate your learning as much as you can about his financial affairs.

I know I may count upon your discretion in these matters.

James Hamilton, Marquis of Abercorn

The following week the Duke and Duchess of Bedford and their two eldest daughters arrived at their London townhouse in Belgrave Square.

"We have no time to lose, Louisa. You must be fitted for your wedding gown and your trousseau. We will spare no expense—you must have an entire new wardrobe."

"What about me?" Georgy demanded.

"You'll be maid of honor, darling, and my sister Charlotte's youngest daughters will be bridesmaids."

"I meant what about my new wardrobe?"

Her mother waved her hand. "You may have everything you put on your list. We'll need more than one modiste this year. First thing in the morning we'll visit Bond Street."

The following day, Madame Madeleine arranged for two seamstresses to take up residence at Belgrave Square and work full-time on Louisa's wedding trousseau.

The bride agreed to white satin for her wedding gown and the dresses of her attendants, but when it came to the rest of her new wardrobe, Louisa decided to please herself, rather than her mother.

"I have very definite ideas about what I want. I love red and other vivid shades."

"Red is too bold a color for a bride," her mother protested.

"Not this bride. Crimson is the ancestral Abercorn color. I shall need at least one gown in that vibrant shade and a velvet cloak to match. I want lots of red accessories—hats, gloves, slippers, fans, parasols, and of course red undergarments."

"You'll shock your bridegroom," Georgina admonished.

"Yes . . . I'm looking forward to it."

At the end of March, the Duke of Bedford and the Marquis of Abercorn attended the debates on the reform bill in the House of Lords. On the final day they sat for thirteen long hours.

"I think we can consider the battle won," the duke told James with satisfaction. "Before I forget, the duchess invites you to dinner tomorrow night. I'll ask Johnny to come and we'll celebrate our victory."

"I'm sorry, Your Grace, but tomorrow I go to Edinburgh to work out details of the marriage contract. My Barons Court attorney has arrived from Ireland to consult with Angus Murray. It was good of you to send your Bedford attorney to Scotland."

"I thought it might speed things up. We cannot announce the engagement until all is settled, and I'm sure you're impatient to set the wedding date."

"Please convey my apology to the duchess. I'll send Lady Louisa flowers." *I'll order a dozen white camellias and one crimson bloom. That should provoke a smile.*

When James arrived home, Claud handed him the letter he had written to his mother.

"A servant from Bentley Priory returned this today. He said Mother was at Haddo House in Scotland."

James's dark brows drew together. Only yesterday he'd seen the Earl of Aberdeen in the Lords. "Hellfire, I hope she hasn't been there all winter. The climate is much too harsh for her health. As soon as I've seen the attorneys in Edinburgh, I'll go up to Haddo House and visit her. I'll be able to tell her in person that I'm marrying Louisa Russell."

When James arrived at the law office in Edinburgh, Angus Murray ushered him into a private consultation room and handed him the detailed report he had compiled.

"When John Russell took over Woburn from his late brother Francis, he took on debt of a quarter of a million pounds. His large income from his many estates allowed him to pay off the old debt, but he immediately borrowed a vast sum for lavish improvements at Woburn. He then took on more debt to build Endsleigh estate in Devon, and to buy and rebuild Campden Hill in Kensington. He has a good income from his estates, which he keeps in excellent repair. Lenders have always been eager to throw money at Bedford, and his debts now equal those of his late brother.

"His heir, Lord Tavistock, has borrowed a great deal on the prospects of what he will inherit. The lenders know those prospects are vast."

James glanced up from the report. "Did you learn the contents of the duke's will? What properties will the duchess inherit?"

"Only the deed to the Kensington house is in her name."

"Not Endsleigh?" James couldn't hide his surprise.

Angus shook his head. "His heir will inherit Endsleigh."

"What about the Belgrave Square House?"

"It is leased," Angus said bluntly.

"What income will the duchess have?"

"No income, my lord."

James was shocked. "Has she money of her own?"

"There are no bank accounts in her name."

"What about his other children? Has he bequeathed them property or put money in trust funds for his sons or daughters?"

Angus looked over the top of his glasses. "His heir inherits everything."

"I see." James was angry, but he knew that temper would avail him naught.

"My lord, are you ready to meet with your man from Omagh and Bedford's attorney, Horace Woodfine?"

"Quite ready, Angus."

When Abercorn entered Murray's book-lined office, the two attorneys who had been working on a document got to their feet and stepped forward.

James shook Rowan's hand. "How are you, Maloney?"

"Foine, and how's yerself, Lord Abercorn?"

"Never better." James saw that Maloney's eyes were twinkling. He held out his hand to the other attorney. "You must be Horace Woodfine. How do you do, sir?"

"I am honored to meet you, Lord Abercorn, and privileged to serve you in the auspicious matter of drawing up the wedding contract."

"Shall we be seated, gentlemen." James took the chair behind Angus Murray's large oak desk and waited until the three attorneys sat down. "Lady Louisa's welfare is paramount to me." He glanced at Maloney and Murray, and they knew he wanted Woodfine to speak first.

Horace cleared his throat. "The Duke of Bedford is a generous man. The marriage portion will be paid directly to you, Lord Abercorn." He spread his hands. "Lady Louisa's dowry is the grand sum of five thousand pounds."

There was a long silence before Abercorn spoke. "I think not, Woodfine."

Bedford's attorney was taken aback at his authoritative tone.

"Make a note of this, Murray. Lady Louisa's dowry will be twelve thousand pounds." He heard Woodfine gasp. "Plus, Lady Louisa is to have a personal allowance of one thousand pounds." James paused then added, "Per annum."

"That is out of the question, Your Lordship."

James continued as if he hadn't heard him. "Take this down, Rowan. If I predecease my wife, she will receive a lump sum of ten thousand pounds, and five thousand each year thereafter from the income of Barons Court."

"That is most generous, Your Lordship," Woodfine acknowledged faintly. "But I doubt the Duke of Bedford will agree to a marriage portion of twelve thousand."

James smiled. "With your negotiating skills, I'm sure he will, Woodfine. Would you excuse us for a moment?"

It took a minute for Horace Woodfine to realize Abercorn was actually asking him to step outside while he conferred with his own attorneys. He nodded stiffly and left.

Rowan Maloney couldn't hide his amusement. Angus Murray raised his eyebrows. "You appear to be very confident."

"I am. The duchess will persuade her husband. Draw up the contract in the amounts I have stated. I won't accept a penny less. I want the money put in trust for Lady Louisa, but neither she nor Woodfine must know. Keep that out of the contract."

James opened the door. "You may come in now." He looked at the three men. "Well, I think we are done for now. I'm on my way to Aberdeenshire to visit my mother. I shall be back to put my stamp of approval on the marriage contracts before I return to London. I thank you for your excellent service."

Chapter Twenty

"This is exactly what I had in mind." Lady Louisa stood before the cheval glass in an emerald green gown. One of the Belgrave Square sitting rooms had been turned into a sewing room, and it was awash in new garments and bolts of brilliant material. She raised her hem and revealed a frilly turquoise petticoat. "Such a shocking contrast. I love it!"

"I had no idea your taste in clothes was so bold, Louisa." Georgina examined a tangerine walking dress. "What color undergarments do you intend to wear with this?"

"Primrose yellow, of course."

Her sister Georgy began to hum "Oranges and Lemons."

"Don't mock me. I never again have to wear the insipid dresses of a debutante. One of the pleasures and privileges of being a married woman is that I will be free to set my own outrageous style." *I warrant it will be the only pleasure of being a wife!*

"Stop the carriage!" James, wearing a heavy wool greatcoat, stepped down from the coach that had just passed through the majestic Grampian Mountains. He climbed up beside his driver, then lifted himself onto the carriage roof and stood with legs apart.

"Look at this place." He pointed to a great stone house, built in the turreted style of a castle. "It's perfect." His arm swept out to indicate the vast scenic view. "Just look at those two waterfalls! I've never seen anything as magnificent as this loch in my life."

The beauty of the place cried out to him and, as often happened to Abercorn when he saw something that was exquisitely lovely, he longed to possess it. He climbed down from his perch, consulted his map, and saw that the long body of water was Loch Laggan. He made a note of it before he told his coachman to drive on.

It took two more days of travel to reach Aberdeenshire. This far north, winter still had its grip on the land, even though it was April. When James saw the huddled sheep on the craggy slopes and the herds of shorthorn cattle roaming the rolling hills, he was reminded that Aberdeen had cleared the land of all its people to accommodate the animals. He had only contempt for a man who felt no obligation to the peasant farmers who had populated these lands for centuries.

As Haddo House came into view, James acknowledged that it was a large, substantial dwelling, but its design lacked any vestige of imagination or beauty. The stableman who helped his driver unharness his carriage horses had a thick brogue. James shook his hand and thanked him with a sovereign, knowing it was the only gold he was likely to receive in Aberdeen's employ.

His heart stood still when he entered the sitting room and saw his mother. She was thin and sallow, frail as an old lady though she was only forty.

"James!" Her face was wreathed in smiles as she struggled from her rocking chair before the fire.

"Mother." He took her into his arms. "Have you spent the entire winter here?"

She nodded. "I got bronchitis and wasn't fit to travel. Aberdeen had to take the boys back to Harrow, and take his seat in Parliament."

He eased her back into her chair and knelt before her. "I should have taken you to live at Barons Court long ago."

She cupped his cheek tenderly. "You're a grown man with no need of a mother. My duty is to my little boy. Arthur is only two. I worry about what will happen to him when I'm—" She didn't finish the sentence, though it was plain what she meant.

James kissed her hands. "Nothing is going to happen to you. It's already spring in London. Once you're strong enough to travel back to Stanmore, the warm English weather will restore your health." *I wish I believed the things I'm telling her.*

"How's Claud?"

"Thriving. He's ambitious to become a Member of Parliament for County Tyrone."

"I never have to worry about Claud. He has you to look after him."

James got up from his knees and took a chair opposite his mother. "I have some news." He knew he must mask both his anger and his pain, and give no hint at the devastation he felt over Louisa. "I proposed marriage to Lady Louisa Russell, and she has accepted."

"James, you're engaged to be married to the Duke of Bedford's daughter?"

"Yes, as soon as the marriage contract is drawn up. Louisa is the second daughter."

Harriet smiled into her son's eyes. "I don't need to ask if it's a love match. You promised me you would never marry without love."

I loved her for years, but if I'm being honest, I don't know how I feel about her now.

"I like the Russell family very much. They welcome me with open arms. I can't wait for you to meet Lady Louisa. I'm sure you will love her."

"I must regain my strength so I can travel to London. Under no circumstances can I miss the wedding of my firstborn son. I'm so happy for you, James."

He was relieved to see that two-year-old Arthur had a sturdy

Scots nursemaid to take the burden of the lively toddler from his mother. Aberdeen's spinster daughters from his first marriage were also in residence at Haddo House. When James saw the pair of females he got another shock. They were both ill with tuberculosis, and the elder one looked to be at death's door. *It is inexcusable of Aberdeen to have abandoned his wife and daughters to the rigors of a cruel Highland winter. I warrant they haven't stepped outside since October.*

"I'm so enjoying your company, James." His mother sat beside him in his carriage, surveying the bleak landscape through the window. He had wrapped her in furs and insisted on taking her for a ride. He hoped the fresh air would do her good. But the outing sapped her strength, and he had to carry her into the house when they returned.

When the doctor from Aberdeen made his weekly call, James took him aside. "My mother believes it was bronchitis that made her too ill to travel back to London. I want you to tell me the truth. Is she, too, suffering from consumption?"

"It was a severe case of bronchitis, or more likely pneumonia, Lord Abercorn." The Scots physician hesitated. "You ask for the truth. The Countess of Aberdeen has never recovered from the birth of her last child. She is, and always will be, a semi-invalid."

James's heart ached for his mother. "*Why* has she not recovered?"

"It's a woman's ailment. Most men prefer not to know these things."

"I am not most men, doctor. I do want to know."

"The countess suffers from a fallen womb from childbearing. She also has a tumor."

James's heart constricted. "How long, doctor?"

"Difficult to say, my lord. A year . . . perhaps two."

James nodded. "Thank you for being straightforward, doctor."

The following day, the wind dropped. A pale sun came out and showed the buds in the trees. Wrapped up warmly and leaning on her son's arm, Harriet accompanied him on a slow walk around the gardens.

"You look happy today."

She smiled up at him. "You warm my heart."

Two days later, the Earl of Aberdeen arrived on estate business. The lambing and shearing that took place in the same month was a source of great wealth. The health of his wife and grown daughters was a secondary concern.

When he saw that Abercorn was visiting his mother, the surprise on the earl's face was replaced by a smug, self-satisfied look. Aberdeen was bursting to impart his news.

Before he could do so, however, his wife said, "James came to tell me he is to be married. Lady Louisa Russell, the daughter of the Duke and Duchess of Bedford, has accepted his proposal."

"Congratulations on achieving a dynastic marriage. Too bad the Russells are staunch Whigs. They've just suffered a crippling setback," Aberdeen declared with glee. "The reform bill was thrown out in committee. Wellington and I led the Tories to reject it. Prime Minister Earl Grey had no choice but to resign."

James was stunned. He had had every confidence it would be passed. *No wonder you look like the cat that swallowed the rat. This will be a terrible blow to Lord John and the Duke of Bedford.* "Has King William asked Wellington to form a government?"

"He has indeed. I must get back to London as soon as possible. We Tories will be in power again, and I must be ready to take up my post as foreign secretary."

That night James packed his bags. He had to finish the business with his attorneys in Edinburgh and get back to London. Though he was a Tory, he was a staunch supporter of the reform bill. For too many years, bribery had been rampant in politics.

James sought a private good-bye with his mother. "Though I'd like nothing better than to see you back at Stanmore, I honestly believe the rigors of the long journey would be too much for you at the moment."

"It would sap what little strength I have."

With a lump in his throat, he embraced her warmly. "Promise me you won't undertake the journey until you are strong enough. My wedding can wait."

"Riots are breaking out across the country. Bristol Town Hall has been set afire," Bedford informed his guests. He had invited Earl Grey, Lord Holland, and his son, Lord John, to dinner at Belgrave Square to discuss the deteriorating political situation.

"The property damage in Nottingham is widespread, I hear," Holland said.

"Middle-class landholders are demanding a say in the electorate. They are sick and tired of the corruption in government," Johnny declared.

Earl Grey said, "I heard in confidence that Wellington is having difficulty forming a government. I am out of favor with the king at the moment." He gave Bedford a speculative look. "But I warrant you still have sway with him, John."

"I have an idea." The Duchess of Bedford set down her knife and fork, and Louisa looked at her mother expectantly. "If there are riots in Nottingham, no one will be more concerned than the Duke of Devonshire. I'm sure you could persuade him to go with you to seek an audience with the king."

Louisa glanced quickly at her sister at mention of the Devonshires; Georgy's face looked like a thundercloud. *Poor Georgy is still furious that Devonshire's heir didn't make an offer for her.*

Johnny looked hopeful. "Devonshire has been lobbying for the reform bill in the Lords, every chance he got."

"He's afraid if we don't reform, the aristocracy could fall," Bedford declared.

Louisa's eyes widened. "Do you mean civil war?"

The men at the table looked at one another. "By God, that's it!" her father declared. "I shall go to King William and tell him he faces civil war unless he creates enough reformist peers to pass the bill. The Duke of Devonshire will back me up."

"Hello, Angus. How are the negotiations coming along?" James took a seat in his Edinburgh attorney's book-lined office.

"Woodfine's offer went up from five to six thousand. Then he dithered for a week and would not commit a penny more. I realized he did not have Bedford's authority to go higher. So I drew up the marriage contract exactly as you stipulated and asked him to present it to the duke. I sent a personal letter to Bedford pointing out how extremely generous the terms of the contract were to Lady Louisa, should she be widowed."

"You challenged him to match my generosity."

"Happily, it worked. Yesterday, I received the marriage contract with John Russell's signature on it." Murray unfolded the crackling document and James Hamilton signed it.

"Excellent work. I have another task for you, Angus. On my journey, I came across a magnificent estate on the south shore of Loch Laggan. I intend to buy it. Find out who owns it and what price he is asking. I'll sell some of my lands in Paisley to pay for it."

"James, how lovely to see you!" The Duchess of Bedford embraced her future son-in-law. "It was good of you to travel to Scotland to expedite the wedding contract."

"Hello, James. I hope you had a pleasant journey." Louisa poured them all sherry. *You are sinfully handsome. I always forget the impact you have on my senses.*

James took the glass Louisa offered and then raised her fingers to his lips.

It was a formal gesture. She saw that his eyes did not light up at the sight of her.

The duchess raised her glass. "Now that the contract has been signed, we can set the wedding date. May is the perfect month for nuptials."

"Your Grace, I took the opportunity to visit my mother at Haddo House to tell her about my engagement to Lady Louisa. Unfortunately I found her in poor health. She has been extremely ill all winter, and she is not yet strong enough to endure the rigors of a journey to London. I'm afraid we will have to postpone the wedding."

"James, I'm so sorry." Lu's heart went out to him. *No wonder his eyes look so bleak. Postponing the wedding is no hardship. Perhaps we can put it off for months.* She immediately felt remorse and said contritely, "I hope with all my heart the Countess of Aberdeen soon regains her health."

The Duke of Bedford entered the drawing room. "James! I'm so glad you're back safely. Did you run into any trouble in the northern counties?"

"I stopped at an inn in Derby and heard about the Nottingham riots. I gave Birmingham a wide berth and came by way of Bedfordshire. This is a direct result of the reform bill being thrown out. I'm sorry, Your Grace. Can anything be done?"

"I'm just back from the palace. I believe Devonshire and I have convinced the king that this unrest may deteriorate into civil war if he doesn't act decisively."

"I was visiting Mother at Haddo House when Aberdeen arrived. He couldn't wait to tell me the bill hadn't passed, and that Wellington had been asked to form a government."

"Tensions are running so high that the Duke of Wellington has been unsuccessful in his attempts. Tomorrow, the king will return Earl Grey to power. William is going to tell Wellington and his close colleagues to abstain from voting so it can be passed."

"I don't want to miss this. I'll be in my seat every day until the bill passes."

"Good man. Our votes will be needed."

Georgina told her husband that Lady Aberdeen remained in poor health and was unable to travel from Scotland to London.

"I'm so sorry, James. I know you are as eager as we are to announce the engagement. Postponing the wedding will be a great disappointment for both you and Louisa."

None regretted the postponement as much as the Duchess of Bedford. Delayed weddings ran the risk of being canceled. The bride's mother wanted her daughter safely married to James Hamilton, and sooner rather than later. Her thoughts darted about, searching for a solution to the vexing dilemma.

An hour later when they sat down to dinner, Georgina knew she had the answer. "I've just had the most marvelous idea. We can have the wedding at Gordon Castle! When I was a girl, I remember visiting Haddo House with my parents. They are only about twenty-five miles apart."

"An excellent plan," John Russell declared. "Ever since your brother George inherited his dukedom and Gordon Castle, he's deluged the family with invitations."

"George will be absolutely thrilled to host the entire affair." Georgina spoke directly to Abercorn. "Since your mother cannot come to London, we'll take the wedding to her. The journey to the Highlands and the preparations will take the best part of a month. By then, with any luck, Lady Aberdeen will be able to make the short journey to Gordon Castle. She'll be able to stay as long as she wishes."

"Your generosity overwhelms me, Your Grace," James said sincerely. "I had the privilege of meeting the Duke of Gordon when I took advantage of his hospitality at Kinrara." He glanced at Louisa and saw that she looked stunned at her mother's suggestion. *I wish things were as they were between us that day we rode together to Kin-*

rara. Her vulnerability cried out to him, and he suddenly realized that none of the anger he felt was directed at Louisa. *The swine who took advantage of her innocence must bear all the blame.*

It slowly dawned on James that love cannot be turned on and off at will. He had given his heart to Lady Lu years ago, and it was still in her keeping. *I am about to take vows to cherish her, and cherish her I will.*

"Louisa, you and James must decide on a date before he leaves, so I may send a letter by courier to my brother immediately," Georgina declared. "I can't wait to tell Charlotte of our plans. She will jump at the chance to take her family to Gordon Castle."

After dinner, Louisa took James into the library. She paced to the window and then turned to face him. "I'm sorry you've been coerced into marrying me."

He closed the distance between them and looked down at her. "I'm not the kind of man who can be forced into things, Lu. I've always wanted to marry you." He took her hand in his and squeezed it.

"What about this Gordon Castle idea? Wouldn't you just rather postpone it?"

"Your mother made the suggestion to accommodate my mother. Your family is exceedingly generous. Mother's health is precarious, and since I want her to see us marry, I don't think postponing it is a good idea."

"James, I'm so sorry. We'd better set a date." She picked up a calendar from her father's desk. "How about the first Friday in June?"

"Perfect. That way we can spend the whole summer in Ireland."

Louisa's heart began to hammer. *It's really going to happen!* Her knees turned to water. *I'm not cut out to be a wife. If you marry me, Abercorn, it will be the disappointment of a lifetime.*

Lady Louisa's wedding finery and trousseau were packed for Scotland. The rest of her clothes and most cherished personal belongings were put into trunks and transported to Barons Court in Ireland.

While the Duke of Bedford and the Marquis of Abercorn re-mained in London so they could vote in the House of Lords on the reform bill, the duchess accompanied the bride-to-be and the rest of her children to Gordon Castle. Lady Bedford's sister Charlotte, the Dowager Duchess of Richmond, and her three youngest daughters traveled with them. In all, five carriages and two baggage wagons were needed to transport the wedding party. Once they arrived, it took two full weeks to prepare for the nuptials.

Chapter Twenty-One

"I've been on tenterhooks. Where on earth have you been? You do realize our daughter's wedding is the day after tomorrow?" Georgina was weak with relief.

"I could hardly leave before the reform bill was passed. We celebrated with Johnny, then set out the next day."

"Father, I'm so happy that Parliament is to be reformed." Louisa kissed his cheek. "You and Johnny must be jubilant after all these years."

"The whole country is celebrating. There were fireworks displays everywhere."

"Congratulations, darling. I'm so proud of Johnny." Georgina glanced through the window. "Where on earth is James? We cannot have a wedding without a groom."

"He's staying at Haddo House tonight. He will accompany his mother here tomorrow. Do stop worrying, darling."

"Oh good. We've prepared a suite with a fireplace for the Earl and Countess of Aberdeen. I'm so thankful my father spared no expense when he had the castle rebuilt."

"It has a Georgian elegance not seen in many castles. The drainage system alone must have cost a king's ransom, not to mention the manicured lawns."

"John, welcome to our humble home," George Gordon jested. "The deer park is full of green plover, and the salmon are running in the Spey."

His wife, Elizabeth, came forward to greet Bedford. "Welcome, John. It is such a delight to have all the children here."

John embraced her warmly. "I suspect you are being kind. They are young savages. It is so good of you both to give my daughter this splendid wedding."

"It is our pleasure. Georgina and Charlotte have done all the work. No detail has been overlooked. The turreted tower has been turned into the bridal chamber."

He saw the blush on Louisa's cheek and smiled at his favorite daughter. "It sounds like it's going to be the perfect fairy-tale wedding."

Lord help me get through this fairy-tale wedding without disappointing my family.

The following afternoon the bridegroom arrived accompanied by his brother Claud, his mother, and his stepfather. The Earl and Countess of Aberdeen were warmly welcomed by the bride's mother and her uncle, the Duke of Gordon. James made the introductions to all the Russells and their extended family.

"This is Louisa," he said simply as he introduced his wife-to-be to his mother.

Louisa curtsied gracefully. *She looks so frail; my heart goes out to her.* "I am most happy to meet you, Lady Aberdeen."

"Please call me Harriet. James told me you were lovely, but your beauty takes my breath away."

The mother of the bride stepped forward. "We mustn't keep you standing here. Let me take you up to the suite the Duchess of Gordon has had especially prepared for you. You'll need a sanctuary away from the noise of the Russell siblings. I'll order you some tea.

Please don't hesitate to ask for anything that will make your stay more comfortable."

"Thank you. You are most thoughtful." Harriet glanced across the room and saw her husband in conversation with their host, the Duke of Gordon, and the bride's father.

"Don't worry about Aberdeen," Georgina advised, as she saw George pour the earl a dram of Scotch. "Men much prefer talk of horses, hunting, and fishing. They pretend that wedding details bore them to death, but in reality I warrant it is fear of commitment that paralyzes them."

Harriet smiled at Louisa and then glanced up at James. "Please bring her up in a little while so we can get to know each other."

"I will, Mother. Let's take you up and get you settled first."

James shows such tender concern for her. Louisa sighed at the gentle way he placed a powerful arm at the small of her back and led her toward the grand staircase.

"I hope my brother knows how lucky he is."

Louisa turned and smiled at Claud. "Welcome to Gordon Castle."

"Are you ready to take on the Irish devil?" he teased.

"Oh Lord, I don't know. It has all happened so quickly."

"Quickly?" Claud laughed. "James has been extolling your virtues for a decade."

Virtues? Louisa inwardly shuddered at his choice of words.

"Everything comes to the one who waits."

"Yes . . . everything," she said faintly.

Georgy came up and took Claud's arm in a possessive gesture. "Lu, must you monopolize all the attractive men? Isn't one Hamilton enough for you?"

"More than enough," she murmured apprehensively.

"Claud, let me give you a tour of the castle. I never did find the dungeons—perhaps we can discover them together. The thought of instruments of torture makes me want to scream with excitement," Georgy said suggestively.

Claud waggled his eyebrows at Louisa and allowed Georgy to lead him away.

Louisa stared after them with a sense of dismay. *I hope she behaves herself.* Luckily she was distracted from her thoughts by James.

"Mother is looking forward to a visit with you, while you can both be private."

"Let's go up now." Louisa took his arm.

James escorted her upstairs and opened the door to his mother's suite. "I'll leave you alone together, but I'll be back to collect you in half an hour."

"Louisa, my dear, do come and sit down." Harriet reclined on a chaise longue before the fire, and her daughter-to-be took a chair close to her.

"My lady, it means so much to James to have you at our wedding. The rigors of the journey to Gordon Castle are bound to take their toll, and it is most generous-hearted of you to make the sacrifice."

"'Tis easy to see you consider others before yourself. James is fortunate that he will have such a caring wife. Meeting you reassures me that all my hopes and dreams will come true. Your marriage will be a happy one because you are in love."

"I will try my best to make it so." Louisa tried to give her a convincing smile, though on the inside she felt anything but confident about their future happiness.

"My first marriage was a love match. I suppose bliss like that only comes along once in a lifetime." Harriet sighed. "James was witness only to my marriage to Aberdeen. That's the reason he is determined to have a joyful marriage. I know he will do all in his power to make you happy."

Louisa chose her words carefully. "It's obvious you love him very much."

"You will delight in Barons Court. It is a magical place. I envy you your summer. My time there was all too short. Promise me you will enjoy every single day."

"I am looking forward to Barons Court. I have never been to Ireland." *At least that is no lie.*

When James tapped on the door and opened it, Louisa was relieved. The last thing she wanted was to say something that would hint at her and James's strained relationship.

Harriet had suffered enough unhappiness and ill health, and Lu didn't want to add to her burden. "Dinner is at seven, but if you would prefer it, I can bring you up a tray."

"Thank you, that's most thoughtful. But I will come down. I want to spend time with both of you. Just seeing you together gives me pleasure."

As they descended the stairs, James said, "Thank you for making her happy. 'Tis obvious Mother approves of you."

Louisa was aware of the irony in his words. "She is a lovely lady. She gives me her approval unstintingly."

James changed the subject. "You still have to sign the marriage contract. Your father and I agreed on the terms weeks ago, and the attorneys have duly witnessed it. Your signature is only a formality, of course. Shall we go to the library and take care of it before dinner?"

"Yes, if you like." She walked passively beside him down the long hallway that led to Gordon Castle's library. Louisa, always sensitive to the emotions of others, could feel the cold anger that emanated from Abercorn. His polite manner emphasized rather than masked his true inner feelings.

In the library, the document sat on the huge black oak desk, which was illuminated by a pair of silver stag-horn lamps. Louisa sat down at the desk and pulled the crackling contract toward her. "I think this is a mistake. My marriage portion is five thousand pounds, not twelve."

"There is no mistake." James walked over and closed the library door before he came back to the desk. "I negotiated a dowry of twelve thousand, and a personal allowance for you of one thousand per annum."

Louisa sprang to her feet. Her passivity vanished in a flash. "My father agreed to pay you twelve thousand?" she demanded incredulously. "He bought you for me! This is nothing short of a bribe!" Green fire flashed in her eyes, as she smote the desk with her fist. "You Irish swine! The insult to me is intolerable. I have never been so humiliated in my life!"

"Keep your voice down, mistress."

"Give me no orders, Abercorn. My family is buying me a husband. The exorbitant price you have demanded is more than double my dowry, and you expect me to keep my voice down? The wedding is off! I'll be no bartered bride."

He stepped close and towered above her. "That is the most selfish thing I've ever heard—selfish, cruel, and thoughtless. Your family adores you. They want only your happiness. For evidence, look at all the planning they have put into this wedding. To thank them you want to fling it in their face and refuse to go through with it."

Louisa was incensed to be called *selfish*. The accusation was totally, completely false. "It's a mockery!"

"If I am willing, you should be able to swallow your self-righteous pride."

Louisa gasped at his insult.

"You may not care how much you hurt *your* mother, but I will not permit you to hurt mine. We *will* be married tomorrow, Lady Lu."

A picture of Harriet came full-blown into her mind. She knew James's mother was dying. How could she hurt her? *For that matter, how can I hurt my own family?* Pride came to her rescue. She raised her chin defiantly. "My father has bought your name. 'Tis the only thing I want from you. I agree to become Lady Abercorn, tomorrow. But the marriage will be in name only."

"An excellent arrangement. Your wishes mirror mine exactly." He picked up the pen and handed it to her.

She plucked it from his fingers with a smile, and in exquisite penmanship signed: *Louisa Jane Russell*. Then she deliberately shook the pen and marred the legal document with myriad, ugly inkblots.

"They look like angels," Louisa whispered to her father, as her young attendants walked down the aisle of the castle chapel. Little Rachel was paired with Alexander; her brothers Henry, Cosmo, and Jack accompanied her female cousins. Claud, who was his brother's groomsman, escorted Georgy, her maid of honor.

John Russell squeezed his daughter's hand and led her toward the altar where James Hamilton awaited his bride.

"Dearly beloved, we are gathered together here in the sight of God, and in the face of this congregation, to join together this man and this woman in holy matrimony," the minister solemnly intoned.

Louisa did not glance up at the groom but kept her eyes straight ahead. The altar was draped in purple velvet embroidered with gold. Tall scented tapers in silver candlesticks flickered beside alabaster vases filled with white lilies and roses. Through her veil she could see that in the bouquet she carried, white heather was tucked between the other flowers. White heather was traditional at Scottish weddings. It was a symbol of good fortune and assured the bride that all her wishes would come true. It brought a lump to her throat.

Her mind wandered back to last night's dinner. Both she and James had balanced precariously on the knife edge of disaster. Not by word or look did they convey to their families that aught was amiss between them. By unspoken, mutual consent they played the role of a loving couple.

"I will."

Abercorn's deep voice brought her thoughts back to the present and she realized the minister had asked him if he would take her to be his wedded wife. She gave her full attention to the Scots clergyman.

"Louisa Jane, wilt thou have this man to thy wedded husband, to live together after God's ordinance in the holy estate of matrimony? Wilt thou obey him, and serve him, love, honor, and keep him, in sickness and in health, and forsaking all other, keep thee only unto him, so long as ye both shall live?"

"I will." *You are always the consummate actress, Louisa.*

"Who giveth this woman to be married to this man?"

"I do." Her father took her hand and gave it to James Hamilton.

You giveth twelve thousand pounds for this woman to be married to this man! Louisa examined her emotions and, here in the sight of God, knew she could not lie. Though the amount of her dowry was exorbitant, the real reason she had declared their marriage would be in name only was because she was afraid. It would be her shield and buckler against intimacy with the devastatingly attractive Irishman.

They pledged their troth to each other, and then James slipped the wedding ring on her finger and the minister pronounced them man and wife. Louisa raised her veil and lowered her lashes as her husband bent his head and gave her a chaste kiss.

Ethereal voices of the choir in the gallery floated above the congregation as Louisa turned from the altar. She saw the beaming faces of her young attendants and the smiles of her family in the front row. The ancient chapel was filled to overflowing by the Duke of Gordon's neighbors and the entire castle staff, all wearing white favors.

When the music of the wedding march began, James took her arm and led her down the aisle. As they emerged from the chapel, a flag went up, and the crowd that had gathered outside began to cheer. A piper led the wedding party back to the castle.

Amid the festive air the bride and groom were soon separated. Every guest embraced Louisa and wished her happiness. James was congratulated by the males and kissed by the females.

Long buffet tables groaned under huge platters of Spey salmon, roast beef, venison, and lamb. Stuffed game birds, running the gamut from grouse and plover to heron and swan, tempted every palate. Dishes of vegetables vied for space with salvers of shellfish and trays of fruit such as figs and peaches imported from warmer climes. Ale, port, claret, and Scotch whiskey flowed aplenty to wash down the copious amounts of food.

All the Gordon staff and tenants were invited to join the aristocratic guests and partake of the food, drink, and Scottish dancing. After a particularly boisterous reel, Claud told his brother, "The members of this family certainly know how to enjoy themselves. You are a lucky dog, James."

When it was full dark, a towering seven-tiered wedding cake was rolled into the ballroom. On top sat a sugared replica of the chapel, with the figures of the bride and groom and their wedding attendants standing before the altar.

Louisa and James made the first cut of the cake with an ancient Gordon sword. The wedding cake was served with champagne. The toasts began and lasted for two hours, before the Highland dancing resumed.

At midnight, all who could still walk made their way outside to watch a brilliant fireworks display. Georgina took her daughter by the hand and led her to James. "Now is your chance to escape. Hurry, before I start to cry."

Abercorn gave his mother-in-law a quick embrace. "Thank you for everything." He took his bride's hand and they made a dash for the stairs.

Only when the bridal chamber door closed did they feel free to drop their pretense.

"Allow me to compliment you on your performance. You made everyone happy today." James removed his formal coat and silk neck cloth.

"Thank heaven it's over." Louisa removed her headdress. *But it isn't over; it has only just begun.* She stared at the wide bed that some romantic had strewn with white rose petals. She glanced up as James walked across the spacious tower room to the far window, ostensibly to watch the fireworks.

He's being civilized, giving me privacy to undress. She removed her wedding gown and undergarments then slipped on the white silk nightdress that lay across her pillow. She stared at her husband's back and realized that the gulf between them was far greater than the distance across the room.

She turned the lamp down and got into bed. "Good night, Lord Abercorn."

Without turning from the window, he said softly, "Good night, Lu."

James waited an hour, giving her ample time to fall asleep, before he began to undress. The chamber boasted a comfortable chaise longue where he could sleep. He picked up the nightshirt, which had been provided to preserve his bride's modesty. When he slipped it over his head, it came down to only his navel. He realized the nightshirt had been cut in half and smiled at the innocent prank of Louisa's young brothers. He removed it and lay down naked, which was the way he always slept.

He lay quietly but sleep eluded him. Finally he got up and moved silently to the bed. In the pale moonlight Louisa appeared ethereal. Her lovely face, in repose, had a look of vulnerability that tugged at his heartstrings.

He remembered his thoughts when he told his mother that he'd asked Louisa to marry him: *I loved her for years, but I don't know how I feel about her now.* As he looked down at his sleeping wife, James knew exactly how he felt. *I'm still in love with her. She is my heart's desire.* If he was being honest, it was his towering pride that had been deeply wounded at the thought that she could love another.

He picked up his coat and removed the boutonnière. Then he laid the sprig of white heather beside her on the pillow.

When he went back to his couch, he lay with his arms folded beneath his head and allowed his fury full rein. *I will find the man responsible for hurting her, so help me God!*

Chapter Twenty-Two

"Ireland certainly lives up to her reputation for beauty. Every view pleases the eye and captures the imagination." Louisa gazed through the window of the carriage at the picturesque Sperrin Mountains. "How far is Barons Court?"

"We are on the estate now. It covers twenty-seven miles. The house lies in a sheltered valley of the foothills." James cast her a glance of admiration. "You are a very good traveler." The day after their wedding, they had left for Glasgow, where they had taken a steamer to Londonderry.

"I warrant that's because of your good planning. The journey didn't take too many days." Louisa was relieved that Abercorn had taken two cabins aboard the steamer and was honoring their agreement. He treated her with respect, which helped to maintain a polite facade, even though the strain between them was just beneath the surface.

She drew in her breath as the setting sun reflected on a lake, turning the water to glistening gold. They passed two more lakes, and then a lovely gray stone house with a clock tower came into view. "Oh, it's enchanting!"

James laughed. "That's just the lodge."

The carriage drove through the arch below the clock tower into vast parkland with its own wood. Beyond the park rose Barons Court, a magnificent Palladian mansion, complete with portico and classical Roman columns. "It's most impressive." *It's overwhelming. I wonder if this is the way Mother felt when she first saw Woburn? No, she was far too sophisticated and worldly to be intimidated.* Louisa raised her chin. "Mother will love it. She promised to come for a visit before summer ends."

Before the coach rolled to a complete stop in the courtyard, James jumped out so he could help Louisa alight. The staff of Barons Court was gathered on the portico to greet the master and his bride.

"This is Kate Connelly, our head housekeeper, and her hard-working staff. I'm proud to present my wife, Lady Louisa. I know you will serve her with devotion."

The men servants bowed and the women curtsied. "Lady Abercorn."

"Oh please, no formality unless we have important guests." She shook each servant's hand. She asked them their names. Their faces were now wreathed with smiles. "Thank you for your warm welcome. I hope you will be patient with me. I have much to learn."

"Everyone inside!" James took her arm and led the way. He leaned toward her and murmured, "Ye've kissed the Blarney Stone, begod. Ye'll have 'em eatin' outta yer hand."

Just beyond the entrance was a large round room covered by a dome. A polished table sat at its center, holding a lead crystal vase filled with blue delphiniums. "This is the rotunda. The sun is setting now, but during the day, it lets in all the light."

"It's a marvelous design."

"Yes, it has been updated. I've hired Sir Richard Morrison to redo portions of the house. I want you to redesign the rooms the way you'd like them. We'll work on the plans together."

You don't really want my ideas. You are just being polite.

"Would ye like a tour of Barons Court, Lady Abercorn?"

"Not tonight, thank you, Mrs. Connelly."

"I suspect all my wife wants is a bath and a comfortable bed."

At a signal from the housekeeper, the staff returned to their duties in the kitchen or elsewhere. Only two young women remained. "Ye'll be needing a lady's maid. This is Meg and the plump one is Molly. The choice is yours, Lady Abercorn."

Louisa looked at their eager faces and knew it would be cruel to choose one over the other. "I'd like both of you. Meg can run me a bath, and Molly can help me unpack."

A manservant had brought in the bags from the carriage. "Did my luggage arrive from England, Mrs. Connelly?"

"Sure an' all. I had everything taken to the master bedchamber. But nothing has been unpacked. I wouldn't let anyone open your boxes and trunks until you were here to supervise." Kate Connelly hesitated. "There was a furniture crate with a lovely dressing table set. I took the liberty of putting it in the chamber adjoining the master bedroom. It will make a lovely boudoir for you, my lady."

"Thank you. That is a wedding present from my parents. The dressing table, mirrors, and gold basins once belonged to Josephine Bonaparte."

"Would ye believe it?" Mrs. Connelly took it in her stride.

James picked up his bag, and the manservant took the two that belonged to Louisa. Abercorn led the way and his wife and her two young maids followed. Louisa's eyes widened with pleasure as they entered the great hall where all the lights had been lit and logs were burning on a great open hearth. Beyond an archway was the main staircase.

The master bedchamber was on the second floor of the east wing so it would get the morning sunlight through its floor-to-ceiling windows. The room was huge. Though the bed was massive, there was plenty of space for cushioned easy chairs and a games table that sat before a large stone fireplace. Tall bookcases flanked the mirrored wardrobe, and a crimson Oriental carpet gave the room a rich warmth.

Meg bobbed a curtsy. "I'll see to yer bath, my lady."

Louisa stood awkwardly as James set his bag down beside a pile of luggage and trunks. Most of them belonged to her, but a few belonged to Abercorn.

"We'll sort all this out tomorrow." James noticed her disquiet and knew immediately what caused it. He moved toward a paneled door and opened it. "Milady's boudoir."

"Thank you." Louisa felt weak with relief as she stepped into the room and saw that it contained a bed. The chamber was smaller than the master bedroom, but it was elegantly appointed and even had a writing desk.

The manservant set down her two bags. Louisa remembered his name was Joseph Smith. "Thank you, Joseph. Molly will help me unpack." She opened the wardrobe, and the maid unfastened the straps on the leather bags.

"Oh, I've never seen anything as lovely in me life!" Molly carefully lifted out a lavender silk dress and carried it to the wardrobe with reverence. When she saw the purple undergarments that went with it, her eyes almost popped out of her head.

Meg tapped on the door and stepped into the boudoir. "Your bath is ready, my lady."

"Thank you." Louisa unpacked a nightdress and a velvet bed robe. "Just point the way to the bathing room. You can help Molly put my things in the wardrobe."

Meg could see that the mistress wasn't going to get dressed again tonight. "After yer bath, I'll bring you up a dinner tray, my lady."

"That's very kind of you."

Meg hesitated, and she threw a couple of glances toward the adjoining door and blushed. "I'll bring it to the master bedchamber."

"No. You may bring it here. This is where I shall be sleeping."

Meg and Molly exchanged a surprised glance.

They might as well know this will be a marriage in name only. The sooner the entire staff knows it, the better. She raised her chin, draped the nightdress and robe over her arm, and went in search of the bathing room.

James unpacked his bag and hung up his clothes. Then he separated his luggage from Louisa's, put his shirts and smallclothes in one of the mahogany tallboys, and hung his suits and jackets in the wardrobe. He noticed that his things took up little space, leaving a great deal of room to accommodate his wife's garments. *By the number of trunks waiting to be unpacked, she will need it.*

He went downstairs and summoned his stewards to join him for dinner. The eighty-thousand-acre Barons Court estate with its tenants, home farm, crops, and livestock needed three overseers to manage it efficiently. Abercorn was pleased with their reports and assured them he would go over their tallies and accounts in the next few days.

They drank a toast to his health and wished him happiness in his marriage. Though there had been little joy in the union so far, James appreciated their Irish wit and their laughter. It helped to keep his bleak thoughts and festering anger at bay.

The hour was late when he went upstairs. He put his ear to the connecting door between the master bedchamber and her boudoir. He encountered only silence and concluded that Louisa was sleeping after their long journey. James turned up the lamp, glanced ruefully at the wide bed, and knew sleep would elude him.

He paced to the window, but the black night showed him nothing of his beloved landscape. He knelt and lit a small peat fire, not because he was cold but because the cheerful blaze and distinctive scent would keep him company.

He crossed to the bookcase, trailed his finger across the familiar titles, but found nothing to engage his interest. His wandering glance fell on the boxes and trunks waiting to be unpacked. Needing something to counter his restlessness, he opened one of the brassbound trunks. The scent of jasmine filled the air. His hand pushed the tissue aside to reveal a gown of crimson taffeta. Its bodice was richly embroidered with pearls and deep red garnets.

It's the ancestral Abercorn color. A picture of Louisa wearing the gown came to him full-blown. Her beauty took his breath away, and he imagined undressing her. James lifted the gown from the trunk and, tucked beneath it, he saw a book. The moment he picked it up, he knew what it was.

This is Louisa's diary!

The key was in the lock.

He carried it to the fire and sank down in a comfortable chair. Without hesitation he unlocked it. Here was his chance to learn who had dishonored her. James thirsted for the swine's name so he could take his revenge.

He opened the journal at the last entry:

Mother told Abercorn I miscarried his child. I am devastated! He is being forced to marry me. His anger is terrifying. Though it is completely justified.

James turned the pages back. A stark entry in December caught his eye:

Aborted tonight!

His gut knotted, and cold fingers squeezed his heart.

James went back a few pages, held his breath, and began to read:

Georgy confided her terrible secret today. I vowed I would tell no one, though if she is four months gone with child, everyone will soon know.

James avidly turned the page and read:

I guessed that the father was Teddy Fox. She said she told him, but he refused to marry her. My heart aches for Georgy. How will she get through Christmas with all the guests who will descend upon Woburn?

He read the next entry:

Georgy says she would rather die than face the scandal. I am terrified that she is contemplating suicide. I'm nearly torn in half over what to do, but I have vowed to keep her secret, and cannot betray my sister.

James could hardly believe what he was reading:

After a long, hard ride across the rutted fields, Georgy flung herself from the saddle hoping to rid herself of the child. She could have killed herself. I put her to bed and sat with her until she slept.

He turned the page and read:

Aborted tonight!

James raised his eyes from the diary and murmured aloud, "How on earth did her mother think it was Lu who miscarried?" He lowered his eyes to the page and read on:

Georgy came to my room in terrible pain. I put her in my bed but she began to bleed. It was a nightmare and went on for hours. Blood was everywhere. Finally it stopped. I stripped off my bedsheets, washed her, and put a fresh nightgown on her.

Mother came in, saw me covered in blood, and assumed I was the one who had miscarried. Georgy's eyes pleaded with me not to betray her, so I took the blame.

James was astounded. His anger slowly melted away and was replaced by a feeling of euphoria. His heart sang with happiness that Louisa, *his precious Louisa,* had never been with child. He knew he shouldn't take joy in the fact that Georgy had been shamefully betrayed, but he was over the moon that it wasn't Louisa.

James closed the diary and sat in wonder. *Lu was so selfless that she took the blame for her sister. She suffered shame in her mother's eyes, rather than betray Georgy. A love that deep was both rare and precious.*

As the situation fully dawned on him, he wanted to laugh and shout and kick up his heels. Instead, he sat brimming over with ela-tion, savoring the secret he had uncovered. Again he opened the jour-nal and read an earlier entry:

Abercorn is dangerous! He is so devastatingly handsome that I must keep him at arm's length or I shall be undone.

James suddenly realized that he should not be reading Louisa's diary. He snapped it closed and turned the key in the lock. *These are Lu's personal thoughts and I am invading her privacy.* He could summon no regret over the secret he had uncovered, however. The knowledge filled his heart and soul with happiness. He rejoiced that with one flash of insight, everything was about to change between them. The corners of his mouth went up in a wicked smile. The Mar-quis of Abercorn was suddenly hell-bent on seduction.

He carried her diary back to the trunk. He folded the exquisite crimson gown and tucked the book beneath it, exactly as he had found it. He closed the lid of the trunk and fastened its brass latches. Then he put one of her boxes on top. *Lu must never find out what I did.*

Louisa's eyes flew open as the sound of her drapes being flung back awakened her. She closed them quickly as the early morning sun blinded her. "Devil take you!"

"Close," James said, laughing. "Get out of bed and come with me." He dragged the covers from her.

"I'm undressed!"

"I noticed." His glance slid over her silk nightgown and he rolled his eyes in appreciation.

"Can't this wait?"

"Absolutely not. Hurry, or I will have to pick you up and carry you."

The light in his eyes told her he would execute his threat. "I'll need my bed gown."

"Oh, if you must." He plucked a white velvet robe from the

foot of her bed and held it while she slipped her bare arms into the sleeves. Then he took her hand and unceremoniously pulled her out of bed.

She barely had time to slide her feet into her slippers as he dragged her toward the door. To keep up with his long strides, Lu had to run. They passed gaping servants as they descended the main staircase, but he was in such a hurry, she didn't have time to blush.

They sped through the great hall, then the rotunda and entrance hall, and dashed through the front door of Barons Court. When they reached the portico, James thrust one powerful arm beneath her knees and swung her up into his arms.

"Custom dictates that a bride must be carried over the threshold by her groom. Never let it be said that I neglected *any* of the hymeneal customs, no matter how you intend to deny me, Lady Lu."

His words were deliberately insinuating, and as he slowly carried her over the threshold into the sunlit rotunda, she had plenty of time to blush. She struggled to be put down, but she was no match for the whipcord muscles of his arms. She could have fought him, but a thrashing resistance would have been most undignified before the smiling servants.

As he carried her through the great hall, he put his lips to her ear and whispered, "You have an audience. I wager you can play your part to perfection if you put your mind to it."

Lu realized it was a game two could play. She raised her voice and challenged, "I wager you won't make it to the top of the staircase!"

He, too, played to their audience. "I concede it will be a challenge after last night's exertions."

Her eyes blazed green. "You Irish devil! How could you?"

James carried her into the master bedchamber and dropped her onto the bed. "I should be thrashed." He handed her a pillow. "Have at me!"

She snatched it from his hand, stood on the bed, and buffeted him about the head.

James picked up another pillow and whacked her across the bottom. Soon they were rolling about the bed, laughing and fighting like children. The covers went one way and they went the other. On hands and knees she scrambled away from him, so she wouldn't end up on the floor. He grabbed her hips, rolled her onto her back, and came over her in the dominant position.

"You are violating our agreement!" she cried.

He grinned down at her. "I have violated nothing. You must agree I have not yet consummated our marriage. Everything is exactly the same between us."

She lay panting as he loomed above her. What he said was true. Everything was the same, yet not the same. She suddenly realized that his anger was gone.

"We can't play in bed all morning. The day is awasting. Get dressed, and after breakfast we'll go to the stables. I have a wedding present for you."

Louisa was torn. Her boxes and trunks needed unpacking, but the lure of what awaited her in the stables was too tempting to resist. She decided her trunks could wait as she retreated to her boudoir and donned an emerald green riding dress.

James stuck his head around the door just as she finished tying her hair back with a ribbon. "If I don't take you to the breakfast room, you could get lost in the labyrinth, never to be seen or heard again."

When he led her to a small, sunlit chamber off the formal dining room, she chided him. "You make the design of Barons Court sound like a muddle, but it isn't nearly the rabbit warren that is Woburn."

"It was built only thirty-five years ago, whereas Woburn Abbey is ancient."

They didn't linger over breakfast. Though James had a healthy man's appetite, he consumed his plate of gammon ham, eggs, and potato pancakes before Louisa finished her strawberries and cream. He gazed at her while she spooned the fruit into her mouth.

"Must you watch me?"

"I must. The dainty way you eat fascinates me. The way you lick your lips affords me untold pleasure."

"You devil. You are deliberately trying to make me blush."

He grinned. "And I am succeeding beyond all expectation."

Louisa threw her napkin at him.

"Come, we've no more time for dalliance." He jumped up and took her hand.

The huge stable block was on the opposite side of the courtyard. When they entered, she withdrew her hand from his and walked slowly past the long row of stalls that were being cleaned by a number of stable boys. "Where are the horses?"

James led the way to a half door. "They are out here."

She joined him and gazed out at two spacious paddocks, carpeted with clover. Each held half a dozen horses, leisurely cropping the grass. "What a lovely picture they make. I'll swear Irish clover is greener than English."

"I've never heard you swear, Lady Lu."

"I seldom swear," she lied.

"But it's one of life's pleasures. I shall give you some lessons, so you can hold your own against me. Irish swear words are more lyrical than English."

"How so?"

"Well, let's see. You say *shit* but we say *shyte*."

Lu began to laugh. "That's deliciously lyrical. My repertoire of salty words is extensive. I have seven brothers who swear like sailors."

He looked shocked. "Surely not Wriothesley?"

"You have a sly wit, Abercorn."

"Follow me." James walked farther back into the stables until they came to some box stalls. He opened the door. "What do you think of this animal?"

"Oh, she's an Arabian. I think she's absolutely lovely."

"Good. Then she's yours."

Lu's eyes widened. "Bloody hell!"

"I have another one in the next stall, but you wouldn't be able to ride her until she foals. If it's a filly, perhaps we should call her Lady Lu."

Louisa pressed her nose to the bars of the next stall. "She could foal any day." She couldn't hide her anxiety. "Aren't you afraid for her?"

"I don't anticipate any difficulty. I'm looking forward to it."

"But she'll suffer pain, and the foal might die."

James studied her face and saw her apprehension. He knew he must diminish her dread and imbue her with more confidence. "Giving birth is natural. Don't harbor fear for her, Lu. I'll be with her when the time comes."

"I'm being fanciful." She turned back to the lovely Arabian he had just gifted her with and ran an appreciative hand down her graceful neck.

James took a riding saddle from a nearby bench. "Why don't you try her out?" He saddled the Arabian and held her bridle.

Louisa placed her foot in the stirrup, and as she mounted, the skirt of her riding dress lifted to reveal long green suede riding boots.

James rolled his eyes in appreciation. "Bloody hell is right!"

She tried not to laugh. "Behave yourself."

"I'll try. But I guarantee nothing." He saddled a mount for himself and they cantered side by side through the parkland.

"Thank you for your beautiful gift. I will treasure her. Does she have a name?"

"Queen of Sheba."

The way his eyes licked over her made her think he was alluding to her. She was secretly flattered and arched her neck. "Sheba is a perfect name."

They reached the woodlands bordering the park. "These woods are carpeted with bluebells in the spring. I'm sorry you missed them. Their scent is intoxicating."

"I'm glad the rhododendrons and azaleas are in bloom. The landscape is splashed with their brilliant colors. Can we ride into the woods?"

"You may do anything you please, but if you want to see wildlife, we should walk."

James dismounted and came to her side. As he lifted her down, he once again rolled his eyes in appreciation at the sight of her knee-high green boots.

As they moved through the lacy ferns, they communicated in whispers. The woods were alive with rabbits, woodcocks, does and their fawns, and the branches above their heads were filled with buntings, yellowhammers, and other colorful song birds. Suddenly, with a great flurry of wings, they scattered. "We frightened them."

James shook his head and pointed to a red kite that had swooped onto a high branch.

As they walked on, Louisa delighted in the pretty wildflowers and colorful toadstools. They came upon a pool in a small clearing that was fringed with rushes and lily pads. A pair of wood ducks glided across its surface, and a little green heron was catching fish. Butterflies flitted about and iridescent dragonflies skimmed the water.

"Oh, it's like a wishing pool from a fairy tale. I can feel the magic."

"Let's both make a wish."

She nodded eagerly.

He watched her close her eyes and saw the tip of her tongue touch her top lip as she concentrated on what to ask for. The picture she made was irresistible. James reached out and plucked the ribbon from her hair.

As her dark curls tumbled to her shoulders, her lashes flew up.

"What did you wish for?" He gazed at her hungrily.

Her breath caught in her throat. "I cannot tell, or it won't come true."

James stared at her mouth; then his eyes sought hers. "It's no secret what I wish for, Lady Lu."

Chapter Twenty-Three

"There's plenty of room for your gowns in this wardrobe." James stood in the doorway of the connecting bedchambers, watching Louisa unpack the trunks that had been moved into her boudoir.

"We have agreed on separate rooms," she told him firmly.

"Lu, I'm offering the wardrobe. I'm not inviting you to share my bed."

She tried not to blush but felt her cheeks grow warm. She hung a turquoise crepe gown on a hanger and tried to squeeze it into the overfull wardrobe. "Oh, very well, I shall accept your offer."

"I won't force you against your will."

She knew he wasn't speaking about wardrobes. *He's promising not to force me into his bed.* "I appreciate your gallantry, my lord."

James carried her half-unpacked trunk into the master bedchamber. He guessed she had retrieved her diary and hidden it away. He opened a couple of empty drawers in one of the mahogany tallboys. "You may have this one. I use its mate."

When she carried some black lace undergarments to the drawer, he staggered back in pretended shock.

"You give me no privacy," she accused.

"Tell the truth and shame the devil, Lady Lu. Your undergarments were designed to be flaunted. You have a most seductive taste in clothes."

"Shyte! You have guessed all my secrets."

James threw back his head and laughed. "You are a saucy baggage, Lu. I enjoy a battle of wits. You have given me a most enjoyable day."

I've enjoyed it too. As she unpacked her fans, stockings, nightgowns, and dozens of other garments that made up her trousseau, she relived her busy day. After their ride, James had given her the grand tour of Barons Court. She had found the house as impressive as its master. It had a magnificent hundred-foot-long gallery with a notable art collection that included portraits by Sir Joshua Reynolds, paintings by the Spanish artist Velasquez, and some rare drawings by Raphael. There were also some unopened crates of paintings that James had recently bought. She was curious to see what he had purchased but decided that would have to wait for another day.

There were two dozen bedchambers and a guest wing containing four suites comprised of bedroom, sitting room, and dining room. There also were nurseries, where Louisa did not choose to linger. But the kitchens were another matter entirely. They were not antiquated, like the kitchens at Woburn. They contained every modern convenience, and the delicious smells coming from the ovens were mouthwatering.

Louisa smiled as she remembered asking about some curious round things piled in a porcelain dish.

"Swatemates," James had informed her. He picked one up. "Open your mouth."

She decided to trust him and bit down into candied ginger rolled in castor sugar. "Oh, it's a sweetmeat!"

James shook his head and whispered in her ear, "Swatemate."

His Irish brogue sent a shiver down her spine.

She recalled that it wasn't the first time he had caused her to shiver. Tonight they had dined in the small private room that opened off the spacious formal dining room. He held her chair then dropped a kiss on the top of her head. From the moment he took his seat across the small table, his dark eyes had never left her face.

He served her, choosing the choicest pieces of game and tempted her to try Irish dishes made from produce grown on their own estate. His teasing compliments were intended to make her laugh. His gallantry was designed to disarm her. His lavish attention was calculated to make her feel desirable, and it worked. Each time their hands accidentally touched, she shivered.

When Louisa finished unpacking her trunks, she glanced toward her boudoir.

To delay her leaving, James said, "How about a nightcap?" He moved toward the games table that held a small stone jug.

She hesitated. "I prefer wine to whiskey."

"Oh, it isn't whiskey. It's Irish poteen. Better not try it," he warned. "It is an exceedingly strong liquor made from malted barley and potatoes. Definitely not suitable for a lady." He could tell she was tempted, so he added a potent lure. "It's illegal!"

"Really?" Her eyes widened. "Then how can I resist?" She moved toward the table and sat down.

James poured them both a dram and handed her the small glass.

The first swallow took her breath away.

"I warned you it was strong." James swallowed his dram in one gulp. Then he reached out his hand for her glass. "I don't think you should finish it, Lu."

Before he could take it, she took another swallow. She felt as if a lovely red rose bloomed in her breast. It made her feel warm and receptive. A warning bell went off in her head. *He gave me the drink so he could take advantage of me.* She licked her lips and remembered the feel of his kisses. *It will take more than poteen to make me lose control of the situation.* She lifted the glass and drained it.

"I did it!" She threw him a triumphant glance. "It wasn't too strong at all." She stood up and suddenly felt its full effect. She tried to take a step and staggered.

James reached for her and she thought he was about to take her in his arms. Instead he simply steadied her. "I think you are ready for bed."

"I think you are right." She threw an apprehensive glance at the wide bed.

"Let me help you." James took her hand and led her through the adjoining door into her boudoir and sat her on her own bed. He hid his amusement and said solemnly, "Lu, I want you to know, I would never violate our agreement."

Alone in her chamber, she managed to undress and get into bed. Her thoughts were fuzzy; she chided herself for being suspicious. *Abercorn had no ulterior motive after all.*

Louisa fell asleep quickly and began to dream. *She was in bed with her husband. He kissed her for a full hour, starting at her temples, kissing her eyelids, then trailing his lips down the curve of her neck. His lavish attentions made her feel beautiful and desirable. She clung to him sweetly, inhaling his male scent. When his lips brushed against her ear, she shivered with pleasure.*

I love you, Lu. His intimate whisper awakened her. She reached out to caress his cheek and realized she was alone in her bed. Her hand moved over the empty pillow beside her. Louisa heaved a great sigh, turned over, and went back to sleep.

"Lu, I can't believe you're still abed." James pulled off her covers as he had done yesterday.

"You devil! I should have expected a repeat performance." She sat up in bed and saw that he had brought a breakfast tray laden with food.

"I am Prince Galahad riding to your rescue." His glance lingered on her breasts.

"Rescue me from what? I know better than to put my trust in princes."

"Rescue you from the racket that will shortly ensue. I have carpenters coming to lay some flooring. Since they'll be hammering most of the day, I thought I would show you our chain of pretty lakes." He threw back the curtains and allowed the sunshine to spill into her chamber. "It promises to be a lovely warm day—perfect for messing about in water."

"Messing about?"

"Take you for a row, among other things."

He was clad in a white silk shirt and her eyes were drawn to his wide shoulders. *He has the muscles of a champion oarsman.* She tried not to picture him without his shirt, but it was impossible. "Among other things?"

"All right, I'll confess. I'd like to teach you to swim. I want you to conquer your fear of the water, if that's possible."

"I'm not afraid of water!" she protested. "I'm only afraid of male louts who push me under."

"Do you consider me a male lout, Louisa?"

"That remains to be seen. So far you have shown me only gallantry," she admitted.

"Flattery, begod." He picked up the tray and put it between them on the bed. "I brought us breakfast to save time, and the cook is packing us a lunch so we can eat out by the lakes." He served her scrambled eggs and held a rasher of crispy bacon to her lips. Its smoky aroma was too tempting to resist. She ate it eagerly and took another piece.

"Greedy wench! Save some for me."

She reached out and held a strip of bacon to his lips. Before he could bite down on it, she snatched it away. Then she relented and offered it again.

He grabbed her hand so she couldn't pull it away a second time; then he proceeded to eat the bacon. On the last bite, his teeth came down on her fingers.

She drew in a sharp breath, anticipating the sharp bite, but instead James licked her fingers with his tongue. He smiled knowingly when she shivered. "Stop teasing!"

He lowered his gaze to her lush breasts; then he rolled his eyes in mock ecstasy. "On the contrary, Lady Abercorn, you are the one who is doing the teasing."

"Since you are the one who pulled off my covers, you are the villain in this game. So suffer away, Lord Bloody Abercorn."

James grinned with appreciation.

"Someday, if you practice long and hard, you may be a match for me." *Long and hard . . . o my God, I can't believe I just said that.* She felt her cheeks suffuse with a blush.

Eyes brimming with laughter, James focused on finishing his breakfast. When he was done he got up from the bed. "I'll let you get ready. Whatever it is you put on under your dress, make sure it's suitable for swimming."

Thinking of the adventures to come filled her with eager anticipation. She opened a drawer to select a petticoat, and mischief bubbled inside her. *I'll make his eyes roll!*

Because it was warm, Lu wore a plain cream linen dress for their ride to the lakes. James left off his coat and wore only his shirt and riding breeches. The blue sky reflecting in the water made the chain of lakes look like a sparkling necklace.

"Look, there's an otter," she said, pointing to the shallows.

"He's a bold fellow. Look carefully and you should see his mate. They are bonded into pairs by summer."

"Yes, there she is! I don't know anything about otters."

"The females are called queens. She's a plump one. She'll be giving birth any day."

"Do they have litters?"

"No, usually just one pup, sometimes two. They are playful and highly intelligent. Look at the flat rocks at the edge of the water. If you watch quietly, you'll see them dive for crustaceans, then carry them to the rocks and crack open the shells with a stone."

"I enjoy watching wild creatures. They are so clever."

He pointed to the branches of a willow tree at the edge of the water. "Do you see that raven? He's so intelligent that he makes use of the otters' skill. If a raven finds something with an extremely hard shell, like a nut, he will leave it on the rock and wait for an otter to crack it open for him."

"It could be a female raven," she pointed out.

"Yes, females are likely more intelligent than the male of the species. They certainly have the self-confidence to survive and make sure their offspring thrive." James wanted Louisa to develop more confidence in herself. Though she tried valiantly, she could not always hide her vulnerability. Teaching her to swim would give her self-assurance.

They rode on and dismounted beside a rustic boathouse. "No need to tether the horses, Lu. They'll enjoy roaming the bank of the lake and cropping the lush grass." James removed their saddles and placed them under a shade tree. He opened the boathouse door and they went inside. There were two boats. One was a skull that he used for racing practice, and the other was a rowboat complete with crimson leather cushions. He got in first to hold it steady, then offered his hand in invitation.

Without hesitation she placed her hand in his and stepped into the boat. She sat down opposite him to watch his every movement. He placed the oars into the oarlock sockets, sat down facing her, and braced his feet.

As they glided from the boathouse into the lake, he tracked a straight course without turning around to see where he was going. When he felt the hot sun on his shoulders, he removed his shirt. "If you like, I'll take us through all three lakes."

Lu gazed at his naked chest and rippling muscles. "Yes, I do like."

"Rowing is great exercise, but it's also good for the mind. The rhythm of the strokes brings a sense of peacefulness and lets you become one with your surroundings."

Louisa sighed with pleasure as his long, slow strokes carried them smoothly down the lake. She noticed the shape of his strong hands on the oars and saw that he dropped his wrists at the end of each stroke, feathering the spoon-shaped oars so they glided over the surface. Rowing was second nature to him, and his technique wasted little energy.

"Careful, there are ducks behind you." She heaved a sigh of relief as they glided past the boat without so much as a ruffled feather.

"Those are tufted ducks. We call them *tufties*; they stay all year round."

"Oh, they have babies . . . how sweet."

"Everything has babies at this time of year. It is the order of nature."

Louisa looked down into the crystal clear water and saw that it was teeming with hatchling fishes. When James rowed into the second lake, it was populated with swans.

"You are right, James. The swans are so majestic. I cannot believe how tiny their cygnets are. They look like little balls of gray fluff."

"Before summer is over, they'll develop brown feathers. They don't start to get white plumage until their second year."

"You are a true nature lover. It makes me happy that you are not a hunter."

Like every other male in nature I'm hunting for a mate, and I have sighted my quarry, Lady Lu.

When they reached the far end of the third lake, James turned the rowboat.

"Don't you need a rest?" she asked with surprise.

"None of the lakes is more than a mile and a half in length. Both ways adds up to less than eight miles."

She laughed. "And I suppose you could row that far with one arm tied behind you?"

He grinned. "Of course not—we'd go in circles."

As she watched his powerful arms, she was reminded of the dream she'd had last night. *He held me in those arms and it made me feel beautiful and desirable.* She lowered her lashes in a deliberate attempt to protect herself from the irresistible lure of the attractive devil. But even though she couldn't see him, she felt the mesmerizing rhythm of his strokes and heard the enticing splash of the water. Her heartbeat took on the same exciting tempo as his compelling nearness threatened to overwhelm her.

When she glanced up and saw the boathouse, it broke the spell that held her in thrall.

James guided the boat inside, jumped out, and tied it securely. Then he reached out to help her alight. When she placed her hand in his with complete trust, he knew that half the battle was won. He picked up his shirt but didn't put it on.

The sun was high in the sky as he walked beneath the shade tree to retrieve lunch from his saddlebags. "I worked up an appetite. Are you hungry?"

"That all depends on what you have to offer, my lord."

James smiled a secret smile. "You choose the spot—sun or shade?"

"Sun . . . and let's go closer to the water."

He spread his silk shirt on the grass to protect her dress. When she sat down, he knelt and unwrapped a huge linen napkin to reveal crusty whole wheaten bread and soft homemade cheese. There was a string of spicy dried sausages and two russet apples. "It's peasant fare, unlikely to tempt a lady."

"It looks good to me. But then my tastes are not too refined."

"That's encouraging," he teased. "Perhaps I still stand a chance."

She ignored his beguiling words but could not close her eyes to the fact that he was wooing her. Louisa helped herself to some bread and cheese. "This is delicious."

James poured them each a cup of blackberry wine. "I promise this isn't as strong as poteen." He bit down on a spicy sausage. "Try one of these." When she looked skeptical, he goaded her. "You have to be adventurous to eat an Irish sausage. God knows what unthinkable porcine parts they put in it."

She took one immediately. "I'm adventurous. I'll try anything once."

His eyes were alight with mischief. "I'll hold you to that."

"Cheeky Irish sod!" When she finished the sausage, she licked her fingers and picked up an apple.

His eyes never left her face as she bit into it with gusto, and laughed when the juice ran down her chin. When she finished, she stood up and tossed the core into the trees. "The deer will eat it. They enjoy apples."

He reached into the napkin and pulled out something wrapped in tissue paper. He undid it and held out his hand. In the center of his palm sat a sugared mouse.

"Oh, James!" She went down on her knees and touched it with her finger. The love token had totally disarmed her. She took it to her mouth and licked it.

"Swatemate," he murmured, his eyes on her lips.

She knew he was not referring to the mouse. *I'm his swatemate.*

He picked up his apple and lay back in the grass, enjoying the feel of the sun on his bare chest. When he finished it, he closed his eyes.

She stole a glance at him, and when she saw his dark lashes resting on his cheeks, she gathered the courage to allow her eyes to roam over his naked torso. His tanned skin stretched tautly over wide shoulders and the rippling muscles of his powerful chest. Once again her dream came back to her and she remembered exactly how it felt to be enclosed in his embrace and pressed to his heart. She felt drawn to him by an invisible force that was so compelling it was impossible to resist. Stealthily, she moved closer. She could smell his sun-warmed skin and see the faint shadow of his beard along his jaw. She reached out her fingers to touch the crisp black hair that curled on his chest.

Her hand stopped midair. Words he had said to her in the library at Woburn came back to her: *Your jasmine stole to me some time ago.* She knew he would be able to smell her perfume. *Don't play with fire, Louisa.* She moved away from him cautiously, silently. Then she stood up and walked to the water's edge, putting a safe distance between them.

Ten minutes later, James sat up. He had been fully aware of Louisa's close proximity and her desire to touch him. He silently rejoiced and hugged the secret knowledge to himself. "Are you ready to swim?" he called.

She hesitated. If she backed out she knew he would think she had lost her courage. Worse, she would consider herself a coward. "Of course I'm ready."

He tucked the remainder of their lunch into his saddlebags and pulled out a couple of towels. He joined her at the lake's edge and removed his riding breeches. "Your turn."

She glanced at his linen undergarment, removed her dress, dropped it onto the grass, and waited for his reaction. He didn't disappoint her. He staggered in shock and rolled his eyes. Instead of the petticoat he was expecting, she stood before him clad in white drawers decorated with crimson ruffles. Her tiny busk was adored with red ribbon.

"If I'd known you were wearing such scandalous trappings beneath your prim and proper dress while I was rowing the boat, I would likely have capsized us."

His teasing made her laugh. "Don't pretend to be shocked, Abercorn. You are the one who believes my undergarments are designed to be flaunted."

"You have extremely theatrical taste, Lady Lu. Are you ready for your water ballet?"

She giggled as she took his outstretched hand and waded waist deep into the lake. "Ooh, it's cold."

"A bit bracing when you first get wet, but you'll soon get used to it. I think you should learn to float before you try to swim. Take a deep breath to fill your lungs with air, then lie back in the water. I'll keep my arms underneath you so you won't sink."

She did as he instructed her, splashing about whenever she felt insecure, but kept at it doggedly. Never once did James allow her to sink or let her nose and mouth go below the surface. Finally she gained enough confidence to put her head back and float on her own. "I did it!" she cried.

"You certainly did. Take a bow, marchioness."

"Let me do it again. Stand over there and be ready to catch me if I sink."

She floated perfectly, and he applauded her performance. "You are ready for a swimming lesson. May I suggest the breast stroke?" He knew she had no idea that her white drawers were transparent in the water, so he made a valiant effort not to roll his eyes in appreciation.

He placed his hand beneath her chin. "Keep one foot on the bottom and pretend you are swimming. When you're ready, lift your leg and kick."

Louisa did it over and over, but each time she felt confident enough to lift her foot off the bottom, she began to sink. She feared her face would go under the water, but James supported her chin, never allowing her mouth or nose to dip beneath the surface.

"Do you think I'll ever do it?"

"Of course you will. It won't be long before you can swim from one side of the lake to the other. Before summer is over, we'll be swimming with the otters."

"Oh, James, is that really possible?" She was so engrossed in their conversation about the otters that she lifted her leg and forgot to sink.

"Sooner than you realize. You just swam at least a yard."

In her surprise and excitement she grabbed him and clung on to him as she almost dragged them both beneath the water. Then she laughed with the pure pleasure of her achievement. "Let me do it again. Don't help me—just let me sink."

She walked about five feet away from him, then took a deep breath and stroked out toward him. He caught her in his arms and they laughed together. "I'm so clever!"

"You are very brave," he told her to bolster her confidence.

"Clever and brave!" she crowed.

"A lethal combination." He put his hands on her bottom and pulled her toward him. "I quite like messing about in water."

She cupped her palm and splashed him until he removed his possessive hands to wipe the water from his eyes. Then laughing, she swam away from him. She did get water in her mouth and up her nose, but her fear was gone as she realized now that slipping underwater was no calamity.

The pair played, laughed, and messed about for another hour until the heat went out of the afternoon. When Louisa emerged from the lake she was covered in gooseflesh.

"I'm cold," she said through chattering teeth.

James picked up one of the towels and began to dry her. He rubbed her arms and back and moved down to her legs. "Take your wet things off and put on your dress." He held up the towel and gallantly averted his eyes to give her a smidgen of privacy. When her gown was in place, he slipped on his riding breeches. He rolled up her wet undergarments in the damp towel.

When he saw that she was still shivering, he wrapped the dry towel about her. He whistled for the horses and saddled them, but decided to take Louisa up before him for the ride home.

She pulled the towel about her shoulders and cuddled up against her husband. His body heat seeped into her, making her feel warm and also protected from the cool breeze.

They left the horses at the stable with a groom and ran to the house.

He followed her upstairs and took the towel from her shoulders. "Let me dry your hair."

"I can do that." He was still shirtless and, because she was determined to avoid further intimacy, she escaped into her boudoir.

James donned a shirt and dry breeches, then opened the adjoining door between their bedchambers. He saw that she was wearing a robe and had wrapped a towel about her head. "I have an idea. Why don't I light us a peat fire, and we can have our dinner up here where we will be warm and cozy?"

Lu hesitated, but the lure of a fire was extremely tempting. *The only reason I learned to swim is because I trusted him. James kept his promise. If I join him in the master bedroom, can I trust him not to violate our agreement?* She decided to be bold and take a chance. "Will you teach me how to light a peat fire?"

She knelt at the hearth and James handed her a piece of newspaper. She scrunched it up and put it in the grate. He pointed to a box. "Make a pyramid with the applewood twigs." He brought over an oil lamp and handed her a taper.

Louisa touched the lit taper to the twigs, and the scent of apples filled the air as they ignited. James pointed to the brass peat bucket, and she quickly piled the pieces of turf around the lighted wood. Then she sat back on her heels and held her breath.

When the pretty blue peat smoke began to spiral up the chimney, she gave him a triumphant smile. She pulled the towel from her hair to wipe her hands and a profusion of damp dark tendrils fell about her shoulders.

They dined in front of the fire and talked about the day's adventures, which were all new and fascinating to Louisa. Because she took pleasure in observing the wildlife on the estate, he promised to show her the place where a sett of badgers made their burrow in the woods.

After dinner they played chess. "Lady Lu, I do believe you are cheating!"

"All my brothers and sisters cheat when we play games."

"I warrant you are shrewd enough to win without stooping to deceit."

She was flattered at his confidence and agreed to play again without subterfuge. She lost, of course, and playfully tipped the board, scattering the chess pieces. Louisa spied a bowl of chestnuts and took a long-handled copper pan from the wall. They knelt by the hearth to roast the chestnuts and then stretched out on the rug to enjoy them.

James peeled them and fed them to Louisa.

They talked and laughed until Lu began to yawn. He watched her in silent enjoyment. Her hair had dried in a hundred tiny ringlets that lured him to reach out and play among the curls. The tendrils spiraled around his fingers, clinging to him of their own volition, and he marveled at their silky, seductive texture. When he moved closer to take her in his arms, he saw that she had fallen asleep.

Chapter Twenty-Four

The early morning sun awakened Louisa because her drapes had never been closed. *Any minute, Abercorn will come in and do his usual. He will throw off my covers and drag me out of bed.* A mischievous thought began to bubble. *Turnabout is fair play!*

She arose, put on her robe, and slipped quietly into the adjoining room. She tiptoed to the bed and yanked off his covers. She gasped when she saw that James was stark naked.

He opened his eyes and began to laugh at the look of shock on her face. Then he gave her back her own words: "Since you are the one who pulled off my covers, you are the villain in this game. So suffer away, Lady Bloody Abercorn."

She turned her back and hurried to the window. "Make yourself decent." A movement in the grass caught her attention. "There are foxes playing on the lawn!"

He came up behind her and placed his hands on her shoulders. "They are often here at sunrise." He grinned when he felt her stiffen. "See what delights of nature you're missing when you shun this bedroom?"

"I prefer to avoid your *natural delights*. You are indecent!"

"I must confess that from time to time, I *am* indecent." He bent his head and whispered in her ear, *"Indacent."* He moved back from the window. "The carpenters will be hammering again today, so I thought I'd take you to meet all our tenants."

Lu twirled around. "Oh, that would be . . ." Her eyes widened at the sight of his naked body. "Lovely," she finished.

"Why, thank you," he teased, anticipating her pretty blush.

I'll be damned if I'll avert my eyes. "What will you do when I am all blushed out?"

He grinned. "Resort to even more *indacent* antics, I suppose."

"You don't think this riding habit is too fancy for visiting your tenants, do you?"

His appreciative glance swept over her. "You are the lady of the manor. They won't expect to see you in sackcloth and ashes. You can't go wrong with green in Ireland."

As the newly wedded pair visited each tenant farm, the scene was the same. The children, especially the boys, eagerly gathered about James. Louisa was impressed that he knew most of their names. It was brought home to her how much Abercorn liked children, and vice versa.

While James spoke with the men, conversing knowledgeably about the livestock and the crops, the women greeted their lord's new lady and wished her happiness. They offered her homemade small beer and whatever they were baking. She inspected their herb gardens and asked them to send some cuttings up to the manor, so she could plant her own. Louisa praised their homemaking skills and complimented their children. She was impressed to learn that every morning, for a few hours, the children gathered to learn how to read and write.

After they had visited the tenant farms and the home farm, James wanted to show her one of his pet projects. "If you are up to a ten-mile ride, there's something I'd like to show you. Not all my tenants are farmers."

"That sounds intriguing. I'd love to go."

As a large stone building came into view, James explained, "It was an old gristmill. Last year I had the whole thing rebuilt into a spinning mill for flax. The Herdman brothers did all the work. I bought the machinery and now the three of them run the mill for me."

Abercorn introduced his wife to three strapping young men—James, John, and George Herdman. George, the youngest, gave Lady Louisa a tour of the mill and explained the different processing stages that took place before the flax was spun onto large bobbins. She noticed that at least half the workers were female.

When they were finished he escorted her to the office, where James, the eldest brother, and her husband were talking business.

"The three of us have a burning ambition to own this mill, Lord Abercorn. But it will be years before we can meet your asking price."

"I have a suggestion," Abercorn said thoughtfully. "Why don't I lease it to you? You've done a damned good job here. The business is thriving and all your employees are happy. You could pay me a yearly rent and keep the flax profits."

The Herdman brothers conferred and agreed. They worked out the rent, then moved on to discuss the length of the lease.

"How about a hundred years?" James suggested. "We can put in a clause to negotiate extending it further, every few years."

The Herdmans readily agreed. A hundred-year lease was more than generous.

"Tomorrow I'll ride into Omagh and have my attorney draw up the papers."

As they rode home Louisa questioned his motives. "Why did you offer such a long lease at such a low rent? Perhaps in a few short years the Herdmans might be able to buy it, and you could recoup the money you have laid out."

"The land is priceless. I never sell when I can lease. The property is our children's and grandchildren's legacy."

Louisa fell silent. *James makes no secret of the fact that he wants children. It's only natural when he has so much wealth and property in three different countries.* Her heart constricted with anxiety. *Whatever am I going to do?*

A mile from Barons Court, Louisa was distracted from her worrying thoughts. She pointed to the sky. "Look at that flock of birds. Are they crows?"

"Ravens. I can tell by their wedge-shaped tails and shaggy throats. They make their rookery close by. Every evening, about an hour before sunset, they gather and seem to revel in the pure joy of flying. Ravens are very social birds that form a close-knit community. They mate for life and make excellent parents. They are the only birds that can do somersaults when they fly."

James and Louisa stopped to watch as the ravens swooped, dived, and somersaulted gracefully through the air, making intricate patterns in the twilit sky yet never colliding. They cawed to each other with gusto.

Lu laughed. "They are singing and dancing!"

"For the pure pleasure of it." *Just like you,* James's eyes told her.

When they entered Barons Court, James cupped his ear. "Listen."

Louisa stood quietly for a full minute. "I don't hear anything."

"Exactly!" he said with a grin. "No hammering. The carpenters must be finished. Shall we go and inspect their handiwork?"

Side by side they walked through the house to a room beyond the great hall. Louisa saw that the carpenters had built a spacious stage at one end of the long chamber. Her heart began to sing and a lump came into her throat. "James, you built me my own theater! I thank you with all my heart. You are always so thoughtful and generous."

"Lu, it gives me pleasure to make you happy."

She removed her riding boots and ran up the steps onto the stage. Then in her stocking feet she twirled about gracefully and ended with an Irish jig. "Thank you!"

That night as Louisa lay abed in her boudoir, her anxiety returned. Then, gradually, it became overshadowed by feelings of guilt. *James is so generous to me, yet I give him nothing in return. He has let go of all his anger toward me, and we have become friends. But I doggedly cling to the barrier I have erected between us.* It began to dawn on her that she was no longer at war with him. She was fighting herself. Selfishness was against her nature and each day she was finding it harder to justify her position. The emotional distance between them was rapidly melting away. The physical distance had dissolved in the lake when he'd taught her to swim. But the *intimate* void had not been diminished by one iota. None of it was his fault, and this added to her anguish.

As usually happened when Louisa was in torment, her recurring nightmare took control the moment she fell into a deep sleep: *She was back in Woburn's garden among the lupins. She heard her mother's cry of alarm and saw her covered in blood. Suddenly the dream changed. Louisa looked down at her white nightgown and saw that it was drenched crimson with her own blood. No! No! Help me . . . please help me! Then she realized it was not her mother's screams she could hear, but her own.*

Louisa awoke in a panic. She felt herself being swept up in powerful arms, and it took her a moment to realize that the person who was carrying her was James. "What are you doing?" she cried.

"You've had a nightmare, Lu. I don't want you to be alone." He carried her into the master chamber and put her into his bed. Then he climbed in beside her and gathered her close. He brushed her hair back from her temples with a gentle hand. "Tell me about your nightmare, sweetheart; it will lessen your fear."

I cannot tell you about the blood. I don't dare hint at the subject of miscarriage. It will dredge it all up again, and stir your black anger. "I . . . I don't remember. I only know that something frightened me. But it's gone now. I can go back to my own bed."

"Absolutely not." His tone brooked no argument. "I'm an authority on nightmares. Claud used to have them when he was young. Making him feel safe was the only antidote." He did not tell her that he too had them, though no one ever came to his rescue. That's how he knew how terrifying they could be. "Once you feel warm and secure, perhaps you'll go back to sleep."

She felt his hands massage her back with long slow strokes that reached from her shoulders to her bottom cheeks. His palms, callused from rowing, felt rough against her soft skin as they moved firmly up and down the curve of her back. She drew in a swift breath as she felt his marble-hard erection brush against her belly.

James willed his cock to soften, but of course the more he stroked her silken skin, the harder he became. He felt her stiffen and heard her whimper, and knew that his erection made her feel anything but safe. If he did not take control immediately, she would bolt from his bed. Quickly he turned her around in his arms, so that her back lay against his chest. Her woman's scent stole to him, and it intoxicated his senses. He curved his body about hers in spoon fashion. As heat leaped between them, he prayed it would make her feel secure.

With her head tucked beneath his chin, he began to murmur about the wildlife she had seen at Barons Court, hoping it would soothe and gentle her. He spoke of the dancing foxes, the diving otters, and the swooping ravens. He promised that the first moonlit night, he would take her to see the romping badgers in the woods.

His words made her stop fighting him. Lying in the big bed with him, knowing his powerful body was curved about hers, made her feel more secure than she'd ever been in her life. She smiled into the darkness and stopped fighting herself.

He felt her body gradually relax against his, and eventually he knew that Louisa slept. He lay still so he wouldn't disturb her slumber, though his body was highly disturbed. He closed his eyes, but as the hours ticked by, he could not sleep. His body raged with unspent passion and desire for the innocent bride he held in his arms.

When morning arrived, James knew the moment Louisa awoke because she immediately withdrew her body from his. She half-turned to look at him as it came back to her what had caused her to share his bed. She could not even pretend anger at his gallantry, but she did feel shy as the sunshine splashed over them.

As his dark glance roamed over her creamy skin, disheveled curls, and brilliant green eyes, a strong urge to seduce her rose up in him. Desire ran through his veins, making his blood hot and demanding. Yet he knew that if he took advantage of her, he could lose her trust and she might refuse to share his bed again.

James made an effort to curb his lust. It wasn't easy, since he knew he would remain hard and throbbing as long as he lay naked beside her. He made a firm decision that he would not allow her to sleep alone again. From now on, her nights would be spent in his bed. For that to happen, he would need to gain her trust. He rose up on one elbow and smiled down at her. "You are still intact after your ordeal."

"The ordeal of the nightmare, or the ordeal of sharing your bed?" she teased.

"You are tempting as sin. I promise not to touch, if you will let me look at you." He didn't wait for her permission but slowly drew down the covers.

Lu wondered if she could trust him to keep his word. She remained silent but did not cling to the covers, which gave him tacit permission to look. His intense gaze roamed over her breasts, then rose to her mouth; it made her feel beautiful. She found his concentrated attention highly flattering. It made her feel extremely feminine. His dark face and black hair set her pulse racing, and the powerful muscles of his chest, covered by the dark pelt of hair, tempted her fingers to touch him. But Louisa knew that if she tempted him further, she would have to take responsibility for the consequences. "We cannot lie abed all day," she said breathlessly.

"Unfortunately," he said ruefully. "Wear something lovely. I am taking you into Omagh to meet all the important people."

As she slipped from the warm bed and made her way to her boudoir, she could sense her husband's eyes on her back and her bottom. It made her feel desirable, which threw her into another dilemma. *For someone who doesn't wish to be either wife or mother, you are embarking on a very slippery slope, Lady Lu.*

When Lady Abercorn stepped from their carriage in Omagh, she was wearing a stylish tawny orange afternoon gown and matching hat that sported a black ostrich feather. She took delight in lifting the hem of her skirt to reveal her black lace petticoat, knowing that James would roll his eyes. As Louisa gazed about, she realized that the town was much larger than she had expected. Their first stop was the town hall, where Abercorn introduced his wife to the lord mayor, Seamus Fitzgerald.

"Your Grace, it is a distinct pleasure to meet you." He bowed gallantly over her hand. "My wife will be grass green with envy that we've had the good fortune to meet."

"You may tell her that Lady Abercorn is planning a dinner party for next Friday and you and your good wife are invited to Barons Court."

Lu's eyebrows rose in surprise, but she took the news in stride and did not rebuke her husband in front of the mayor. "The Fitzgeralds will be our guests of honor."

They moved on to another section of the town hall, where the Tyrone County councilors had their offices. James introduced her to Clive O'Brien, Patrick McGowan, Ross Begley, and Joseph Quinn.

The marchioness graciously issued them invitations to her upcoming dinner party.

When they departed the town hall, James thanked her for falling in with his plans. "When we get home, we'll send an invitation to the Earl and Countess of Caledon. I have an ulterior motive."

"I should have guessed as much, you devious devil."

"Caledon is the lord lieutenant of Tyrone. Might as well invite the lord lieutenant of Donegal too. I'm hoping to become the future lord lieutenant of either County Tyrone or County Donegal."

"If you become the viceroy, will that make me the vice queen?"

He waggled his eyebrows suggestively. "I'll have a deal of things to teach you before you can claim to be a vice queen."

While James visited the county magistrate, Louisa explored some of the town's shops. Privately, she was happy about the dinner party. Since Abercorn was politically ambitious, finally here was something she could help him with, in return for his generosity toward her. Her mother had taught her how to be an effective political hostess and she was eager for a chance to prove herself.

James was waiting for her when she came out of the bookstore. He took her to his attorney's office.

"I am utterly delighted to finally meet the beauteous Lady Abercorn." Rowan Maloney bowed deeply and ushered her to a comfortable leather chair.

"I believe you are one of the attorneys who drew up our marriage contract." Louisa's manner was polite but cool.

James cut in quickly, "If you are left a widow, Maloney will make sure you receive your inheritance money from Barons Court before the estate is passed on to my future son and heir."

Lu realized the arrangement was far more generous than what her mother would receive from Woburn. "And do you look after my thousand-pound allowance from my father, Mr. Maloney?"

"I do indeed, Your Grace." Rowan's eyes twinkled. "Lord Abercorn was most insistent with your father's attorney that you receive such a generous allowance."

Lu glanced at her husband. "Seems the two of you were in cahoots to fleece the Duke of Bedford good and proper," she drawled. She did not see the wink James gave Rowan Maloney.

Abercorn asked his attorney to draw up the legal document to lease his flax mill to the Herdman brothers, and then he invited Maloney to the dinner party they were giving.

That evening when they arrived home, the post had been delivered. James had a letter from Angus Murray, his Scots attorney, and Louisa had two letters—one from her mother and the other from Georgy. She decided to keep them so she could read them in the privacy of her boudoir when she went up to bed.

A few hours later, Louisa undressed and chose a pink satin nightgown. When her trousseau had been made, she had vowed never to own a pristine white nightdress ever again. She sat down on the bed and opened her letters. She got as far as the salutation when James opened the door between the adjoining chambers.

He waved the letter in his hand. "Won't you join me, Lu? I'm dying to share my news with you."

She arched her brows. "Are you substituting your letter for a sugared mouse?"

He grinned. "Witty as well as shrewd—a seductive combination. Absolutely this is a ploy to get you in my bed again." He hid his amusement. "My news can wait." He left the doorway and went back into his room.

Lu read Georgy's letter. It was short. She sounded resentful that Louisa was not only a wife but also a marchioness. *"When I come to visit I hope you will introduce me to the wealthy, titled bachelors who have estates adjoining Barons Court. By the way, when I got back home, I learned that Teddy had deserted England. He's gone to France on a diplomatic mission. Which is ridiculous since he totally lacks diplomacy. He would never have gotten the post without Lord Holland's influence with the prime minister and King William."*

Louisa set her sister's letter down. She felt bad for Georgy. Clearly she meant that Teddy had deserted *her* as well as England.

Next she read her mother's letter. It recounted the family's journey from Scotland back to Woburn. Her mother thanked her for giving Rachel her dormouse, Cracknut, and told her how much she and her father missed her. *"I urge you to fight any feelings of homesickness, darling. Enjoy your honeymoon to the full. Your summer in Ireland will be over before you know it."*

Louisa set the letter down. *I don't have any feelings of homesickness. I find everything about Ireland irresistible.* She lifted her eyes to the open door. Then she picked up her letters and moved toward it, lured by an insatiable curiosity to know what was in Abercorn's letter.

Chapter Twenty-Five

"I'll show you mine, if you'll show me yours." James's words were deliberately teasing and provocative. He was sitting up in bed as if he were waiting for her. His eyes licked like a candle flame over the pink satin nightgown. He patted the bed in invitation.

Louisa climbed on and sat down facing him. "My letters are from Georgy and Mother. Would you care to read them?" She held them out.

He glanced down and read: *Enjoy your honeymoon.* James almost choked. "Your mother is no doubt giving you advice."

Louisa set her letters down. "What is your news? I'm curious as a cat."

"Do you remember when I came to the Doune because I feared you were ill, and we rode together to Kinrara over the mountain trail?"

"Of course I remember."

"We came to a clearing in the pines and a magnificent vista opened before us."

"Yes, we stopped to enjoy the view of the loch and the heather-covered mountains, and you said, *Now I understand why you love the Highlands.*"

James nodded. "And you said: *It holds a special place in my heart.*"

Absently, he reached for her bare foot and caressed it. "I'll never forget the look on your face. It made me want my own place in the Highlands. So when I was traveling from Edinburgh to see my mother in Aberdeen, I came upon a place that took my breath away and fired my imagination. I made my driver stop the carriage so I could drink it in. It was the most scenic glen and loch I'd ever seen in my life, and beside it stood a magnificent, gray stone turreted castle. Whenever I see something exquisitely beautiful, I long to possess it." His eyes roamed over her satin-clad body with appreciation.

"My map told me the long body of water was Loch Laggan, so I instructed Angus Murray, my Edinburgh attorney, to find out who owns the estate and offer to buy it from him." James held up the letter. "Turns out it is owned by Cluny, chief of the MacPherson clan. It is called Ardverikie, but he absolutely refuses to sell the place."

Louisa's face was etched with disappointment. "I thought you had good news."

The corners of his mouth lifted. "It is good news, Pussycat. Cluny offered to *lease* it to me, and we have agreed on fifty years."

"So Ardverikie is yours for the next fifty years?"

"Ours!" He held her ankle and pulled her toward him. His arms slid around her and he sought to capture her lips with his.

Louisa stiffened and tried to climb from the bed. He held her captive, refusing to let her leave. "Lu, why are you so afraid of intimate relations?" he demanded.

She stared at him wide-eyed for long, drawn-out moments. She longed to be one with him yet dared not. "I'm not afraid of intimate relations." Her words were as big a revelation to herself as they were to him. "It's the thought of having a child that terrifies me, James."

He enfolded her against his heart and dropped a tender kiss on the top of her head. "My sweetheart, I'd never dream of giving you a baby until you are ready. There are many ways for us to be intimate, without actual intercourse."

"You mean kissing. I must confess that I do enjoy your kisses, but I don't dare let things go any further."

"Kisses are only a small part of being intimate. I long to teach you how to enjoy your body, Lu. By heightening all your senses, they can give you as much pleasure as mine give me."

"Senses?"

"All five of them. Let me describe how. *Looking* at you fills me with delight. When I see you walk into a room, my heart skips a beat. When I watch you dance, I am mesmerized. Just a glimpse of your black lace petticoat makes me roll my eyes. When my gaze fastens on your mouth, my imagination fills my head with untold fantasies. Whenever you raise your black lashes and I see your emerald green eyes, I go weak. When I look at you wearing a pink satin nightgown, it takes my breath away."

Louisa smiled shyly.

"Just *hearing* you has an effect on me. When I hear you sing, I want to applaud. If I hear you laugh, I want to join you. When I hear your undergarments rustle seductively, I become aroused. If I pass the bathing room and hear water trickle, I want to rush in, grab the sponge from your hand, and bathe you."

Louisa laughed softly.

"My sense of *smell* plays merry hell with me. When I scent your jasmine perfume, it lures me to draw closer. When I inhale the fragrance of your hair, it makes me dizzy. When I detect the aroma of wine on your breath, it intoxicates me." He drew in a heady breath. "Your woman's scent fills me with lust."

Louisa blushed.

"When I *touch* you, your skin feels like silk to my callused fingers. When I cup your shoulders, an urge to protect you overwhelms me.

If our hands accidentally touch, I become instantly aroused. When I was holding you in the lake, teaching you to swim, I wanted to remove your ruffled drawers and fondle your naked flesh. When I take you before me in the saddle, the feel of your soft bum against my hard cock, makes my blood surge hot and wild."

"James, stop." She lowered her lashes.

"Not before I describe the sense of *taste*. When I kiss your hand, the taste of your warm skin makes my pulse race. When you feed me bacon and I lick your fingers, it makes me ravenous to taste every inch of you. When I taste the honeyed sweetness of your mouth, it drives me mad."

She raised her lashes. "You *are* mad."

"Not stark, raving mad. Just a little demented where you are concerned, Lady Lu. I find everything about you physically seductive."

"Everything?" Louisa craved to hear more sweet talk. It was deliciously addictive.

"At least a dozen things, starting with your feet. They are extremely dainty, with little pink toes and a high instep." He moved down in the bed and took one in his hand. He gazed at it, caressed it, inhaled its fragrance, and kissed it. Then he sucked her toes into his mouth and tickled them with his tongue.

Louisa was beginning to enjoy the game he was playing. "That's one; what is number two?"

He reached beneath the hem of her nightgown until his fingers reached the soft place behind her knees. "Very seductive," he murmured.

Lu, finding it difficult to speak, held up three fingers.

James moved up in the bed. "Your hair." He threaded his fingers into the dark mass of curls, inhaled its scent, and drew a tendril through his lips. Then he lifted her above him so that it cascaded down onto his throat and his shoulders. "It makes me quiver."

She looked into his eyes. "Four?"

He set his lips to the curve of her neck and left a trail of kisses. "More beautiful than the swans out on the lake."

She felt a shiver run down her back. "Five?" she whispered.

He rolled her onto her back and came above her in the dominant position. He raised her arms above her head and dropped a kiss into each armpit. When she gasped, he murmured, "An extremely intimate and seductive place."

"Dare I ask what the sixth is?"

He moved his hands down her body, sliding them over the slippery satin. "Your slim waist—I can almost span it with my fingers. And it has a swate spot in the middle."

"A sweet spot?" she asked breathlessly.

"Your navel." He circled it with his finger. "I can't wait to dip in my tongue."

"James!"

"That would be me."

"I lost count," she lied.

"Seven." He slid his hands beneath her and caressed her bottom with the palms of his hands. He moved in circles over the slippery satin. "Seven rhymes with heaven."

Louisa felt a tiny frisson of desire ripple through her belly. *Eight— I can't wait.*

James cupped her breasts and weighed them on his palms. His thumbs stroked over her nipples until they became erect and ruched like hard little diamonds. As he played with her lush titties, Lu felt burning threads of fire spiral down from her breasts into her belly and threaten to go lower. She licked lips gone suddenly dry as he slid the nightgown from her shoulders and exposed her bare breasts to his kisses.

"James . . . I want . . . I want . . ."

"Nine. I want it too." He captured her mouth with his in a lingering kiss that went on and on. He lifted his lips from hers. "Your mouth is one of the most wickedly tempting things about you, Lu. I'll never have enough of it." His lips took possession of hers firmly, parting them so he could slide in his tongue to capture all her sweetness.

With his mouth still against hers, he murmured, "Are you curious about ten?"

"Mmm."

James slid his hand down her body and raised the hem of her nightgown to expose her legs. "Your inner thighs are especially seductive." He traced his fingers down one thigh and up the other.

Louisa shivered at his touch.

He stroked and caressed her soft flesh with his callused palms and knew she was becoming aroused. "Eleven is even more intimate."

Louisa's breath caught in her throat as her thighs began to tingle.

His hands slipped beneath her to capture her bare bum. Then his fingers slid into the deep crevice between her bottom cheeks.

Louisa arched up from the bed as his hands evoked ever more sensitive sensations that were all new and deliciously wicked.

His hands pushed the pink satin up to her waist. "Twelve is Mons Venus, which guards your hidden jewel." His fingers threaded through the dark curls that sat upon her high mons. Then his fingertips dipped into her honey pot to toy and tantalize.

"No!"

"Enjoy the sensation . . . feel the pleasure, sweetheart." He stroked the private place, allowing her to get used to the intimacy. He knew when she began to thrill to his touch, and he pressed the pads of his fingertips against the sensitive spot hidden inside her scented flesh.

The tiny moan in her throat told him she was experiencing her own female sexuality for the first time. He dipped his head and took possession of her lips with his mouth. He thrust his tongue in a rhythm that matched the pulsations produced by his fingers. He felt her become dewy and moved in delicate circles around her bud, enticing her to feel passion. He stroked slowly to prolong her pleasure.

Louisa felt a hot ache start in her woman's core, then threads of flame raced up into her belly, spiraling upward into her breasts, making them hard and tingling. She cried out as she peaked and shattered into a million delicious shards of ecstasy.

James withdrew his fingers and cupped her mons with his strong hand as she pulsated and quivered until her last tiny spasm was spent. He carefully drew the satin nightgown to cover her nakedness. Then enfolded her in his arms and held her securely so she could savor the enchantment of what had just happened to her.

When he felt her body soften in his arms he said huskily, "There . . . I have violated nothing. I gave you pleasure without consummating our marriage. Everything about you is exactly the same as it was before."

"Before the twelve steps?" *I am still intact but nothing about me is the same . . . I will never be the same again.*

James was amazed that he had been able to hold himself in check. He had lusted to mount her and bury himself in her silken sheath, unleashing the fierce desire that rode him whenever he was in her presence. Somehow he had been able to put her enjoyment first, and his need to bring her pleasure had overridden his dark, primal urges. He realized that he must lure her gently. She had resisted him for so long, he knew that if he allowed his ravenous hunger to become savage, she might withdraw from him and erect a defensive barrier that he would have to scale like a castle wall.

James turned her over and curved his long body about hers in spoon fashion.

Lu wriggled against his powerful body until she found a comfortable spot. She smiled as she felt his arm slip about her and cup her breast. It made her feel cherished.

Before she drifted off to sleep, she thought about her husband's body. *I would love to stroke the contoured muscles of his chest and thread my fingers through its black pelt.* Then she thought of his inner thighs and his cock that thrust out in rampant splendor.

A frisson of desire spiraled through her and she shuddered at the thought of exploring his powerful male body.

The next day, they swam again in the lake, but this time Lu was daring enough to take off her drawers and swim naked. They played in the water like lovers, splashing, and touching, and laughing, and kissing. When they were done, she allowed him to dry her with a thirsty towel, patting and rubbing every inch of her silken skin. Then they lay together in the sun while James described again their five delicious senses, and proceeded to show her the dozen physically seductive places that drove him wild.

Lu has far more self-confidence today, both in and out of the water. James murmured, "Explore me, Lady Lu," and she joined in the sensual game with gusto.

On the ride home, Louisa spotted a bird sitting on the ground. She dismounted immediately and knelt beside it. The young raven tried to run away, but it couldn't fly.

James dismounted and bent down to have a look at it. "It has injured its wing."

"I'm going to take it and look after it until it can fly again, so the foxes don't get it," Lu said decisively.

James corralled it and Lu picked it up. When the raven tried to peck her fingers, she laughed. "Are you a male or a female?"

"I think it's a young female."

"How can you tell?"

"On a female, the beak starts to curve around the middle. The curve of a male's beak is more pronounced."

"I'm very impressed. You know so much about creatures."

"Cratures."

"She's black as tar. I'll call her Tara. I'll have to dig up worms from the garden."

She wrapped the bird in the towel and they remounted.

"You needn't. She's a raptor—she'll eat any kind of meat or flesh—preferably raw."

When they arrived at the stables, James unsaddled their mounts and turned them over to a groom. "Are you going to put her in one of the empty box stalls?"

"Of course not. I shall keep her in my boudoir." She glanced at him seductively. "Seeing as I'm not using it."

Louisa carried the young raven upstairs and entered her chamber. She looked about the room for a suitable place to put her patient. She carefully unwrapped the towel and set Tara down in one of the gold basins that had once belonged to Josephine Bonaparte.

James smiled his approval. It showed that Louisa valued the bird more than the imperial treasure.

She brought it a little pot of water and descended to the kitchens. She told the cook what she needed and asked for a knife. They went into the larder where a roebuck was hanging from a hook and Louisa carved off a small piece of flesh. She cut it up into tiny bits and took it back upstairs.

The raven huddled in the gold basin, and its bright yellow eyes watched Louisa's every move. "Hello, Tara. You are intimidated right now, but there is nothing here to be afraid of." She put the tiny bits of raw venison in the gold basin and moved away.

Louisa and James had just finished dinner, when Mrs. Connelly escorted one of the grooms to the dining room. When James saw him, he knew immediately that his Arabian mare must be showing signs of foaling. "Will you come with me, Lu?"

She hesitated because birthing intimidated her. *If something goes wrong, James will need me beside him.* "Yes, I'll come," she said quickly.

When they arrived at the stables, James hurried down to the box stall and Louisa followed. Jasmine was moving about restlessly, but she whickered when she saw him. He entered the stall and stroked his hand across the Arabian's swollen belly.

Louisa summoned her courage. "I warrant we are in for a long night of it."

"What makes you think that, sweetheart?"

"Giving birth is a long, agonizing procedure."

"Not for a mare. There is pain, certainly, but once she starts in labor, if she doesn't deliver within half an hour, the colt will be dead." James removed his coat and stripped off his shirt. "Sit down in the straw—I think she's started." With his strong hands and soothing words he gentled and encouraged his treasured mare.

In about quarter of an hour, which seemed far longer to Louisa, a birth sac slid onto the straw. James swiftly broke it open so the baby could breathe, and a pleasant aroma filled the air. Then he picked up his shirt and wiped the mucus from its coat. "It's a male! I couldn't be more pleased."

Lu watched Jasmine sniff and nudge the little colt. The touching affection between mother and baby brought a lump to her throat. "We just witnessed a miracle."

"What shall we call him? Prince something or other?"

"Let's call him Sultan, son of Jasmine."

"That's perfect." James wiped his hands on some clean straw and got up from his knees. After they watched the long-legged colt suckle, they returned to the house. While James went to bathe, Lu went into her boudoir to check on her raven.

She found the bird perched on the edge of the gold basin. "Well, aren't you the clever little *creature*?" Tara had eaten a few bits of venison and her water was half gone. The young bird cocked her head from side to side when Lu spoke to her.

James came in wearing only a towel about his hips. "That's a good sign. She knows it's nighttime and she's gone to roost." He laughed as a few droppings fell onto the dressing table.

Knowing he was naked beneath the towel made her pulse race. "*Shyte!*" Lu wiped up the bird's droppings with a linen napkin. She poured water from her jug and washed her hands. "Shall we go to roost?"

She's actually asking to share my bed. Wipe that smug look off your bloody face before she sees it, Abercorn.

James folded a small linen towel and tucked it beneath his pillow. *With any luck I'll need this before the night is over.*

He watched Lu come through the adjoining door into the master bedchamber. He experienced a flaring desire that threatened to consume him. It took him a moment to get it under control. He saw her begin to undo the buttons of her riding habit. "Let me undress you."

The corners of her mouth went up in a bewitching smile. "I have heard an Irish superstition that green gives a woman power over a man. Are you not afraid that I will drive you to your knees, Abercorn?"

That's exactly the position I'll crave once I have you naked. "Show me no mercy." He was beside her in two strides, and his fingers finished undoing her buttons and lifting off her riding dress. He turned her about and lifted her hair. "Here is another sensual place my lips cannot resist." He dipped his head and touched his tongue to the back of her neck. "You taste and smell deliciously feminine."

A tiny frisson of desire ran down her spine.

From behind, James wrapped one arm about her waist and raised her arm. His lips touched her wrist, and then he dropped a trail of kisses along her arm until he reached her shoulder. He set his mouth close to her ear and blew on the curly tendrils of her hair.

He removed her busk and ruffled drawers then trailed his lips down along the curve of her bare back. He felt her quiver when he kissed her tempting round bottom. When she was naked, save for her stockings and garters, he picked her up and carried her to their bed. He laid her down and spread her tantalizing hair across the pillow.

"You are beautiful in your witchery."

She reached up and traced her fingers over the sleek contours of his chest muscles. "Aren't you going to take off my stockings?"

"Later. Green satin garters hold me in thrall."

She was beginning to realize that a woman's power over a man had its own potent magic. Her feminine instincts were urging her to be more daring.

His mouth curved into a smile. *Lady Lu, you do possess great power, you just haven't learned to brandish it. Once you do, it will be devastating.* James allowed his smoldering glance to travel the length of her body. With the towel still about his hips, he knelt above her, straddling her soft thighs that were decorated with the garters. "I'm going to taste you."

She licked her lower lip and closed her eyes in anticipation of the kiss.

"I'm going to taste you everywhere."

Her lashes flew up as she felt his lips kiss the tendrils on her mons. She saw his dark head dip low between her thighs. "You must not," she whispered breathlessly.

"Darling, I must."

She saw his face become taut and hungry with need. As his mouth moved closer to her secret center she feared he would devour her. She arched her body and in that moment his thumbs touched her cleft and opened her slightly. Then he covered her with his hot mouth and licked her bud delicately with his tongue. The sensations he aroused were so exquisitely pleasurable, she wanted to scream with excitement.

He began to thrust his tongue in and out, longing to make her feel wild and wondrous. She was so small and tight, he could tell that she was still virgin, and he vowed to keep her that way for a while. Making love to her with his mouth aroused him to madness. He would never get enough of her.

As all her senses heightened, she arched into his mouth and cried, "James . . . James!"

James felt her climax as her sugared sheath tightened on his tongue; then he enjoyed her tiny pulsations as she shuddered with pleasure. Before he withdrew, he licked her swollen bud, relishing her cries of bliss.

She lay sprawled before him in wanton splendor, and he threw off the towel and moved up over her to capture her mouth in a passionate kiss. He thrust in his tongue, imitating what he longed to do with his cock, knowing that soon he would impale her with his hard shaft. But not yet, not until she was ready.

Lu tasted herself on his lips and it made her feel wicked. Making love to her with his mouth was addictive. She wanted him to do it again and again.

James was in a fever of arousal. His gut ached from their love play that hadn't reached its natural conclusion. If he didn't have release soon he knew that his hard erection would become painful. His body screamed with the pent-up desire that was surging through him. "Touch me, Lu."

He took possession of her hand and drew it slowly down his body. Then guiding her fingers he wrapped them around his marble-hard shaft. "Grip me firmly," he directed. As he manipulated her hand, slowly at first, then faster and faster, the hot sliding friction made his blood pound. He could not find release until he imagined he was inside her, with her slim legs wrapped about his body. He pictured her beneath him, writhing, panting, and moaning. Only then did his orgasm start. He held her hand still as his cock bucked and his seed spurt forth like a small fountain. "Thank you, sweetheart." James reached beneath his pillow for the linen towel.

Louisa buried her face against his shoulder, marveling at the power she had over him. The intimacy between them was a thing to be savored. Here in the big bed, the world receded and left them alone in their own private cocoon. She smiled her secret smile. Tonight when he whispered, *I love you, Lu,* she might not be dreaming.

Chapter Twenty-Six

When Louisa awoke, James was leaning on one elbow gazing down at her.

She stretched luxuriously. "Good morning."

He reached for her hand, dropped a kiss into her palm and closed her fingers over it. "Don't you think it's about time that you shared your secret with me, Lady Lu?"

"Secret?" She searched his eyes.

"You never had a miscarriage . . . you were never with child."

She stared at him in shock. *How on earth did you find out?* She licked lips gone suddenly dry. "What makes you think such a thing?"

"Because, my darling, your hymen is intact. You are still virgin."

"James . . . I . . . ." She bit her lip. "It's very complicated. Mother didn't deliberately deceive you." *O Lord, how can I explain?* "I was the one who deceived you." She rushed on, "But at the time, it was the lesser of two evils." *I shouldn't have said that.*

"Marrying me was the lesser of two evils?"

"No, I didn't mean that." She took a deep breath. "James, I couldn't tell you the truth without betraying . . . ." Her voice trailed away.

"Without betraying your sister."

"How did you know?" Lu's voice was filled with surprise.

"A wild guess," he said dryly. "It's no secret to me that Georgy was sexually active."

"She only confessed to me just before Christmas. She said she would kill herself if anyone learned of her shameful secret."

"Georgy is far too selfish to kill herself."

"She's not selfish!"

"She allowed you to take the blame—I call that selfish."

"But I'm stronger than Georgy. She was terrified and had no one else to turn to."

"But you did. You could have turned to me, Lu, and told me in confidence."

"You would have killed . . ." Her voice again trailed away.

"Teddy Fox? Absolutely, I would have killed him, if he had done it to you. But what's between him and Georgy is none of my business."

She searched his face. "James, can you forgive my deceiving you?"

"There is nothing to forgive. You are my heart's desire. If you hadn't been coerced, you might never have agreed to marry me." He winked at her. "By choosing the lesser of two evils you are the Marchioness of Abercorn *until death us do part.*"

She went into his outstretched arms and nuzzled his shoulder. "James, I'm so glad you know. You have lifted a weight off my conscience." She raised her eyes to his. "I should have agreed to marry you long ago. To be precise, I'm sorry I didn't accept your proposal the night you arranged for me to dance at Covent Garden."

"I shouldn't have let you leave. I should have made you my prisoner until you gave in to my demands."

"Irish devil." She lifted her lips and kissed him. "I love it when you are dominant."

"I'll remember," he promised.

I'm so lucky. He forgives me because he loves me.

. . .

"What a clever girl you are, Tara." The raven had hopped onto the windowsill. "You must be feeling adventurous." Louisa filled the bird's pot with water. "I'll go downstairs and get you some food."

As she moved toward the door, the young raven hopped to the floor and began to follow her. "Come on, then." When they got to the staircase, Tara hopped down the first two steps and then stopped. "Perhaps you'd like a ride." She reached down her hand and the raven hopped onto it. Lu carefully lifted the bird to her shoulder then continued descending the stairs with slow steps. She was absolutely thrilled that the raven considered her an ally rather than an enemy.

"I see you have cast another spell," James teased.

The raven cawed. "Don't you dare try to steal her affections from me, you womanizer! She's hungry. I do hope her wing is healing. Perhaps tomorrow we could take her outside and teach her to fly."

"She knows how to fly, Lu. She just needs to regain her confidence. When you've finished tending your charge, we'll go to the stables and check on the colt. Then I'd like you to join me in the library. I want your ideas on how to redesign a couple of rooms."

"You don't really. You're just trying to boost my confidence."

He shook his head. "Any more confidence, Lady Lu, and you'll be wearing the trousers around here."

Louisa cut up more venison for the raven and watched her eat a few pieces. Then she took her back up to her boudoir where she knew the bird would be safe.

A short time later in the stables, they found Jasmine, suckling her colt. "Sultan looks like he has grown overnight."

"That's because his coat is dry and fluffy today. Tomorrow we'll let them out into one of the paddocks. You'll enjoy watching him learn to run."

She drew in a deep breath of appreciation. "I love everything about Ireland."

In a flash he had his arms around her, and dipped his head to capture her mouth. He caressed her round bottom with his hands. "Tell the truth and shame the devil—it's the *Irishman* you love."

"Cocksure sod!"

"This room is far too small for a library." Louisa gazed up at the bookshelves as James stood at the library table looking down at the architectural plans of Barons Court.

"It certainly cannot compare to your father's magnificent library at Woburn," he said with regret.

"But James, there's no reason why we cannot duplicate Woburn's library. We just need to design it in another chamber that is more spacious."

"You may have hit upon the solution. We have no shortage of rooms."

They went in search of a chamber that could be redesigned. Next to the long gallery was a room that was large enough, but it was a bit dark and dismal. "I want my library to have an upper level like your father's. We could do that here, but it wouldn't be anywhere near as cheerful and welcoming," he complained.

"Would it be possible to put a dome in the ceiling like the one in the rotunda? That lovely oval room lets in so much daylight and sunshine."

James smiled and slipped his arm around her. "See what we can produce when we put our minds together?" He drew her close so that her soft breasts rested against his chest. "Together, I warrant there is no limit to what we can create."

Louisa drew in a swift breath. There was no mistaking his meaning. *By create, you mean procreate.* A frisson of desire swept through her. *You are breaching all my defenses, James Hamilton. I must double my guard.*

That night however, in the big bed, her caution deserted her, as her body responded to his shamelessly. When he brushed his lips against her thigh, or when his fingers stroked her bud with a tantalizing rhythm, or when she felt his hot erection slide across her belly, she writhed, and panted, and cried out her pleasure.

In return she exalted in making him gasp and groan as she cupped his heavy testes and wrapped her teasing fingers around his rigid cock.

During the next few days they went fishing in their own river where the shadowy pools teemed with trout. They swam in the lake with the otters that had grown used to them, crept through the woods at night to watch the badgers romp about with their young, and took the young raven out to the park to tempt her to fly.

"James, look! Another raven has just flown into the tree." She had perched Tara on a low branch.

"Let's move back toward our horses and watch."

The new arrival hopped from branch to branch until it reached Tara. They cawed to each other and bobbed their heads in communication.

"I think it's a male," he murmured.

The larger raven flew to a higher branch and waited. Tara flapped her wings but did not follow. Lu held her breath in anticipation. The raven called to Tara but she did not answer. "She's afraid to fly. Perhaps her wing still hurts." Tara fluttered to the ground and walked back to Louisa. "Do you think if we bring her back, he'll come again?"

"Perhaps. Try again tomorrow."

"Not tomorrow, James. I shall be busy all day. Have you forgotten we are hosting a dinner party?"

The next morning, Louisa was up with the lark. She inspected the five guest suites with Kate Connelly and asked the housekeeper to air the beds in case their guests decided to stay overnight. She spent the rest of the morning in the kitchen with the cook and her scullery maids, planning the food and wine they would serve to their guests. Then she moved on to the large dining room, selecting the china, the cutlery, the crystal, the serving dishes, the linen, the candles, and the flowers. She even chose which cheese, fruit, and nuts would be served.

When James appeared with an amused look on his face, she told him he was underfoot. "Make yourself useful. Legend has it that all the Irish are musical. Find me some fiddlers or flute players. They can play in the small dining room, where they can be heard without being seen."

James bowed. "I warrant I can also find you a harpist, Lady Abercorn."

"That would lend a note of refinement, Lord Abercorn."

With a straight face he asked, "Are you planning to dance for our guests? If it's refinement you want, may I suggest an Irish reel? *The Ladies' Pantaloons,* perhaps?"

She pointed to the door. "OUT!"

James rolled his eyes in rapture and this time he was completely serious. He had come up to dress for the dinner party and found the maid, Molly, tightening the strings on his wife's corset. He motioned for Molly to leave. "I'll do that. I've never seen a red corset before."

"I find that difficult to believe, considering your association with certain members of the theater," Lu teased.

James refused to take the bait. He fastened the corset strings and kissed the nape of her neck. "I'm tempted to remove it."

"I thought this dinner was to further your political ambitions to become a lord lieutenant."

"Ah, that achievement is years away. You are here and now, vixen."

"Hand me my petticoat." She stepped into it and allowed him to tie the tapes at her waist. "Now for the *piece d'occasion*." She lifted the gown that had been laid out on the bed and raised her arms so that he could put it on over her head. It was the crimson taffeta embroidered with deep red garnets that she'd had made in the ancestral Abercorn color. "Do you think the *décolletage* is too low?"

"Every female guest will think so, but I warrant every male will drink a toast to you with his eyes."

"Please call Molly back. She's helping me put up my hair. We'll use my boudoir, so you can dress in privacy."

As James and Louisa stood in the oval rotunda waiting to greet their guests, he murmured, "Here come the Earl and Countess of Belmore. Don't mention that Claud is coming next month to campaign for the County Tyrone seat."

"Why not?" she whispered.

"The earl is the present MP for Tyrone."

Lu hid her smile behind her fan. "You are so bad." She had done her homework and knew the Earl of Belmore was Amar Lowry, and that his wife Emily was from Kent.

The next couple to arrive was the Marquis and Marchioness of Londonderry. Charles Vane Stuart was a charmer, and his wife, Frances, was a dark-haired beauty about ten years older than Louisa.

James introduced his wife to George Chichester and his wife Anna. Louisa knew their titles were Marquis and Marchioness of Donegal.

The fourth noble couple was the Earl and Countess of Caledon. Louisa had no trouble remembering the earl's name was Alexander Du Pre, and that he was the present lord lieutenant of Tyrone.

"I'm delighted that Barons Court has a new lady of the manor," Lady Catherine declared. "You must visit us at Caledon House."

"Thank you for your warm invitation. James and I would love to come."

"Lady Abercorn, it is a pleasure and an honor to meet the daughter of the Earl of Bedford. Your father was the most popular lord lieutenant that Ireland ever had." The Earl of Caledon winked at her. "Rumor has it James married you for your father's political influence, but now that I've seen you it's clear he wed you for your beauty."

Louisa smiled sweetly. "And here's me thinking he wed me for my brother's political influence. I warrant Lord John Russell will be prime minister of England one day."

Lady Catherine bestowed a look of admiration and Lady Frances declared, "Touché, my dear. Your beauty is only exceeded by your wit."

Louisa treated Mayor Fitzgerald with as much deference as she accorded her noble guests, perhaps a bit more, knowing that town officials revered attention.

At dinner she carried the conversation with ease. She was knowledgeable about Irish as well as English politics. She spoke of horses and racing with the men, and fashion with the ladies. She even promoted the flax mill. "Our mill is able to spin flax so fine, they can produce a hundred hanks from each pound. I warrant there is no finer linen or cambric spun anywhere than here in Northern Ireland. I intend to send some to Woburn for my mother and sisters."

She discussed cosmetics and herbal creams with the ladies, since aging skin was the nightmare of every female living and breathing. When they spoke of their children, she listened attentively. When they hinted at her producing an heir, she smiled sweetly and changed the subject.

Louisa was knowledgeable about many subjects and answered all their questions about the king and queen of England, as well as the young heiress to the throne, Princess Victoria Alexandrina.

When she spoke with a male guest, she gave him her undivided attention, which was far more flattering than outright flirtation. Louisa had learned from her mother at an early age that every man's favorite subject was himself.

Soft, lilting music could be heard throughout dinner, but because the musicians were in another room, it did not intrude on the conversation. After dinner she led her guests to the great hall for drinks and *swatemates*.

When the hour grew late, Louisa extended an invitation to those who lived farther away than Omagh to stay the night at Barons Court. The titled couples all opted to stay, while the Abercorns' local guests decided it was time to depart.

It was one o'clock in the morning before Louisa was able to join James in the master bedchamber.

"Our first dinner party was a resounding success, and I owe it all to you, Lady Lu. I certainly made the right choice when I chose to wed the daughter of the Duke and Duchess of Bedford."

"The right choice to further your political ambitions, or the right choice to provide Barons Court with a perfect hostess?" she teased.

"Both, of course . . . as well as a more intimate reason. For the past two hours I've been anticipating undoing the strings on that red corset of yours."

"'Tis said that *anticipation heightens the pleasure*." Lu allowed him to help her remove her crimson gown, which she carefully hung in the wardrobe. "Savor your anticipation a little longer, James. I must go and check on my young raven."

His gaze licked over the provocative corset and lingered on the curve of her breasts. "The word *ravenous* is derived from ravens. Ravenous is exactly how I feel."

"Then perhaps I should sleep in my boudoir tonight."

"Don't cocktease."

Louisa smiled. *That's exactly what I was doing.*

The following day, after their guests had departed, Louisa wanted to take Tara back to the park. "She perched on the valance above the window last night. She must have flown up there. Perhaps she's ready to spread her wings."

Tara perched on the pommel of Louisa's saddle as they rode out to the park. As she dismounted, James advised, "Put her facing the wind. Birds prefer to take off and land that way. Facing windward helps keep their feathers unruffled."

"Where did you acquire all this knowledge? I think you are *fey*."

"A misspent childhood, rambling with the leprechauns, I warrant."

She perched Tara on a branch, facing into the breeze. Then they moved back from the tree to observe. They exercised patience and sure enough, after a while, another raven swooped onto a high branch.

James murmured, "I believe it's the same male."

The birds exchanged a few *caws*, and Lu held her breath as the larger raven made his way down to the lower branch. As before, the two birds bobbed their heads in communication. Then the male flew up to a high branch and waited.

Tara stretched her wings, flapped them a couple of times, and flew up to the branch where the male raven sat. "I told you she could fly," Lu whispered.

After the birds sat together for a minute or two, the male flew up and circled about the tree, cawing loudly. "All she needs is confidence," James murmured.

Again, Louisa held her breath, willing her young raven to fly.

Suddenly Tara took off into the wind and joined her companion. They flew in a wide circle over the tree. "Oh, how brave she is!" Lu cried.

Her young bird flew onto a tree branch then flew to the ground beside Louisa. "No, no, Tara, you mustn't come back to me. I want you to be free." Lu was so disappointed she wanted to cry. She looked at James hoping he could make it right.

"Have faith and a little patience, sweetheart."

Just when Lu thought it was hopeless, her young raven began to caw and joined the male in his flight. She and James stood with their faces turned to the sky as the pair of ravens flew higher and higher. "He gave her confidence to be free. It's a miracle!"

James slipped his arm around her. "Every *crature* needs a mate. We all crave love."

When they returned to the house, Louisa was delighted that she had once again received two letters—one from her mother and the other from Georgy. "I shall read them right away so I can reply to them before dinner. I have lots of things to write about."

Her mother's letter was filled with news about Lu's brothers:

Henry has passed his first year at Oxford and Cosmo is looking forward to joining him in the autumn. Alexander is still keen on becoming a doctor, though I warrant a young man who is not yet eleven may easily change his mind in the coming years.

Edward is still in the Mediterranean and tells us he is about to get a promotion to lieutenant commander. Last week I received a letter from Charles. He seems to be fascinated with India and its people.

Wriothesley and Eliza are expecting their first child, and they are hoping for a boy.

Your father is well—I believe the time in Scotland was good for his health, and since Jack has taken over the management of Woburn, your father has more time to rest and relax. I am looking forward to seeing you and James, and of course Barons Court. I shall be there in less than a month! My darling Louisa, I think of you every day.

Lu smiled as she read her sister's letter. It was all about Georgy:

Through mother's dear friend, Edward Ellice, I have met a
gentleman, Charles Romilly, who has quite taken my fancy.
He is both tall and broad, and extremely handsome to boot.
He has no title and is only a clerk of the Crown, so marriage is
out of the question. But I have to admit that I am in lust with
the man. I don't really want to leave London for our upcoming
visit to Ireland, but who knows? Perhaps my absence will make
him all the keener for my company when I return.

Lu sat down at her writing table. Her mother's letter was easy to answer. Georgy's, on the other hand, posed a problem. She wondered if she should admonish her to be careful, or scold her for her discrimination over titled suitors. The latter might be hard to swallow, coming from the Marchioness of Abercorn. In the end she did neither. Instead she urged her to come to Ireland and told her that she missed her.

After dinner, Louisa remembered the unpacked crate of paintings in the gallery. "I never did see what art you bought in England. I'd like to see them and have them hung before mother visits."

She watched James open the wooden crate. "How many are there?"

"Only two, but the subjects are extremely lifelike." He lifted them from their packing and handed one to Louisa.

Her eyes went wide in surprise. "Edwin Landseer painted this."

"Yes, he painted both of them. I saw his work at Woburn. I loved the portrait he painted of you with your horse. So I visited his studio in London and purchased these two. I particularly like this one titled *Shoeing*. And how could I resist *Arab Tent* portraying the white Arabian mare and her colt?"

"Oh, James, the colt looks just like Sultan! Edwin truly is a genius." She blushed. "When he was painting my portrait, I developed a girlish infatuation for Edwin. Not long after, my feelings changed completely."

James laughed indulgently. "It's amazing how one week we can develop a fatal attraction for someone, and before you know it, the appeal vanishes into thin air."

Ah, that happened to you, I warrant. Lu was immediately ashamed of her thought. "You have very good taste in art. These two paintings should be hung side by side."

When they entered their bedchamber, Lu was in a restless mood. She undressed and donned a black silk nightgown. "For some reason I feel like dancing tonight. When I lose myself onstage, it frees my mind to soar about and ponder things so that I see them more clearly. I wish you could play for me."

"But I can. It would give me the greatest pleasure to play the piano for you. Especially if you perform your Spanish shawl dance." He rolled his eyes.

"A command performance done especially for the Marquis of Abercorn. Your wish is my command, Your Lordship." She opened the wardrobe and pulled out her fringed crimson shawl. She wrapped it around her bare shoulders and together they went to the chamber where her new stage had been built.

The melody James began to play was hauntingly beautiful. Lu had never heard it before, but she had no trouble dancing to it, and it fit her mood perfectly. Her thoughts took flight. Ireland was a magical place, and she enjoyed it more every day. She was happy that she had married an Irishman who was teaching her about his country.

Louisa thought about their lakes and streams that were teeming with new life. Millions of hatchlings darted through the water. Families of otters chased about playing endless games. Skulks of foxes and setts of badgers had produced litters of young and seemed to be thriving. Their Arabian Jasmine watched her new colt Sultan dash about the meadow; then he would cuddle close and the mare would suckle him. Whenever Lu saw them together, her heart was touched with yearning.

As she swayed about the stage, swirling her shawl, she thought about Wriothesley and Eliza having their first child, and for the first time she felt envious. Her thoughts moved on to the ravens. Lu knew she could have tamed Tara and kept her as a pet, but that would be wrong. Tara showed great courage when she learned to fly and joined the male raven in a flight to freedom and happiness. *Every crature needs a mate. We all crave love.* She suddenly knew the truth of her husband's words, and she realized that she had found her mate and he proved every day that he loved her.

As James watched Louisa dance, he became mesmerized by her lithe, graceful movements. When she danced she had an ethereal quality that touched his heart. Her dark, delicate beauty cried out for him to possess her body and soul. He stopped playing and sat transfixed as the glow of the lamps alternately concealed and revealed the curves of her tempting body through the transparent black silk.

James walked a deliberate path to his wife. He swept her up into his arms and carried her upstairs to his bed.

Chapter Twenty-Seven

"I was thinking about the ravens and how they stay together for life. I'm glad she found a mate." Lu shivered as he removed her nightgown.

James picked her up and lifted her into bed. "*He* found *her*."

"She found the courage to fly with him." She watched him slide into bed. "I wish I had the courage to fly with you, James."

He cupped her cheek gently. "You have courage, my love."

She lowered her lashes. "Not enough."

"Look at me, Lu. You have *more* than enough. You were fearless enough to dance at Covent Garden. You were brave enough to take on your sister's trouble and put her well-being before your own. Surely you are daring enough to let me consummate our marriage?"

"I do want you to make love to me . . . it's just that . . ."

He brushed the tendrils back from her temple. "You are apprehensive about having a child," he finished.

"Yes," she whispered.

"I'm sure you are not alone. I warrant you will make the best mother in the world. But first things first . . . I have to make you a wife before I make you a mother. Are you brave enough to yield to me, Lady Lu?"

She smiled seductively. "I am sorely tempted."

He drew down the covers and began to make love to her with his eyes, lingering on every secret, intimate part of her body. He savored the sense of spicy anticipation as he felt excitement stir in him. He relished the tightening of his balls and shaft, the heat stealing across his loins, and the potent sensation as his cock thickened and hardened. He dipped his head to taste her lips, and he heard her sigh when he took his lips away.

Louisa wondered if it was the wine she drank at dinner that made her feel so bold. *No, it's this devilishly attractive Irishman whose eyes are stained black with passion.* She cast him small, tempting glances from the corner of her eye and licked her lips provocatively with the tip of her tongue. She gasped with pleasure as he threaded his fingers through the curls on her mons, dipped in a finger, and then tasted it.

"Honey pot," he murmured.

She slipped her arms about his neck and offered him her lips. His hungry mouth was hot, fierce, and demanding, and she closed her eyes and gave herself up to him to assert his mastery over her in any way he wished. For the first time ever she welcomed the act of domination and submission.

His hands roamed over her body, caressing, exploring, and teasing until he had set up a fever of need. He fused his mouth to hers and she opened her lips to receive his tongue. It ravaged her mouth until she moaned from its thrusts.

She felt an emptiness inside her that needed filling in exactly the same way he filled her mouth. She reached for him with fevered fingers then gasped as she felt the engorged size of him.

Her gasp brought him to his senses and he schooled himself to be gentle with her this first time. He wanted her eager for him the rest of their lives and knew this consummation could not be savage but must bring her pleasure. He gathered all her softness in his powerful arms, imprisoning her beneath the hard length of his body. Her thighs parted, inviting his thick male shaft to seek succor inside her. His hands slid down to cup her buttocks and he rubbed her against his hardness. When he heard her moan with need, he positioned the velvet tip against her cleft and, with one thrust, penetrated her hymen.

Louisa bit her lip to stifle her cry, and miraculously, though the pain was sharp, it was short-lived. After the initial stab, it was replaced by a sensation of fullness, and as James held still so she could get used to his size, she could feel his heartbeat deep inside her. The whispered love words he poured over her made her melt inside.

"My sweet, wrap your legs around my back."

Louisa slowly slid her thighs around his hips and crossed her ankles, imprisoning him tightly. She pressed her lips against his throat and felt his throbbing pulse beat. When he began to thrust, her body began to undulate to the sensual rhythm. As her desire spiraled higher and higher, she dug her nails into his shoulder, and finally surrendered everything with a passionate sob.

When James felt her climax, he withdrew quickly and thrust against her soft belly until he spent. With a cry he scattered his seed across her silken skin.

I surrendered everything to him, and I am glad. At long last I am a wife and a real woman. His lovemaking had empowered her, and her self-esteem soared. Consummation had conquered all her fears and her heart overflowed with love for her dark, devilishly attractive husband.

Lu awoke when the curtains were drawn back to let in the sunshine. James had brought their breakfast on a tray and she sat up in bed and smiled shyly.

Her hair was wildly dishevelled and James thought she had never looked more beautiful than she did on this glorious morning. "Lady Abercorn, you truly take my breath away."

I can finally lay claim to that title. "It smells good. What did you bring?"

"Food fit for a marchioness, of course." He set the tray before her and began the acknowledgment of last night's lovemaking with a kiss that told her he remembered every detail. It also evoked tonight's possibilities. His dark eyes told her that she lingered in his consciousness. James knew that without the epilogue, the cycle of making love was incomplete.

When Lu lifted the silver cover of a small dish, instead of food she found a small velvet box. She opened it eagerly and found a pair of emerald and diamond earrings. "Oh, James, how can I thank you? I simply adore emeralds!"

"I'll think of a way. I chose emeralds to match your lovely eyes. They will also go splendidly with your diamond necklace from the Russell collection."

Lu sighed with happiness as she put on the earrings. "I'm the luckiest lady alive."

James sat down on the bed and lifted the breakfast covers. "Let's eat before it gets cold. I've ordered a slipper bath for you, so you won't have to leave our chamber to bathe this morning."

His words brought a smile to her lips. "You have no ulterior motive, of course."

"I always have an ulterior motive, Lady Lu. I've had a fantasy for years about watching you bathe. I've decided this morning is the perfect time to indulge it."

As she ate her crispy rashers of Irish bacon, she said, "Tell me about this fantasy."

"Very well. I walk into a chamber and find you reclining naked in a marble slipper bath. In your languid, sensual pose your lush breasts seem to float upon the water. Your long black eyelashes cast delicate shadows upon your cheekbones, and your full lips form a pouting moue inviting my kisses. Your black silken hair cascades over the edge of the tub to the carpet, inviting my fingers to tangle in it and lift it to my face. I feel my cock engorge and throb with desire."

She licked her lips. "And when did you begin having this fantasy?"

"The day your brother Charles brought me to Woburn on my summer holidays from Oxford."

Lu's eyes widened. "If you've been having a naked fantasy about me for two years, it is high time we indulged it." She glanced across the breakfast tray and saw the bulge between his legs. "I warrant you've been throbbing long enough."

"After your . . . *our* bath, what would you like to do today?"

"I've decided to make some rose-scented candles. The wild roses are blooming everywhere . . . wild *Irish* roses."

James smiled into her eyes. "*Sure, and may there be a road before you and it bordered with roses, the likes of which have never been smelled or seen before, for the warm fine color and the great sweetness that is on them.*"

"That's lovely. I hereby decree that you must quote me poetry every morning."

"I promise. If you're occupying yourself making candles today, I'll ride out to the mill with the leasing contract I've signed. When the Herdman brothers have affixed their signatures, I'll take it into Omagh and give it to Rowan Maloney for safekeeping."

There was a knock on the door. "Oh, I warrant that's the bath. James, hurry and finish breakfast, so we can proceed with the next delicious course."

Three hours later, Lu waved to her husband as he rode from Barons Court and she took her basket into the park to cut the wild roses. Her heart was brimful of joy and her heart overflowed with love for her husband. She was so glad she had overcome her reluctance to allow James to make love to her. *The Irish devil has made me happier than I've ever been in my life.*

Lu took her roses to the stillroom and hummed a lilting tune as she separated the fragrant petals from their stems. Her song halted as she pricked her thumb with a rose thorn. "Damnation!" She stuck it in her mouth to suck away the blood.

In the silence she could faintly hear female voices. They sounded angry, and she could tell they were having an argument. Her curiosity was piqued; the household was a calm and peaceful one, and the staff seemed a contented lot. She left the stillroom and walked toward the voices. She stopped outside open French windows when she saw the housekeeper, Mrs. Connelly, scolding a female who had her back to Louisa.

"You shouldn't have come to Barons Court! Have you no *shame*?"

"James promised that Barons Court would always be my sanctuary."

"You mustn't call him James. He is Lord Abercorn."

"Don't be ridiculous! He asked me to call him James. We are on extremely intimate terms. He pays my rent and takes me out to dinner, among other things. Why on earth would I call him Lord Abercorn, and why wouldn't I come home when I need him?"

Lu stepped inside. A cold finger of apprehension touched her. "Kitty, is that you?"

The young woman turned, and Louisa's eyes widened as she saw that she was heavy with child. "Kitty, what are you doing here?" *Please God, no!*

"Jane . . . I could ask the same of you. Barons Court is my home. Kate Connelly is my mother. Kitty Kelly is just my stage name."

"Kitty! This lady is the Marchioness of Abercorn," the housekeeper admonished.

Kitty's hands went to her hips defiantly. "So, your name isn't Jane after all. You must be Lady Louisa, the noble daughter of the Duke and Duchess of Bedford. Imagine you dancing at Covent Garden!"

"I'm sorry, Lady Abercorn. My daughter doesn't know her place."

"On the contrary, I do know my place, and my bloody place is *here!*" Kitty raised her chin. "Where is your husband, my lady? I need to talk with him."

Lu had such a painful lump in her throat she could hardly speak. "Lord Abercorn is out on business."

Kate Connelly could not hide her humiliation. "When did this happen?"

"When I was here at Christmas, of course!" Kitty said defiantly.

She and James were here together in December. He never told me Kate Connelly was Kitty's mother. Her knees felt like wet linen. *Don't be naive, Louisa. Why would he tell you his mistress is his housekeeper's daughter?*

"Have neither of you any decency?" Kitty demanded. "How can you keep me standing here in my condition? Have a room plenished for me."

Louisa rang the bell and Molly answered the summons. "Would you ready one of the guest suites for this lady, and take up her bag?"

Molly goggled at Kitty's belly. "Yes, my lady." She picked up the bag and Kitty followed her.

Kate's face was ashen. "Lady Abercorn, I'm so ashamed of my daughter's behavior."

Louisa pressed her lips together and shook her head. Then she followed Kitty Kelly as she made her clumsy way up the staircase. When Molly was out of earshot, Lu steeled herself to ask Kitty the dreaded question. "Is James the father of your child?"

The redheaded chorus girl looked her up and down. "Yes," she replied.

As Louisa watched her disappear down the hallway, icy fingers closed about her heart. Only a short time ago, she was the happiest female in Ireland. Now she was heartbroken. She went into her boudoir and sank down on the bed.

Was it only this morning that I let him share my bath and make love to me? Her eyes flooded with tears. Her thoughts were in disarray, her emotions were in turmoil, and her happiness lay in shards all about her.

As Louisa sat in utter defeat, her sorrow slowly transformed into anger. Then it progressed to red-hot anger! She saw Molly go past her door. "Molly, I need your help."

The young maid came into the boudoir and kept her eyes lowered.

"Help me pack my things, Molly. I'll just take the clothes in this wardrobe. I'll send for my other things later." Louisa summoned a footman. "Would you have them ready the carriage for me, and then come back for my luggage?"

Her hands went to her ears intending to remove the diamond and emerald earrings. Then she changed her mind. *You bastard! You bloody Irish bastard! You begetter of bastards! I've earned the jewels. I finally yielded and gave you everything, and Kitty Kelly is my sodding reward!*

Louisa packed her brushes and combs, and put her powder and lip rouge into her reticule. All she had in the bottom of her purse was a couple of gold guineas.

I have no money . . . but I know where to get some . . . Rowan Bloody Maloney!

When Louisa stepped from her carriage in Omagh, she was garbed in a fuchsia-colored traveling suit. Her matching hat was decorated with a cream ostrich feather and she wore cream kid gloves. "Wait for me," she told her driver.

"Lady Abercorn, what a delightful surprise." Rowan Maloney bowed to her.

"Surprise indeed, though not a delightful one, I warrant."

The attorney showed her to a chair. "How may I help you, my lady?"

She ignored the chair. "By handing over my thousand pounds, Mr. Maloney."

"Of course, my lady. Will a bank draft serve your needs?"

"No, it will not. I will take it in cash, please."

Though his eyebrows twitched, he kept the look of alarm from his face. "If you will take a seat, I shall endeavor to accommodate you, Lady Abercorn."

When he left the room, Louisa deigned to sit. In a few minutes she heard her husband's voice. *Judas! I forgot he was coming here today.* Louisa jumped up from the chair and braced herself for the storm.

James came into the room smiling. "You came to meet me, Lady Lu."

"Do not delude yourself. I came for my money. I'm going home to England."

His smile turned into a frown. "What's amiss? Have you received bad news?"

"As a matter of fact, I have." Her green eyes glittered. "It was delivered by a red-headed chorus girl."

His frown deepened. "Kitty?"

"How many red-headed mistresses do you have?"

"Lu, we are at cross purposes."

"And always have been, I warrant!"

"What on earth are you talking about?"

Her eyes narrowed. "Why didn't you tell me that Kitty Kelly was Kate Connelly's daughter? Why didn't you tell me that she spent Christmas with you at Barons Court?"

"I didn't think it mattered."

"Then once again you are deluding yourself. Kitty has arrived bearing the fruit of your scandalous liaison."

"You are talking rubbish!"

"Not enough that you demanded a fortune from my father to marry me. Not enough that you desired the political connection more than you desired me. Well, let me disabuse you, Lord Bloody Abercorn. You cannot have your cake and eat it too!"

Rowan Maloney beckoned James from the room. "Shouldn't I tell her that you put the money from her dowry in trust for her, my lord?"

"Absolutely not."

"Here is the money she requested," Maloney said uncertainly.

"I'll take it." James went back into the room, with Rowan on his heels.

"Do you have my thousand pounds, Mr. Maloney?" she demanded.

"I have it," James declared.

She held out her hand imperiously. "You avaricious swine. Give it to me."

"One more word, madam, and I shall give you a clout round your ear hole."

"You wouldn't dare!"

James took a swipe at her hat and sent it rolling across the floor. "Silence!"

Lu took a step back from him. He had never spoken to her in fury before. She summoned her courage. "I won't put up with your bastards. I'm going home!"

"You are going home, all right. Home to Barons Court. You are demented. I shall take you into protective custody until you regain your senses." He stepped toward her.

"Don't you dare touch me!"

His dark eyes were stained black with fury. James swept her up and carried her outside to the carriage. He set her down on the seat and slammed the door. He jerked his thumb at the driver. "Home!"

Inside the coach, Louisa's anger doubled. She put her hand on the door latch, intending to get out, but the driver was going so fast, the carriage was actually careening. Lu withdrew her hand and schooled herself to wait until it stopped. But inside, her fury bubbled like the brew in a witch's cauldron.

Demented, indeed! He is the one who is demented if he thinks he can bully me and keep me from leaving. The swine thinks he can deny it, but let's see him refute the accusation when he is confronted with the evidence of her swollen belly. Lu's hand went to her hair. *The uncivilized devil ruined my hat, to boot!*

When they arrived at Barons Court and the driver stopped the carriage in the courtyard, Louisa flung open the door and jumped out in a flash. She was incensed that Abercorn had arrived before her and was standing, waiting for her. She lifted her skirts and began to run, but his quickness, determination, and strength easily thwarted her. With her wrist in a vise grip she struggled to free herself, flying at him with her free hand and trying to tear his dark face with her nails. She succeeded in neither. Thwarted, she balled up her fist and smote him in the chest. She refused to give him the satisfaction of showing that she hurt herself.

With long, determined strides he took her into the house. Since the indignity of being dragged was anathema to her, she had no option but to keep up with him. They climbed the stairs in silence. She wanted to scream abuse at him but instinctively knew such behavior would put her at a distinct disadvantage.

Abercorn took her into the master bedchamber, then through the adjoining door into her boudoir. He freed her wrist and looked her directly in the eyes. "Of what exactly am I accused?"

"Kitty Kelly is having your child!"

James stared at her for a full minute. "If that's what you think— if that's what you truly think of me, we can never be husband and wife." He paused and then continued, "You have a natural impulse to close yourself off as a defense against being hurt. I will give you some time to find the strength to rise from your defensive crouch and think about this accusation. Don't concentrate on whether you can trust me, Louisa. Trusting yourself is the key to making the best decision for your marriage."

He walked to the outer door, locked it, and put the key in his pocket. Then he entered the master bedchamber.

When he went into the other room, Lu immediately slammed the adjoining door. The minute she did it, she realized she had no clothes in her boudoir wardrobe. She had packed them all and they were in the carriage. Of course she had plenty of clothes in the master bedchamber. *I'll go naked before I'll enter that room again!*

James went in search of Kate Connelly. He found her in her housekeeper's quarters.

"Lord Abercorn, my daughter has brought shame upon Barons Court."

"Kate, tell me what happened."

"Kathleen . . . Kitty arrived in the middle of the morning, swollen with child. We had words, and unfortunately Lady Abercorn heard the altercation. Apparently your wife knew Kitty but didn't realize she was my daughter until she found us together."

"Where is Kitty?"

"Lady Abercorn asked Molly to plenish one of the guest suites for her. I'm so sorry, my lord." Kate hesitated. "Kathleen said you had been paying her rent in London."

"That's perfectly true. Her original lodgings were in a rough area, entirely unsuitable for a young woman living alone. I found her a respectable house and paid the landlady to keep an eye on her. I saw no need to worry you about it."

"That was very obliging of you, Lord Abercorn. She shouldn't have come here, shaming us, causing trouble."

"Of course she should have come. My grandfather admonished me to make sure Barons Court would be a haven for her."

"She's gone and got herself in the same trouble I did." Mrs. Connelly wrung her hands. "When she went running off to London, it's the one thing I feared."

James put a comforting hand on her shoulder. "Yet I warrant it didn't happen in London. Most likely it happened here at Christmas."

"That it did!"

"Don't fret your guts to fiddle strings, Mrs. Connelly. It isn't the end of the world. I shall see what I can do to set things right." He moved toward the door. "Make yourself a pot of tea and put your feet up, Kate."

James went upstairs to the guest wing and knocked on the door to one of the suites. When Kitty opened it, he said, "May I come in?"

She nodded and tried to cling to her defiance, but it began to waver. She lowered her lashes. "I'm sorry, my lord."

"Sorry for what, Kathleen?" he asked softly.

"You're not angry with me?"

"You were in trouble. You had no one in London. You did the right thing to come home to Ireland." He paused. "Now you have to decide about your future."

"I know." She sat down and rested her hands on her swollen belly.

"After the child is born, do you want to keep it, or do you intend to return to London and the stage?"

"I want to mother my baby. I don't want to go back to London, but my decision depends on"—she hesitated—"certain circumstances."

"I understand." He nodded toward the bed. "Why don't you get some rest? The journey must have been exhausting."

James returned to the master bedchamber. He put his ear to the adjoining door, but all he heard was dead silence. *I thought that at long last you loved me, Louisa. But love without trust is no love at all. Once I would have given you anything—forgiven you anything—but this time, Lady Lu, you won't get your way!*

Chapter Twenty-Eight

$\mathcal{L}$ouisa removed her vivid fuchsia dress, since it was the only one she had, and hung it in the empty wardrobe. She was wearing ruffled bloomers beneath a lavender petticoat. Inside, she was seething. Now she was not just angry over Kitty Kelly. *How dare the Irish swine keep me captive? It's just more proof that Abercorn isn't civilized!*

She paced about the small chamber working herself up into a fine froth of fury. She had known all along it was a mistake to give a man everything, and now she was kicking herself for allowing him to consummate their marriage. She caught a glimpse of herself in the mirror and spoke to it. "Giving your heart to a man is like giving a delphinium to a dog. He will simply piss on it!"

Finally she stopped pacing and looked through the window. The afternoon light had started to fade and she realized it had begun to rain. The room was cast in dark shadows, and to banish the gloom she lit her lamps. She was restless but surmised it would not be long before James opened the door. She would neither look at him nor speak to him. Her outraged silence would speak louder than any words.

Louisa jumped as she heard the door open. James came in carrying a dinner tray. She deliberately turned her back on him.

"It's a damp night. If you feel the cold you may avail yourself of my turf fire."

When she heard the door close quietly, she swung around. "I'll freeze to death before I'll avail myself of your bloody fire . . . or your food!" she said to thin air.

After a few minutes, the aroma from the food was very tempting. She summoned her resistance and it was more difficult than she had first anticipated. She also imagined she could feel the dampness but forbade herself to picture his fire. She glanced about hoping for something to fill the long hours of the evening, but there were no books in her room. The only reading materials were the letters from her mother and sister. She retrieved them from her writing desk and sat down in a comfy chair to read them.

Georgy's first letter about Teddy Fox's desertion only emphasized to Louisa how perfidious the male of the species could be. Georgy's second letter, describing Charles Romilly as tall, broad, and extremely handsome, reminded her of her own husband and it rekindled her anger. *The handsomest men are always the most arrogant and selfish. I should have written and warned her about him!*

Louisa reread her mother's letters. *Enjoy your honeymoon to the full. Your summer in Ireland will be over before you know it.* "It cannot be over soon enough for me!" Then Lu read, *I'm looking forward to seeing you and James. I shall be there in less than a month.* She put the letters back in the drawer. "There is no need for them to come—I won't be here!"

She removed her ruffled drawers and kept on her petticoat as a nightgown, and then she climbed into bed. The prospect of returning to Woburn was distinctly unappealing. *I don't fancy being involved in Georgy's escapades. I was so happy here. Why did Abercorn have to go and ruin everything?*

Louisa lay for hours feeling sorry for herself. Suddenly she didn't like sleeping alone. The bed was cold, but mostly it was lonely. She had become accustomed to lying in the glow of her husband's adoration and now that he had withdrawn it, she felt like a snowdrop craving the warmth of the sun. She remembered the first time she had shared his bed. She'd had her recurring nightmare and her cries of distress had brought him immediately. He had carried her to his bed to dispel her fear. Then he had rubbed her back to make her feel safe and secure.

If I pretended to have a nightmare and cried out, would he come running? Lu was appalled at her thoughts, not because they were devious but because she would be surrendering and subduing her will to his. Her mind played over his reply to her accusation: *If that's what you think—if that's what you truly think of me, we can never be husband and wife.*

"He said those words to me before. When was it?" It came to her immediately. *It was when I accused him of a sexual encounter with Georgy. That proved to be a false allegation. Is it possible I'm wrongly accusing him again?*

Lu thumped her pillow and turned over. *That's just wishful thinking. Don't be so bloody naive! Kitty Kelly admitted that James was the father.*

She didn't fall asleep until early in the morning. When she began to dream, a smile curved her lips because she was in bed with her husband: *He kissed her for a full hour, starting at her temples, kissing her eyelids, then trailing his lips down the curve of her neck. His lavish attentions made her feel both beautiful and desirable. She clung to him sweetly, inhaling his male scent. When his lips brushed against her ear, she shivered with pleasure.*

I love you, Lu. His intimate whisper awakened her. She sat up in bed and realized it was only a dream. His phantom kisses had aroused her. She lay back down and her body ached for him. When dawn crept through the window, she relived the mornings when he had swept into her chamber and pulled off her covers. *Damn you to hellfire, Abercorn! I want everything to be the way it was before . . .*

Louisa got out of bed and went to the window. After last night's rain she was glad to see the sun. *At this early hour, the foxes are probably playing on the lawn, but I can only see them from the master bedchamber.* She chalked up another black mark against him.

She heard the adjoining door opening and braced herself. Her shoulders slumped when she saw it was Molly bringing her breakfast. "I thought it was Abercorn."

"Lord Abercorn is up and about already, my lady."

Lu lowered her voice. "He's not in the next room?"

Molly shook her head.

"Wonderful! I can make my escape." She opened the wardrobe to get her dress.

"You can't escape, my lady. I would be sent away in disgrace for ignoring Lord Abercorn's orders."

"What orders, pray?"

"I am to see to your needs, but under no circumstances must you leave your boudoir until . . ."

"Until what?" Lu demanded.

"I don't like to say, my lady." Molly looked pained beyond bearing.

"I order you to tell me what he said."

"He said . . . *until you come to your senses and beg his pardon.*"

"Beg? Beg? I'm not in the habit of begging *men* for anything, especially not men who sow their *bastards* about the country."

Molly gasped at her accusation. She quickly changed the subject. "You didn't eat your supper, my lady."

"I refuse to eat until I am freed from my prison!"

Molly bobbed a curtsy, set down the breakfast tray, and took away her dinner tray.

The bacon smelled delicious. Lu thought of the dinner she had left untouched. *That was an exercise in futility. The Irish devil won't even know I'm starving on principle.* She abstained as long as she could; then she lifted the covers and devoured the lot.

Louisa decided that while James was out, she would go into the other room and get some of her clothes from the wardrobe. When she turned the knob on the adjoining door and found it locked, she was outraged. *Molly locked me in!*

She began to pace her boudoir to rid herself of her choler. She stopped at the window and looked down into the courtyard. She was shocked to see James and Kitty in deep conversation walking toward the stables. She felt a stab of jealousy. "Where the devil is he taking her?"

She stood staring after them until they disappeared. "Lying swine. You told me you loved me. How can you do this to me?" Slowly, it came to her that the only time James had told her he loved her was in her dreams. She searched her memory and could not recall him vowing his love. Her heart sank. She began to turn from the window and saw Kitty Kelly. She was returning to the house without James. Kitty turned and waved, and Lu realized that James must be riding out somewhere alone.

She got a letter opener from her writing desk and tried to pick her boudoir door lock. She realized it wasn't going to work and moved across the room to try the lock on the door that adjoined their bedchambers. She concentrated hard, trying over and over, but her endeavors were unsuccessful. She threw herself down into a chair feeling thwarted and frustrated. She cursed her husband for being the author of all her misery. On such a lovely sunny day, she wished she could be swimming in the lakes. Instead, she was locked up with absolutely nothing to occupy her, save her thoughts.

Her memory flew back to the day James had rowed her up the three lakes and back again. *It was such a perfect day.* Her memories moved on to the day he had taught her to swim, and how patient he had been with her. *I put my full trust in him . . . that's why I learned so quickly.*

When I let him make love to me, it was a huge leap of trust for me. How can he accuse me of not trusting him? The answer came back immediately. *Because you accused him of fathering Kitty's baby. She said that James was the father, yet he was a picture of outraged pride when I threw the accusation at him. What was it he said? "Don't concentrate on whether you can trust me, Louisa. Trusting yourself is the key . . ."*

A phrase floated to her from her girlhood Latin lessons: *Chi ama, crede . . .* Who loves, trusts . . . "James was telling me that if I loved him, I would trust him."

Lu sat quietly, digesting her thoughts.

I do love him! I love him with all my heart!

Then why don't you trust him?

Because he's a man.

But James has proven to you over and over that he is different from other men. What if Kitty is lying and Abercorn is not responsible? Girls have been known to lie about inconvenient pregnancies. I myself lied about a pregnancy.

Louisa opened her window and made her bed. Then she poured water from her jug into one of the golden bowls that had once belonged to Josephine Beauharnais. The water was cold, but as she washed, she thought about the empress and Napoleon Bonaparte. *Were they in love? Mother told me he wrote Josephine impassioned, reproachful love letters, but I warrant he never fully trusted her.*

Louisa thought she heard voices and moved to the window. She caught a glimpse of James and the eldest Herdman brother as they left the courtyard and disappeared around a corner of the house. *He's been to the mill. The Irish devil is conducting business with never a thought for me, holed up here in my prison. I shall go mad if I am confined much longer!*

Lu thought of her private journal. *I shall put the venom I am feeling down on paper so I won't soon forget it.* She went to the wardrobe, opened an old shoebox, and took out her diary. Then she opened her jewel case and retrieved the small key.

When she opened it and read the last entry, she blushed. She had written about her feelings and emotions the morning after she and James had made love. The pages were filled with the outpouring of her heart:

I never realized how I hungered for my husband's love and adoration, yes, and I freely admit I was starving for his body. Last night was rapturous and this morning he gave me proof that he cherishes me. I have trusted my heart to his keeping and know that I will never regret marrying my Irish lord. From now on, my journal will be one long love letter to him. When I think of James, my very breath stands still.

Louisa was caught up in the heartfelt words she had written. The venom she was harboring melted away like snow in summer. She closed the book, locked it, and put it back in its hiding place.

Through the open window she heard a female voice and hurried across the chamber to see who it was. She saw Kitty walking through the courtyard flanked by Abercorn and Herdman. The trio was heading toward the stables. *Where the devil are they going? They must be taking her to see the mill.* Suddenly Louisa was filled with concern. *Kitty shouldn't be riding in her condition. If it happened at Christmas, she's almost seven months along.* Then she realized that Abercorn would take the carriage. Louisa sighed. *James didn't even look up at my window.*

To pass the time, Lu picked up an emery board. Her nails were in need of repair since she had planted her herb garden with the cuttings the tenants' wives had sent her. As she worked on her nails, thoughts of Kitty filled her mind. *She must have been frightened to death when she discovered she was with child. Just as Georgy was. Being alone in London, unable to work, must have been extremely daunting.* Lu didn't know whether she felt more pity for Kitty or for herself.

When the afternoon light began to fade, Lu went to the window to watch the sun go down. She heard the sound of boots and looked down. She saw James coming back from the stables, and he was alone. She hadn't expected Herdman to return, but it seemed odd that James had not brought Kitty back to Barons Court with him. Her mind ferreted out an explanation that made sense.

"O my God. The eldest Herdman brother is called *James*!" Lu stood at the window, stunned at the revelation that had just dawned on her. "It couldn't be," she murmured.

"Yes, it absolutely, positively could be! When I asked Kitty if James was the father and she said yes, she wanted me to think it was my husband."

Louisa crossed over to the mirror so she could have a serious conversation with herself. "No wonder Abercorn was offended to his very core when you accused him of being the child's father." She bit her lip. "Judas Iscariot, what have you done, Lady Lu?" She had done James a great injustice and felt remorse, but she searched for an excuse. "The Irish devil could have told me!" Then she realized his towering pride would prevent him from issuing denials. *James expects, nay demands, trust from his wife.*

Lu raised her chin at her reflection. *He may not be guilty of fathering her child, but the Irish devil is certainly guilty of imprisoning me! If Abercorn thinks he's going to get off scot-free, he's in for a bloody revelation!*

When she heard movements in the adjoining bedchamber, she gathered her indignation. She would go on the attack the moment he opened the door. She saw it move but was thrown off kilter when Molly came in carrying her dinner tray.

Molly set the tray down, along with some bed linen. "I brought you fresh sheets, my lady, but I see you've already made your bed."

"Thank you, Molly, I'll put them on in the morning." Lu nodded toward the other room. "Is Abercorn in there?"

"Yes, my lady." Molly hesitated. "His lordship sends you an invitation."

"An invitation?"

Molly lowered her eyes. "He says . . . if you are ready to beg his pardon, he is ready to listen."

Louisa gasped. "You may tell his lordship that I shall be ready to beg his pardon in a hundred bloody years!" She dug her fists into her hips. "Be sure to lock the door to ensure Abercorn's safety. I'm demented; it will take me that long to regain my senses."

Molly retreated through the adjoining door and closed it quietly.

Lu ran to the door, put her ear against it, and heard Molly say, "I'm sorry, my lord, but Lady Abercorn says . . ."

"Yes, I heard what she said, Molly. Thank you, that will be all," Abercorn replied.

That won't be all. Not by a hell of a long chalk!

Lu pulled up a chair and thoroughly enjoyed every morsel on her dinner tray. Full as a tick, she rubbed her belly. *Ah bliss! I must remember to give my compliments to Barons Court's cook.*

An hour before dawn, Louisa took the sheets from her bed and took them to the window. She added the pile of fresh sheets Molly had brought. She tied them together with tight knots and secured one end to a sturdy bedpost.

Lu removed her petticoat and, clad in her busk and ruffled drawers, climbed onto the windowsill, gathered her confidence, and then began to slowly and carefully climb down the sheets. *If I don't look down, I'll be all right.* She knew her self-assurance was buoyed by a thirst for revenge. She was looking forward to her encounter with her husband, and she intended to give as good as she got.

Lu experienced a moment of panic when she got to the end of the sheets and found she was still ten feet from the ground. She closed her eyes, crossed her fingers, and jumped. She offered up a prayer of thanks when she landed unhurt in a flowerbed.

She was pleased as punch with herself. *Now comes the tricky part.* She knew that avoiding the servants would take ingenuity, although not many would be up this early. She entered Barons Court through a back door. It was a food storage room next to the kitchen. She picked up an apple from a basket and listened at the door. When she heard nothing but silence, she slowly and cautiously opened the door and crept up a back staircase. Then she went into the guest wing and entered one of the unoccupied suites. She stretched out on the bed and waited.

James opened his eyes and his first thought was the same one he'd had yesterday and the day before. *Damn, I hate waking up and not finding Lu in bed beside me. It took such a hell of long time to get her to share it with me, and before you know it, it's separate bloody rooms again. I must be raving mad to put up with it.*

He threw back the covers and swung his feet to the carpet. *Since Kitty is no longer in residence, and the bone of contention has been removed, there is no sodding reason why I should put up with it. I'll set-tle this trust business once and for all—even if it means a knockdown, drag-out fight!*

James reached for his robe but then changed his mind. He'd have more authority if he was dressed and booted. He donned shirt and riding breeches, and then pulled on knee-high boots. He was no sooner finished than Molly was at his door with a breakfast tray to take through to her mistress.

"Thank you, Molly. I'll do the honors this morning." He saw the look of relief on the young maid's face and watched with amusement as she made herself scarce. He unlocked the adjoining door between their bedchambers and then, balancing the tray, he kicked the door with his foot and watched it swing open. He stepped through and found the chamber empty. "Jaysus!" James abandoned the tray and rushed to the window. A certain amount of relief swept over him when he saw Louisa was not lying in a heap below the string of tied-together sheets.

Then his heart plummeted. "She's gone!"

James took the stairs two at a time, shouting to the servants as he descended. "My wife has left the house! Has anybody seen her?"

He rushed outside and looked up at her boudoir window. His heart constricted. *It's such a long drop. I warrant she hurt herself. My God, what if she's injured and crawled away somewhere?* James was covered with guilt. *It's my fault. I never should have locked her up when I know what a reckless little bitch Lady Lu can be when provoked.*

Any lady with enough guts to perform at Covent Garden incognito has enough pluck to throw caution to the wind and climb out a bloody second-story window.

James ran to the stables and asked the grooms and horsemen to search the grounds of Barons Court. "She could be injured. Look in the woods when you're done scouring the park." He went to the paddocks where the horses were grazing and searched meticulously. James found no sign of her, and the stablemen reported they had no luck.

With a heavy heart, James returned to the house. He summoned Mrs. Connelly and the indoor staff. "No one can find Lady Abercorn. Would you be good enough to search Barons Court for me? There are so many rooms; she could be anywhere."

After two hours the staff assembled in the rotunda. No one had anything to report. Lady Abercorn had simply vanished.

"Thank you all for your help." His face was grim; his mood had gone from optimistic to hopeless. He went into the great hall and leaned his head against the black oak mantel of the stone fireplace. *Louisa has left me. She's doubtless on her way back to England. Lu has neither clothes nor money, but she won't let that stop her. Perhaps she went to see Rowan Maloney for travel money.*

James summoned a footman. "Would you have one of the grooms ride into Omagh to see if Rowan Maloney has seen Lady Abercorn? Thank you."

James didn't feel optimistic. *Lu could have climbed out the window last night. She could be long gone by now. Dear God, I love her so much; I can't bear to lose her.* Abercorn made his decision instantly. *The stubborn little wench has gone home to Woburn, so I have no choice. I'll simply have to go and get her and bring her back to Ireland where she belongs!* A sudden thought hit him. *What if she refuses?* His jaw clenched along with his fists. *I'll drag her back by the bloody hair if I have to!*

Chapter Twenty-Nine

When Louisa heard the hue and cry and knew that James and everyone else at Barons Court were searching for her, she slipped from the guest wing, went into the master bedchamber, and closed the door.

With great anticipation, she relished the thought of the confrontation she knew would erupt when she and James came face-to-face.

She saw her abandoned breakfast tray and sat down to enjoy it. She sighed with satisfaction and then used his water to wash. She brushed her hair until it crackled, applied powder and rouge, and finally placed a drop of jasmine perfume between her breasts. She picked up her apple, set it on the bedside table, and propped herself up on the pillows of the wide bed where her husband had recently slept. She took a deep breath to appreciate his provocative male scent that lingered on the linen.

It was hours before Louisa saw the knob turn and the door swing open. She picked up her apple and took a bite.

"Lu! You didn't leave after all." Abercorn's amazed expression turned to one of relief. "Thank God you are safe!"

She gave him an indifferent glance and took another bite of her apple.

The gesture angered him. "I should tan your arse for being so willful and causing such unnecessary alarm."

Louisa held up her hand imperiously. "Don't come one step closer."

His dark brows drew together as the storm gathered.

"I know you are not the father of Kitty's child, but don't think for one moment I will *ever* forgive you for taking me captive and keeping me locked up, you Irish devil!"

"And don't you think for one moment I will ever forgive you for *suspecting* I was the father of Kitty's child."

"I want a profound and heartfelt apology, Abercorn."

"I'm *truly sorry* you behaved like a lunatic and needed locking up, Lady Lu."

"I have emerged from my *defensive crouch*." She threw the apple at him.

He deftly caught it and took a bite. He arched a dark eyebrow and a wry smile played about his lips. "The woman tempted me."

"Don't quote the Bible to me, you uncivilized heathen!"

"Me, uncivilized? You are the one climbing down sheets in your drawers."

She raised her chin defiantly. "I'm a marchioness; I can do what the hell I please."

"Only with my permission. I am lord and master of Barons Court, madam."

"You are delusional, Lord Bloody Abercorn!"

"You need a good beating or a good bedding. I think I'll give you both!" James launched himself onto the bed and pinned her beneath him.

Lu squealed and tried to free herself.

"You may as well stop struggling. To the victor go the spoils." He rose onto his knees and pulled off her ruffled drawers. "Which will it be, the beating or the bedding?"

She made a little moue with her lips. "You decide. But if you choose the latter, would you mind removing your riding boots?"

James grinned. "Since you ask so nicely, Lady Lu, I'll remove more than my boots."

She watched avidly as her husband undressed and then came back over her in the dominant position. "You cannot resist me."

"I don't want to resist you—there's a difference. I intend to be master in my own house, Lu. But I wouldn't change you if I could. I want you just the way you are." He removed her busk and her luscious breasts spilled into his palms.

Her silvery laughter spiraled about them and James thought it the loveliest sound he'd ever heard. "Vow you will never keep me locked in a room again. I won't yield to you until you swear it."

"Won't yield to me?" He swept his hands from her breasts to her waist and lifted her so that her face was close to his. "I warrant it will take about three kisses to wear down your defenses."

In fact, it took only one.

His hot mouth took possession of hers and their tongues mated wildly. He slipped the head of his cock inside her and urged her to wrap her legs about his back so he could bury himself to the hilt. He made passionate love to her until she could no longer think. She could only taste and smell and feel. When her climax came, he spilled his seed into her slippery satin sheath.

James rolled beside her and cradled her in his arms, whispering love words that made her very bones melt. He kissed the corners of her mouth then put his lips close to her ear. "I love you, Lu."

His intimate whisper made her heart sing.

"I'm sorry I accused you of fathering Kitty's baby. When I saw her and found out she'd been here at Christmas, I felt threatened and vulnerable. To love is to trust, and I love you with all my heart, James."

"I'll tell you a secret. My pride was mauled because Kitty is my grandfather's child. Kate Connelly was more than his housekeeper."

Lu's eyes widened. "That makes Kitty your aunt." She found the situation quite funny.

"For some reason, Kate Connelly has never told Kitty, but I think it's time she knew. I'll speak to Kate about it."

"Will James Herdman marry Kitty?"

"Yes, as soon as he learned she was carrying his child, he insisted they marry." James looked into Louisa's eyes. "Would you mind if I settled some money on her? My grandfather left Kate an annuity, but nothing for his child."

"Of course I wouldn't mind. You are filthy rich, Abercorn, especially since you took my father's money as an inducement to marry me."

"Ah, about that money." He brushed back the dark tendrils from her forehead. "Before we were wed, I put that money in trust for you."

"For me?" she asked in wonder.

"You may never need it, but if and when your mother is widowed, you may have to help her, Lu. Your father's will leaves everything to his heir, except for the Campden Hill house."

"However do you know?"

"I pay my attorneys well, sweetheart." He brushed his lips across her temple. "While we are on the subject of money, I may as well confess that I will bear the cost of whatever my brother Claud needs to gain him a seat in Parliament."

"I don't have any objection." Her eyes lit with amusement. "Confession is good for the soul. What other secrets have you been keeping from me?"

"Well, there is one little thing. The night we arrived at Barons Court and you withdrew to your boudoir, you left your unpacked trunks in here. I opened one and found your diary."

Louisa stiffened. "You didn't read my private journal?"

"Well, actually I did."

She pulled from his arms in outrage. "You Irish devil! Always going on about trust! You are nothing but an uncivilized lout!"

James pulled her back into his arms and held her captive. "I was eaten alive to know who had fathered the child that you miscarried. When I read your diary and learned it was Georgy, it made me the happiest man breathing. That was the night I became hell-bent on seducing you."

She stared at him for a full minute as her mind absorbed the things he was saying.

The corners of her mouth lifted. "Then what the hell are you waiting for? You had better get on with it, Abercorn."

His face became serious. "In all truth I must warn you my lovemaking could result in a baby, Lady Lu."

"James, I trust you implicitly." She smiled her secret smile. "Just make sure it's a girl!"

Chapter Thirty

Ardverikie Estate, Scotland
Summer 1846

"May God save our gracious Queen Victoria." Lord Abercorn offered the toast to their sovereign who had brought her family to their Scottish estate for a visit.

"Thank you, James. We truly appreciate your generous hospitality. We have fallen in love with the landscape and are firmly convinced we need our own Scottish estate."

James hid his amusement. Victoria always used the royal we. His glance moved from the queen to his wife, Louisa, who was engaged in an animated conversation with Prince Albert. He could not help comparing the two females. The queen was both short and plump, and though she had pleasant features, she had no claim to beauty. Lady Lu, on the other hand, was exquisite. *Though Lu is five years older than Victoria, no one would ever guess.*

His glance moved to handsome, twenty-seven-year-old Prince Albert, who was seated on Louisa's right. *He hasn't taken his bloody eyes off Lu since we sat down to dinner.* James felt extremely proprietary about his beautiful wife. She was an accomplished flirt and had the supreme self-confidence of a goddess who walked among mere mortals. *Lady Lu is certainly not the vulnerable girl I married. Acting as my political hostess and being fawned upon by every male who was invited to Barons Court soon gave her self-esteem and polish.*

Two years ago, the Marquis of Abercorn had been appointed the lord lieutenant of County Donegal, and in no small measure his wife had helped him secure the post. His term as viceroy was now over, and James had his eye on becoming the lord lieutenant of Ireland. Louisa's brother, Lord John Russell, was the new prime minister of England and doubtless would be able to use his influence to get Abercorn the appointment.

"May I have wine with my dessert, Mama?" Lady Harriet, age twelve, appealed to her mother.

"Yes, Harry, providing it's *negus* wine." Negus wine was mixed with sugar and water and served especially to children.

"Me too!" Edward, the five-year-old heir to the throne, demanded.

Prince Albert frowned. He had very definite ideas about how children should be brought up. "I don't think so, Teddy."

Louisa gave the prince a sideways glance from beneath her dark lashes. "A little bit of what you fancy never hurt anyone. Indulge the boy, Your Highness."

Prince Albert allowed himself to be persuaded and gave in to Lu's suggestion without further demur.

It was Abercorn's turn to frown. *The bloody prince is lovesick! Lu has him wrapped around her little finger.* James felt a hand on his sleeve and turned to look at Victoria.

"Albert runs the nursery like a sergeant major. He's a stickler for manners. We are rather strict with the children."

"I must compliment you on your children, Your Majesty," James said gallantly. "I warrant you won't regret securing a Scottish estate. This country is such a healthful place for young ones."

Only two of the queen's children were taking dinner with them. Princess Adelaide was six, and Prince Edward only five. The other three were in bed in the nursery wing.

"Your own children are a credit to you and Lady Abercorn. We are amazed at the way they handle their Highland ponies."

"Thank you. Louisa starts giving them riding lessons soon after they learn to walk."

"You don't mean she teaches them herself, surely?"

"She does, Your Majesty. Her energy is boundless," James said proudly.

"Lady Abercorn doesn't look old enough to be the mother of eight children," Victoria said primly. "Such a slim waist. We are trying to persuade her to come to court and be mistress of the queen's robes. Perhaps you could plead our cause, James?"

James smiled. "I will do my best, Your Majesty." *In a pig's eye. The only wardrobe Lu has any interest in is her own.* Tonight his wife was wearing a magnificent gown of crimson, the ancestral Abercorn color, and it suited her dark beauty to perfection. James became instantly aroused as he pictured the crimson corset she was wearing beneath it. He shifted in his chair and frowned. *I warrant Albert's cock is hard enough to crack walnuts. Lu has that effect on men, regretfully.*

Louisa arose. "Shall we take our wine into the drawing room? I've promised the children a game of hide-and-seek before bed."

Prince Albert immediately moved behind Victoria's chair to assist her in rising. She had given birth to another baby daughter only two months before and still moved slowly.

James took his son and heir aside to give him a word of warning. "Don't play rough with Prince Edward. He's only five and you are eight."

Young James looked up at his father. "Teddy can be willful for a five-year-old."

Abercorn whooped with laughter. "You are the reigning champion when it comes to willful, young sir."

"I have four older sisters bossing me about. If I wasn't willful they'd squash me."

James sobered. "Quite right. If you don't keep females in their place they will run roughshod over you. Go and take charge."

When the queen was seated in a comfortable chair so she could enjoy watching the children's game, Lady Harry volunteered to hide her eyes and count while the others hid.

Lady Lu grabbed Prince Albert's hand. "Come on, run! I know a place where they'll never find us!"

Victoria looked askance at James. "Lady Abercorn joins in the children's games?"

James rolled his eyes. "Yes, I'm afraid so, Your Majesty. Apparently her mother, the Duchess of Bedford, joined in her children's games, and my wife carries on the tradition."

"How extraordinary."

When Her Majesty decided it was time to retire, Louisa and James took their children up to the nursery wing. At Barons Court all had their own bedchamber, but here at Ardverikie, the four older daughters shared one large room.

Beatrice, who was eleven, remarked, "I don't think Princess Adelaide had ever played hide-and-seek before. She's quite shy."

"Too shy to shout and brawl like my angelic lot." Louisa tucked her daughter into bed and tapped Louisa Jane on the bum. "Tomorrow, your father has promised to take the queen on a tour of the estate in the pony cart. You girls can accompany them in your own cart if you like. Harry is old enough to drive."

"I will only go if Harry lets me take the reins for a few minutes," Katherine Elizabeth declared emphatically.

"Well, since you're nine, I warrant you're old enough to learn," her mother agreed. "But Harry is in charge, so it will be her decision. I'll leave the lamp turned up; your father will be in to say good night shortly."

"Good night, Mother," the four girls chorused.

"Good night, darlings. Sleep tight—don't let the bedbugs bite."

Louisa went into the next bedchamber where James was making sure their son actually got into bed, rather than lying on the floor playing with his toys.

"I told Prince Edward he could ride my pony tomorrow." Young James had decided to be magnanimous.

"He will need his father's permission first," James reminded his son.

"Mama will get Prince Albert to agree. She's very persuasive."

James slanted an eyebrow at his wife. "Out of the mouths of babes."

Lu hid a smile. "Tush and piffle!"

Lord and Lady Abercorn entered the nursery where Claud and baby George were sound asleep. "They look like cherubs when they're sleeping," James whispered.

"They may look cherubic, but awake they are Irish devils, like their father."

"I'll just go and bid the girls good night. Then I shall attempt to prove the disreputable opinion you have of me."

"Don't be too long. I need your help getting out of my best gown."

Within ten minutes, James entered the master bedchamber and crossed the room to unhook his wife's gown. "I don't think you realize how Prince Albert looks at you."

She glanced up at him over her shoulder. "Darling, a female always knows when a male is attracted to her."

James undid the top hook. "Your face was flushed when the pair of you returned from the linen press, or wherever it was you took him to hide. Stop playing games with the poor devil."

She arched her brows. "Perhaps I should leave my corset on, if you are determined to manipulate my strings, Lord Abercorn."

James watched her step from her gown and move across the chamber to hang it in the wardrobe. He let go of his jealousy and said wryly, "I don't suppose Her Majesty indulges him with many games."

Lu kicked off her high-heeled slippers. "Oh, I don't know. She's given him five children in six years of marriage, so I assume she lets him play *tickle my fancy!*"

James couldn't resist reciting a limerick that was popular in Ireland:

> *Queen Vicky was ever a prude*
> *Who couldn't stand anything rude,*
> *But once in a while*
> *She ventured a smile*
> *When Albert appeared in the nude.*

"Well, I'm willing to wager he's a braw laddie when stripped, and nothing to smile at, *at all, at all.*"

He took her in his arms. "You are incorrigible, Lady Lu."

"And then some." She slid her hand down between their bodies and stroked his hardening cock with teasing fingers. "That's why you'll never have enough of me."

After an hour of particularly passionate lovemaking, Lu smiled into the darkness. *Whenever we have attractive male visitors, James has a compelling urge to put his stamp of ownership on me.*

The following day, the Abercorns' best pony cart, rigged out with cushions and a lap robe, was brought to the front door to convey Her Majesty Queen Victoria around the Highland estate. When she was comfortably seated with her young heir beside her, James took up the reins.

Another pony cart, driven by the Abercorns' twelve-year-old daughter Harry and loaded with an assortment of children, followed her father.

His Royal Highness Prince Albert had declared that he was in need of exercise and preferred a good hike on foot. Lady Abercorn graciously agreed to accompany him.

The pair waved to the departing carts and set out on foot. Albert carried a sturdy hand-carved walking stick. "Don't you carry a stick, Lady Abercorn?"

Only figuratively. "If I get into difficulty, Your Highness, I'm sure you will lend me your good strong arm."

"I love to hike. In which direction shall we go?"

"Ardverikie has two lovely waterfalls. Why don't we take a look at the first one, and if that hasn't exhausted all your disgusting energy, we can slog on to the second one."

Albert laughed. "I've never met anyone quite like you, Lady Abercorn."

"My friends call me Lady Lu."

An hour later, as Louisa and Prince Albert were enjoying the view of the second waterfall, it began to rain. At first they didn't notice because there was a light spray of water in the air from the cascade, but as the rain began to pelt down, they both looked up at the sky in dismay.

"Come, there is a gamekeeper's hut through those firs where we can wait out the rainstorm." Lu pointed to the stand of trees.

"Good! Lead the way, my lady."

They were both out of breath from running and laughing by the time they reached the shelter. Prince Albert removed his tweed cape, shook off the raindrops, and hung it on a peg to dry. He moved toward Lu and helped her remove her damp jacket.

"I hope Victoria isn't caught in the downpour."

"She won't shrink, Your Highness." Lu bit her lip. "I'm so sorry, Albert. Truly I wasn't remarking on the queen's lack of height."

Prince Albert grinned. "My wife *is* rather short in stature."

"Physically perhaps, but certainly not figuratively," she said, laughing.

"No, indeed," he replied wistfully, "her stature certainly overshadows mine." He took possession of Louisa's hand and drew it to his lips. "Lady Lu, I find you attractive beyond belief. Just looking at you makes my pulse race."

Lu gently withdrew her hand. "Thank you for the gallant compliment, Albert. Abercorn is not a man who would tolerate dalliance in his wife, I'm afraid."

"I'm sorry." He looked abashed. "Victoria and I make a fine pair. She has developed a *tendre* for James. She intends to appoint him to her privy counsel and has asked me to attach him to my household as groom of the stole."

"Oh, Your Highness, James will feel immeasurably honored by these appointments."

Albert smiled. "Victoria has also instructed me to persuade you to become her mistress of the robes. There is no more fashionable lady at the Royal Court."

"Ah, I must regretfully decline. As the mother of eight children and the wife of a privy counselor and groom of the stole, I would not be able to devote sufficient time to her gracious majesty's wardrobe."

Albert grinned ruefully. "You are the only lady in Britain who would dare say *no* to the queen."

Lu smiled her secret smile. *And say no to her royal husband.*

After dinner that night, Queen Victoria took Lord Abercorn aside and told him about his appointment to her privy counsel. "As well, Prince Albert would like to make you his groom of the stole."

James bowed gallantly. "I am deeply honored, Your Majesty."

An hour later, in the privacy of the master bedchamber, James had changed his tune and voiced his anger.

"What the hellfire went on when the pair of you sheltered in the gamekeeper's shack?" Abercorn's face was dark with fury.

"You're being ridiculous! Don't make a cake of yourself." Lu tossed her head.

James grabbed her shoulders in powerful hands and shook her

fiercely. "I don't want royal appointments because the queen's husband wants to get you into bed," he said through gritted teeth.

Lu dared to laugh at him. "I can't help it if he wants to get me into bed."

His hands tightened painfully on her shoulders. "I won't have you playing the cocktease. Do you hear me?"

She raised her chin and looked him straight in the eye. "I hear you loud and clear. If you must know the truth, it is Queen Victoria who has a *tendre* for you. So it must be you who has been playing the cocktease, Lord Abercorn."

He stared at her in amazement, and then they both laughed until they became weak. Lu fell down on the bed and rolled about in merriment. James dived on her and pinned her beneath him. "Let me warn you, Lady Lu. When we are at Court there will be no dalliance allowed."

"You mean on *my* part. But I warrant if you play your cards right, there could be a dukedom in your future."

"Mm, the Duke of Abercorn does have a nice ring to it."

Her challenging laugh rang out. "Let's have a demonstration of your famous cockteasing, Lord Bloody Abercorn!"

Epilogue

Montagu House, London

August 1894

"Thanks for the buns and the use of the hall," Dowager Duchess Louisa said irreverently to her daughter, the Duchess of Buccleuch.

"Montagu House *is* rather grand," her daughter and namesake Louisa Jane declared as she glanced about the magnificent, top-lit central salon where the historic levee was being held. "Are you ready to retire, Mother?"

"From the present company, yes. Would you ask young Maud to bring me the letters from Queen Victoria and Prince Edward, darling?"

Lu, with admiring eyes, watched her daughter cross the salon. *James, our daughter Louisa Jane is undoubtedly the beauty of the family. 'Tis little wonder she caught the attention of a duke. You promised me more girls than boys, and somehow managed to keep your pledge.*

Maud, and her cousin whose name had escaped Lu, brought her the royal letters of congratulations. "Would you like me to help you upstairs, Your Grace?"

"Under no circumstances. I shall ascend the grand staircase alone. I certainly don't need the aid of halflings like you two." Then she took pity on her great-granddaughters.

"You were wondering earlier how many lovers I'd had. Let's see . . . there was a baron, a viscount, an earl, a marquis, oh, and a duke. I mustn't forget the Irish Duke." Lady Lu smiled her secret smile. *They aren't to know they are all the same man.*

Her descendants watched in reverence as Dowager Duchess Louisa ascended the grand staircase, wafting her crimson ostrich feather fan.

When she reached the top, she turned and smiled. *I'm ready for my bed.* She was eager to fall asleep, so that James could visit her in her dreams and whisper in her ear, *"I love you, Lu."*

Author's Note

Louisa Jane, Duchess of Abercorn, lived to be ninety-three years old.

She was invested as Lady of the Royal Order of Victoria and Albert.

James Hamilton, Duke of Abercorn, was appointed lord lieutenant of County Donegal in 1844, and two years later he was appointed to the Queen Victoria's Privy Counsel and became Prince Albert's groom of the stole. In 1866 he served as the lord lieutenant of Ireland and received his dukedom.

James and Louisa had thirteen living children—seven daughters and six sons.

His brother, Lord Claud Hamilton, served as Member of Parliament for County Tyrone.

Lord John Russell became prime minister of England in 1846.

Lady Georgina Russell, Louisa's older sister, married Sir Charles Romilly when she was thirty-two years old. He became principal secretary to the lord chancellor of Britain.

Louisa's brother, Edward Russell, achieved the rank of admiral in 1867.

Louisa's brother, Charles Russell, achieved the rank of lieutenant colonel.

Louisa's brother, Alexander Russell, became a doctor.

Louisa's youngest sister, Rachel, became a novelist of romantic fiction.

James Hamilton's mother, Harriet, Lady Aberdeen, died less than a year after her son's marriage.

Louisa Jane, Duchess of Abercorn, lived to see Queen Victoria's son, Prince Edward, ascend the throne. Thus a total of five monarchs reigned in her lifetime.

*Lady Diana Spencer and her son and heir to the throne, Prince William, are among Louisa's descendants.

Photo by Glamour Shots

Virginia Henley is a *New York Times* bestselling author and the recipient of numerous awards, including the *Romantic Times* Lifetime Achievement Award. Her novels have been translated into fourteen languages. A grandmother of three, she lives in St. Petersburg, Florida, with her husband.

Read on for an excerpt of another exciting
and sensual historical romance from

· VIRGINIA HENLEY ·

The

Decadent Duke

AVAILABLE FROM SIGNET

The social scene in the month of November had been extremely active, but once December arrived it turned into a veritable whirlwind of invitations to parties and balls.

Georgina did her best to be on hand when the post arrived so she could sort through the invitations before her mother got to see them. That way she could discard the ones she suspected would be dead boring.

Today, however, she opened one that intrigued her. It was addressed solely to Lady Georgina Gordon, and was an invitation to attend an Evening of Fashion. At the bottom in small print it said: *Masks Optional*. She did not know who had invited her, but strangely the address was fairly close by on Pall Mall.

She tucked the pink card into her reticule, and later that morning took a stroll past the tall stone house. She had no idea who resided there, but her curiosity was piqued. On the spot, she decided that she would attend.

The Duchess of Gordon received an invitation to a musical evening being given by Lady Lavinia Spencer for the same evening, which she accepted on behalf of herself and her youngest daughter.

At the last minute, Georgina complained of a headache and begged off.

"Since Lavinia and her sister-in-law, the Duchess of Devonshire, are not on speaking terms, the Duke of Bedford isn't likely to attend. I don't suppose it will hurt if you miss the party. Perhaps you should have an early night and get some beauty sleep."

After her mother left, Georgina went up to her bedchamber, opened her wardrobe, and with a critical eye, tried to decide what to wear to an Evening of Fashion.

"I wish Louisa were still at home. She'd join me in a heartbeat. We had such jolly times together." Georgina hadn't seen her sister often since her wedding, as she and her young husband lived at Brome Hall in Suffolk. Louisa had attended Charlotte's ball, but she had focused her attention on Charles the entire evening, much to Georgina's disgust.

"I suppose I ought to take Helen with me, but she would blab to Mother that I'd accepted an invitation and gone out after complaining of a headache."

Georgina smiled her secret smile. *Masks Optional.*

She donned her most sophisticated evening gown, which was the one in the vivid shade of peacock. Then, to hide her identity, she put on a wig as well as the black sequined mask that belonged to a cat costume she'd worn to a children's party years ago.

Wearing her velvet cloak, Georgina waited at the top of the stairs until the foyer was empty of servants; then she quickly descended and hurried through the front door. Feeling free as a bird, she felt like singing as she made her way along Pall Mall.

She crushed her apprehension about the unknown by dashing up the steps, and making liberal use of the door knocker. The major-domo who appeared was wearing gold and purple livery, as if he pre-sided over a royal residence. Georgina presented her pink invitation, and in return she received a formal bow.

"This way, my lady."

She followed the footman up a spiral gilt staircase to a ballroom that was lit with crystal chandeliers. The walls were mirrored from floor to ceiling, giving it an aura of palatial opulence. The room was half full of people, with more men than women, and she noted that most of the ladies wore masks. She was surprised to see that the servants, who were carrying glasses of champagne on silver trays, were not footmen, but what could more aptly be described as *footwomen*.

The orchestra was playing a baroque piece by Handel, and Georgina saw that no one was dancing. She recognized three of the gentlemen immediately. Francis Russell was laughing with Prince Frederick and Prince Edward. She remembered that she was wearing a mask and would be incognito until she spoke with them and they recognized her voice. *What fun!*

The hostess came forward to greet her. Georgina knew she had never seen the woman before in her life. "My dear, welcome to an Evening of Fashion. The show will get under way shortly. There is something to tempt and titillate every taste. I urge you to be bold and bid on whatever strikes your fancy."

She's urging me to bid . . . That must mean the fashions will be for sale. How delightful. Georgina watched the hostess engage an older woman in conversation, and she recognized the female immediately. The gestures of Lizzie Melbourne were unmistakable. Georgina did not know the man with her, though she knew it was not Lord Melbourne.

Rather than stand alone, she decided to join a trio of masked ladies who were whispering and laughing behind their fans. They fell quiet as their hostess went to the center of the ballroom and held up her hands. "I thank you all for coming tonight. Don't forget that Christmas is coming and presents will be expected. I urge the gentlemen to be generous and loosen their purse strings. The fashions you will see tonight are unique. They have been imported from Paris at great expense to the establishment."

Everyone laughed.

"Ladies and gentlemen, I proudly present the *Demoiselles de Maison Rouge!*"

The applause was deafening, but as the first female high-stepped across the floor, the clapping turned to whistles of appreciation.

Georgina stared in disbelief. The girl was clad in a flowing red gown that was completely transparent. As she walked, the creamy flesh of her breasts and thighs was clearly visible. The tendrils on her mons showed dark red through the sheer silk.

Before Georgina could regain her composure, another girl undulated across the ballroom floor. This one was wearing a frilly white corset, a pair of lace stockings, and sequined garters. The space between her hips and thighs was completely nude. As she crossed the room, her bare buttocks bounced. She carried a red rose and tossed it toward the whistling men.

When Francis Russell caught it and immediately bid, "Twenty guineas," Georgina was shocked. The bidding was fast and furious, and it began to dawn on her that the men were buying more than the fashions.

A girl garbed in a black busk decorated with pink bows touched her breasts with the tiny fan she carried. When she drew it suggestively across her mons, two of the women present began to bid, and the laughter turned raucous.

Georgina's shock turned to anger. *Who the devil sent me the invitation?* She gazed across at Prince Frederick, who was bidding an obscene amount of money for a statuesque blonde wearing silver tassels. *Charlotte's husband, Charles, once dueled with Frederick. Could this be his way of getting even with our family?* She soon dismissed the suspicion. It had happened years ago, and the prince didn't seem the type to carry a grudge.

She wondered if the hostess was amusing herself by inviting a debutante who lived on the same street as her establishment. *What would she gain by offering such an insult to a Gordon daughter?*

Georgina's glance traveled slowly around the ballroom, and when it came to rest on the Duke of Bedford, she knew exactly who had sent her the outrageous invitation. She was not amused.

The more she thought about it, the more furious she became. She was angry with herself as well as Francis Russell. *I should not have come. I must get out of here.*

She glanced toward the door and was stunned to see her sister Susan's husband walk in. The Duke of Manchester was not alone. The woman on his arm was the one she had seen in his carriage that day outside the House of Lords.

Outraged, she hurried across the room until she reached her brother-in-law. She removed the woman's hand from his arm. "William, you must escort me home immediately."

"Christ Almighty, Georgina! What the hell are you doing in a brothel?" he demanded.

"I am here by accident. Obviously, you are here by intent. Nevertheless, I need your protection."

"Of course, my dear." He offered her his arm.

She glanced back across the room, her wicked juices bubbling. "Just one moment. I will be back directly."

With head high she marched across the ballroom until she stood before the Duke of Bedford and Prince Edward. She raised her hand and slapped Francis Russell's face. "Pig!"

She knew he recognized her green eyes glittering through her mask. The prince, who did not recognize her, took immediate offense for the assault on his friend and grabbed her arm. She shook him off and slapped his face also. "Pig's friend!"

The crowd about them parted like the Red Sea as Georgina swept across the floor, took the Duke of Manchester's arm, and departed.

As they walked up Pall Mall, Georgina said, "I warrant discretion is the better part of valor. If you won't divulge where I was tonight, I won't reveal where you were, William."

The Duke of Manchester saw her to her door and kissed her hand.

The Duke of Bedford felt both elation and desolation. *The little vixen came!* The moment Georgina slapped his face, it ignited a raging lust that ran through his veins like wildfire and spread to his loins with the inevitable result. But something else had happened when he looked into her glittering green eyes. His heart had skipped a beat as he realized the lady was utterly desirable. He experienced a twinge of despair that she might refuse to speak to him again.

"Who the devil was that bold bitch?" Prince Edward demanded, rubbing his cheek.

"Don't you know?" Francis asked, surprised.

"She just left with Manchester. Is she one of his whores?"

"I haven't the faintest idea who she was," Francis lied as an urge to protect Lady Georgina suddenly came over him. "She obviously has a grudge against you, though," he added with glee.

"She slapped you first."

"That's because I'm your friend. What female have you offended recently?"

"More than I can count on one hand," the prince admitted with braggadocio.

Francis Russell perused the females parading in dishabille and suddenly lost his appetite for the strumpet in the frilly white corset. *Now, if Georgina were wearing those white lace stockings and sequined garters, it would be another matter entirely.*

"I fancy the one you bid on, Francis," Edward remarked glumly.

"Then be my guest. I'm off to Brooks's."

.   .   .

It was four in the morning when Bedford returned home to Russell Square. At the club he'd lost money because his mind was not on the game but elsewhere. Thoughts of Georgina Gordon persistently intruded, playing merry hell with his concentration. Finally, he gave up, tipped the porter who summoned his carriage, and allowed his mind to fully focus on the object of his desire.

As he disrobed for bed, he played a game of "what if." John had been nagging him to consider taking a wife, and for the first time in his life, he thought about it seriously.

Georgina would be an exciting woman to bed. She is a combination of innocence and recklessness. It would be fun to teach her to be wild and wanton. His hand went to his groin. *Christ, my cock is so hard, I could crack walnuts with it!*